SIEGE OF CASTELLAX

THE SHRIEKING SIREN of an ork fighter-bomber ripped across the sky, the primitive aircraft swooping so near the battlements that Gamgin could clearly make out the snaggle-toothed squig painted across its nose. Streamers of black smoke belched from the plane's wing, but it was impossible to tell if it was from damage or the crude exhausts of its combustion engine. Whatever its condition, the Iron Warrior watched as the plane's guns opened up, splashing the wreckage of a gun crew across the interior of a weapon pit. An instant later, the bright beam of a las-cannon burned a hole through the plane's fuselage, sending it plummeting from the sky to crash in a great fireball against the desert floor.

A WARHAMMER 40,000 NOVEL

SIEGE OF CASTELLAX

C L WERNER

BLACK LIBRARY

For Rob and Crystal, Matt and Chris, comrades in arms and fellows of the Darkson.

A Black Library Publication

First published in Great Britain in 2012 by
Black Library,
Games Workshop Ltd.,
Willow Road,
Nottingham, NG7 2WS, UK.

10 9 8 7 6 5 4 3 2 1

Cover illustration by Jon Sullivan.
Maps by C L Werner and Adrian Wood.
Colour illustrations by Sam Lamont.

A CIP record for this book is available from the British Library.

UK ISBN 13: 978 1 84970 259 1
US ISBN 13: 978 1 84970 260 7

See Black Library on the internet at

www.blacklibrary.com

Find out more about Games Workshop
and the world of Warhammer 40,000 at

www.games-workshop.com

Printed and bound by CPI Group (UK) Ltd, Croydon, CR0 4YY

It is the 41st millennium. For more than a hundred centuries the Emperor has sat immobile on the Golden Throne of Earth. He is the master of mankind by the will of the gods, and master of a million worlds by the might of his inexhaustible armies. He is a rotting carcass writhing invisibly with power from the Dark Age of Technology. He is the Carrion Lord of the Imperium for whom a thousand souls are sacrificed every day, so that he may never truly die.

Yet even in his deathless state, the Emperor continues his eternal vigilance. Mighty battlefleets cross the daemon-infested miasma of the warp, the only route between distant stars, their way lit by the Astronomican, the psychic manifestation of the Emperor's will. Vast armies give battle in His name on uncounted worlds. Greatest amongst his soldiers are the Adeptus Astartes, the Space Marines, bio-engineered super-warriors. Their comrades in arms are legion: the Imperial Guard and countless planetary defence forces, the ever-vigilant Inquisition and the tech-priests of the Adeptus Mechanicus to name only a few. But for all their multitudes, they are barely enough to hold off the ever-present threat from aliens, heretics, mutants - and worse.

To be a man in such times is to be one amongst untold billions. It is to live in the cruellest and most bloody regime imaginable. These are the tales of those times. Forget the power of technology and science, for so much has been forgotten, never to be re-learned. Forget the promise of progress and understanding, for in the grim dark future there is only war. There is no peace amongst the stars, only an eternity of carnage and slaughter, and the laughter of thirsting gods.

CHAPTER I

I-Day Minus 15

OBEDIENCE. LABOUR. FIDELITY.

The three words stretched across the cyclopean wall, each letter ten metres high and stamped in steel. Lines of corrosion bled downwards from each word, scarring the ferrocrete blocks to which they were bolted. At the base of each wall, a narrow gutter carried the oxidised runoff into drainage pits, where it mixed with the waste of the smelters to create a slither of toxic steam that danced in the hot susurrus of the foundry's machinery.

Yuxiang stared up at those words, feeling them pressing down upon him in all their corroded malignance. From no point in the mammoth processing plant was it possible to escape the steel letters. Like watchful gods, they glared down upon the slaves chained beside the conveyor belts, pneumatic presses, industrial ovens and bubbling slag pits. Every time the great blast furnaces vented a sheet of flame from their stacks, the steel letters reflected a hellish glow, the light of mirrored fires rippling along their length.

Above the din and roar of the conveyors, the fiery growl of the furnaces and the shriek of steam leaving the ovens, it was impossible to escape the low snarl being vomited by the vox-casters scattered about the plant. An endless litany of dry, grim voices chanting the same mantra stamped upon the factory wall.

Obedience. Labour. Fidelity.

The slaves in Processing Plant Secundus Minorus lived by the words that had been drilled into their very souls. Very often, they died by them.

Across the face of Castellax, there were millions who slaved to feed the war machine of their oppressors. Hour after hour, day after day, without rest or respite, they toiled to spread tyranny and destruction across the galaxy. Their only reward was the continuance of life, but for men like Yuxiang, it was enough. They had seen what became of those who defied the lords of Castellax.

Work had halted in Yuxiang's section. Sometimes the machinery would require maintenance or some fault in the processors mandated a shut down. Such occasions were cause for cheer among the slaves. The reason for the current break, however, didn't make even the most jaded labourer happy.

Yuxiang watched the whip-thin figure of Prefect Wyre, supervisor of Processing Plant Secundus Minorus, pace along the steel gantry above his section. Wyre's face was lean and hard, his features stamped with callousness and cruelty. Among the thousands of slaves in the factory, there wasn't one who hadn't felt the burn of Wyre's shock baton against his ribs. As he paced, the prefect slapped the deactivated baton against his palm, the hollow *thwack* making a menacing accompaniment to the click of his boots against the metal grating.

Kneeling before the prefect was a dishevelled, emaciated man, his scrawny frame draped in the coveralls of a factory slave, the brand of Secundus Minorus etched across his forehead. Blood streamed from the man's broken nose and with each breath a bubble of blood dribbled from the corner of his mouth. The black-clad overseers who flanked the prostrate slave hadn't been gentle when they subdued him.

'Who is that?' The question came in a whisper, uttered by Chingwei, Yuxiang's alternate at the pneumatic press.

'Mendes, from Blast Furnace Gamma-four,' Yuxiang whispered back.

'An off-worlder,' Chingwei sighed, a trace of envy in his tone. Yuxiang could understand the sentiment. Whatever fate awaited Mendes, at least the man hadn't been born into servitude on Castellax. At least he had known some kind of life before he was condemned to the factories.

'What did he do?' Chingwei hissed. Despite the horror of the situation, the slave couldn't restrain his curiosity about the reason for this break in routine.

Yuxiang hesitated before answering, glancing about to make sure none of Wyre's overseers were near. 'He made the sign of the aquila,' he said.

'Poor, stupid off-world bastard,' Chingwei said. 'Wyre will have him shot for that. When will these off-worlders learn?'

The gaunt prefect was launching into a harangue now, his voice raised in a caustic hiss that was amplified into a fiery roar by the factory's vox-casters.

'When will you vermin learn?' Wyre asked. 'When will you understand that your superstitions will not help you?' The prefect leaned in, activating his baton and driving the butt of the weapon against Mendes's midsection. The slave cried out as electricity crackled across his body. He writhed in the grip of the overseers who held him, his captors safe inside their insulated uniforms.

'You are no longer a man,' Wyre snapped, turning away from the slave and pacing along the gantry. 'You do not think. You do not dream. You do not hope.' He rounded on Mendes, smashing the baton across his mouth. Lightning sizzled through the captive's clenched teeth. 'You do not pray!'

Yuxiang watched the torture, impotent rage boiling inside him. He longed to do something, anything to stop the hideous tableau. But he knew there was nothing that could be done. He had seen Wyre at work too many times to hold any delusions that the prefect could be stopped. Any gesture of defiance and he would simply join Mendes in his suffering.

'Did you really think anyone would answer you?' Wyre sneered, stabbing the butt of his baton into Mendes's shoulder. The slave's body twisted and jerked in a spasm of agony as the shock scorched his flesh. 'What did you pray for, scum? Did you pray for freedom? Did you pray for justice? Did you ask for revenge?' The baton crackled against the man's thigh, searing through the leg of his coverall as Wyre intensified the strength of its discharge. The smell of burned meat drifted down from the gantry.

'There are none of those things here,' Wyre announced, turning from his victim and glaring across the upturned faces of the factory's slaves. He raised his baton, jabbing it over his shoulder, pointing at the steel words on the wall. 'Obedience. Labour. Fidelity. Those are the only things here! And when you forget that… there is pain.'

Wyre spun around, thrusting the baton into Mendes's gut. The slave screamed, thrashing wildly in the grip of the overseers. The prefect grinned sadistically as he held the activated shock baton in place, watching it burn into the slave's body.

'God-Emperor have mercy!' Mendes shrieked.

Wyre's face turned crimson with rage. He drew back the baton, revealing blackened skin where it had rested on the captive's body. His gloved hand seized the slave's hair, forcing the man's face upwards, forcing him to look into the prefect's blazing eyes. 'There is no God-Emperor here,' he spat. His finger ran across the power stud of his shock baton, pushing it to maximum intensity. Electricity danced from the head of the weapon. 'There is only *me*!'

Wyre raised the baton to jab it into Mendes's face, but

before the prefect's blow could land, a thunderous voice called out, 'Restrain yourself, peon.'

The red rage drained from Wyre's face, replaced by an ashen pallor. He turned slowly, facing in the direction from which the booming voice had sounded. Immediately, the prefect deactivated his shock baton and dropped to his knees, bowing his head in abject submission.

From the shadow of a loading elevator, a giant stalked out onto the gantry, the steel grates groaning under his armoured weight. The huge figure towered over the black-clad overseers, men chosen for their size and ferocity. His dimensions were superhuman, two metres from crown to toe, as broad as an ore-cart. The ornate armour he wore was a masterwork of ceramite plates, deeply engraved with gilded flames. The giant's helmet encased his head completely, red optics glaring out from a mask of iron. The face of the helm was pulled forwards in a long beak, its sides carved into the image of a fanged, snarling mouth. Upon one bulky shoulder pauldron, a leering metal skull glowered down at the slaves of Processing Plant Secundus Minorus.

A thrill of terror swept through the assembly. Chains clattered as men covered their eyes, moans of horror rose unbidden from stunned spectators. For once, even the overseers were taken aback, staring with outright fear as the giant marched towards Prefect Wyre.

Yuxiang's body trembled like a leaf in a storm. He longed to hide his face from the armoured nightmare but found himself as transfixed as a sump-rat watching an ash-viper.

Wyre was nothing. His brutality was nothing. His cruelty was nothing. The prefect was little better than a slave himself, a vassal to the masters of Castellax, a clever pet to the monsters who ruled over Yuxiang's home world.

Among the slaves, particularly the off-worlders, there were whispers about the warrior angels who defended the Imperium, the semi-divine Adeptus Astartes, supermen who brought battle to the enemies of mankind and enabled the spread of humanity across the stars. They were demigods, sons of the God-Emperor Himself, protectors of His faithful children.

The masters of Castellax were a profane mockery of that holy image. They were angels defiled and corrupted, twisted into things monstrous and obscene.

They were the Iron Warriors.

'My Lord Rhodaan,' Wyre addressed the armoured giant, his voice little more than a frightened squeak. 'You do Processing Plant Secundus Minorus great honour with your presence.'

Rhodaan stopped his march only a few metres from the cowering prefect. When he spoke, his voice was deep and malignant, infected with a metallic snarl by the amplifiers in his helmet. The Iron Warrior didn't deign to look at the prefect when he spoke, instead fixing his gaze upon the tortured Mendes.

'Why have you halted production?' Rhodaan demanded. 'Why is this Flesh not at its work station?'

Shivering with terror, Wyre risked a look at the slave he had been punishing. 'I-I was making a-an example of this one.' He pointed his baton at the slaves below. 'I felt th-that the others n-needed discipline...'

The Iron Warrior stood in silence for a moment, still staring at Mendes. 'What did this Flesh do?' he asked at last.

The question brought beads of sweat dripping down Wyre's forehead. He swallowed nervously. 'He was ca-caught making the sign of the aquila.'

Rhodaan's head turned, the lenses of his helmet boring down upon the trembling prefect. 'That is unfortunate.'

'I-I was making a-an example... Reminding th-the rest...'

The Iron Warrior was no longer listening to Wyre. With two steps, Rhodaan reached Mendes. The giant's ceramite gauntlets closed around the slave's scrawny forearms.

With a single wrenching motion, he broke both of the man's arms and dropped the screaming wretch at the feet of the overseers.

'Hang this animal above one of the smelters,' Rhodaan ordered Wyre as he began to march away. 'Every minute the creature fails to make the sign of the aquila, you will lower him one centimetre. It will be interesting to see if his faith in the False Emperor sustains him when he feels the kiss of molten titanium on his toes.'

Yuxiang held his gaze on Rhodaan until the Space Marine vanished once more into the shadows around the loading elevator. Only then did he look back at Mendes, watching with horror as Wyre ordered his overseers to secure the mangled man to one of the chains suspended above the closest smelter. With his broken arms, there was no chance Mendes could make the gesture demanded of him. Centimetre by centimetre, he would be lowered towards the molten metal and hideous death.

Truly, the off-worlder would have been better left to the brutality of Wyre. Compared to the Iron Warrior, the prefect's punishment would have been an act of mercy.

Captain Antares leaned back in his grox-hide command throne and watched as the icy grey globe grew steadily smaller. At this distance, he could just barely make out the superstructures of the transfer stations orbiting the moon. If not for the guide-lights mounted to their docking arms, he doubted if he'd have been able to pick them out from the black starscape which stretched across the bridge's viewscreen.

Impex V, outermost of the vagabond moons of the Castellax system. For an interplanetary tanker like the *Stardrinker*, it took two weeks to make the voyage, take on cargo and return. Two weeks of unrelieved monotony and boredom. Impex V to Castellax. Castellax to Impex V. Back and forth, week in and week out. An unbreakable pattern that had ruled Antares's life for the past seven years, ever since he'd had the misfortune of surviving an Iron Warriors slave raid and become one of their thralls.

Antares rose from his throne, hearing the heavy grox-hide adjust itself to his vanished weight. Idly the captain descended the short flight of stairs separating the command dais from the main deck of the bridge. He filed past the technicians labouring at their displays, sometimes pausing to look over a shoulder and study the information scrolling across a screen. Antares didn't understand half of what he was looking at, but it was more important that his crew thought he did. Efficiency through encouraged paranoia was something the Iron Warriors used to dominate their fleet. Antares found it worked just as well for him on his own bridge.

The captain looked up from the terminal of a sandy-haired officer, frowning at the younger man. 'Don't you think we can do better?' he asked the lieutenant. Antares didn't wait for an answer, but continued walking the bridge. Any questions might have proved awkward. He wasn't sure if better meant an increase or decrease.

The black sprawl of the bridge's pict screen stretched before Antares as he reached the last of the terminals. He paused a moment, staring out at the grey blob which marked Impex V's position. *Two weeks*, he thought, *and then I'll be staring at the exact same thing all over again*.

It was a problem that had plagued Castellax for a hundred years. Even before the world fell to the Iron Warriors, it had been a desolate place. If not for its vast mineral resources, the Imperium would have bypassed the planet. But Castellax was rich in promethium and heavy metals, so the Imperium had established a colony on the world to exploit the planet's wealth.

That same wealth had drawn the Iron Warriors. They needed the resources of Castellax to feed their great war machine, to build new warships for their raider fleets, tanks and guns for their marauding armies. After seizing control of the planet, they had instituted a policy of savage exploitation that made the Imperium's industry pale by comparison. Such rampant ravaging of the planet had not been without its consequences. The seas were drained to feed the factories and strip mines, the water table under the planet's surface was hopelessly corrupted by industrial waste. After a century of occupation by the Iron Warriors, there wasn't a spoonful of freestanding water left on Castellax that wasn't nine-parts toxic sludge.

The Iron Warriors had been forced to look elsewhere to feed Castellax's thirst. In the frozen outer moon of Impex V, they found their solution. Orbital stations were brought to surround the moon, each station deploying hundreds of small barges which would fly down to harvest the ice. A fleet of tankers like the *Stardrinker* would then collect it, ferrying the huge frozen blocks back to Castellax, a continuous chain of supply to keep the fires of industry burning.

'Captain Antares!' one of the officers suddenly cried out, breaking Antares's contemplation of the ice-moon. He turned towards the excited crewman, marching over to his station and staring at the pict screen.

'These objects just appeared in our starboard quadrant,' the officer reported. Antares did not know much about the actual operation of his ship, but he was able to recognise the fast-moving blips whose trajectory put them on an intercept course.

'Could they be elements of the supply fleet?' Antares asked. The officer shook his head.

'No, sir. They are too far from Castellax to be fighters and too small to be destroyers.'

As Antares digested the problem of what the blips might represent, the crewmen at the communications relays suddenly clapped their hands to their ears, swiftly turning down the volume of the vox-implants bolted to their skulls.

'Captain Antares!' one of them shouted. 'We've tried hailing the blips. Every frequency is being overwhelmed by some kind of strange intercept.' The comms officer reached down to his terminal. As he depressed an activation rune, vox-casters began to broadcast the weird chatter. It was a confusion of deep grunts and croaking laughter, a bedlam of gruff, brutal vocalizations.

Antares listened to the chatter, a feeling of dread crawling up his spine. He glanced again at the display of the starboard quadrant. The objects were quickly gaining on the *Stardrinker*. There was no question of them being meteors or any other stellar phenomenon – to maintain their position, the objects had made a deliberate course correction. Only something with awareness could pursue a ship.

'Raise the defence fleet,' Antares ordered the comms officer. Tell them we are being menaced by unidentified craft.'

The officer shook his head. 'We can't raise anyone, captain. The chatter is across the board. On every frequency.'

Antares stared once more at the display. At their present speed, the unknown ships would intercept the tanker within a matter of a few minutes.

'All crew to battle stations,' Antares ordered.

'Keep trying to break through the interference. Find an open channel. Spread the alarm.

'We are under attack.'

BODRAS CURLED HIS gnarled hand around the jug of caff and took a long pull of the fiery drink. It was an old mixture he'd picked up from some gunrunners on the Eastern Fringe, back when his vessel had been an Imperial patrol ship – caff mixed with fermented vespid jelly and twenty grams of cordite. On a ship like the *Vulture*, it was smart to have a drink none of your crew would touch.

Wiping the treacly residue of the drink from his beard, Bodras shifted in his command throne, staring down into the crew pits flanking the captain's bridge. The pits were so filled with scanners, relays, exchanges, comms hubs, fire control systems and observation-slates that there was scarcely room for the crew to breathe. The original complement of machinery the frigate had been fitted out with when it left the shipyards of Calth had been greatly augmented in the decades since she had entered the thraldom of the Iron Warriors. Every vessel the *Vulture* had captured had contributed something to her conqueror's improvement, augmenting her far beyond the frugality imposed by the Imperial Navy.

Bodras smoothed the front of his brocaded jacket as he rose from his throne. The jacket was two sizes too big for him, but the smoothness of its virgin scand-wool and the jade-studded epaulets were too fine for him to worry overmuch about the garment's fit. The jacket had belonged to the deputy governor of Galar IX, right up until five seconds before Bodras blew his head off. Such a noble heritage, he felt, was bound to have rubbed off on the jacket – and by extension to himself.

Aristocratic pretensions notwithstanding, Bodras bellowed down at his junior officers, 'Any sign of that damn scow?' and punctuated his shout with a cordite-scented belch.

'Negative, captain,' called back a hook-nosed lieutenant, the mechanical eye set into his scarred face whirring and buzzing as it focused upon Bodras. 'We've picked up no sign of the *Stardrinker*.'

'Did you try raising her?' Bodras growled. He didn't care for patrol duty to begin with – any interruption to routine only made it worse.

The one-eyed lieutenant jabbed a thumb over his shoulder to one of the frigate's comms relays. 'All we've been able to get is a bunch of noise. It's across all frequencies. Probably solar interference.'

Bodras glared down at the lieutenant. 'Did that shrapnel take out part of your brain as well as your eye? We're sixty-four AU from the sun! Any solar activity that could interfere with us here would also burn Castellax to a cinder.'

The lieutenant ran his thumb along his scarred cheek. 'My... my apologies, captain. I will have the arrays examined for malfunctions.'

'All six of them?' Bodras growled. He was beginning to wonder why he'd made this idiot an officer. Something about two kilograms of fire-emeralds if he remembered right. He was reconsidering that bribe right now. What good was all this equipment if the man in charge of it was a moron?

'Narrow the range of the frequency sweep. If they are using unsecured transmissions on Impex V, we might be catching echoes.' Bodras stepped down from his throne, passing between the pair of armed bodyguards flanking the raised dais. It was astounding what the threat of two shotguns could do to enforce morale in a confined space.

The captain loomed over the sunken crew pit, watching as the comms men adjusted their equipment. Bodras tapped the holster of his laspistol, growing irritated at the delay.

'Captain, we're detecting a vapour cloud one hundred kilometres starboard,' another officer reported. Bodras favoured the communication section with a last menacing look, then turned his attention to the long-range scanners. The crewmen shifted aside to allow Bodras a clear view.

'The molecular scan identifies a high oxygen/hydrogen content,' the scanner officer said. 'It could be water vapour. The tanker might have had an accident.'

'If the idiot dumped his cargo, he'd better hope it was a serious accident,' Bodras said. Even that probably wouldn't save the tanker's crew from the ire of the Iron Warriors. Men seldom lived to disappoint the lords of Castellax twice.

Studying the screen, Bodras pointed at a large blotch a few thousand kilometres from the vapour cloud. 'What is that?' he asked.

'Asteroid,' the officer replied. 'High metal content. They

will be happy to hear of such a find back on Castellax.' The man's face spread in a steel-toothed grin. 'The ship who reports this discovery will be well favoured by the Iron Warriors.'

Bodras shook his head. Something wasn't right. Castellax needed water more than metal – any captain who dumped his cargo so that he could race back and gain the dubious gratitude of the Iron Warriors for discovering a new asteroid was too stupid to be believed. No, there was something very wrong. An asteroid loaded with metal ore just sitting right next to the most travelled space route in the system…

The vox-casters on the bridge suddenly broke out in a chaotic din of savage growls and grunts. Bodras spun around, his eyes bulging as the hideous cacophony struck horror in his heart. The comms men had narrowed down their scan to isolate a very narrow frequency range, then filtered it further to a single transmission band. Now that he heard it, Bodras almost wished he hadn't. The interference had been caused by a bedlam of crude vox-transmissions scattered across a range of frequencies, their erratic and unstable nature causing them to bleed across each other. In effect, their very primitiveness, the obsolescent inefficiency and instability of the transmissions had overwhelmed the frigate's sensitive equipment. The *Vulture*'s sharp ears had been deaf to the howls of the worst predator in the galaxy.

Bodras knew those voices. He'd heard them before, on the Eastern Fringe.

Now he understood why there was an asteroid lying just off the trade route between Impex V and Castellax.

'Battle stations! Battle stations! Battle stations!' Bodras roared, storming across the bridge and smashing his fist through the glass casing of the alert signal. Claxons wailed as harsh crimson lights flashed from the ceiling.

'Hail all gun crews,' Bodras snarled down at his officers. 'I want every battery trained on that asteroid! I want torpedoes at the ready! I–'

'Captain, we are picking up thirty... no... forty energy discharges from the surface of the asteroid,' one of the officers shouted. 'Captain, it's firing at us!'

Bodras raised the jug of caff and took a quick swig. They were too late. The enemy had gotten off the first salvo. All they could do now was hope their void shields could withstand the barrage.

Because what was out there, lurking off the space lane, wasn't an asteroid any more. It had been hollowed out and turned into a space-faring fortress by the most murderous species in the galaxy.

The orks.

CHAPTER II
I-Day Minus 14

IT CAME LUMBERING out of the void, a great darkness that blotted out the stars with its advance. A leviathan from space, a behemoth that roared between worlds like a vengeful devil. It had been born in the cauldron of an angry cosmos, a slab of rock and metal seventy kilometres in diameter, a fledgling planet that had never found its place and so had been cast into the emptiness between galaxies.

There, in the darkness, savage intelligences had found it, had descended upon this abandoned almost-world and through their barbaric technology had given it purpose, a place in the cosmos. A place of horror, havoc and destruction.

The *Vulture* was like a fly buzzing about the wings of a hawk, the disparity between the patrol ship and the rok was so immense. The rok was vast enough to exert its own gravitational pull on the ship, dragging her slowly towards it, affording the terrified crew an increasingly clear view of their mammoth adversary.

The rok was pitted and scarred, pockmarked with the impacts of smaller asteroids against its surface, gouged by the crude excavations of the orks. Towers and bunkers projected from the asteroid's surface, hangars gaped in the walls of its canyons, gun emplacements bristled from its jagged mountains. Cyclopean engines, their exhausts a hundred metres wide, projected from the rok's sides, spitting streams of atomic fire as the orks inside the asteroid struggled to direct its trajectory, to exert some measure of control upon the elemental force they had attempted to enslave.

It was a futile effort. The best the orks could do was cause the rok to revolve, to spin on its axis as it hurtled through the void. For the xenos, however, it was enough, allowing them to adjust the position of their heaviest guns and bring them to bear against those victims unfortunate enough to encounter the rok.

The crew of the *Vulture* was almost upon the rok before they were aware of their peril. The deranged array of guns and missile batteries the orks had fitted to the hollowed-out asteroid opened fire in a savage burst of destruction. An armada of alien craft exploded from the canyon hangars and from launch craters littering the surface. The rok had provided shelter to a ramshackle flotilla of smaller ork ships, an ugly assortment of scrap metal that somehow managed to be space-worthy. What the ork ships lacked in grace, they made up for in firepower. Some of the weapons they boasted were so massive that the ships which carried them fairly disintegrated the moment they fired.

It was punishment the frigate's void shields were never meant to handle. More and more of the alien barrage was getting through, ripping Bodras's ship apart.

THE VULTURE REELED as another broadside smashed into her. The ship's artificial gravity struggled to compensate for the rolling vessel, creating a wild confusion of forces upon the bridge. Bodras watched as one of his body-guards hurtled forwards, then was grabbed and dragged by a malfunctioning inertia dampener. The screaming man smashed into the wall as though he'd been fired from a torpedo tube, his ribcage collapsing as the damp-ener tried to pull his body through the bulkhead.

The captain took another pull of his jug and shuddered. Squashed like a bug wasn't a pretty way to die.

'Damage report,' he snarled at the bloodied men down in the crew pits. Between overloaded circuits, dislodged machinery and debris from the ship's infrastructure, not a man in the pit had escaped some sort of injury. The dead had been unceremoniously dumped onto the walkway where the inertia dampener grabbed hold of them. The worst of the wounded had been similarly disposed of until Bodras ordered the practice stopped. Even if they were in the way, the wounded had to be shown some consideration. It was bad for morale if they weren't.

Lieutenant Collorus studied one of the flickering pict screens and cried back to the command throne. 'There is a hull breach aft, exposing three decks to vacuum. The gravity generators can't compensate, so we're vacillating between a seven and ten degree list. Alpha and Beta bat-teries have been obliterated by direct hits. Gamma battery is still firing but we've lost all communication with the gunnery crew.'

'Send runners,' Bodras snapped. 'We need to maintain fire control. The only way we'll survive is by concentrat-ing our fire!'

Even as he gave the order, Bodras wondered if it would really make any difference.

'Only one macro-cannon still operational,' an ensign with a raw gash across his forehead reported, cringing back as his terminal spat a shower of sparks at him. 'Vox communications have been lost throughout the lower decks!'

Bodras groaned. That would be those filthy missiles the

rok had fired into them. The moment they had struck, the crew had breathed a sigh of relief, thinking they were duds. Then the electronic pulses had started, gradually increasing in scope and intensity. Somehow the missiles were both absorbing and projecting energy. The effect was like a massive haywire grenade, shorting out machinery close to the point of impact and utterly severing the lines of communication passing through that part of the ship.

'Fires in the kitchens, crew barracks and officers' deck!' another ensign shouted.

'Get a fire control team down there,' Bodras ordered. If a fire was allowed to go unchecked in that part of the frigate, the ship would be effectively cut in two.

'The team assigned to that area was killed by a hull breach,' Lieutenant Collorus reported. 'We're trying to redirect another team there now.'

'Don't try, do!' Bodras roared. He stared at the view-screen beside him. The rok was slowly closing upon the frigate, rotating to bring an obscenely huge cannon mounted on its surface to bear on the *Vulture*. Some of the smaller ork ships were scattering, intimidated by the approach of their hulking comrade. Others, too lost in their mindless urge to destroy, continued to swarm about the frigate.

'More hull breaches in decks nineteen through twenty-four!'

'Fire control has been hit! Can't raise fire control!'

'Last macro-cannon has gone silent!'

'Delta battery reports two plasma batteries have overheated!'

Bodras turned the jug upside down, draining the last few drops from the bottom. He tossed the empty vessel aside, watching as the inertia dampener caught it and smashed it against the bulkhead.

'Report to Castellax,' the captain said, his voice cold as he watched the rok rotate into position. 'Tell them we've occupied the orks as long as we can.'

Bodras watched as a brilliant glow gathered in the mouth of the rok's oversized cannon.

'Tell our dread masters they can expect some company real soon,' Bodras spat. He glanced down at his elegant jacket. It was such a shame that so fine a garment was going to be ruined.

Mummified husks of humanity, bound in sinews of steel and garbed in mantles of iron, mouths stretched wide in frozen screams, the Eternal Choir loomed from the vaulted heights, incense dripping from their desiccated chests, madness crawling in their shrivelled eyes. Each servitor was bolted fast to the face of a curved pillar, their broken arms wrapped about the obverse side. A low chant hissed from the throats of the automatons, a sibilance that somehow melded the harmony of song to the howling of beasts.

The monstrous chant swept across the grim chamber below. Promethium lamps cast an infernal glow, sending weird shadows slithering about the pillars and dancing along the heavily adorned walls. Bas relief battles raged anew as the play of crimson light and black shadow swept across them, once more igniting the ancient campaigns of Sebastus IV and Olympia. Power-armoured giants contested bloodied battlegrounds, their gilded bolters and chainswords glistening with reflected light. Stone Titans rained destruction upon screaming masses of humanity, thorny towers bristling with armaments wrought carnage upon Space Marines of the Imperial Fists Legion while gloating killers adorned in the heraldry of the Iron Warriors visited doom upon those striving to escape the trap.

Everywhere in the frescoes, one terrifying visage was repeated. The glowering countenance of an Iron Warrior encased in baroque Terminator armour, wielding a storm bolter and a power claw encrusted with shining rubies. Half the Space Marine's face was flesh, the rest was nought save a snarling skull of metal. Wherever the hulking warrior appeared, there the enemy lay heaped and torn about his feet. Always there was a sense of malignance and power in his piercing stare.

Seated in a throne of pure diamond, clear as ice and strong as adamantium, its legs shaped into clawed feet and its back carved into folded wings, the half-faced monster from the wall cast a steely gaze across the gloom. The flesh of his face was puckered and raw, scarred with hideous burns and the corrosive caress of things beyond human imagining. The metal of his exposed skull bristled with cables and power feeds, a nest of synthetic serpents that coiled about the Iron Warrior's neck before sinking into sockets scattered across the bulky armour he wore. Even in rest, safe within the halls of the Iron Bastion, mightiest fortress-keep on Castellax, Warsmith Andraaz kept himself locked inside his ancient suit of Terminator armour. It was whispered that his body hadn't stirred from the plasteel and ceramite shell in five millennia.

To either side of the throne towered the hulk of another Space Marine encased in Terminator armour, a member of the elite Rending Guard. Bodyguard to the Warsmith, the Terminators were veterans of countless campaigns, their armour studded with battle honours and draped in trophies torn from the bodies of their conquests. When the Terminators committed themselves to combat, it was only on the express command of Andraaz. They recognised no other authority short of Perturabo himself.

The Warsmith stretched out his hand, closing the armoured gauntlet into a fist and smashed it down against the immense table of obsidian which dominated the centre of the chamber. The crazed network of glowing wires and relays streaming through the semi-transparent rock blinked as the impact sent a tremor through the table.

'Enough,' Andraaz growled, his voice like a metallic scratch. The word echoed through a suddenly silent room, even the chanting of the servitors retreating before the monster's anger.

Seated about the obsidian table, a half-dozen armoured giants shifted uncomfortably in their chairs. Masters of life and death, gods of destruction and doom to the millions of slaves entombed upon Castellax, the Iron Warriors felt their hearts quicken as Andraaz focused his ire upon them.

'It does not matter how the filthy xenos infiltrated the system,' Andraaz hissed, turning the red lens of his synthetic eye upon the man seated to his right.

Broad of build, massive of frame, Captain Morax, Skylord of Castellax, glared spitefully at his opposite across the table. Morax ran a jewelled glove through the stubble of hair covering his scalp, wiping away the beads of perspiration gathering there. 'Honoured Warsmith,' Morax said, sucking at the moist fingers of his glove, 'I was merely observing that if control of the fleet had been shared with my administration, then these intruders would have been dealt with much sooner.' A trace of a smile curled the Skylord's flaccid cheeks as he watched his rival across the table react to his taunt.

'That is a dangerous insinuation, Sky-rat,' the other Iron Warrior spat. Admiral Nostraz was a towering man whose face was, if anything, even more scarred than that of Andraaz, though he hadn't augmented any of his mutilations with cybernetic implants. 'The raider fleets stand as ready for action as they ever have.' His eyes darkened and his voice dripped with menace. 'Or perhaps you would prefer we send half our ships out every time we hear a noise or one of our tankers is overdue?'

'It is a sad thing to see timidity masquerading as strategy,' Morax said, grinning. Nostraz's eyes narrowed into murderous slits and he lurched up from his chair.

'The Warsmith said there was to be an end to this squabbling!' roared the Iron Warrior seated to the left of Andraaz. Captain Gamgin was a vicious specimen of savagery, one arm a mass of gears and cables bound in plasteel plate and armaplas fibres, one leg given over to a grumbling bundle of machinery, his lower jaw a set of piston-driven steel fangs. The Ruinous Powers had been quite attentive to Gamgin over the millennia, corrupting his body with fierce mutations. Each time the warp corruption settled into his flesh, a bit more of Gamgin had been cut away and replaced by metal. The millions of conscript soldiers Gamgin maintained on Castellax held that the first part of him that had been changed to steel was his heart. Only one purpose beat there now: complete and merciless loyalty to Andraaz.

Both Nostraz and Morax shifted their hateful gaze from one another to Gamgin. As much as the two rivals might hate each other, their mutual contempt for Gamgin and envy at his favour with the Warsmith gave them common cause. At the slightest nod from Morax, Nostraz pointed at the shifting pattern of lights displayed above the surface of the obsidian table. It was a three-dimensional star-map of the Castellax system, not a true hologram but rather a projection of the table's weird elements. As Nostraz pointed, the table reacted, shifting and magnifying one portion of the starfield while allowing the rest of the map to recede.

'The orks struck from the fringe of the system, in the vicinity of Impex V. The high proportion of asteroids in that sector has always been a detriment to our sensors.' The admiral gestured and brought the image of an old Imperial frigate into view. 'Our initial response, a single system patrol sentry, was overwhelmed by the intruders. They have since penetrated the static defences surrounding the ice-moon and its neighbours. Mostly through the crude callousness of their assaults. They think nothing of driving their smaller ships straight into the waiting guns of a satellite and obliterating the position with the debris of their own comrades.' At the snap of his fingers a dozen more ships appeared on the map, each image slowly collapsing into a menagerie of lights gradually streaming towards Impex V. 'The second wave consists of five Infidel-class raiders and seven system-defence destroyers. They will engage the orks. After whetting the aliens' appetite for battle, the raiders will withdraw, using their greater speed to outdistance the destroyers. They will maintain a presence just beyond the enemy guns while the orks are occupied with the destroyers. With the greenskins busy, the raiders will use their macro-cannon to pick them off from afar.'

'And if the xenos have weaponry able to match the range of the macro-cannons? Or if the orks have infiltrated in numbers capable of focusing on both elements of your fleet?' The questions came from a scowling man, his richly adorned armour studded with battle honours and the leathery trophies of past conquests. Over-Captain Vallax, his face split by the jagged scar of a World Eater's chainaxe, his long hair shifting in hue as his emotions darkened, leaned over the obsidian table. The Over-Captain's gauntlet touched a line of ships further towards the core of the system.

'I see these possibilities have already occurred to you,' Vallax mused. As he touched the lights, each was revealed as another vessel in the Castellax fleet. In all, there were fifty-nine ships in the second line Nostraz had established.

The admiral nodded his head. 'The second wave has a two-fold purpose. The first is to engage the xenos, but more importantly they are to gauge their numbers and deployment.'

'Orks don't have any rational deployment,' scoffed the ghoulish Skintaker Algol, Slavemaster of Castellax. The Iron Warrior's armour was lost beneath the hideous folds of the cloak he wore, a garment fashioned from human skin flayed from slaves. The stink of blood still clung to the freshest patches of Algol's vestment. When the aroma wore off, he would stalk back into the strip mines in search of fresher replacements.

'Rational or not, we need to know where they are,'

Morax snapped back. 'Our sensors can't give us proper intelligence for that sector, and there is too much psychic disturbance in the area for the Navigators on our ships to provide us with anything useful.'

Captain Rhodaan stood and faced the Skylord. 'What about using the Speaker?' he suggested. Morax ran his glove across his scalp again, hesitating to answer the question.

When the question was answered, it was Warsmith Andraaz who spoke. 'The Speaker may be needed for other duties.'

A dull, mechanical rasp crackled from the end of the table. Alone among those gathered in the war room, the speaker wasn't an Iron Warrior, but rather a withered shell of humanity. Pale, corpse-like flesh fused to a mechanical armature, its gaping mouth housing the meshwork of a vox-caster, the servitor was acting as the proxy for the only member of Castellax's hierarchy absent from the chamber. When it spoke, however, all within the room knew they heard the voice of Fabricator Oriax.

'To focus the Speaker's thoughts upon such a task would require a drastic change to the chemical mixture in its bath. To safely perform such a procedure would take days. To unsafely perform such a procedure might kill it. Or, even worse, return it to awareness.'

There was no emotion on the corpse-face of the servitor as it transmitted Oriax's words, but a flicker of uneasiness crossed the countenance of each Iron Warrior who heard them. Veterans of thousands of wars, victorious conquerors of hundreds of worlds, they knew better than to tamper with an alpha-grade psyker, especially after what they had done to him.

'Using the Speaker is out of the question,' Andraaz declared. 'We will proceed with Admiral Nostraz's plan.'

THREE SCARRED AND battered Infidel-class raiders raced across the stellar emptiness. Behind them, the ships abandoned wounded comrades and slower support vessels, consigning each to the doubtful mercies of the orks. Survival, not loyalty, was the law of the moment. Flee now, or remain forever with the dead.

From the bridge of the *Requiem*, Arch-Commander Vortsk watched as the survivors drew steadily closer to the defensive line his fleet had established. The old pirate's brow knitted with dismay, disturbing the nest of cables implanted into his forehead that hardwired his mind with the cogitators of his battleship. He could feel his vessel's agitation pulsing through the wires, like a hound smelling blood. The *Requiem* was an old hand at slaughter, having perpetrated thousands of atrocities in her time, both for and against the decaying Imperium. Since defecting after the Badab War, the battleship's lust for violence had only grown. Vortsk sometimes wondered if her time in the Eye of Terror had endowed his ship with a consciousness of her own.

'Patience,' Vortsk whispered, his fingers tapping against the command baton resting in his lap. 'You shall glut your hunger soon enough, my sweet.'

The Arch-Commander forced the ship's agitation into his subconscious and focused his attention upon the pict screens scattered about his control-nest. The armoured, tomb-like pod was ringed with flickering displays, cycling through views of every deck on the battleship. Vortsk ignored these and the thousands of relays transmitting views of the *Requiem*'s exterior hull. What interested him were the long-range observium reports, the transmissions from the fleeing raiders and the vox-chatter of the on-coming enemy.

Together, the data created a fearsome picture. The raiders and their destroyer escorts had encountered a far bigger mass of orks than the doomed *Vulture* had reported. The rok was still active, but now it served as just another warship in an armada that dwarfed the combined might of the entire Castellax fleet. If the data from the raiders was to be trusted, the aliens had infiltrated the system with three hundred vessels of destroyer-size or greater, including two monstrosities boasting a mass approaching that of an Oberon-class battleship.

There were other ork vessels operating deep in the system. An alien species as wild and vicious as the orks rarely maintained focus and cohesion, and the invaders of Castellax were no different. Small splinters of the armada were attacking the remote mining outposts scattered through the planetoids at the fringe of the system, while a hulking kill kroozer had been closing upon the Impex V station when the last message was transmitted from the ice-moon.

Vortsk scowled as he examined the data. The odds were against the human fleet, but he knew there was more to securing victory than simple numerical advantage. The human mind was organised, analytical and calculating. That of the ork was simple barbarous instinct, with no greater thought than closing with an enemy and giving immediate battle.

The Arch-Commander studied the pict screens displaying the proximity of the ork forces. While some of the armada had lingered behind to finish off the abandoned destroyers and crippled raiders, a small number of ships were pursuing the three raiders that had escaped. Vortsk licked his lips as he saw that among the pursuers was one of the big battleship analogues. The ork armada as a whole might outnumber the human fleet, but in the present circumstance, the advantage belonged to Vortsk. There were only a half-dozen escorts with the ork battleship, none of them larger than a frigate. Even allowing for the ork propensity to pile ridiculous amounts of armament onto their ships, the human battle line had them outgunned twenty to one.

'Raise the captains of the *Pride* and the *Damnation*,' Vortsk said, hissing into the vox-sceptre which would convey his order to the bridge surrounding his command-crypt.

'What about the *Vindictive*?' a sub-altern's question crackled back. Vortsk smiled as he glanced again at the positions of the approaching ships.

'Maintain strict silence as regards the *Vindictive*,' Vortsk said. 'It is best that her captain doesn't know our plans.'

ARCH-COMMANDER VORTSK FELT a shiver of excitement crackle down his steel spine as he watched the pict screens. The raiders and their pursuers had only just drawn within range of the battle line's guns. Instead of losing momentum, the ork pursuers had picked up speed. Vortsk smiled as he imagined the desperate efforts the aliens had made to force this last burst from their ships. They were so eager to sate their appetite for battle that they were charging headlong into destruction.

Only one thing more was needed to complete the trap and, by prearranged conspiracy, the *Pride* and *Damnation* provided what Vortsk required. As soon as the three raiders were within range of the fleet's heavy guns, the *Pride* and *Damnation* fired upon the *Vindictive*. The close-range barrage tore through the raider's void shields, smashing into her engines and leaving her a cripple.

Predictably, as her betrayers raced away and left her behind them, the *Vindictive* blasted away at them with the few guns she could bring to bear in such an unexpected emergency. Her fire was ineffectual as far as punishing her betrayers, but it did serve the purpose Vortsk needed it to. It reminded the pursuing orks that, though crippled, the *Vindictive* was still very much alive.

Vortsk's breathing became shallow, his mind feeling the eagerness of his ship as he watched the drama playing out upon the pict screen. The *Vindictive* abandoned her vengeful fusillade and turned her guns back upon the approaching orks, unleashing a desperate and futile barrage into the grotesque battleship. The crackle of energy shields intercepted most of the raider's fire, what little penetrated did nothing more than scratch the battleship's armoured hull.

The frantic efforts of the *Vindictive* to save herself did ensure she had the orks' full and undivided attention. The battleship and her escorts closed upon her like a pack of wolves. Vortsk grinned, lifting the vox-sceptre to his trembling mouth. 'Arch-Commander Vortsk to all ships,' he said. 'The orks are engaging the *Vindictive*. When they close to three kilometres of her, open fire. All batteries are to concentrate upon the battleship designated as Target Omega.'

Dim memories of his pampered childhood flashed through Vortsk's mind as he waited for the aliens to close the distance. He remembered waiting impatiently for his father, a noble of Decima X's ruling cadre, to bring home the traditional grox-hide cassock each St. Julian's day. The same unbearable eagerness gripped him now. He could almost hear the *Requiem* growling in expectation.

'Unleash hell!' Vortsk hissed into the vox-sceptre as the orks finally came within range. From every ship in the fleet, a withering barrage of macro-cannon, lances, plasma batteries and lasers slammed into Target Omega. The ork battleship seemed to glow like a tiny sun as its shields struggled against the awesome violence. Two of its escorts, whether by accident or design, diverted into the path of the barrage and were almost instantly gutted by the concentrated fire.

Target Omega, venting vapour from breaches in her hull, fires rippling across her starboard side, began to turn, shifting away from the *Vindictive*.

'Close with Target Omega,' Vortsk screamed into his vox-sceptre. 'Don't let it get away!' He could hear the blood pounding in his heart. The idea that the ork ship could survive the initial barrage wasn't half as repugnant as the idea that it might escape from his trap.

The fire coming from Target Omega was far less than what the battleship had been directing against the

Vindictive. Vortsk smiled. The initial assault must have obliterated most of the xenos gun batteries. More than ever, he was determined not to allow the ship to escape. Gripping his vox-sceptre, he demanded greater speed from his ships.

In the blink of an eye, the situation suddenly, horribly, changed.

The front of Target Omega burst apart in a great fireball. At first, Vortsk thought it was the result of damage inflicted upon the battleship by his fleet, but he was quickly forced to think again. From the smoke and debris, a dozen bulky assault ships erupted onto his pict screens. He felt his insides grow cold as the *Requiem*'s cogitators analyzed the fast, fat-bodied vessels. The ugly ships were almost all engine except for the immense mass of armour piled up about their prows.

Ram ships! As that hideous realisation came to him, a second explosion ripped through Target Omega. A smaller flotilla of ork craft burst from the battleship's portside, racing straight towards Vortsk's fleet. As they streaked away from the battleship, the larger vessel began to roll, its stability overwhelmed by the violent, speedy launch of its cargo.

Target Omega wasn't a battleship at all. It was an assault carrier!

Panic crackled across the displays monitoring communications within Vortsk's fleet. The ram ships, impossibly fast with their oversized engines, were smashing into the human vessels almost before their crews were aware they were being attacked. The ork craft charged straight into the fleet, breaching hulls with their armoured prows. More than the actual damage they inflicted, it was the confusion they wrought upon the fleet. Even as he tried to exert his authority and bring cohesion back into his force, Vortsk was seeing segments of his command scatter. Pirates and renegades, traitors to a man, there was no loyalty to bind them to the battle.

'Arch-Commander!' the screaming voice of the *Requiem*'s captain echoed from the vox-casters within the command-crypt. 'Target Omega is losing integrity. She's breaking up!'

Vortsk looked over at the pict screen showing the clearest view of the ork craft. With the loss of stability, the slow roll had turned into an apocalyptic vision. The spine of the ship had snapped in the middle of its roll, turning the scrap-work mass of metal into a spiralling corkscrew of shrapnel. Shrapnel hurtling directly towards the *Requiem*.

'Evasive manoeuvres,' Vortsk growled. Even as he spoke, however, he could feel the *Requiem* cry out. The battleship shuddered as one of the rampaging ork ram ships slammed into her side.

'Hull breach in decks fifty through fifty-five,' the captain's voice cried out. 'The ork ship has buried itself in our starboard!'

Vortsk closed his eyes, pulling the information he needed from the *Requiem*'s cogitators. The drag of the ork ship would compromise her manoeuvrability, too much so for her to escape the spiralling wreckage of Target Omega.

The Arch-Commander raised the vox-sceptre one last time. 'All weapon batteries, open fire on Target Omega.'

The order tasted like ash on his tongue. Even the firepower of an Oberon-class battleship wouldn't help them now. The best they could hope for was that the *Requiem*'s armour would hold and they wouldn't suffer so much damage that they'd be left immobile and defenceless when the rest of the ork armada showed up.

'Damn xenos,' Vortsk thought bitterly.

'They used my own trick on me.'

'GRIM LORD, THERE can be no question that the orks will penetrate the second line of defence.' Admiral Nostraz's voice was subdued as he made the pessimistic report. He bowed his head in contrition as the Warsmith stirred upon his translucent throne.

'How long can we expect the third line to hold?' Andraaz demanded.

Skylord Morax reached out and brought the cluster of lights representing the third of Castellax's defence fleets into focus. 'Raiders and slaveships,' he grumbled. 'Nothing here that can possibly stand up to the orks.'

'Then the aliens will make planetfall?' Captain Gamgin asked, a trace of anticipation and eagerness in his tone. After five generations of training, he was curious to see how his janissaries would perform against an enemy more formidable than a rabble of feral slaves.

Morax ran his glove across his scalp and glowered at Gamgin. 'An armada that size might have a billion howling greenskins. If they make planetfall…'

'We will destroy them,' Andraaz stated, his voice brooking no argument. His red eye focused upon the youngest of his war council. Sergeant Ipos was the only member of the inner-circle who had been created with hybrid gene-seed, a necessity for a Legion whose own genetic material was rife with corruption and mutation. Despite the admixture of gene-seed, Ipos had proven himself a brilliant strategist and tactician, as well as a shrewd political manipulator. He had used a careful campaign of conspiracy and subterfuge to worm his way into his position as Castellan of the Iron Bastion, one long coveted by full-blooded Iron Warriors like Algol and Vallax.

Ipos rose from his chair, sweeping his gauntlet across the surface of the table. The starfield faded. In its place appeared an orbital view of Castellax itself, its satellites and space stations. Another sweep of Ipos's hand and hundreds of lights began swarming around the world.

'We shouldn't expect a concentrated attack by the orks for several hours, perhaps even days,' Ipos declared. 'Until their warlord exerts its influence, the xenos will attack by individual squadrons, each warboss trying to cheat its fellows of loot and glory. We can exploit that.'

Admiral Nostraz smirked at the last statement. 'How do we do that, half-breed?' he grumbled.

Ipos ignored the admiral, directing his attention instead to the other Iron Warriors. 'We can't keep the orks from making planetfall. What we can do is prevent them from gaining a firm foothold once they are here.' He pointed to the ring of defence satellites and armed weapons stations orbiting the planet. 'If we adjust the orbits of five per cent of our installations we can present the orks with deliberate gaps in the defences. Eager for plunder, the xenos will use those gaps to try and reach the surface as quickly as possible.'

'You want to make it easier for the orks to reach Castellax?' Algol almost choked on the words, such was his incredulity.

The sergeant shook his head and made an adjustment to the illuminated display. Now some of the swarming lights were streaming down towards Castellax. 'By focusing the orks into pre-arranged windows of opportunity, we will funnel them into specific areas of the planet. Far from the industrial centres, though we will need to present the orks with some lesser installations to maintain their interest. As the xenos converge upon these sacrificial settlements, the Air Cohort will deploy and bomb them into oblivion. We'll be able to destroy the first wave of orks piecemeal, a tactic which Skylord Morax's squadrons should be fully capable of implementing.'

Morax clapped his hands together, almost chortling with pleasure as he imagined the glory which would belong to his Air Cohort. 'Indeed, indeed. We'll burn down every xenos that sets one foot on Castellax!'

Over-Captain Vallax leaned over the table, studying the pattern of lights swirling about the projected planet. 'That might settle for the vanguard, but you don't expect the entire armada to hit us at the same time. I've fought orks. They might be stupid, but they're also cunning. They won't fall for the same bait twice.'

'Afraid of getting your chainaxe dirty?' Morax chuckled, waving his jewelled glove at the Over-Captain. 'By the time the orks figure out what to do next, our surviving ships will be well on their way to Medrengard for help.'

'The Third Grand Company fights its own battles, Sky-lord,' Vallax snapped. 'To contemplate anything less is cowardice.'

'I shall quote you when the warlords of Medrengard demand to know why their shipments of arms are behind schedule,' Admiral Nostraz retorted. 'If the greenskins are allowed to set up a siege of even a few months, produc-tion will grind to a halt.'

'We might manage food for the slaves,' Algol said, pon-dering the problem. 'Synthetics will last out for the better part of a year and can be supplemented, but water will be a problem. The only extra water supplies we can tap into are those at the embryo farms and that will deprive us of our next generation of workers. Unless we go out and col-lect our own on a large scale. Like in the good old days.'

'Castellax has been fortified against full assault by the False Emperor's minions,' the crackling drone of Oriax's servitor announced. 'We are the sons of the Iron Cage. We are the Betrayers of Isstvan. However great the xenos horde, it shall break upon our walls.'

Warsmith Andraaz stepped away from his throne, steam venting from the coil of cables sunk into his armour as idle servo-motors pulsed into life. The hulking Iron Warrior stalked across the chamber, his Rending Guard falling into step behind him. Andraaz kept one eye fixed upon the obsidian table while his mechanical eye flashed across the faces of his officers.

'There will be no call for help,' Andraaz stated. 'There are those upon Medrengard who believe the Third Grand Company to be weak, that our days of glory and might are behind us, that we are but a sorry remnant of the past!' The Warsmith drove his fist straight into the middle of the projection, stabbing deep into the sphere representing

Castellax. 'This battle will belong to us, and us alone! We shall exterminate the xenos and send their skulls to Great Perturabo as tribute. There will be no retreat. There will be no surrender. And there will be no mercy.'

'What of our fleet, Grim Lord?' Admiral Nostraz asked. 'If they remain engaged with the orks they will be destroyed and we will lose them all. We can't replenish our losses without raiders to secure fresh materials.'

'The Warsmith has already said there will be no retreat,' Gamgin growled. His temper subsided when he felt Andraaz's gaze focus upon him. Abased, he sank down into his chair.

'The fleet will disengage and withdraw to the far side of the sun,' Andraaz decided. 'That will put Castellax between them and the ork armada.'

Morax nodded appreciatively at the strategy. 'With the orks caught up in the planetary fortifications, we can recall the fleet and have it engage the ships the xenos leave in orbit.' The Skylord cast a sneer in Nostraz's direction. 'Or they can withdraw into the warp and get help.'

A cold smile twisted the half of Andraaz's face that was still flesh. 'There will be no withdrawal.'

'But, Grim Lord, many of our ships are crewed by pirate scum,' objected Nostraz. 'If one of them should lose nerve, or perceive our situation as being–'

'There will be no retreat,' Oriax's proxy droned, the servitor's lifeless eyes staring emptily at the ceiling. 'The Speaker will issue a compulsion to every Navigator in the fleet. They will bite down upon the capsule hidden in their teeth. The poison will put them into a coma until such time as an antidote can be administered.'

Warsmith Andraaz slammed his fist against the obsidian table once more, vanquishing the display in a crackle of sparks. 'The pirates will have to come to the Iron Bastion for that antidote. Without the Navigators, they dare not tempt the warp. No, my brothers, there will be no retreat from Castellax, no display of weakness to cheer our persecutors.'

The Warsmith turned and slowly marched back to his throne. 'Castellax belongs to the Third Grand Company of the Iron Warriors Legion. No one will forget that fact. Not the filthy xenos. Not the pawns of the False Emperor. And not the warlords of Medrengard.

'Castellax is ours. Any who think otherwise live on borrowed time.'

CHAPTER III
I-Day

THE BINARY RASP of a Lingua-Technis chant hissed through
the mesh-work funnel of copper and titanium which
had replaced the mouth of Enginseer Heroditus three
centuries ago. The protruding, insect-like muzzle of his
respirator melded into the blocky contours of a face
rebuilt in adamantium and platinum. A confusion of
pipes and hoses snaked away from his cheeks, coiling
around his head to secure themselves to sockets built into
his spine and servo-limbs. Crab-like arms jutted from
spurs built into his shoulders, steel mechadendrites that
rippled with the gleam of idle energies.

There was little of Enginseer Heroditus that remained
organic. Five centuries of zealous service to the Omnissiah had replaced most of his decayed flesh with bionics.
Bundled in a heavy robe of vat-grown synthfibre, the only
exposed portion of the tech-priest betraying his tenuous
relation to humanity were the pale, empty eyes staring
from the depths of his metal face. Sight had fled from
those eyes long ago, his vision replaced by mechanical

sensors embedded in his forehead and on the backs of his bionic hands. Heroditus had declined to have his organic eyes removed, despite their obsolescence, believing he must maintain them until the Omnissiah's advent. Only then would he offer them up to the Machine-God as a final sacrifice of flesh.

The enginseer's valve-pump slowed its pulsations as his brain sent a surge of emotion crackling through his nerve-relays. The hiss of binary faltered for an instant as Heroditus fought down the pathetic despair that flickered into life within his brain. It was true, he was unlikely to ever make that sacrifice, to gaze upon the glory of the *Deus Mechanicus* incarnate. That was no excuse for such weakness. To be a servant of the Machine-God was to cast aside the flawed illogic of the flesh and embrace the cold reason of technology. A tech-priest did not know regret. His purpose was to accept the path before him and to walk it in such a way as to bring greater glory to the Machine-God.

Heroditus bowed his head in acknowledgment of his weakness. However much they cut away, it seemed there was still too much flesh left inside to make him complete. Without disrupting the binary chant hissing from his mouth, he transmitted a liturgy of penance from the vox-caster built into his chest, an appeal to the machine-spirits of his bionics and augmetics to forgive the discord caused by his sorrowed emotions. To ensure the sincerity of his prayer, Heroditus had the flagellation bundles fixed to his spine send pulses of electricity throbbing through his organics.

It was an act of self-castigation that Heroditus had performed many times since Castellax fell to the Iron Warriors. When the traitors had descended from the stars and rained death upon the colony, the adepts of the Machine Cult had been spared the most infamous of the Chaos Space Marines' outrages. Indeed, the invaders had expended some effort taking as many of the tech-priests intact as possible. It was not an act of mercy, of course, but rather a question of practicality. The Iron Warriors wanted to transform Castellax into a forge world to feed the war machine of their infamous Legion. To do that, they required more than billions of simple slaves. They needed specialists, men who understood the arcane sciences of manufacturing and design, processing and refinement.

Under the terrible scrutiny of their Fabricator Oriax, the Iron Warriors had pressed the captured tech-priests into their service. The exchange was simple: life for obedience. Some of the adepts had refused. Their deaths had been terrible spectacles of barbarism, outrages against the machine-spirits of their components as they were disassembled piece by piece.

Most of the adepts, like Heroditus, had agreed to obey, believing that even under the lash of the Iron Warriors they could serve the Machine-God. While they could function, they might yet serve a greater purpose.

Heroditus raised his head, staring at the acid-scoured walls of the immense drainage sluice, watching the crust of oxidised metal slowly drip into the toxic mire on the floor. Twenty metres across, nearly half again as high, the barrel-like tunnel ran the length of Vorago's processing district, funnelling pollutants and waste from the city into the abandoned strip mines that pock-marked the face of Castellax. Poisonous vapours rose from the rainbow-hued confusion of sludge and slime, filling the passage with an atmosphere so hostile to life that the hardiest sump-rat would be dead before it drew its third breath.

Only something as devoid of organic frailty as a tech-priest could prowl these passages in relative safety; yet even here Heroditus was wary. He knew Oriax was a fiend incarnate, a living devil, a Chaos Space Marine who had compounded his outrages with a perverted corruption of the Quest for Knowledge. There was no place on Castellax one could be certain the Fabricator did not have his spies. The floating 'Steel Blood', Oriax's ghoulish imitation of servo-skulls, flitted throughout Vorago, watching everything and everyone. Oriax claimed each of the fiendish skulls had a bit of his own genetic material pulsing through its circulation, heightening its responsiveness to his commands. Servitors, both those crafted in the Fabricator's workshops and those scavenged from the conquest of Castellax, were often fitted with transmitters that fed intelligence directly to Oriax's stronghold in the sub-catacombs of the Iron Bastion. More hideous still were the seemingly organic specimens Oriax had transformed, implanting them with complex mechanics without consideration of the subject's suitability and worthiness for such augmentation, or the dignity of the machine-spirits of the devices he abused in these monstrous experiments.

A terrible darkness had descended upon Castellax, but Heroditus calculated that there might finally be a chance to see the light again. It was why he chanted orisons to dull and mislead the sentinel-implants Oriax had attached to his body. It was why he braved the toxic miasma of the drainage sluice, hiking through kilometres of corrosive sludge.

Hope, that most irrational of feelings, had begun to burn once more in the mind of Enginseer Heroditus.

TAOFANG PULLED THE goggles from his face and stared up at the night sky. Even the sting of Castellax's polluted atmosphere wasn't enough to dissuade him from watching the awesome light show unfolding far above the planet. It was a spectacle of such beauty as to move even the hardened janissary to tears. Great spheres of light streaked across the sky, sometimes spewing streams of energy, sometimes expanding into brilliant blazes before collapsing in upon themselves and fading into darkness. Whorls of star-fire coruscated through the blackness, racing about the planet in dazzling displays of colour and patterns of the most compelling fascination. To Taofang, it was like watching the birth of some cosmic–

'Put those goggles back on!'

The sharp command broke the fascination. Hastily, Taofang pulled the protective lenses back across his eyes and turned his gaze from the sky to the men around him. There were over five hundred of them, janissaries of the Scorpion Brigade, each man fitted out in the corrosion-resistant duster and ore-scuttle helmet of their regiment. Mustered from the grim ferrocrete barracks which cast its shadow across the marshalling yard, the soldiers waited for their quartermasters to distribute arms from a sunken bunker at the far end of the plaza. Officers in black storm coats stalked among the troops, chastising those who, like Taofang, allowed their awe of the light show over Castellax to overcome their discipline.

'There is a beta-level caution tonight!' one of the officers, a thick-necked, dark-skinned colonel named Nehring barked over a vox-caster. He raised a gloved hand and tapped the opaque lenses of the goggles he wore. 'Three minutes of exposure to the air and the pollution will begin to deteriorate your vision. Half an hour, and you would be as good as blind. If that isn't enough to make you scum keep your goggles on, consider this: any man who can't pull his own weight is a burden on the regiment...' Nehring's hand dropped to the jewelled holster hanging from his belt. There was no need for the colonel to continue his threat. The janissaries had seen him use his laspistol too many times to need the consequences explained to them. It was a custom weapon, plunder from some forge world, calibrated to fire a wider, more powerful beam than a standard pattern weapon. The charred wounds it left behind were big enough to put a man's fist through.

Colonel Nehring removed his peaked cap and raised his face to the sky. A sneer twisted his features. 'That spectacle you find so fascinating is our orbital defences and satellites being obliterated. A few of the big ones might be remnants of the system fleet falling to xenos guns.' Nehring's shielded eyes glared over the faces of his soldiers. 'Hold a happy thought,' he growled. 'When the orks are done up there, they'll be paying us a visit down here. Then each of you will get the chance to show our masters the quality of your training.'

A few jeers of defiance rose from the ranks. The janissaries weren't strangers to combat, even if their previous experiences had been limited to putting down slave revolts or tracking renegades in the wastelands between the mining settlements. Only a few of the soldiers in the Scorpion Brigade had ever been seconded to the raider ships and engaged in battle off-world – and even those expeditions had been strikes against the Imperium. None of the janissaries had ever seen a xenos in battle, but they doubted it would be much different to killing their fellow man. All of them had done that often enough to become calloused to the prospect of battle.

Taofang was still in shock. Orks attacking Castellax! It was fantastic, unbelievable. Born and raised under the lash of the Iron Warriors, he had come to view them as invincible, a malignant force as irresistible as an earthquake or an ash-storm. The very idea that anything would dare to attack them was almost absurd to Taofang. That the orks had succeeded in driving through the system fleet and threatening Castellax itself was incredible. Yet, the evidence was all around him. The first frantic rumours of battle above the planet, the frightened mutters of orks from the comms tower garrison, the mustering of every soldier in Dirgas – all of it was grim testament to the reality of the situation.

As Nehring began barking new orders to the men filing past the quartermaster's bunker, the officer's voice caught in his throat. His dark features turned ashen as he snapped to attention and bent his body almost in half sketching a profound and self-humiliating bow. Taofang had never seen a colonel display such deference to anyone before. He turned his head, following the direction of Nehring's gaze. Instantly, the janissary snapped to attention. All around him, the click of boots filled the air as the rest of the brigade followed suit.

As he stood at attention, an icy wave of fear rushed through Taofang's body, chilling him from toe to scalp. Striding across the plaza was the armoured hulk of an Iron Warrior, his ceramite boots scarring the flagstones as he marched. The soldier had seen the Space Marines before, but always at a distance and never one as terrifying in appearance as the legionary he now gazed upon. A revolting mantle of flayed human skin was draped across the giant's shoulders. Taofang didn't need to look at the skull-like helm with its maze of jewelled campaign-markers to recognise the monster. It was Algol, the fiend of Castellax, feared as the Skintaker, the merciless Slavemaster.

Every eye in the plaza was locked upon the Skintaker as he marched towards the bunker. Even the shriek of Air Cohort fighters as they streaked overhead wasn't enough to make the janissaries look away. They watched Algol's gruesome cloak billow about his shoulders as the fighters screamed through the sky. They watched as the Iron Warrior approached the still bowed Colonel Nehring and held their breaths in anticipation.

'I require the Scorpion Brigade,' Algol said, the vox-casters in his helm sending his voice booming across the plaza.

Nehring's words came in a frightened squeak. 'Of course, Dread Lord! We are distributing weapons right now. They can be–'

Algol reached out with one of his armoured hands, his gauntlet closing about Nehring's head as he drew the bowed officer upright. The crimson optics in his helm bored into Nehring's terrified eyes. 'You have two minutes to get this rabble armed,' Algol hissed. 'I want them loaded on the trucks within five.'

'Ye-yes, Dre-Dread Lord,' Nehring sputtered. Algol removed his crushing grip and turned away, leaving the colonel to dab at the blood trickling from his crumpled cap.

'Five minutes,' the Iron Warrior reminded as he marched away.

Nehring reached to his holster and drew his pistol. The colonel spun around, firing the weapon into the face of the closest unarmed janissary. The soldier didn't even have time to scream, simply dropping to the flagstones, a smouldering crater where his forehead should have been. 'Faster, you maggots!' Nehring shrieked. 'Lord Algol wants you scum in the trucks and by the warp, you will not disappoint him!'

The orderly ranks of men collapsed into a crush of humanity as the janissaries swarmed towards the bunker, snatching lasguns and autoguns from the quartermasters. As soon as they had a weapon in their hands, the soldiers were sprinting across the plaza towards the motor pool and the waiting trucks. Such was their panic that many of them neglected to snatch extra ammunition from the crates lined against the bunker's wall.

As Taofang pushed his way into the mass, he looked once more at the terrible figure of Algol. The Space Marine continued to stalk across the plaza at the same measured march. *He has such contempt for us*, Taofang thought, *that he didn't even bother to see what we're doing. He didn't even care who was shot. We're too small for him to even notice us.*

Taofang stared skywards again, watching as another bright burst of light slowly faded into nothing. How terrible must the orks be to cause war-gods like the Iron Warriors such concern? What could mere men like the Scorpion Brigade do against such an enemy?

* * *

THE FAT-BODIED TRUCKS lurched and bounced as they rumbled through the deserted streets of Dirgas. Curfew had been imposed upon the city on Algol's command, freezing all shipment to and from the factories, arresting all transportation from the production plants and hab-pens. Slaves were ordered to remain where they were, either locked inside their cells in the hab-pens or else shackled to their machinery in the factories. Travel meant communication, and communication was something now forbidden in the city.

Taofang hugged the cold steel of his lasgun closer to his chest, grimacing as he stared down at the three clips of ammunition he'd taken. Among the last men to leave the plaza, he'd been in too much of a hurry when he'd raced past the ammunition boxes. Instead of three energy cells for his lasgun, he had three clips of bullets for an autogun. Trying to haggle with his comrades in the truck had been fruitless. None of the men were from his own platoon and several of them were in an even worse state than he was, having neglected to grab any ammunition at all. As it stood, Taofang had twenty shots from the energy cell already inside his weapon.

With a shudder and screech, the truck came to a stop. The steel doors at the back of the cabin swung open, the bark of an officer ordering the janissaries from their conveyance. Taofang dropped down from the truck, finding himself in the warren-like sprawl of a factory. Metal girders and ferrocrete pillars soared dozens of metres upwards to support a vaulted roof. Stamps and presses, a river of conveyor belts and production lines filled the immense structure. Toppled carts, their cargo of tank treads and hatch-doors strewn about them, littered the floor. Here and there, a gore-soaked body lay sprawled amid the wreckage. Looming from the destruction like some scrap-work colossus, was the still-smoking casing of a huge rocket, its hull glowing a dull orange from its fiery descent through Castellax's atmosphere.

Taofang's truck had pulled up halfway along the sloped ramp leading to the factory's transport node, a monorail connecting it to Dirgas's main railway. A quick glance showed him that a half-dozen other trucks were likewise positioned around the transport node, an officer snarling orders at the soldiers as they disembarked. In all, there were about two hundred janissaries being deployed. He thought he could hear the sound of the other trucks' engines below the din of the factory's machines and thought the rest of the regiment might be deploying on the far side of the building.

Closer at hand, however, was the sinister bulk of an armoured transport quite unlike the crude trucks employed by the janissaries. It was a box-like vehicle, its hull fashioned from plates of reinforced plasteel, every centimetre pitted and scarred from millennia of warfare. Great titanium treads powered the machine up the ramp, its engine belching thick black fog as it powered its way forwards. Stained in dull grey livery, marked with the metal skull of the Iron Warriors, the transport was a formidable contrast to the khaki-painted trucks.

'Establish a cordon!' the officer was bellowing at the janissaries as they disembarked. 'No xenos leaves this factory!'

Only a few metres away, a pair of janissaries jerked in agony as large calibre rounds ripped through their bodies. Soldiers scattered from the doomed men, taking cover behind the trucks and abandoned loading cranes scattered about the transport node. Taofang thumbed the activation rune on his lasgun and dove for shelter behind a wrecked cargo carrier, falling flat as his boot slipped on the slick floor. He bit down a livid curse as he found himself staring into the mushy remains of what was either the carrier's operator or a regurgitated mass of vita-gruel.

Heavy slugs continued to slam into the floor, pulverising the dead bodies of the ambushed janissaries. A confusion of other shots plastered the same area, displaying a crazed variety of calibres and ammunition types. The helmet of one of the corpses melted under the glowing discharge of a low-intensity plasma weapon, the skull inside smoking as the man's hair caught fire.

Taofang followed the afterglow of the plasma beam, tracing it back to its source on one of the steel gantries criss-crossing the factory. As he did, he felt his skin crawl. There were creatures crouched upon the walkway. He could see one of the beasts clearly, a thing the likes of which he had never dared imagine. Its shape was vaguely human, or at least humanoid, though swollen in proportions with thick knots of muscle and sinew. Its arms were short and thick, its legs stumpy and broad. Its head seemed to jut directly from its powerful shoulders, an apelike skull that was mostly jawbone and tusks. Beady little eyes glistened from shadowy pits sunken into its monstrous face. A patchwork of crudely assembled textiles clothed its massive frame, each scrap stained and dyed into a checkerboard of white and black. Bandoliers of bullets and knives criss-crossed its chest and straddled its waist. A machete bigger than Taofang's arm was thrust through the alien's belt, keeping company with a cluster of primitive-looking grenades and a nest of still-dripping human scalps.

The alien's leathery green skin marked it as an ork, but the vicious brute crouched upon the walkway bore only the slightest resemblance to the absurd, clownish marauders Taofang had heard of. Looking up at the monster, he couldn't see anything amusing. It looked like death, and a more brutal death the janissary was unable to picture as his gaze strayed back to the mutilated bodies of his comrades.

Orks in Dirgas! How had the aliens penetrated the defences of Castellax so quickly? Even if they had pierced the orbital defences, there were the city's defence batteries and the Air Cohort to fend them off. Indeed, Taofang hadn't heard so much as a peep from the gigantic surface-to-orbit defence cannons, guns so immense their recoil felt like an earth tremor. It was impossible that the orks could strike so suddenly.

The rattle of renewed gunfire slammed against the sides of the trucks, some of the shots of such strength that they ripped clean through the vehicles and into the men cowering behind them. Screams of agony echoed through the factory as injured janissaries writhed on the ground, clutching at the bleeding stumps of arms and legs or trying to push splintered ribs into the wet meat of mangled chests.

The aliens on the gantries coughed and growled, savouring the carnage. Las-beams sizzled up at the monsters, searing ugly scars into their flesh and scouring their primitive vests of chain and scrap metal. Taofang joined in the vengeful fire, targeting his shots at the ugly xenos with the plasma weapon. Again and again he fired at the ork, watching its hulking body jerk with each shot. For a brief moment, Taofang felt exhilaration. For the first time he experienced a feeling of true accomplishment. He was a real soldier, fighting one of mankind's most ancient foes. And he was winning.

Then, as the ork reared up and pointed its weapon in his direction, Taofang's exhilaration evaporated. He could see now the effect his shots had on the alien. A half-dozen black splotches on its leathery green skin, a nice cluster of fresh scars to go with the confusion of old wounds already marring the alien's hide. Staring down the sight of his lasgun, Taofang could see the ork staring back at him, its face pulling back in a leer of amusement as it brought its weapon to bear.

Before the ork could shoot, however, the greenskin was bowled backwards by the meaty impact of an explosive round. Bone and sinew burst from the alien's body as the shell detonated against its shoulder. Uttering a shriek that was half snarl and half howl, the ork struggled to spin around and face its attacker. Even as it made the effort, a second explosive shell tore deep into its chest, detonating an instant later. Ripped almost in two by the explosion, the dying ork fell from the gantry and hurtled to the factory floor far below.

'Iron within! Iron without!' The bellow rolled like thunder through the factory. Marching from behind the box-like hull of his Rhino, Algol pressed a fresh clip into his ornately adorned boltgun and began looking for new targets. The armoured giant moved without hesitation, stalking towards the raised walkways and the xenos fiends infesting them. Like a heathen war-god, the Iron Warrior raised his weapon and sent burst after burst of high-calibre death speeding towards the orks. Alien howls of confusion and pain now filled the factory as the orks suddenly found themselves the attacked rather than the attackers.

The janissaries, only a moment before quaking in their boots, rallied to the gruesome Algol. The terror the Space Marine inspired now emboldened them. The Skintaker was the most fearsome fiend on Castellax... and he was fighting on their side!

Bullets from the ork guns gouged the floor as the aliens struggled to get the Iron Warrior in their sights. It seemed an effort beyond their savage brains. Algol's huge frame was constantly shifting from one direction to another, fading into the shadow of a truck or support pillar in that fragment of time before an ork loosed a barrage of automatic fire. Instantly, the Space Marine would return fire, leaning out from behind cover to deliver unerringly accurate bursts from his bolter. Each shot seemed to send another xenos hurtling from the walkways.

'Castellax!' the voice of Colonel Nehring rang out. The officer rose from behind the shelter of a pile of steel crates and made a beckoning sweep with his arm. Dozens of janissaries took up his cry, lunging from cover and rushing towards the aliens on the gantries, loosing a withering stream of las-fire as they charged. With the invincible

Iron Warrior leading them, the men forgot their fear of the orks, remembering only their training and the thrill of battle.

Taofang rose from behind the crane, his heart hammering in his chest. He felt his awe of the Space Marine flooding through his mind, driving him to bold heroics. Screaming an inarticulate war cry, he charged the closest gantry, firing at the skulking ork crouched at the top of the stairs. He saw his shots burn into the alien's flesh, saw one of his las-bolts melt the tinted visor of the alien's helmet and sear into the beady eye behind it. He saw the ork pitch and fall, tumbling down the stairs like a rag doll. He laughed as he continued to shoot the wounded brute, burning fresh holes into its leathery flesh.

It took him a few seconds to realise his weapon wasn't firing any more. Taofang stared incredulously at his lasgun, noting with some confusion the blinking red light of the depleted energy cell. For an instant, fear tried to well up inside him. The ork he had been shooting wasn't dead, its hideous physiology preserving it through the fusillade. Wounded, bleeding, several of its bones broken in its fall, the monster was struggling to rise, its one good eye glaring murderously at Taofang.

Before panic could grip the janissary, he noticed the terrifying figure of Algol marching across the factory. One of the orks, more crafty than its comrades, had played dead and now, as Algol passed beneath the walkway the xenos was lying on, the alien leaped down onto the Iron Warrior's shoulders.

Algol didn't even break stride. As the ork's weight slammed into him, the Space Marine reached back and closed his gauntlet about the alien's jaw. Pivoting at the waist, he used his grip to swing the ork across his hip, breaking its hold and dashing it to the ground. Before the ork was even aware of what had happened to it, Algol's boot came smashing down into its face. The alien thrashed wildly, but a second stomp from the Skintaker crushed its skull and ended its struggles.

Taofang looked back at the ork he had injured. With a vicious scream, he shifted his grip on the lasgun and ran at the alien. Swinging the weapon like a club, he brought its heavy stock cracking into the monster's head, ripping open its cheek and knocking its helmet askew. The ork swiped at him with one of its paws, but the clumsy effort only spilled the brute back onto the floor. Standing above the prostrate beast, Taofang drove the butt of his lasgun into its head, pounding its skull until he felt it splinter and crack beneath his blows. Carried away by the violence and feeling of unspeakable power, Taofang kept up the assault until there was only a gooey mush clinging to the stock of his weapon.

Breathing heavily, his lungs burning with the intensity of his exertions, Taofang stepped away from the pulverised mess. The factory echoed with the bark of gunfire, the shouts and screams of men, the howls of savage aliens. He could see janissaries rushing up onto the gantries, hurdling the butchered bodies of slaves and overseers, firing at the scattered orks. He watched as Algol emptied his bolter into a huge ork with massive tusks and a rifle that looked like it had started life as a small howitzer. He saw the ork keel over, its face reduced to pulp by the Iron Warrior's shots. The howitzer-rifle roared as the ork's twitching fingers tugged the trigger, sending a shot straight into the roof with all the devastation of a mortar shell. Debris clattered down around the triumphant Space Marine, glancing off his ceramite helm and pauldrons.

Then, Taofang saw something else, something that offended his eyes and made his brain recoil in disbelief. As he stared at the victorious Iron Warrior, he saw a strange image, like a phantom vision projected across the scene. He could see the ghostly echo of some immense room, an impression of spectral orks scurrying about strange machines.

A sound like tearing metal shrieked across the factory and with it came an ozone stink and a weird ripple of light that penetrated Taofang's eyelids when he closed them against the glare. As he tried to blink the searing pain away, he caught a blur of motion on the walkway above him. Forcing his eyes to focus, he felt his gorge rise as he began to make out more clearly what it was he was looking at. There was another ork on the gantry.

No, he corrected himself. Not *on* the gantry. *In* the gantry, its body inextricably fused into the metal framework, the grille woven through its leathery flesh. Taofang was at a loss to explain how such a gruesome thing could happen, even more so because he was willing to swear on the fiends of the warp, that the alien hadn't been there a few seconds before.

The incredible supposition was further emboldened by the magnified sounds of combat roaring through the factory. Taofang could see orks charging at the janissaries from every quarter, even from places the soldiers had definitely cleared already. The men were taken completely aback by this incredible ambush, and the xenos spared them no chance to recover from their surprise.

Even Algol was beset by fresh foes, firing into a mob of orks who came charging at him from the transport node, a place that had been absolutely devoid of enemies only a moment before. To the strangeness of the attack was added the disheartening spectacle of the Space Marine retreating from the aliens, firing short, undirected bursts at them as he sprinted back towards the ramp and his transport.

Taofang wasn't the only one who saw Algol's withdrawal. Colonel Nehring's stern voice rose above the crackle of gunfire, calling for the Scorpion Brigade to fall back to the trucks. Judging by the number of orks between most of the men and their transports, it was unlikely more than half of them would make it.

The janissary turned to make his way back to the ramp,

but as he did so the tearing sound swelled to a deafening din, the ozone-stink so profound he fumbled for the respirator hanging from his belt. Whichever way he turned his eyes, he saw the same spectral image, the mammoth room with the scrap-metal walls and strange machines. And he saw orks. Not one or two, not dozens, not even hundreds. There were thousands of the aliens, their fanged mouths open in noiseless roars.

A blinding blast of light exploded through the factory, this time accompanied by an electrical crackle that set every hair on Taofang's body standing upright. The janissary gave small notice to even this strange effect, instead clapping his hands to his ears as a thunderous clamour resounded through the factory. It was the bestial cry of a thousand savages, the primordial bellow of mindless brutality.

'Waaagh!'

His clearing vision displayed a factory that had been torn to shreds, mangled and twisted as though the funnel of a tremendous ash-storm had rampaged inside the building. Walkways had been wrenched from their foundations, curled into knots by the malignant force. Pillars and beams had been toppled, bringing with them great sections of roof and wall. Conveyor belts had been flattened, stamps and presses twisted into jumbles of unrecognizable wreckage. Dripping heaps of meat gave loathsome evidence that the same havoc had been visited on flesh as well as metal and ferrocrete.

Taofang had only an instant to gauge the destruction, for the flash of light had brought more than simple carnage. It had brought the cause of that monstrous bellow. Massed among the wreckage was a horde of greenskinned aliens, their hulking bodies draped in ragged armour and tattered rags, their fists wrapped about a crazed assemblage of weaponry, from crude stub guns to complex meltas and everything between.

The city was infested with aliens now. The brutes hadn't

penetrated the defences, they had bypassed them entirely. It was teleportation, that most mysterious and esoteric of human technology, but on a scale so vast that even the most crazed tech-priest would balk at the possibility. Taofang had heard stories of boarding parties of five or six Adeptus Astartes appearing inside a raider during an engagement against the Imperium, but this went far beyond. The orks had teleported thousands of their loathsome breed from orbit to the surface of Castellax.

There was ghastly evidence of the hazards of the ramshackle alien technology all around. Many orks had been fused into pieces of the factory, their bodies melted into gantries and pillars. Hundreds of orks at the very fringe of the teleportation's effect had only partially reformed, their horribly translucent bodies collapsing into puddles of quivering mash after a few abominable moments of agonised animation. Where some of the strange machines had failed to materialise along with the ork horde, at least two had been caught in the area of effect, emerging as sputtering, smoking towers of runaway energy.

Yet, however crude the process, there was no denying the brutal fact that the orks had circumvented all of Dirgas's complex defences. The xenos invaders had gained a beachhead within the very walls of the city!

Algol's Rhino was firing into the massed orks as it hurriedly backed down the ramp. With the Iron Warrior's withdrawal, the trucks weren't far behind, their drivers scarcely waiting for the frantic janissaries scrambling to climb onto them. Most of the orks were too disoriented by their transference to react to the fleeing humans, but enough of them opened fire to turn the retreat into a complete rout.

Taofang raced down the ramp, climbing onto the running board of a truck as it made a crazed three-point turn and tore out of the factory. The janissary was spun around as the truck turned, clinging to the massive door panel to maintain his footing. Behind him, he could see fleeing soldiers being cut down by the deranged marksmanship of the orks. He watched as a smoke-belching missile rose from the massed aliens and slammed into one of the trucks. The vehicle exploded in a burst of flame and shrapnel, shredding the janissaries racing after it.

The sight of the blazing wreckage was Taofang's last view inside the factory. In the next instant, his truck lunged out into the streets of Dirgas and was racing along the desolate lanes.

Behind him, Taofang could hear the vicious aliens raise their croaking voices in another guttural howl.

'Waaagh!'

WARSMITH ANDRAAZ GLOWERED at the liveried slave trembling beside his diamond throne. The Space Marine's eye smouldered with cold hate as he digested the report the man had brought into the Iron Bastion's war room. It was news that sat ill with the overlord of Castellax, news that demanded an appropriate response.

In a blur of motion, the gigantic Warsmith surged from his chair. Before the slave could even blink an eye, Andraaz closed the armoured fingers of his gauntlet around the man's throat. With a savage wrench, he twisted the messenger's head, snapping his neck like a twig. Arrogantly, he let the corpse flop to the floor and turned to regard the Iron Warriors gathered about the great table. One of the Rending Guard stepped away from the diamond throne and dragged the carcass out of view.

'The orks are in Dirgas,' Andraaz repeated, his voice an angry growl. 'Algol says the local janissaries are unable to contain the aliens to the manufacturing district. He requests extraction of all portable resources.'

Sergeant Ipos nodded in agreement. 'As distasteful as it is, the Skintaker may be right. If Dirgas is lost to us then it would be prudent to remove whatever we can while we can. There is no knowing how long the xenos will lay siege to Castellax or what measures will be necessary...'

'Pull out and flatten the city from the sky,' Over-Captain Vallax declared, slamming his fist against the table. 'Let the orks taste a few hundred megatons of vengeance from our bombers. That will make them think twice before using their teleporters again.'

'Wasteful and impetuous,' scoffed Captain Morax. 'You couldn't drive a thought into an ork's brain with a power maul. All bombing Dirgas will do is destroy valuable infrastructure and material. By my calculations, losing the city will reduce overall production by fifteen per cent. We will have a hard time meeting our tithe to Medrengard if we turn the city into a cinder.'

'What do you propose, Skylord?' Admiral Nostraz sneered. 'Leave the aliens to establish a foothold in Dirgas?'

'There is something to be said for such a tactic,' Morax said. 'Dirgas is the other side of the Mare Ossius and the Witch Wall. If we can contain the orks on that side of the sea, we can fortify Vorago and our other strongholds.'

'Which will disrupt our production even further,' said Vallax. 'If you are so set against bombing Dirgas, then maybe a deep strike is in order.'

From his place at the end of the table, Captain Rhodaan turned to face his commander. 'You have heard Algol's report. The ork numbers are already formidable. There is no telling how many more they might still be teleporting down into the city.'

'Allowing that the xenos technology continues to function,' came the mechanised voice of Oriax's servitor, voicing its master's objection. 'Ork machinery is wildly unpredictable. The more complex the mechanism, the less likely it is to maintain integrity after repeated use. The xenos do not understand the necessity of placating the machine-spirit.'

Rhodaan shook his head and ignored the servitor. 'Attacking Dirgas will be costly,' he said.

'Necessary losses,' Vallax countered.

Rhodaan felt his blood begin to boil. 'And whose squad will suffer these losses?' he hissed through clenched teeth. The two Assault Marines locked eyes, each of them glaring deep into the blackened soul of the other. Centuries of rivalry and hate pounded inside their hearts and sent adrenaline coursing through their veins.

'There will be no attack on Dirgas,' Warsmith Andraaz declared. 'Captain Morax is right. If we allow the orks to concentrate in the city, we will be able to more easily contain and monitor them. Moreover, until we can be certain this teleportation machine is no longer a threat, a direct assault would benefit us nothing.' Andraaz shifted his gaze to Oriax's cyborg mouthpiece. 'The teleporter is your area of expertise, Fabricator. Whatever it takes, I want to know if it is still in operation.'

A cruel smile crawled onto the Warsmith's scarred face. He stared at Vallax, then shifted his attention to Rhodaan. 'If the teleporter is non-functional, then you will have your chance for glory. But do not be so eager to claim it that you forget your obligation to the Third Grand Company and the Legion.

'No Iron Warrior dies unless I allow him to. Forget that, and the orks are the least of your worries.'

CHAPTER IV
I-Day Plus 9

THE GREAT DOORS of the assault hangar slowly descended, sinking into the ferrocrete floor of the Iron Bastion. Alarm claxons sounded as thousands of tons of reinforced steel and titanium shifted upwards, lifting the bulky assault boats from the arming bays deep beneath the hangar. Slaves in the cobalt-coloured livery of the Castellax Air Cohort scrambled to remove the restraining bolts from the missiles slung underneath each boat's stubby wings. Other humans, garbed in the blue tunics and breeches of the Cohort proper, made a final examination of each craft before boarding.

'It is a great honour to be chosen by the Warsmith himself,' Brother Baelfegor said, his voice fairly crackling with pride. Captain Rhodaan didn't even deign to look at him as they marched through the hangar towards their assault boat.

'Any honour will be bestowed upon Over-Captain Vallax,' Rhodaan growled. Across the hangar he could see Vallax and the Assault Marines of Squad Vidarna climbing the boarding ramp of their own craft. 'We are to support them, nothing more.'

'This raid upon Dirgas is too important to trust to Vallax,' grumbled Brother Gomorie, the fingers of his afflicted hand unconsciously lengthening into knife-like claws.

Rhodaan rounded upon the other Iron Warrior. 'You were not asked for opinions, only obedience.' He pointed at Gomorie's hand. 'Perhaps the virus has spread its tendrils into your mind, brother. Perhaps soon you will be a berserk monstrosity like Brother Merihem.'

Gomorie stopped in his tracks, shifting uneasily under his commander's reprimand. 'Forgive me, captain. I know my obligations. I will not dishonour the Legion or Squad Kyrith.'

The other Iron Warriors continued to march towards the assault boat. Rhodaan remained behind with the chastened Gomorie. 'See that you remember that,' he warned. 'I would hate to see one of my battle-brothers cast into the Oubliette with Merihem.' His voice dropped to a vicious snarl. 'In fact, I *will* not see such a thing. Do we understand each other, brother?'

'Yes, captain!' Gomorie cried, his hand crashing against his chest in salute. Rhodaan gestured for the Space Marine to join the rest of the squad. He turned to watch as Vallax's assault boat finished its preparations and began to taxi onto the hangar's launching catapult.

The raid upon Dirgas was a plan conceived by Warsmith Andraaz himself. The city had been the first to fall to the orks and in the days since the invasion's start, the xenos had transformed it into a vital command and supply centre for their forces. Aerial reconnaissance showed that the orks were cannibalising the infrastructure of Dirgas for their own use, destroying valuable resources so they might cobble together their ramshackle war machines. Morax was especially dour in his predictions of how the damage would affect Castellax's industry after the orks were repulsed. It was a prediction grim enough for the

Warsmith to dispatch ten of his Iron Warriors against the alien beachhead, ten of a complement that numbered only sixty-four.

Ten demigods of death to capture a city infested by thousands of murderous aliens.

It would be a battle worth remembering.

THE ASSAULT BOAT shuddered as it catapulted from the Bastion's hangar. The human air crew were jounced violently by the craft's rapid ascent into the skies of Vorago. Rhodaan could almost pity the men the weakness of their bodies. To be human was to be frail and inferior. To be an Iron Warrior was to walk among the gods.

Seated in the cargo compartment of the assault boat, the hulking Iron Warriors barely stirred as the craft gained momentum. Mag-clamps built into their boots and designed to thwart the vacuum of space kept each of them firmly fixed to the plasteel deck. A steady grip upon the metal guide-bar running the length of the compartment further restricted the effects of inertia to a minimum.

'The Cohort does not spare itself,' Brother Baelfegor observed. 'We should make good time to Dirgas.'

'Morax has probably promised them extra rations if they perform well,' Brother Pazuriel said. He lowered his gaze to the chainaxe lying across his lap, his gauntlet caressing the diamond studs embedded in each tooth. 'Or perhaps he has provided a different incentive should they fail his expectations.'

'All humans are weak maggots,' Brother Uzraal growled. 'They exist only to serve the Legions and even in this they are found wanting.' He turned his angry glare to the front of the compartment where a half-dozen Cohort auxiliaries sat in high-backed crash chairs. 'Tell me, flesh-maggots,' he barked at the men. 'Tell me what gives you the right to breathe the same air as a legionary? What reason can you give me for not opening this door and feeding you to the wind? Why– Ow!'

Captain Rhodaan leaned back in his seat, the little motors built into his gauntlet making tiny whirring noises after their abrupt impact against the side of Uzraal's helmet. The stricken Iron Warrior turned about in a display of wolfish fury. His anger quickly faded when he saw it was his captain who had struck him.

'Focus on the objective,' Rhodaan warned. 'These distractions are beneath an Iron Warrior.' He turned his fanged helm in the direction of the ashen-faced auxiliaries. 'They will perform what is demanded of them. They understand their purpose.'

Suddenly, the assault boat shook with violence far greater than might be occasioned by turbulence in Vorago's polluted sky. The auxiliaries appeared to hop and squirm in their seats, their helmets cracking against the rests of their chairs. The Iron Warriors themselves were jounced from side to side, their hands sliding along the guide-bars.

'By the walls of Medrengard!' Pazuriel cursed. 'What are those fools doing up there!' The huge Iron Warrior turned towards the cockpit and started to rise from his seat, but a gesture from Rhodaan curbed his action.

The captain was listening to the Air Cohort frequency, and what he was hearing wasn't good. Since the orks' first assault on Castellax the relentless alien attacks had choked the stratosphere with a cloud of debris and chaff, effectively cutting the planet off from the network of observation satellites orbiting it. As a result, the Iron Warriors had been forced to rely upon fly-bys and ground-based intelligence stations to follow enemy movement and deployment. As Morax had complained loudly and frequently, it was like trying to fight with only half an eye open.

The Skylord's fears were now being realised. The Castellax Air Cohort had been thrown into complete panic by the sudden descent of several hundred ork craft which had been orbiting the planet. Like a meteor storm, the armada was hurtling towards Vorago. Before the sub-orbital defences could be brought to bear against the invaders, the vanguard of the aliens was already over the city.

Rhodaan partitioned his concentration, letting only a fragment of his attention rest upon the Cohort vox reports. Humans were his emotional, frightened inferiors and he didn't trust their observations. What he did trust were his own eyes. Rising from his seat, he marched over to the assault boat's side door, rolling its armoured weight aside as though it wasn't even there.

Beyond the door, the vast industrial sprawl of Vorago stretched before Rhodaan's eyes. He could see plumes of fire belching from hundreds of blast furnaces, pillars of smoke snaking upwards from thousands of smoke stacks. But he could also see dozens of other scenes of fire and smoke, less regimented, scattered throughout the city. It didn't take much imagination to guess what the fires represented. In their ferocious, headlong plunge from orbit, the orks had abandoned any pretensions of caution. Hundreds of their ramshackle craft must have found the descent too much for their air frames, cracking apart as they dived towards the city.

Yet even in death, the orks served the greater cause of their Waaagh! Each broken craft became a shower of shrapnel, hurtling at the city with a velocity that could shatter plasteel. They smashed into Vorago with the fury of an orbital bombardment, shaking the city to its foundations. Worse, the doomed attack ships acted as decoys for the other aliens. The panicked janissaries manning the defence batteries chose the closest of the descending craft as their targets, training their fire on already disabled ships rather than the still intact orks following behind them.

It was a mistake no Iron Warrior would have made. Bitterly, Rhodaan regretted the schism that had broken the

Third Grand Company, reducing it from over a thousand battle-brothers to the tiny remnant occupying Castellax. With a full complement of legionaries manning every aspect of the city's defences, no alien would have made planetfall.

Now, however, the sky was thick with a confusion of ork craft. Huge, fat-bodied bombers, their exhausts belching thick streams of smog and diesel fumes, lumbered over the city, disgorging tons of ordnance with reckless abandon. Scrap-metal fighters raced along the ferrocrete canyons, training their crude slug-throwers on anything that moved.

More troubling were the bulky transports. Looking like big boxes of pig-iron fitted with wings and a mad array of guns, they rumbled across the sky. While Rhodaan watched, the side of one of the transports bulged outwards, distorted by some violent impact from within. A moment later, a ten-metre section of the aircraft's hull was sent hurtling away, kicked loose by the mob of frenzied orks within.

The aliens roared with glee as the hull plate was torn free, paying no notice to the handful of their comrades pulled from the ship by the resulting suction. They were a fierce-looking mob, steel helmets crushed down around their apelike heads, their mouths distorted by a profusion of yellowed tusks. Each of the orks gripped some sort of weapon in its leathery paw, from stubby pistols to crude axes and clubs. One monster flexed the talons of a massive power claw, electricity crackling about each finger.

It did not take the orks long to spot Rhodaan's assault boat and realise it wasn't part of their armada. A fierce howl sounded from the mob and their transport screeched in protest as it swung around to adopt a parallel course to the assault boat.

'Man the door guns,' Rhodaan snarled into his vox. 'I think the xenos want to play.'

Solid shot rattled off the hull of the assault boat as

the orks in the transport began to blast away at the Air Cohort ship. One of the shots glanced off the pauldron of Rhodaan's power armour. The captain responded by delivering a quick burst from his bolt pistol, blowing gory chunks from the massed ork mob. The stricken aliens were tossed from the compartment with callous disregard by their comrades, the wounded greenskins plummeting earthwards like rag dolls.

The human auxiliaries were beside Rhodaan now, unlimbering the pintle-mounted heavy bolter from its fastenings and feeding ammunition into its magazine. One of the men cried out as a lucky shot from an ork bolter ripped half of his torso away. The rest of the gun crew instantly ducked behind the armoured door, leaving Rhodaan alone to face the alien onslaught.

'Worthless simpering flesh-maggots!' Uzraal bellowed, kicking his way through the cowering auxiliaries. His gauntlet gripped one of the men by the back of his tunic. Slinging the man as though he weighed nothing, he tossed the soldier back towards the doorway. The man screamed as he pitched over the side and fell into Vorago's polluted sky.

'A bit too much force,' Uzraal apologised as Rhodaan darted a glance at him. The other Iron Warriors were in the doorway now, their bolt pistols sending withering fire into the ork transport. Uzraal took their timely intervention to march over to the heavy bolter. In a few seconds, he completed the arming of the weapon and directed its murderous fire against the alien vessel.

The scrap-metal transport was shredded by the high-impact, automatic fire from the heavy bolter. Plates were ripped from the alien craft, the crystallised canopy of the flight compartment burst apart in a shower of fragmented shards, the pilots reduced to gory smears at their controls. Howling like a daemon from the warp, Uzraal ripped the heavy bolter from its mounting and leaned out from the side of the assault boat. With savage precision, he sent a continuous stream of shells slamming into the crippled transport, pulping the ork warriors in the exposed cargo compartment.

'Left at the four!' Rhodaan said, slapping his hand against Uzraal's shoulder to get the Iron Warrior's attention. Descending above and from the left of the assault boat was another ork transport, this one painted a dull grey and adorned with crude glyphs and crosses. As it dropped down, Rhodaan saw doors slide open in its sides and little metal gantries clatter out from the hull. At first he wondered if the orks were mad enough to try a boarding action, as though they were aboard ancient sea vessels, not aircraft hurtling through the sky thousands of metres above a modern city.

As Uzraal's weapon began to chew chunks from the bottom of the ork ship's hull, Rhodaan saw the real purpose of the gantries. Ork warriors were emerging from the transport, climbing out upon the shuddering metal platforms. They were somewhat slighter and paler of colour than the vicious mob in the first transport, wearing dull grey fatigues in what seemed some crude attempt at a uniform. More importantly, however, each of the monsters had a huge rocket fastened to its back.

The Iron Warriors immediately turned their fire from the transport to the orks on the gantries. They had fought the greenskins many times and each of them remembered the vicious stormboyz who employed their own crude versions of jump packs to stage brutal assaults in the very heart of their enemy's position. These orks weren't going to get the chance.

An autocannon positioned in the tail of the transport growled into life, punching holes in the Iron Warriors' assault boat. There was a shrill scream as one of the ork shells tore through a Cohort auxiliary, splashing the man's innards across the compartment. Uzraal shifted his aim, directing his heavy bolter against the ork gun. The other Iron Warriors continued to pick off stormboyz from the gantries. With each shot, another ork went careening from the transport. One especially good bit of marksmanship from Baelfegor exploded the rocket strapped to one ork's back, transforming it into a living torch and bathing four of its fellows in burning promethium. The stricken greenskins fell earthwards, igniting patches of industrial smog as their burning bodies plummeted through the brown sky.

A nimbus of flame suddenly erupted from the rear of the ork ship, the telltale impact of a krak missile. The sensors in Rhodaan's helmet instantly calculated the trajectory, spotting Vallax's assault boat in the distance. He could see the Iron Warriors of Squad Vidarna standing at the open doors of the craft, blasting away at a swarm of ork stormboyz flitting about their ship. Though the Space Marines were slaughtering their foes by the bushel, more of the rocket-packed xenos were converging on the assault boat.

'Pilot,' Rhodaan snarled into his vox. 'Reduce speed! Bring us closer to the other assault boat.' Whatever his personal animosity towards Vallax, his pride as an Iron Warrior wouldn't allow him to abandon his brothers on the field of battle.

'Lord Rhodaan,' the pilot objected, his voice quaking with fear. 'We are taking too much punishment ourselves to render aid to the other gunship.'

Rhodaan's voice was sharp as steel as he growled back at the pilot. 'Iron Warriors do not forsake their battle-brothers,' he said. 'Bring us about, or I will take command of this ship.' He didn't need to explain to the human crew what would happen to them if he was forced to pilot the assault boat himself.

'By your command, Lord Rhodaan,' the pilot replied. Immediately, the assault boat's speed began to slacken and the craft began to veer towards Vallax's ship.

Almost instantly, Rhodaan saw a mob of stormboyz shoot away from a saucer-shaped transport vessel, their rocket packs spewing black fumes as they surged across the sky. It quickly became clear that the aliens had spotted their assault boat and were manoeuvring to intercept. The stormboyz veered crazily through the polluted sky. Rhodaan watched as one of the rocket packs exploded, sending a burning mass of ork-meat plummeting earthwards. Other orks tried to compensate for the erratic trajectory of their flight by attempting to steer with their flapping arms. Still others were too occupied firing their bolters at the assault boat to be bothered by something as inconsequential as speed and direction.

'Brother Uzraal, bring down that rabble!' Rhodaan ordered. Uzraal marched across the compartment to the opposite doorway and braced himself against the recoil of the heavy bolter. A bloodthirsty hiss sounded from his helmet's vent as he took aim.

Before Uzraal could fire, the assault boat was shaken by a tremendous explosion. Two of the auxiliaries were hurled from the compartment and it was all the Iron Warriors could do to maintain their footing. The frantic voices of the crew sounded over the vox, shouting that the dorsal stabilisers and airfoil had been hit. The boat was becoming unbalanced, slipping over into a roll the pilot couldn't bring her out of.

Rhodaan glared at the oncoming mob of stormboyz, firing into the laughing orks. Beyond them, he could see Vallax's assault boat veering away, escaping the crush of enemies swarming about her. Clearly the Over-Captain didn't have the same sense of martial pride as his subordinate.

'Brace for impact,' Rhodaan ordered his squad as the boat's roll increased, shifting the craft to a forty-five degree angle.

'I don't think we can expect a soft landing.'

THE FACTORY WALLS throbbed from the reverberations of Vorago's cannon. Tiles rained down from the roof as bombs exploded across the district. A section of ceiling came crashing inwards as an immense block of ferrocrete, blasted from a neighbouring structure, smashed its way into Processing Plant Secundus Minorus. The huge chunk of debris scored a deep gouge in the floor as it tumbled through the factory, obliterating ovens and conveyors in its path. Dozens of slaves struggled futilely in their chains as the rolling wreckage tottered towards them.

Yuxiang turned his face so he wouldn't have to watch the men at the nearby conveyor ground into paste by the runaway block. It wasn't the sight of death that unsettled him – he had been a spectator to grisly death since he'd taken his first breath on Castellax. No, it was the knowledge that the slightest deviation in the block's rampage would have made him one of its victims. This was what threatened to turn his knees to jelly and his mind sick with terror.

Now, at this moment, Yuxiang couldn't allow his emotions to overwhelm him. If he was going to survive, he had to keep his wits. He had to keep focused.

Defiantly, Yuxiang raised his eyes to the wall and the glowering steel words bolted to its surface, the words that had oppressed him for so many years, burning themselves into his mind.

Obedience. Labour. Fid–

As he stared at the words, the entire factory was rocked by a tremendous impact. An entire section of wall was blasted inwards, ripping the last letters from the wall in a shower of sparks and a shriek of steel. Yuxiang gaped in awe as he watched an armoured assault boat come thundering into the factory, smoke and flame streaming from its scarred hull. The deathly insignia of the Iron Warriors glared at him from the boat's wing as the craft began to roll. A moment later, the craft smashed into one of the blast furnaces, spewing molten metal across the factory in a shower of fire.

The slave could only stare in disbelief at the devastation,

his eyes straining to pierce the veil of steam and smoke that now engulfed the assault boat. That had been an Iron Warriors gunship, only the terrifying Traitor Marines were allowed to bear that insignia. Yuxiang's stunned mind couldn't come to grips with that fact. All his life he had looked upon the Iron Warriors as something indestructible, unconquerable. Like a force of nature, or a cabal of cruel gods spat from the depths of hell. To think that they could die, that they could be beaten was something Yuxiang had never dared believe possible.

The harsh bark of gunfire broke Yuxiang's fascination. Whipping around, the slave found his eyes again turned to the wall. Through the great gash torn by the assault boat, he could see hideous forms streaming into the factory. They were things possessed of only a general semblance of human design and upon the broad back of each creature a massive rocket had been strapped. They used these to power down through the rent in the wall, laughing and shooting as they made their descent.

Raw horror raced through Yuxiang's body. He had never seen an alien before, but he knew he was seeing the dreaded xenos now. No man who had ever heard tell of an ork could fail to recognise the creatures when he saw them.

The monsters must have been the ones who shot down the assault boat, then pursued the crippled craft into the factory. Once inside, however, the bloodthirsty orks quickly forgot their quarry. Even after the havoc wrought by the explosions around it, there were still thousands of slaves shackled to the machinery of Processing Plant Secundus Minorus. The sight of helpless, cowering prey was too much for the orks to ignore. Laughing their brutish calls, the aliens raised their crude weapons and happily began to massacre the defenceless humans.

Prefect Wyre was nowhere in sight, but several of his overseers had remained behind to safeguard the factory during the attack. At the sound of gunfire, they emerged from the shelters they had retreated to at the height of the bombing. Quickly they fanned out, seeking cover from which to engage the orks. Yuxiang knew it wasn't concern for the slaves that motivated the overseers, but rather fear of what would happen to them if the aliens caused further damage to the factory's infrastructure with their reckless carnage.

One of the hulking orks pitched over onto its side as its body was peppered with shot from the overseers' guns. Despite being blasted by three shotguns, the greenskin still had fight in it, aiming its fat-barrelled pistol in the general direction of its attackers and emptying the magazine at the humans. When the weapon was spent, the ork threw its weapon at the oven the closest overseer had taken shelter behind, then threw one of its boots when the pistol failed to hit a target. The wounded brute was groping about looking for something else to throw when another fusillade from the shotguns smashed into it, nearly ripping its head from its shoulders.

The first ork the overseers killed was also their last. With savage glee, every ork in the factory turned away from their slaughter of the slaves to converge upon the small cluster of humans who had the temerity to fight back. Slugs and shells smashed into the machinery the guards were using as cover. The projectiles with lower velocity glanced from the sides of the obstacles, but there was no consistency among the alien armaments and several rounds tore through the machinery as though it were made of paper. Human screams rose from behind the cover as one by one the guards were torn to ribbons by the high-calibre ork weaponry.

Yuxiang cowered deeper in the shadows as he saw the last of the overseers pitch and fall, his shotgun clattering across the floor only a few metres away. The slave watched in terror as several orks prowled among the bodies, stripping weapons and ammunition belts from the dead men. He glanced back at the shotgun. Indecision gripped him.

He could make a mad dash for the weapon, seize it before the orks saw him.

The very possibility of attracting the attention of the aliens made Yuxiang shift even lower against the side of his work station. He was no soldier, he couldn't expect to equal the fighting prowess of the overseers. If he had a gun, he still wouldn't be any match for one of the aliens. No, his only hope was to hide and keep quiet.

A greasy, musky stink struck Yuxiang's senses a moment before he saw the ork step out from the other side of his work station. The reek of the alien's leathery flesh was overwhelming, as though it would take root in his lungs and choke him with its foulness. The slave clapped a hand over his mouth to keep from coughing, fighting against his body's instinctive revulsion.

It was a wasted effort. The ork took a few steps towards the shotgun, then suddenly swung around. The monster's beady red eyes narrowed as it stared down at Yuxiang, but it was the alien's flaring nostrils that told the slave how he had been found. Just as he had smelled the alien, so the alien had smelled him.

Yuxiang rose slowly to his feet, a coil of chain clenched in one hand, the twisted piece of rebar he had used to break his chain in the other. The ork scowled at him for a moment, then its face pulled back in a sadistic leer, exposing its yellowed fangs. He could see the alien's body shivering with amusement as the ork holstered its pistol. Its eyes darted from the loop of chain to the piece of rebar.

Chuckling, the ork reached to its belt and dragged out an immense knife, a weapon with a blade bigger than Yuxiang's forearm. The greenskin stabbed one of its fat fingers against an activation stud and the teeth along the edge of the knife began to churn back and forth. Hefting its brutal weapon, the grinning ork stepped towards Yuxiang.

The next instant, a single shot exploded from just over

the slave's head. The ork staggered, the knife dropping from its numbed hand. Smoke rose from the hole in its forehead, its beady red eyes crossed as though trying to look at the wound between them. A second later, the explosive round detonated, blasting the helmet from the greenskin's head and sending most of its brains and part of its skull spurting across the floor. The alien's body crumpled to its knees, then pitched forwards onto what was left of its face.

Yuxiang's relief quickly collapsed into fear as his deliverer marched into view. Like the ork, his rescuer came from behind the machinery and towered above the slave. Again, Yuxiang found himself gazing upon the skull-icon of the Iron Warriors, but where before he had seen it emblazoned across the wing of one of their gunships, now he saw it engraved upon the pauldron of a Space Marine's own armour.

The Iron Warrior's plate was almost black from where it had been scorched and charred. It was incredible, but Yuxiang realised this Space Marine must have been on the assault boat and survived the conflagration that consumed it. He could see the scarring along the muzzle of the Iron Warrior's bolt pistol, the bubbling that bespoke exposure to the most extreme temperature. Somehow, the armour had endured the same heat – and so had the man inside.

No, not a man, Yuxiang corrected himself. A monster, something as cruel and alien as any ork. An Iron Warrior.

Like a god of death, the hulking Space Marine gazed at his handiwork. He brought his armoured boot down upon the wreckage of the ork's head, smashing what was left of it into a greasy smear. Peering around the corner of Yuxiang's workstation, the Iron Warrior studied the dispersal of the other orks. After a moment, his fanged helm dipped in a nod of satisfaction.

'Thirty targets,' the Iron Warrior growled over his vox-caster. 'Brother Baelfegor will frag the three near the conveyors. When the rest react to the grenade, the remainder of the squad will assault from the flanks. I will maintain a firing position at their rear. If any of the aliens attempt to disengage, flush them towards my position.'

Almost as soon as the Iron Warrior issued his orders, the factory echoed once more with the discharge of bolters and the boom of grenades. From the smouldering wreckage of their transport, the Space Marines had risen like avenging phoenixes. Now it was their turn to bring death into Processing Plant Secundus Minorus.

Yuxiang sank against the base of his work station, all ideas of escape and freedom dashed. There was no defying the Iron Warriors. They were indestructible. They were unbeatable.

The only thing a mere mortal could hope for was to keep out of their way.

RHODAAN BROUGHT THE screaming edge of his chainsword crunching through the ork's body. The greenskin flailed on the gnawing blade, yet even as its spine was cut in half, the alien struggled to bring its wide-barrelled pistol towards the Iron Warrior's head. The Space Marine twisted aside at the last instant as the ork's finger tightened on the trigger, the violent flash of the discharged weapon causing the left lens of Rhodaan's helmet to darken its display for a moment. The slug whipped past his head, burying itself in the side of a pneumatic press. The next moment, the bisected ork's body was flopping on the floor.

The Iron Warrior stared contemptuously at the mutilated alien, then pointed his bolt pistol at its head. Where the ork had missed, Rhodaan's aim proved more accurate, exploding the brute's skull with a single shot.

Sounds of battle slowly faded from the processing plant, only a few scattered howls and the occasional stutter of gunfire where moments before bedlam had reigned. The other members of Squad Kyrith were taking their share of the alien invaders. The stormboyz who had pursued the crippled assault boat were learning what it meant to oppose the Iron Warriors. They had thought the Space Marines destroyed in the crash. Now they knew better. Not that the lesson would do them any good. A dead ork didn't perform new tricks.

Rhodaan fired a few rounds at an ork rising off the floor, trying to use its rocket pack to reach the hole in the wall and escape. The shots crippled the creature's pack, causing a stream of flame to erupt from the side of the mechanism and sending the rocket careening through the factory on an erratic trajectory which ended in a ball of fire when the alien smacked headfirst into one of the walls.

Rhodaan had already dismissed the alien from his thoughts. With the ork incursion in the factory effectively eliminated, he turned his attention back to the bigger situation.

'Squad Kyrith to Bastion,' Rhodaan growled into his helmet's vox-unit. 'Assault craft destroyed. Request extraction and redeployment. Our location is Processing Plant Secundus Minorus. Minimal xenos presence at our position.'

The captain waited while his report was relayed by the Bastion's servitors. Warily, he watched the breach in the wall, ready to spot any more orks trying to enter or leave the factory. The building was still being shaken by the bombs the aliens were continuing to rain down on the district. Simple logic dictated that the orks wouldn't be deploying troops in this area, only an idiot or a madman would bomb his own soldiers. But Rhodaan had fought orks before and knew that the aliens were both idiots and madmen. The only thing they could be depended upon to do was to be undependable.

'Captain Rhodaan, this is the Bastion.' Rhodaan stiffened slightly as he heard the voice of Sergeant Ipos over his vox. 'Over-Captain Vallax reported your craft destroyed with all personnel. It is good to hear that his report was in error.'

Rhodaan took a second to drain the emotion from his voice before responding. Again, he considered the eerie accuracy of the shots which had disabled the assault boat's dorsal engine. So, Vallax had thought Squad Kyrith destroyed, had he?

'Squad Kyrith is fully operational,' Rhodaan said, his tone as tempered and mechanical as that of a servitor. 'We require only extraction to pursue our objective.' If Vallax thought he would reap the glory of assaulting Dirgas on his own, then the Over-Captain was going to be disappointed.

'Negative, Captain Rhodaan,' Ipos replied. 'The Dirgas mission has been cancelled. The xenos have descended upon Vorago in considerable force. They must not be allowed to establish a beachhead. Warsmith Andraaz has made the extermination of the xenos within Vorago top priority for all brothers of the Third Grand Company.'

'Squad Kyrith obeys,' Rhodaan said, slamming his fist against his chest plate in an almost automatic gesture of fealty. Beneath his helmet, his lip curled in a sneer. If his men were denied the opportunity to win glory in the raid on Dirgas, then at least Vallax wouldn't be adding any laurels to his name either.

'Brothers!' Rhodaan called over the inter-squad vox frequency. 'Cleanse this place swiftly. We have been given new orders from the Bastion. The foul xenos seek to gain a foothold within Vorago.

'We will see that the only ground they keep is the pit we dump their carcasses into.'

CHAPTER V
I-Day Plus Thirty

A BLOSSOM OF flame and smoke rose from the hab-pen, an incandescent mushroom of atomised stone and vaporised metal that spiralled into the greasy sky. Somewhere within that pillar of devastation, the ashes of six thousand slaves reached towards the heavens before sinking back into the rubble of their bombed-out cage.

Better them than me, thought Group-Captain Xiaowang as he stared from the cockpit of his ebon-winged Spineripper. The swept-back intrusion-bomber represented the latest word in Castellax design templates, a vicious fusion of human engineering and xenos technology. Capable of incredible atmospheric speeds, the Spineripper had earned its name for its uncompromising manoeuvrability, far in excess of what the human body could safely endure. Even competent pilots like Xiaowang, with years of hypno-conditioning and training behind them, had to be vigilant lest the aircraft get out of control. Sometimes, when he looked at the alien crystal relays scattered across the control console, the pilot wondered if some malignant intelligence was staring back at him, waiting for him to make the slightest mistake.

'Hab-blocks six and seven now eliminated,' a quivering voice reported over the squadron comms channel. Xiaowang pressed his thumb against the activation rune for his vox-unit.

'They're better off dead,' he snarled at the other pilot. There were twelve Spinerippers in his command and he wasn't certain which man made the report. He didn't want to know. Skylord Morax was extremely unforgiving when it came to displays of emotion. A favourite punishment for such displays of weakness was for the offender to be shackled to a bomb and dropped in the very next run. Xiaowang had seen it happen more times than he cared to admit. Mercy was something only a complete idiot expected from the Iron Warriors. Do your job with efficiency and diligence and they might ignore you – anything less was playing with death.

Xiaowang turned his attention back to the flight path of his squadron. Pillars of fire sprouted from the city below, like some hellish grove with leaves of ash and smoke. It was sobering to think of the many thousands of dead those pillars represented, the atomised destruction of so many men and women who had been alive before the Iron Bats appeared in the skies over Oramis.

The orks had descended en masse on the city of Oramis in the early days of the invasion. The local defence forces had been overwhelmed in a matter of days and the *Kreisleiter* of the city had been slow implementing the murderous abandonment measures demanded by the Iron Warriors. Instead of leaving a desolate city, the Kreisleiter had allowed the foul xenos to capture a populated metropolis with most of its industry still intact. The orks had quickly started using the city to manufacture weaponry to facilitate their conquest, impressing the population into their workforce.

Xiaowang grimaced as he pictured the brutal, monstrous

aliens. The people of Oramis had fallen from th
the fire. The Iron Warriors were merciless and
ing, but at least they didn't think of their sla
supplemental food supply.

The very thought of food brought a growl from
Xiaowang's stomach. Since the onset of the siege, the
people of Castellax had been subsisting from an even
lower quality protein sludge than normal. The loss of
the orbital algae swamps had reduced their rations to a
noxious mix of synthetics and protein supplements. At
best, the villainous paste lacked any semblance of taste.
At worst, it was like trying to eat sand after a silica rain.

Xiaowang shook his head. It was a poor metaphor,
but naturally his mind had turned to thoughts of water.
There was little left on Castellax, most of it so polluted
by the planet's industry that a sump-ghoul couldn't drink
it. Even more than food, water was becoming a dire
scarcity. The reserves maintained in Vorago and the other
cities wouldn't last forever, whatever the Iron Warriors
might claim. It was fine for the Space Marines – as far
as Xiaowang knew, they didn't need to eat or drink or
sleep for that matter – but for mere mortals it was mighty
important to know where the next drink was coming
from. Or if there was even going to be a next drink.

Another blossom of fire boiled upwards as the last
of the Spinerippers released its payload. The visor of
Xiaowang's helmet darkened as the bright blast burned
across the sky. How many had perished in that blast, he
wondered? Perhaps it was better not to know.

He turned his face from the explosion, scowling as his
gaze stared out across the sweeping panorama of factories
and processing plants which made up the industrial section of Oramis. Many of the structures were blackened
and burned, but not from the attentions of the Castellax
Air Cohort. Skylord Morax had given them strict orders
against bombing Oramis's industry. What damage the
factories had suffered was caused by the orks when they

captured the city. From the deranged confusion of derricks, gantries and improvised balustrades arrayed around the buildings, it appeared the conquerors had gone to great pains to put everything into working order again.

Xiaowang clenched his fist. The target priority established by Morax was beyond callous. The Iron Bats were to eliminate the workforce to disrupt ork activity in Oramis. Another squadron was to bomb the rail-lines to hinder transport of materiel from the city to other ork positions. But the factories, they were sacrosanct. Any pilot who dropped his payload in the industrial area was to be skinned alive before his entire wing and then thrown into the acid-flats of Teramis.

The city, Xiaowang understood, was to be the focus of a future campaign. The goal of that campaign was recapturing the factories. For the Iron Warriors, that was the only thing that made the city worth possessing. The fate of the humans living in Oramis was less than nothing to them. They could always cultivate a new generation of slaves from the embryo farms.

'Bandits! Bandits!' a voice screamed across the vox. Xiaowang's head snapped around, his eyes darting to the proximity display. True to the panicked report, there were a dozen blips rising from the midst of the industrial centre. Xiaowang didn't need visual confirmation to know they were ork fighters. After three sorties against Oramis, the aliens had figured out the pattern and moved their hangars into the inviolate part of the city.

'Iron Bats,' Xiaowang snarled into his vox-bead. 'Hostiles at our five. Xenos-pattern craft!' He almost laughed at that classification. When it came to ork aircraft, there was no pattern. Every plane was as different from the next as one alkali crystal from another. Until each example was actually engaged there was no way to gauge its speed or manoeuvrability. Or its armament.

'All wings, drop bombs and scatter,' Xiaowang ordered. Loaded down with ordnance, there was small chance of outmanoeuvring the fighters. Oramis had been too distant from the aerodrome for the Spinerippers to bring their own fighter cover. Even Morax would have to agree that a discreet withdrawal was the smart thing. He might execute Xiaowang anyway, of course.

The Spineripper was jostled violently as the last bombers dropped their loads onto the smouldering hab-blocks. Watching the pillars of fire and ash rise into the sky, Xiaowang smiled. The ring of destruction was between the Iron Bats and the approaching orks. He hadn't planned it this way, but he couldn't have asked for a better screen to cover the squadron's retreat.

'All wings, peel off at your nine. Keep the blast-area between you and the bandits as long as possible.' Xiaowang pulled back on the control stick, putting his bomber into a steep-angled turn. With one eye on the proximity-slate, he watched the ork fighters continuing their approach. Some of the aliens were initiating steep climbs or drastic turns to avoid the ash clouds, others seemed intent on just ploughing straight through the radioactive pillars. A flicker of relief spread through him. The orks weren't going to catch them now.

'Incoming!' came a frantic shriek, shattering the moment of calm Xiaowang had taken possession of. He looked back at the proximity-slate. It was peppered with a confusion of little specks. In his ears, Xiaowang could hear the clatter of bullets glancing off the fuselage of his Spineripper.

Whatever air detection devices the orks had, it wasn't very good. The Iron Bats had been able to sortie over Oramis with relative impunity before. In the past, however, their flight path had taken them well away from the city before turning back to the aerodrome. This time, they were crossing their own tail and flying over a city infested with kill-crazy aliens fully aware of them. Looking down from the cockpit, Xiaowang could see rooftops swarming with orks, every one of them armed with a gun of some kind and firing wildly into the sky. It wasn't a question of accuracy or precision, the sheer amount of fire being thrown into the air made it impossible to avoid. It was like trying to fly through an ash-storm of lead.

The only saving grace was that the ork weaponry was of too low a calibre to bring down a Spineripper at such distance. Even as that comforting thought came to Xiaowang, an agonised scream shrieked across the vox. Through the cockpit, he could see his wingman descending in flames, his Spineripper trailing smoke from its mangled fuselage. On the ground below, an ork rocket battery belched a salvo of twenty warheads into the sky. He saw several of the rockets detonate soon after, probably struck by the wild fire of small arms, but there were still a half-dozen left when they reached the Iron Bats' altitude. Xiaowang stabbed his thumb against a rune on the control panel, releasing a bundle of metallic chaff to misdirect the rockets. He felt his body go cold when they ignored the bait, shifting course to match his own. Whatever machine-spirit the orks had pounded into their weapons to guide them, it was too primitive to change targets once it was unleashed.

'I don't want to die in Oramis,' Xiaowang cursed as the first of the rockets slammed into his tail.

A moment later, his world vanished in a sheet of flame, his broken Spineripper spiralling downwards until it evaporated in the mushroom cloud rising from the rubble of hab-block six.

CAPTAIN RHODAAN PROWLED along the marble crypt, inspecting the artefacts entombed in their stasis-field niches. The segments of a massive crystal, the spider-web of flaws marring its face still weeping the same tears of blood as when he had ripped it from the shell of an eldar wraithguard. The sceptre of an ecclesiarch, its thorns as keen as the day the priest had vainly tried to bludgeon Rhodaan with it, little specks of the cleric's brain still clinging to the ornate baton. The talon of a tyranid hive tyrant, its alien flesh still squirming and striving to regenerate itself five centuries after it was chopped from the monster's arm.

Rhodaan paused before one of the niches, letting his gaze linger upon the pride of his collection, the centrepiece of his own private reliquary.

The still-leering head of a Space Marine, a captain from the Imperial Fists Chapter, one of the servile fools who yet slaved for the False Emperor. Preserved at the very moment Rhodaan had hewed it from the man's shoulders, he could still see the hate in the dead Imperial Fist's eyes. It was validation, a testament to his prowess and might. It was tangible proof that he, Rhodaan, was a true Iron Warrior, a son of Perturabo, proud inheritor of the legacy of the Legion.

He turned away from the decapitated head, all doubt vanquished in his mind. It did not need the calculated flattery of Skylord Morax or the grudging acknowledgement of Over-Captain Vallax or even the regard of Warsmith Andraaz to justify Rhodaan's sense of purpose. It took only one look into the dead eyes of a butchered enemy. Hate was his purpose, to avenge his Legion's betrayal upon the galaxy. Millions had already been sacrificed to his hate, but it was not enough to scratch the surface. The Imperium's suffering had only begun. So long as there was a breath in his body, a beat in one of his hearts, Rhodaan would prosecute the Long War.

'Revenge is my honour,' the Iron Warrior growled, his words echoing from the marble walls. Rhodaan's voice was an alchemy of pride and bitterness. After millennia of unending war, he knew the Legion's thirst for revenge would never be quenched and so he was doomed to die without honour. The moment the Legion's flesh-rippers had claimed him, he had become one of the damned. They had given him strength and power beyond anything a mere mortal could possess, but in return they had taken everything.

Rhodaan closed his eyes, picturing that final moment when the flesh-rippers had come. He could see their chainaxes tearing through the sealed door of the hab-unit, shredding the furniture that had been piled behind it to strengthen the barrier. He could hear the death agonies of his parents and sister as the slavers butchered them before his eyes. The Iron Warrior felt no kinship to these people now. The only feeling that stirred within him was disgust at the sloppy tactics displayed by the flesh-rippers. It was insufferable to think such vermin served the Third Grand Company, dared call themselves vassals of Warsmith Andraaz.

The Space Marine stalked through the empty halls of his reliquary, abandoning thoughts of the past and turning his mind to promises of the future. Skylord Morax was pushing for the recapture of Oramis, promising that his Air Cohort could immobilise the orks infesting the city long enough for ten divisions of janissaries to sweep in and seize the initiative. The Iron Warriors themselves would strike at the vital industrial district, exterminating every alien lurking within the factories. Morax was quite confident that the entire operation could be organised and put into action in as little as a week.

Of course, there had been voices raised in protest. Algol and Gamgin were concerned about maintaining the strength of the garrison manning the Witch Wall and the Mare Ossius fortifications. Already bemoaning the reserves that had been detached from the Mare Ossius area of operations in order to assist Project Malice – Ipos's plan for dealing with the orks should they breach the Witch Wall and cross the dry ocean – the two captains weren't about to lose more men to Morax's offensive.

Admiral Nostraz went one better, calling for a surgical strike against Oramis. A single run targeting the spoil heaps looming over the city's northern and western districts would smash Oramis flat under an avalanche of industrial waste. Even if the orks could dig themselves out, they wouldn't be using the factories to arm any more of their brood. It was a proposal that seemed to be gaining more favour with the Warsmith each day. Having lost his fleet, Nostraz appeared to be manoeuvring to assume Morax's position as Skylord.

The sharp tang of fresh blood struck Rhodaan's nostrils as he rounded a marble partition. A flicker of tension passed through the Space Marine's towering physique, an instinctive reaction to the potential for violence and strife. He paused beside the partition, his fingers closing about the carved figures of daemons writhing along the cold stone. The sound of a murmured litany relaxed the Iron Warrior. There was the potential for violence and strife here, but it was violence he would unleash.

Down a dimly lit hallway, Rhodaan marched, the sounds and smell growing more distinct with each step. Now the niches were filled with different trophies. A diamond-toothed chainsword from the foundries of Olympia. A masterwork plasma pistol crafted by the vanquished abhumans of Freya Seven. The vicious talons of an enormous power claw, each knuckle moulded into the semblance of a grinning skull, a product of the bloodthirsty daemonlings of Zhok, deep within the Eye. Each weapon was more than a simple trophy to Rhodaan. These were battle honours, living symbols of his might and power. Gazing upon them, he could remember not only the moment he had torn them from the lifeless fingers of an enemy, but all his other battles, the wars in which these instruments of death had known him as their master. They had shed blood upon a thousand worlds and would do so upon a thousand more.

The subdued sound of the litany increased as Rhodaan made his way deeper into the confines of his arsenal-chapel. Now he could hear a wet, gurgling noise as well, punctuated by the dull pulsations of a machine. How often had he heard that sound? How often had it presaged the coming of conflict and glory?

Rhodaan turned a corner and stared into a marble-walled alcove draped in pressure-film and the crackling coils of temporal bafflers. The drapery had been pulled back, carefully bound in lengths of leathery hide and parchment conjure-strips. Within the recess beyond, a tall metal stand rested. Between the stand's splayed arms, a sinister-looking device was displayed. It was a bulky mass of ceramite and titanium, its surface etched with the most elaborate calligraphy. Huge thrusters sprouted from its back, their intakes looking like the fanged mouths of ancient star-devils. Straps of plasteel dangled from its front, merging into a skull-shaped buckle, forming a cob-web of segmented metal and glistening gemstone.

Most striking of all, however, were the folded wings which jutted from the sides of the device. Sheathed in reptilian leather, veins pulsing and quivering beneath the skin, an evil-smelling musk rising from its pores, the wings seemed not only organic but alive.

The Iron Warriors captain smiled as he gazed upon his prize possession. It was named Eurydice and he had claimed it from one of his own battle-brothers, Sergeant Gaos. The Raptor had died in the talons of Rhodaan's power claw during the violent overthrow of the old War-smith. Since that time, it had been Rhodaan's right to wear the daemo-mechanical marvel into battle. It was a thing of the warp, beyond mundane rules of physics and chemistry. Swifter and more agile than any jump pack fabricated by the priests of Mars, Eurydice had served its new master well.

It would have cause to do so again.

A clutch of shaven mamelukes knelt on the floor sur-rounding Eurydice, the slave-serfs looking like shapeless heaps of grey in their heavy robes. It was from their parched lips that the chords of the litany rose. The humans swayed in rhythm to the archaic syllables, a chorus of adoration and genuflection to the somnolent essence of the jump pack. Rhodaan had scores of mamelukes detailed for no other purpose than to tend Eurydice and keep it ready for him. Artisans who diligently mended every nick and scrape, machinist-fabricators who ministered to every gear and piston, tech-adepts who placated the essence of the device through prayer and ritual.

And the butchers, who satisfied Eurydice's hunger.

The smell of blood emanated from a circular framework standing in the hall outside the alcove. Two wizened mamelukes attended the cobalt-hued skeleton of rods and tubes, their faces locked behind snarling fetish-masks. Upon the frame itself, limbs spread wide, was the limp paleness of a naked slave. From the shackle attached to each wrist and ankle, a fat tube snaked away from the body, undulating across the framework before dipping down into a reservoir. With each breath the slave took, the tubes shuddered and a spurt of crimson fell into the reservoir.

The exsanguinator was a fiendish device of torture, exploiting the victim's own pulse to bleed him dry. But it was not mere torture which caused Rhodaan to order its use. One of the butchers held a long, brush-like instrument in his withered hand. As the reservoir filled, he would dip the bristles into the collected blood. Once the brush was saturated, the mameluke would approach Eurydice and paint the reptilian wings with the sanguine fluid. It was almost possible to see the blood soaking through the skin and swelling the veins beneath.

Rhodaan paid scant attention to his slaves and even less to the dying wretch in the grip of the exsanguinator. He had eyes only for Eurydice. Would its essence be placated? Would it accede to his demands, or would it be capricious and betray him the way it had Gaos?

He could almost picture the scene in his mind, the reptilian wings folding in upon themselves, dropping him to his destruction. He could see Vallax gloating over his corpse as the Over-Captain stripped Eurydice from him.

Rhodaan reached out, seizing one of the chanters by the

neck. His fingers tightened about the slave, crushing his windpipe, pulverising his vertebrae. As he felt the man's death spasm against his palm, an icy determination filled his hearts. His hated superior would never plunder Rhodaan's treasure. He glared at Eurydice, eyes boring into the empty sockets of the skull-buckle. Whatever awareness the jump pack's essence had, it could not fail to mistake the Space Marine's warning. He would not be a mere victim like Gaos. If Eurydice failed him, Rhodaan would destroy them both. The jump pack would never serve a jackal like Vallax!

Thoughts of the Over-Captain brought a tightening of Rhodaan's hand and torn skin and sinew oozed through his fingers. He stared down at the dead slave, then let the carcass slump to the floor. Vallax had been conspiring against Rhodaan's Raptors, picking the choice assaults for his own squad and assigning the less prestigious missions to his subordinate. It was a strategy calculated to ensure Rhodaan remained in obscurity while Vallax's name was ever before Warsmith Andraaz.

The next mission was no different. While Vallax led a raid against an important ork staging area, Rhodaan would coordinate the evacuation of material from a mining outpost in the path of the latest xenos incursion east of the Convallis Robigo. There would be glory for Vallax, leading an attack against the invaders. There was none for the man who organised a retreat.

Of course, this effort on the Over-Captain's part to relegate Rhodaan to the most ignominious duties could simply be a clever ploy to put his rival off guard. It was no secret that something would need to be done about the ork presence in Dirgas. Since Algol's abandonment of the city, the xenos had transformed it into a fortress bristling with anti-aircraft batteries. Morax's Air Cohort had suffered tremendous losses in their last run against Dirgas, exchanging only the most minor damage to the city for their efforts. Since then, the Skylord had been making one excuse after another to avoid Dirgas entirely, pleading a campaign of strategic isolation to neutralise the ork stronghold's impact on the overall war effort.

It was a tactic which was only a stop-gap. Eventually, Warsmith Andraaz would order the Dirgas problem settled. When that time came, it would be the Raptors who would be in the vanguard. All of them, both Vallax and Rhodaan. The Over-Captain wouldn't be able to sideline his rival when it came to knocking out the invader's stronghold. He would need to find another way to keep the glory for himself.

Which brought Rhodaan's thoughts back to a conversation he'd had, a clandestine liaison with Uhlan, one of the Raptors from Vallax's squad. Uhlan was a half-breed, his gene-seed cobbled together from the plundered glands of butchered enemies. It was a fact Vallax never allowed his subordinate to forget. Such treatment had eroded the other Space Marine's loyalty to the Over-Captain, moving him to look for a more supportive patron.

Rhodaan felt contempt course through his gut. He was a pure Iron Warrior and the temerity of a half-breed like Uhlan disgusted him. Such creatures were a necessary evil to maintain the ranks of the Legion and allow them to prosecute the Long War, but for such abominations to think they were equals was absurd! He would have laughed in Uhlan's face if he hadn't realised the mongrel's delusions might prove useful. He had disclosed something to Rhodaan that the captain had suspected from the first. The crash of his assault boat during the attack on Vorago hadn't been entirely the work of orks. Vallax had the opportunity to take down the ork who shot down Rhodaan's transport, but the Over-Captain had refrained from action.

Strategic inaction. It was the most cunning sort of treachery, the kind only a psyker could prove. And the only psyker of such power on Castellax was the Speaker, whose talents could be exploited only on the express orders of Warsmith Andraaz. It was clear from the

Warsmith's remarks that the Speaker would be detailed to other duties for the duration of the siege. Vallax had nothing to worry about from that quarter.

But he did have a victim who was aware of his treachery now. Rhodaan would know what to watch for and he would know what steps to take to ensure that when the smoke cleared, he would be the man left standing.

Perhaps he would even thank Uhlan before sending the half-breed to join the Over-Captain in hell.

Rhodaan nodded as he watched the mameluke paint another coat of blood on Eurydice's wings.

It was never wise to trust a traitor, the Iron Warrior reflected.

BROTHER UHLAN STOLE through the maze-like network of vaults running between the sub-levels of the Iron Bastion's cellars. Thick bundles of pipe and wire snaked along the vaulted ceiling above his head, the parchment attendance-liturgies brushing against his helmet as he passed them. A thick, cloying stink of promethium fumes filled the narrow corridors, in places becoming so dense as to make spots flicker across his lenses.

The Raptor growled in irritation. It galled his pride to slink through these black vaults, creeping around in the darkness like some kind of sump-rat.

Ahead, a red light winked into life, its beam strobing through the darkness. Uhlan quickened his pace. It was the signal he had been watching for. Soon he could be quit of these forgotten cellars.

The source of the light was mounted in the shoulder of a tall, gangly figure, its metal knees folded back upon themselves to allow it to clear the overhanging pipes. The thing's face was pale and corpse-like, its gaping mouth stuffed with the copper honeycomb of a vox-caster. Insect-like lenses protruded from the pits of its face, clicking and whirring as they adjusted to focus on the approaching Iron Warrior.

'You were not followed,' the servitor announced, its voice shrill and fleshless.

Uhlan smirked at the statement. He did not need the cyborg to tell him that. After centuries of warfare, he could smell a lurking enemy at fifty metres; hearing a slinking spy following him in the abandoned tunnels would have proved no challenge. Sneering at the servitor, he told it as much.

'There is always the chance,' the robotic voice intoned. 'Flesh is weak and can be deceived. Only the machine is infallible.'

The Space Marine's hard features curled in an angry snarl. 'Machines are only tools,' he growled. 'They cannot compare with the perfection of the Iron Warriors. The machine is nothing beside the flesh that commands it, the flesh that designs it, the flesh that builds it. There is no weakness in the flesh of an Iron Warrior.' His eyes hardened as he stared into the servitor's optics, making sure their image was conveyed to the cyborg's secluded master. 'Have you forgotten what it is to be an Iron Warrior, Oriax? Buried in your cobweb of machines, have you forgotten what it is to stalk among the stars, to spread the terror and the glory of the Legion wherever you tread? To know that billions live only because you have not brought death upon them? Do you remember the power and the glory, or has that memory rusted away, Fabricator?'

There was no change in the monotone of the servitor's broadcast. If Uhlan's reprimand had drawn any emotion from Oriax, it wasn't conveyed by the cold, metallic voice. 'I remember more than you have forgotten, Uhlan Half-blood. While I function, there is purpose. While you function, there is purpose.'

'I have done what you asked,' Uhlan said. 'Captain Rhodaan has been made aware of Over-Captain Vallax's actions during the attack.' The Iron Warrior paused, directing a concerned look at the servitor. 'It is a dangerous game, playing the two against one another.'

The servitor lumbered forwards on its segmented legs. 'The rivalry has been there a long time. It is only now that it becomes propitious for exploitation.'

Uhlan's hand tightened into a fist. 'So long as Vallax is brought low,' he vowed.

The servitor's lenses glistened in the crimson light. 'He will be,' the modulated voice promised. 'And when he is, you shall have your reward.'

'You have promised me considerable–'

'It has all been arranged, all factored into my calculations,' Oriax's words droned from the servitor's speaker. 'From this crisis, the Third Grand Company will embrace its destiny and you will have a part in that destiny.

'All of us will.'

CHAPTER VI
I-Day Plus Forty

'Incoming!'

Blared across the vox-casters bulging from the stone faces of the gargoyles leering down from the rooftops, the warning was almost drowned out by the steady crump of artillery. The streets seemed to bounce as a barrage slammed into the hills five kilometres away. Plumes of dust and smoke exploded into the air, sending a foul brown smog rushing down into the settlement.

Taofang dived into the dubious cover of an open trench he hoped had been dug as a shelter rather than a latrine. The soldier landed in a tangle of bruised flesh and virulent curses, the protesting mass of a motorman breaking the impetus of his fall. Snarling his own oaths, Taofang drove the butt of his lasgun into the rail-worker's back until he made room for the janissary. Somehow, the motorman managed to squeeze himself into a small gap between the wall of the trench and a trembling tech-adept.

Taofang hugged the bottom of the trench and opened his mouth, hoping to keep his eardrums from bursting under the shock of the barrage. Ork artillery was wildly unpredictable, over-shooting the target and falling short with utter abandon, often within the same salvo. About the only consistency was a general direction, yet even that was never totally dependable when it came to orks. The settlement was pock-marked with the evidence of their chaotic ideas of accuracy.

Gamma Five was the only designation the mining settlement bore on the maps. If its inhabitants had some other name for it, Taofang neither knew nor cared. Crouched in the shadow of a string of rocky hills, stinking like a chemical bath and coated in a green scum of pollutants, the settlement was like a sore on the buttocks of Castellax. If the orks wanted the rotten jumble of hab-pens and ore-crushers, the xenos were welcome to them as far as Taofang was concerned. The thought of dying over such a forsaken piece of land made the janissary's insides turn.

But they were dying. Nearly ten thousand janissaries had been dispatched to Gamma Five. If a quarter of them ever left the mining settlement, it would be a wonderment. Over the course of five weeks, the soldiers had been engaged in a protracted campaign against the orks.

At first, it had been the humans who were on the attack, striking out in mechanised columns to harass the advance elements of the alien invaders. The orks were establishing themselves in the bombed-out ruins of a transport nexus along the Dirgas-Aboro rail-line, using it as a base from which to expand outwards. The stated objective of Colonel Nehring's 'reconnaissance in force' had been to disrupt the alien advance, to prevent them from establishing advance camps further along the line. A series of lightning raids against the xenos march which would blunt the thrust of their attack and force the orks to withdraw and dig-in. Such was the intention of the campaign.

In practice, it had been so much less. The orks were always more numerous than expected; their absurd vehicles, knocked together from seemingly random jumbles of scrap, outgunned anything the janissaries had. It was easy enough to surprise the aliens and throw them into confusion, but the janissaries quickly discovered that a confused ork didn't break and run. A confused ork just started shooting at the closest target and didn't stop until it ran out of ammunition.

Hit and run quickly became the watchwords. The soldiers would strike from the shelter of a spoil heap or ash dune, assault the flanks of the ork column, then fade away before the xenos could muster an effective response. It was the strategy of harassment, not victory, dealing little real damage to the orks. Perhaps if the raids had been carried out by Iron Warriors rather than mere mortals, the results would have been different. Indeed, Taofang wondered if the campaign had been conceived by the dread masters of Castellax, with little consideration for the abilities of the men who would be tasked with carrying out the actual fighting.

As the weeks grew, however, a grimmer prospect occurred to Taofang. The Iron Warriors had conceived the campaign *and* they knew the limitations of their human janissaries. The harassing attacks might not have done much damage to the orks, but they had drawn the aliens' attention. In steadily increasing numbers, the invaders had been striking northwards, advancing for the janissaries' staging area of Gamma Five. There had never been any intention of recapturing territory from the orks. Taofang and the other soldiers were nothing more than a diversion, a distraction to keep the aliens in the vicinity of the Convallis Robigo.

The proof of that lay in the near total absence of the Air Cohort. Almost from the start, the presence of Skylord Morax's fighters and bombers had been negligible. For the past two weeks, however, the orks had complete control of the skies, their crude planes and gyrocopters roaring over Gamma Five with impunity and keeping the janissaries bottled up inside the settlement.

Taofang bit down on a curse as something solid slammed into his back, flattening him into the dust. The taste of Gamma Five's polluted dirt filled his mouth, sizzling against his teeth as it reacted to his saliva. The soldier thrashed about beneath the weight. Then he felt the cold touch of sharp metal against the back of his neck.

'If one of us is getting thrown out of here, it's going to be you,' a voice as hard and cold as the blade pressing against his flesh threatened.

Taofang froze, holding himself as still as the artillery barrage would allow him. He turned his head slowly, finding himself staring at a black boot and a camouflage legging. Whoever his assailant was, they were a janissary. 'Taofang, Dirgas XX Division, Scorpion Brigade,' he introduced himself, trying to keep any element of panic out of his voice.

'Mingzhou, Ossuarian Jackals,' the other soldier replied, removing the knife from the base of Taofang's neck.

Slowly, with careful deliberation, Taofang rolled onto his side. The Ossuarian Jackals were hunters and trackers especially recruited from the scattered outposts deep within the desert wastes of the Ossuarium. Trained to the exacting standards of Lord Gamgin, they were some of the hardest fighters on Castellax next to the Iron Warriors themselves, capable of tracking an escaped slave across the toxic quagmire of the slag-moors and the poisonous desolation of the Mare Ossius. With such a killer holding a knife at his back, Taofang was amazed to still be alive. Almost sheepishly, he lifted his gaze to regard the fearsome desert haunter.

He wasn't quite prepared for what he saw. The camouflage tunic and fatigues clung to a lithe, lean body in which every trace of excess had been burned away, leaving only hardened muscle behind. A bandolier of 'hot-las' cartridges straddled the swell of the soldier's breast, locking into a second ammo belt which circled a slender waist. The ugly snout of a suppressed lasrifle jutted over one shoulder, secured to the soldier's back by a weathered leather strap. The face that stared back at Taofang was as hard and weathered as her gear, high-cheekbones framing a slim nose and slender mouth. Eyes of deep blue stared from beneath a subdued brow. A wild mass of long hair, burned crimson by the pollutants of the Ossuarium, fell about the woman's neck.

Taofang swallowed anxiously as he felt Mingzhou's icy eyes study him, evaluating him like a plate of contaminated protein paste. Instantly, he felt the sting of the toxic dirt in his throat. He pressed himself against the side of the trench, hacking a mix of mud and mucus onto the motorman's boots. It took the better part of a minute for the fit to pass and most of the dirt to be purged from his mouth. Ignoring the slurs thrown at him by the motorman, Taofang shifted himself into an upright position and turned his attention back to the other soldier.

Mingzhou's attention was no longer fixed on the janissary. She had unlimbered her rifle and was squinting through the scope, watching the desolate streets of Gamma Five. Taofang moved closer to the woman, flinching as another barrage of shells slammed into the hills beyond the settlement. One shell, falling short or lacking the same amount of propellant as the rest of the salvo, smashed into a nearby hab-pen, sending a sickening shower of cement and body parts spraying into the air.

The hunter kept her focus on the scope of her rifle, not even noticing when a fist-sized chunk of cement glanced off the lip of the trench only a few centimetres from her head.

'Are you crazy?' Taofang hissed at the woman. 'Get your head down!' He tugged at the camouflage legging when she ignored him.

'Want to keep that hand?' Mingzhou asked, her eye never leaving the rifle-scope. There was something about the tone of her voice that made the question so much more than a threat. Chastened, Taofang relented and slipped back against the wall of the ditch. Another cannonade sounded from the ork position, shells and rockets screaming overhead. This time, the detonations were much closer, landing solidly within the confines of the settlement. Taofang expected Mingzhou to duck down, but she maintained her vigil. Cursing under his breath, the janissary removed his helmet and, stretching to his utmost, held it behind the hunter's head to shield her from any flying debris.

'D'spawn!' Taofang swore. 'Are you trying to get killed?'

'Far from it,' Mingzhou said, keeping her eye fixed to the scope. 'If there's one thing I intend to do, it's getting out of here alive.'

'You have an interesting way of doing it,' Taofang grumbled. 'Most people have brains enough to keep their head down during an artillery barrage.' He glanced over at the motorman and the tech-adept. 'Even these wretches know better.'

'They know nothing,' the hunter hissed back. 'Neither do you,' she added. 'How will your brains look spattered across an ork's axe?'

The image sent a shiver through Taofang, then his mind rebelled at the thought. 'Even the orks wouldn't drop a barrage on their own troops,' he protested.

'You think so?' the woman sneered. 'Do you think their artillery is that accurate? They'd probably do it deliberately if it seemed amusing to them.'

Taofang shuddered. After his experience in Dirgas, watching the orks teleport straight down from orbit by the thousands, heedless of their own ghastly losses in the process, he knew there was nothing beyond the aliens.

A moment later, he had a demonstration of just how little he understood the invaders. Mingzhou shifted slightly, swinging the muzzle of her lasrifle to the right. Her finger slowly pulled the trigger. A soft glow erupted from the weapon as the concentrated energy beam sped away, most of the flash and sound consumed by the dampener fastened to the lasrifle's muzzle. Somewhere, in the dust-choked gloom of Gamma Five's streets, the deadly charge struck its target.

Without changing her position, Mingzhou motioned for Taofang to stand. Gripped by a feeling of dread, the janissary rose and stood beside her. When the sniper leaned her face away from the rifle, he pressed his cheek against the warm barrel and squinted down the scope. The filters built into the device cut through the confusion of smoke and dust, the magnification revealing a clear view of the street. Sprawled at the end of the lane, its forehead burned clear through, was the hideous bulk of a massive ork. Beyond the corpse, Taofang could see other aliens creeping through the murk.

Hastily, Taofang withdrew. Mingzhou smoothly leaned her head back against the rifle. Almost at once, her finger was pulling at the trigger again. 'Their eyesight is poor,' she said. 'While the smoke lasts, they'll never know we're here.'

Taofang gripped his own lasgun and stared dubiously into the brown cloud of dust. 'What about when it clears?' he wondered aloud.

Mingzhou fired another shot, then looked away from the scope to direct a sharp look at Taofang. 'It would be best not to be around,' she said, punctuating the statement by nodding towards the cowering tech-adept and motorman. 'Keep an eye on those two,' she advised. 'The only way out of here is by train. The colonel won't be able to take everyone out when he sounds the retreat. We keep those two close and we won't be left behind.'

The janissary nodded grimly and turned his weapon towards the motorman. 'I think I can guarantee our new friends wouldn't think of deserting us.'

AS EACH SLAVE was marched out from the subterranean hab-pens cut into the corroded mountainside, he stared in awed terror at the crenellated rooftop of the processing centre. The once fearsome aspect of their prefect, an only semi-human mutant called Spyder, now seemed absurd and inconsequential beside the monsters who stood beside him. Encased in their armour of ceramite and plasteel, the Space Marines exuded an aura of brutality and tyranny far beyond anything the mine-workers had imagined. After a single glance, they hurriedly averted their eyes lest they draw down upon themselves the notice of such terrifying manifestations of Evil. Until this day, the slaves had laboured in the dark of the mines, allowed themselves to forget that theirs was simply a small piece of a greater whole. The knowledge that Epsilon Station was only a small cog in the great machine of Castellax had become inconsequential to their daily allotment of toil and suffering. Now, as they marched past the processing centre towards the rail yard, they were reminded of their place in the world and the superhuman devils to whom their lives, their thoughts and their souls belonged.

The Iron Warriors.

Prefect Spyder rubbed his scaly hands together in satisfaction as he watched the slaves being herded towards the rail yard, a sadistic smile splitting his broad face every time one of his overseers set a whip cracking against some slow-moving wretch. 'The evacuation is going more quickly than I anticipated,' he chuckled into the ruff of fur which circled his neck. Immediately, he regretted the comment, cringing against the battlements as he felt the eyes of his masters turn upon him. There was a promise of death in those optic-lenses, none more so than in the red eyes which glared from either side of Captain Rhodaan's Corvus-pattern helm.

'Acceptable,' Captain Rhodaan's voice growled at the prefect, 'only if one makes allowances for the Flesh. Five seconds for their eyes to adjust to the sun. Three more for them to note our presence. Five more seconds for their craven minds to slip from fear back into obedience.' The demi-organic wings on the Iron Warrior's jump pack quivered in a spasm of psycho-sympathetic irritation. 'The Legion does not make allowances for weakness. All resources from this outpost are being transferred to Vorago. The timetable will not be adjusted.' The snarling beak of Rhodaan's helm tilted to stare down at the column of emaciated labourers. 'If the Flesh threatens that timetable, they are no longer a resource but a liability.'

Spyder's scaly face recoiled into the shadows of the leathery hood he wore. 'But Dread Lord, these men have worked all night! The order for evacuation reached us only this morning...'

'Obedience does not offer excuses,' Rhodaan growled, threat dripping from each word. 'In five minutes, the rest of the Flesh will embark. Whatever must be left behind will be herded back into the pens.'

'But... the mines have been rigged to...' The mutant's protest died on his lips, his beady eyes bulging as he understood that the Iron Warriors had already made that calculation. Such deliberate destruction offended Spyder's sense of materialism, years of overseeing Epsilon Station had given him a very keen appreciation of how much each slave was worth, the correct expenditures of provision which would keep the mine operating at peak efficiency. To see that thrown away so readily and callously offended him on a spiritual level and sent a chill of fear rattling through his soul. Like the slaves, he had learned a new appreciation for who the masters of Castellax were.

'The Warsmith has ordered scorched earth,' Rhodaan declared. 'Nothing is to be left that may be of use to the enemy. The mines will be destroyed. Any resources that cannot be removed will also be destroyed.'

Rhodaan's demi-organic wings flittered with a touch of annoyance. It was a waste of breath to explain these things to this creature. The prefect's duty was to obey, not question.

He had learned long ago it was the way of such base animals, the dregs that called themselves humanity. They lacked the vision to see beyond their immediate needs, the strength to endure the travails demanded of them. If there was one thing the False Emperor had done correctly, it was to engineer something better than mankind. His mistake was failing to recognise that what he had created were not guardians of mankind but their replacement.

The Iron Warrior turned and regarded his fellow Space Marines. He could see at a glance that they shared his annoyance. This task was beneath them, watching over a rabble of slaves as they were herded into transport carriages. The strategy of stripping the entire region of resources was one that grated on Rhodaan's sensibilities. However sound the tactics, it offended his martial pride to concede anything to an enemy so base as the orks, even a land made desolate and barren. Pride in the Legion was the ultimate purpose in an Iron Warrior's heart. Take that from him and you took his very soul.

Rhodaan strode across the centre's roof, the optics in his helm adjusting as they focused upon the rail yard. He could see Spyder's militia forcing the slaves into the box-like transport carriages, compelling them to lie flat so they could be stacked in staggered tiers across the bed of the car. Those on the bottom were gradually crushed as the mass of Flesh was packed ever tighter into the car. More would be smothered to death once the doors were shut. Nine out of ten would have expired by the time the train reached Vorago, but it was of small consequence to Rhodaan. His orders were clear: remove all portable resources from Epsilon Station and send them to Vorago. Whatever condition the Flesh arrived in, his job was done.

The Raptor swung back around, glaring out across the polluted wasteland beyond Epsilon Station. He could see the mire of slag spilling across the crevasses which snaked through the blighted earth, watched the eerie shimmer of toxins radiating from the scummy surface of chat mounds. Somewhere, beyond the desolation, were the orks. How he longed to find them, every molecule in his body cried out to give battle to the invader. It was only the discipline of his conditioning and the loyalty of his training that restrained him, kept him from leaving Spyder's wretched little outpost and leading his troops to the battle they sought.

Dirgas, that should be their objective. Strike down the orks in their filthy nest, not slink away and wait for the aliens behind the Witch Wall! Warsmith Andraaz was wrong to concede even a millimetre of ground to the xenos vermin. The honour of the Third Grand Company was crumbling under the burden of inactivity. They should strike, fast and swift and with merciless brutality. Teach the aliens the meaning of fear.

Duty silenced the thoughts raging within Rhodaan's mind. His first obligation was to the Legion and his commander, not the dictates of his own heart. There would be battle enough when the time was right. Andraaz was no coward, whatever else he might be. However hard for him to stomach, Rhodaan had to trust the Warsmith's strategy.

'Pazuriel. Baelfegor,' Rhodaan called out. The two Raptors snapped to attention, fists slamming in salute against their breastplates. 'Span out. Ensure the bombs are in place and armed. The train will be departing. Our orders are to leave nothing behind.'

'I obey, lord captain,' the two Iron Warriors growled back, their voices drowned out by the roar of their jump packs as the enormous thrusters launched them from the surface of the roof and flung them across the sprawl of Epsilon Station.

Rhodaan watched the two Space Marines until they landed near the base of the mountain. The long column of Flesh froze as the Iron Warriors approached. It took only a flourish of their weapons for Pazuriel and Baelfegor to turn the slaves around and send them fleeing back into the darkness of the mineshaft.

'All those workers...' Spyder grumbled, watching as the Iron Warriors ruthlessly pressed the slaves towards their doom.

In a single motion, Captain Rhodaan swung around, the snarling mouth of his plasma pistol thrust towards Spyder's hideous face. A blaze of brilliant light, the sizzle of super-heated power-coils, the stench of vaporised flesh, and the mutant's headless body collapsed. 'The prefect would have taken two minutes to board the train,' Rhodaan told the other Raptors. 'Embarkation is to be completed in one. No intact resources are to be left for the enemy.'

'I obey, lord captain,' the Iron Warriors said again as they launched themselves from the roof.

Rhodaan gazed at the rail yard. It would be a ridiculously short massacre. There were barely five hundred slaves and overseers still waiting to board the train. Hardly worth Squad Kyrith's attention, really. But orders were orders and obedience was what separated an Iron Warrior from the lesser orders of humanity.

Obedience, Rhodaan reflected with a grin, and ambition. Today had called for the one. Tomorrow might very well belong to the other.

GAMMA FIVE'S STATION was a scene of complete panic. A monstrous mass of reinforced ferrocrete, it had withstood the worst of the ork shelling, though some of the tracks hadn't been so fortunate. Teams of slaves and soldiers worked frantically to repair the damage, slapping down magnetised plates that would conduct the current where the rails had been smashed. It was a temporary fix; the plates would be ripped from their fastenings as soon as the train passed over them, dragged along by the magnetic pull of the last car. There would be no second train following after the first.

Janissaries were already destroying the other engines in the station, demolishing their controls and propulsion rods, exorcising their machine-spirits with flame and profanity. Gangs of slaves pushed ore-cars into position behind the only engine remaining, coupling them into a long line of titanium and plasteel. Even before the cars were in place, packs of terrified humanity were clambering aboard, abandoning weapons and equipment in their frantic haste.

Taofang watched the spectacle with a feeling of contempt. Many of these men were comrades in arms, but their lack of perspective disgusted him just the same. Any janissary who threw down his gun was no better than a slave, forsaking the ability to fight for the dubious promise of safety. He hugged his own weapon tighter against his chest. Beside him, Mingzhou kept her sniper rifle at the ready, frequently looking down the sight and staring across the station into the streets beyond. From their perch on the roof of the fifth car, they had a good view of the mining settlement and the fierce fighting raging in its outskirts.

The ork scouts had penetrated Gamma Five in significant numbers, launching their attack in the midst of the barrage. But for the efforts of Mingzhou and the other Jackals, the aliens would have overwhelmed the entire settlement. As it was, the orks had been contained to the southern perimeter, hemmed in by such armour as Colonel Nehring still possessed. While the xenos were pinned down, the colonel ordered the withdrawal.

At first, the operation had a veneer of organisation about it. That illusion collapsed once the barrage stopped. The silence of the ork guns meant one thing: the main body of their force was now starting its advance on Gamma Five.

Slaves and soldiers alike fought for a place on the train. Taofang quickly lost count of the acts of murder and brutality he witnessed as order broke down. He thought of the rearguard, holding their positions in the ruins, trying to delay the ork assault. He wondered what they would think if they could see the selfish confusion they were giving their lives to protect.

Taofang shook his head sadly. He was no better than any of them, he reflected. As the motorman's 'escort', he and Mingzhou had easily wormed their way onto the train. It was a shining example of Castellax morality. Survival at any cost. It was a maxim Colonel Nehring and his staff had certainly adopted. The officers made certain they were given the first car behind the engine, detailing an entire company of shock troops to secure the car against trespassers.

Sounds of explosions and a marked increase in gunfire rose from the distant battle line. Whatever their feelings might be, the rearguard was committed now. The orks were attacking the perimeter.

The sounds of violence threw the massed humanity within the station into a final excess of crazed panic. Soldiers and slaves rushed the cars, thrusting their bodies into doorways, scrambling up ladders and clinging to walls. Like a swelling tide, the frightened mob surged about the cars, darting from one to another in their search for escape. Taofang was forced to smash the butt of his lasgun into groping hands and crazed faces as terrified men sought to drag him down from the roof and take his place. From the front of the train, the sharp crack of shotguns sounded, Nehring's shock troops ensuring the dignity of their officers with lethal efficiency.

Above the shouting mob, the vox-casters suddenly sounded, blaring an alarm across the length of the station. For a moment there was silence, then a shaky voice gasped the news from the speakers. The orks had penetrated the perimeter.

All pretence at discipline shattered. The mob clawed and fought their way to the train, the strong smashing down the weak. Shotguns fell silent as desperate men swarmed over the shock troops, crushing them beneath a flood of fear. Yet even as the first of the rioters scrambled onto the steps of the officers' car, the train suddenly lurched into motion.

Aware of the threat, Nehring had given the order to leave, abandoning thousands of men to their doom.

CLOUDS OF TOXIC dust billowed into the desert sky, churned from the sun-baked surface by the growling treads that gouged the earth. Through the bleached, polluted wasteland, seven armoured behemoths raced, the roar of their engines echoing across the desolation, blue smog spewing from their exhausts. At random intervals, flame would explode from the barrels of the guns embedded in the turrets which topped the hulking machines and some distant patch of desert would be blasted to oblivion.

Until a few weeks past, the tanks had formed the core of the Dirgas garrison's armoured company. Abandoned by the fleeing humans, looted by the conquering orks, the war machines had been pressed into service by the xenos. The khaki and brown camouflage of the original paint was still visible beneath the crude graffiti and primitive symbols that had been scrawled across the hull. Slabs of sheet metal had been bolted to the original armour in a simplistic effort to break the regimented, organised appearance of the tanks, to lend them a more individualistic profile. Deranged arrays of weaponry had been fitted to the turrets and hulls, from pintle-mounted heavy stubbers to nests of rocket tubes and deadly arrays of plasma batteries. One tank crew had even removed their vehicle's main gun in order to fit a lunatic amalgamation of boltguns, meltaguns and multilasers into a single piece of patchwork ordnance.

Around the tanks, clinging to their flanks like scavengers slinking behind a pack of steel sharks, was a motley confusion of warbikes and buggies, ramshackle vehicles slapped together with the wreckage of Dirgas. Goggled ork bikers circled around the tanks, impatient with the slower speed of the armoured giants while bored gunners in the beds of buggies fired bursts into the dingy sky. Occasionally, the growling head of an ork tanker would sprout from an open hatch to snarl abuse at the mob.

The aliens were unfocused and inattentive, too eager to locate some mining camp or settlement to attack to display any interest in the desolate terrain. A few catcalls and rude gestures was the only reaction from the crew of the nearest tank when one of the warbikes suddenly ploughed into a hole in the sand, the vehicle's weight punching through a thin layer of silica dust. None of the ork mob stopped to render aid to the crashed bike, instead continuing to thunder across the desert, the accident already dismissed from their minds.

In the hole, the ork biker had been slung into the handle-bars, the wind rushing from its lungs as its chest smashed into unyielding metal. Before the xenos could try to draw breath back into its body, a powerful arm was wrapped about its neck. The hole wasn't some accident of nature and corrosion but a carefully prepared pit.

A pit that was far from empty.

Over-Captain Vallax held the stunned ork in one hand, with his other he thumbed the activation stud on his chainaxe. Gripping the weapon just behind the head, he pressed its churning edge into the face of the struggling alien, relenting only when he felt the ork's thick skull split beneath the sawing blade.

Contemptuously, Vallax dropped the dead ork and pushed it to the far side of the pit. The ork's stupid blundering would have been disastrous if the aliens had even a semblance of caution about them. Fortunately, they were as crude and mindless as they looked, not bothering to check on their comrade. The roar of the chainaxe was drowned out by the far louder roar of alien engines – the greenskins were so enamoured of loud noises they'd even stripped the mufflers from the exhausts on the tanks they'd captured. That obsession with noise was going to cost the aliens dearly.

'Situation stabilised,' Vallax hissed into his vox-bead.

'Have you suffered injury?' Uhlan's voice crackled over the vox. The half-breed sounded more disappointed than concerned.

Vallax glared at the warbike, its treads still clawing at the wall of the pit, sending a spray of dirt into the air. The machine had missed crushing him by only a few centimetres when it had broken through the silica covering and plunged into the hole. He brought his chainaxe slashing into the vehicle's engine, silencing it in a burst of sparks and smoke.

When he fell, it would be in full honour in battle, not the victim of some pathetic accident.

Ignoring Uhlan's question, Vallax demanded reports from the rest of his Raptors. Each of the Iron Warriors was hidden in a pit like that which Vallax was in, separated from one another by a few hundred metres in a convex formation so that if one of them had been discovered by the orks, the others would still be in a position to retaliate.

The Space Marines replied, one after the other, each ready and eager to carry out their mission. Vallax's scarred face twisted into a smile. Today, Squad Vidarna would earn new honours for him, and all at the expense of Skintaker Algol. It had been the Skintaker's slave-officer who had failed to destroy the tanks before retreating from Dirgas. That failure had so incensed Algol that he hadn't left a patch on the man's body whole enough to stitch into his cloak.

Algol's wrath amused Vallax. Let the self-indulgent sadist harbour his puny hate, his star was fading. The Third Grand Company had outgrown the need for such brutes and Warsmith Andraaz knew it. The future belonged to warriors like Vallax, not thuggish butchers like Algol.

The sound of las-beams and autoguns suddenly echoed

from the distance. Again, Vallax smiled. The Flesh had started their diversion. The janissaries were positioned in a tank ditch a kilometre behind Squad Vidarna's pits. They had been quickly assembled and dispatched from a nearby settlement. They lacked the numbers or equipment to seriously threaten the tanks, but the orks wouldn't care about that. Vicious savages, all the xenos would care about was the fact they had been attacked. That would be enough to goad them into an immediate response.

While they were closing on the janissaries, the orks would be unaware of what was happening behind their backs.

Vallax climbed to the top of the warbike, crouching low so that the thrusters of his jump pack wouldn't protrude above the lip of the pit. He glanced down at the ruined mush of the biker's head. The orks had been fortunate thus far. They'd had only a few opportunities to learn why Vallax and his Raptors were called the Faceless.

'Iron within!' Vallax snarled across the vox-channel. 'Iron without!'

On the Over-Captain's command, the Raptors exploded from their pits, the mighty thrusters of their jump packs launching them hundreds of metres into the sky. As they reached the apex of their leap, the Iron Warriors stared down at the tanks far below. Each of them angled his body towards one of the armoured machines and began his descent.

Hurtling through the polluted sky, Vallax kept his gaze locked upon the hull of the lead tank. He watched the ork crew as they manned pintle-mounted stubbers and fired at the distant ditch. He didn't care about the Flesh being gunned down by the steady stream of automated fire. The janissaries were obeying their command, that was all he expected of them. Keep the orks' attention fixed upon them until the Iron Warriors could strike.

The Space Marine came slamming down against the

engine block behind the tank's turret, the report of his violent impact sounding like the crack of a cannon. The ork sitting in the turret shifted around at the noise, its jaw dropping in a surprised howl. Before the brute could think to train its weapon on the Iron Warrior, Vallax sent a burst of bolt-shells punching through its head. The gory mess slumped in the hatch and disappeared as it slipped down inside the turret.

Furious roars echoed from inside the tank, but Vallax didn't have the moment needed to attend his enemies. Letting his pistol drop and dangle from the chain which fastened it to his wrist, he reached to his belt and withdrew the blocky mass of a melta-charge. Thumbing the activation rune, the Raptor slapped it against the tank's engine.

Bullets ricocheted from the hull at his feet, shells glanced from his armour as Vallax rose from his task. Another burly ork had appeared in the turret, shooting at the Space Marine with an oversized stub pistol. A second ork had climbed out from one of the drivers' hatches and was dragging itself along the hull with one paw while firing at him with the bolter clenched in the other.

In what seemed a single motion, Vallax brought his pistol back into his hand with a flip of his arm and fired at the aliens. The brute in the turret yelped in surprise and ducked down, part of its jaw shot away. The ork crawling across the hull screamed as Vallax's shells blew off the fingers of the hand clutching the hull and sent the xenos tumbling away from the tank to be splattered across the desert landscape.

More bullets slammed into Vallax's armour, scratching the ceramite casing. Two of the buggies had turned their guns on him, opening fire without regard to their comrades in the tank. As the machines closed, Vallax activated his jump pack, launching himself hundreds of metres into the air.

It wasn't fear of the approaching enemy that motivated

the Raptor but rather the steadily-declining countdown of the melta-charge. As he soared into the sky, the rear of the tank burst into flame, sending a cloud of smoke and shrapnel scything into the nearby bikes and buggies. Fire belched from the tank's hatches and burning orks struggled to escape the armoured giant, whose insides had become a furnace.

Across the desert, Vallax could see four more tanks blasted into ruin, testament to the prowess and efficiency of Squad Vidarna. Only the best Iron Warriors became Raptors. Only the toughest Raptors were allowed to survive among the Faceless.

Over-Captain Vallax angled his descending body towards one of the surviving tanks. The ork in the turret hatch saw him, using a pintle-mounted heavy bolter to send a stream of shells screaming up at him. The beast had neither the discipline nor the accuracy to hit a fast-moving target like the plummeting Raptor.

There was nothing it could do to prevent what was coming.

Vallax's fingers tightened about the heft of his chainaxe. He could already see the churning blade slicing through the ork's flesh, stripping skin from skull. It was already another victim of the Faceless, it just didn't know it yet.

TAOFANG FELT A sense of nausea as the armoured train picked up speed and hissed down the magnetic rails. On every side, frantic men raced after the train, making wild grabs for the cars. He could see a half-dozen uncoupled ore-cars still standing on the siding, their holds packed with masses of screaming humanity, cheated at the last moment of the escape they believed they had won.

Over his shoulder, Mingzhou's cold voice spoke. 'Here they come,' she said. Taofang didn't need the las-rifle's scope to see the orks this time. From the station's entrance, a motley array of rude vehicles roared into the building, black fumes belching from their exhausts. The screams that greeted the appearance of the aliens were quickly lost beneath the chatter of autoguns, bolters and stubbers. Every ork machine that drove into the station was fitted with some manner of weapon, weapons that were now turned loose upon the hopeless humans. Those not cut down by gunfire were run over by the ork machines, crushed beneath their tyres and treads. Taofang watched in horror as an ork warbike rode down a fleeing janissary, the man's body becoming caught in its treads. The ork glanced back at the gruesome obstruction, then revved its engine until the steel treads churned the soldier's body into pulp.

A thousand scenes of similar havoc played out behind the train as it picked up momentum and raced away from the burning wreckage of Gamma Five. A motley pack of buggies, perhaps desirous of bigger prey than the forsaken men left behind, sped away from the station in pursuit.

Now the lack of foresight by those soldiers who had cast aside their weapons came back to haunt them. From the rearmost cars, only a feeble, sporadic fire challenged the oncoming greenskins. The withering roar of heavy bolters answered the desultory opposition, the explosive rounds chewing through the hindmost ore-car in a spray of torn metal and shattered flesh.

Mingzhou sighted down the scope of her rifle, picking off the driver of a gaudily painted warbuggy. The vehicle careened wildly as the ork slumped at its controls, the gunner in the carriage behind it roaring in panic as it realised what had happened. The monstrous alien had just started to climb out from the carriage in an effort to reach the steering wheel when the machine struck a rail tie and went spinning end over end through the air, throwing the gunner ahead of it to slam into the desert floor with bone-shattering force.

The beleaguered rear car suddenly broke away, receding into the distance as the rest of the train sped onwards.

Observing its peril, the officers in the advance car had uncoupled it by remote signal to its cogitator. The callous tactic bore only meagre fruit, just a handful of the orks remaining behind to finish off the abandoned car while the rest maintained their pursuit of the train.

A precedent had been set, however, and through the long hours of the chase, the scene was repeated at intervals. Embattled car after embattled car was detached from the train, left behind as a distraction for the pursuing orks. By gradual attrition, the train became slimmer and sleeker, picking up speed with each discard.

Finally, Taofang found himself watching the sixth ore-car recede into the distance. His own refuge now formed the tail of the train, the unenviable post of next to be martyred. He scowled at the advance car. For a brief moment, he considered his chances of climbing over the intervening roofs. Quickly he dismissed the idea. He had watched too many men try to cross the roofs of the cars that had been behind him only to be swept away by the train's momentum. The lucky ones had been killed outright by the fall. He didn't like to think about the unlucky ones.

Only a dozen or so vehicles were still following the train, the others having fallen away to allow their passengers to deal with the abandoned cars or to attend to some malfunction of their ramshackle machines. There was small comfort in the fact, however. Each of the pursuers boasted weaponry heavier than anything aboard the train, capable of slaughtering an entire ore-car of men.

Taofang ducked down against the roof as a wartrak turned its heavy stubber loose against the car. The bullets rattled against the titanium wall, denting it with each hammer-like blow. An ugly wartrike, a side-car bolted to its frame, brought the nozzle of a flamer around to bathe the side of the car in a blast of searing promethium. The passengers aboard a wide-bodied battlewagon opened up with a riotous array of sidearms, howling with brutal glee.

It could only be a matter of moments before the aliens would close upon their prey and the callous officers in the advance car decided to cut loose the embattled men.

Taofang glanced at Mingzhou, his gaze telling her what words would not. He knew he was a dead man, but he was determined to go down fighting, to send as many aliens into the darkness ahead of him as it was within his power to do. He saw the same grim intent in the sniper's eyes. She favoured him with a sombre nod, then slapped a fresh power pack into her lasrifle.

Suddenly, the crump of artillery roared overhead and the desert exploded in a burst of sand. Another loud boom, a second explosion of sand, this time right behind one of the pursuing warbuggies.

At first Taofang wondered if the train's speedy retreat had accomplished nothing more than to draw them into another nest of orks. Then, as the barrage intensified, as shells peppered the landscape behind the train, the truth dawned on him. It wasn't ork artillery he was witnessing, but a barrage from friendly guns.

The concentrated barrage only drove the orks closer to the train, the aliens recognising the position of their enemy as the only safe place to be. Taofang wondered if they were wrong, if the artillerists behind the barrage might not prove as callous as Nehring and his officers, willing to sacrifice their own.

The idea sent a surge of raw hate thundering through the janissary's veins. Leaning over the side of the train, Taofang stared down into the bestial visage of an ork biker. Vindictively, he fired his lasgun at the monster. The ork braked hard, preventing the shot from striking its head. Instead, the energy beam struck the warbike's forks, melting through the scrap-metal pipe. The damaged fork snapped, causing the bike to jerk to the left, straight into the path of a pursuing buggy. Both vehicles disintegrated in the resulting collision, spilling a junk-heap of debris across the tracks.

A loud explosion to the right turned Taofang's attention away from his own handiwork. He watched in awe as the big battlewagon went spinning through the air, its cargo of burned and mangled orks hurtling across the desert. An instant later there was an explosion to the left – a wartrak had struck another mine.

Between the barrage and the minefield, the remaining orks lost heart and turned their machines around. Taofang watched the aliens as they tried to make good their retreat, stubbornly trying to navigate the cratered landscape where the first barrage had fallen. With their own fire marking the range for them, the artillery made an easy job of annihilating the fleeing aliens.

Taofang turned to congratulate Mingzhou on their miraculous escape, but instead found his eyes fixated upon the sight directly ahead of the train. Stretching away across the horizon, as far as the eye could follow, was an immense wall half a kilometre high. Rising from the barren waste, black as night, bristling with guns of every size and calibre, it could only be the Witch Wall, the almost cyclopean fortification engineered by the Iron Warriors to defend their world from invasion.

Today, the Witch Wall's defences had claimed their first victims.

They would not be the last. Of that Taofang was sure.

CHAPTER VII

I-Day Plus Fifty

'… AND I SAY it is the failure of Morax's vaunted Air Cohort that has brought us to this impasse!' Admiral Nostraz's words boomed through the vaulted halls of the Iron Bastion, drowning out the chorus rising from the gargoyles. 'We are losing air superiority in our own skies to a bunch of slack-brained xenos trash!'

Skylord Morax rose from his seat and leaned across the table, his gauntlets hissing as they tightened about the edge. 'If I had been given half the resources squandered on your system defence fleet, brother, then the orks wouldn't dare show their filthy faces in the sunlight. As it stands, my squadrons are being taxed to their limit just trying to keep the xenos away from the Witch Wall and maintain control on this side of the Mare Ossius. I need more pilots. I need more bombs. I need more planes. Give me the tools to do the job and I will have the orks scurrying back to Dirgas like whipped curs.'

'More empty promises from the hero of Janicar,' Skintaker Algol scoffed. The clutch of robed attendants hovering about him, sewing fresh patches of leather into his cloak, froze as they heard their fearsome master speak. It would take much for him to lash out at another Iron Warrior, but almost less than nothing for him to turn his ire on mere slaves.

Morax's face grew crimson as he heard Algol's insult. The siege of Janicar had been fought over two millennia past, yet it was still a raw wound against his pride. There, too, Morax had commanded the Iron Warriors' air arm, using it to smash the massed armour of the Imperium. He had caught an entire tank army upon the plains of Boresh, annihilating it in a merciless campaign of saturation bombing. At least, that is what he reported to his battle-brothers. In truth, he'd been tricked by the Imperial commander, gulled into destroying a phoney formation – civilian vehicles dressed to look like tanks and artillery. While he was bombing the fake army, the real armour was slipping away to surprise the Iron Warriors ground forces encircling the planetary capital. It had been a near disaster and a stinging blemish on Morax's career.

'Damn it, Algol!' Morax exploded, his armoured fingers digging into the table's surface, cracking the transparent stone. 'I can do nothing without more equipment. I need more Flesh to fly the planes. I need more munitions to drop on the orks. My resources are not unlimited!' He swung around, pointing a finger at Nostraz. 'Complain about the great admiral's cowardly pirates. If they had done their job, we would still be able to draw supplies from off-world, instead of rationing every las-pack and protein-tube!'

Admiral Nostraz started to respond, but thought better of rising to Morax's bait. From the corner of his eye, he studied Warsmith Andraaz on his diamond throne. Anything the admiral might say to defend the performance of his defence fleet would challenge the Warsmith's policy of isolation. Any challenge to Andraaz's authority was reckless, but especially on a day like today. The Rending Guard seemed especially eager for an excuse to defend their master's rank and honour. Discretion proving the better part of wisdom, the admiral sat down and contented himself with glaring death at his rival across the table.

'We must all make do with what we have,' Warsmith Andraaz declared, his voice like the rasp of a chainsword. 'In the hands of an Iron Warrior, the rudest tool becomes an instrument of death.'

'I cannot work miracles with nothing,' Morax grumbled under his breath. Andraaz leaned outwards from his throne, the talons of his power claw clacking against one another with unspoken menace.

'You will perform as it is demanded of you to perform,' the Warsmith said. 'Fail me and you will not have the chance to repent your weakness.'

Sucking in a great breath, the chastened Skylord sank down into his seat. 'As you command, Grim Lord.'

'As I command,' Andraaz repeated. 'Do not forget that. Any of you.' He turned his head and fixed his smouldering gaze on Over-Captain Vallax. 'What news of the ork advance? What have your scouts reported?'

Disappointment flashed across Vallax's hair in a ripple of lavender colour, the mutation betraying the emotion if not its cause. He had hoped to exploit the Warsmith's call for deep penetration in the ork-held wastes. Captain Rhodaan had been so eager for action the cretin hadn't even questioned the assignment. Vallax had been very careful to choose the most ork-ridden region of the planet for Squad Kyrith's mission, stealing data-slates from Morax's Air Cohort to verify the hazards. It had been frustrating to see Rhodaan and his rabble return to Vorago intact. Perhaps his rival hadn't been as credulous as he had seemed.

'An enormous concentration of ork machinery is gathering in the heights overlooking the Convallis Robigo,'

Vallax recited Rhodaan's report. Having Squad Kyrith reassigned to duties in the Mare Ossius afforded the Over-Captain the opportunity to make the report himself and claim it for his own. 'A mass horde of warbikes, buggies, trucks and primitive armour, supported by an array of artillery and rockets. Enemy numbers are estimated to be above six hundred thousand. There can be little question the xenos intend to move against the Witch Wall.'

'Captain Gamgin has been alerted,' Admiral Nostraz interjected. 'The janissaries manning the fortifications have been placed on double watches. Supplemental provisions and water rations have been drawn from the stores at Aboro against the potential for a prolonged xenos assault.'

'The orks won't have the patience for a long attack,' Algol said. 'They'll lose twenty or thirty thousand trying to break through the defences and then lose interest. They don't have the discipline for a long siege.'

Sergeant Ipos stood and bowed his head as he addressed Warsmith Andraaz. 'It is impossible to predict the alien mind,' he cautioned. 'It is just possible the orks may bypass the Witch Wall. We have to be prepared against that possibility.'

'Your ambition is showing,' growled Algol. 'Afraid Gamgin will reap all the glory for himself and leave nothing for a scheming half-seed?'

'The only glory I seek is that of the Third Grand Company,' Ipos retorted, just the faintest hint of mockery in his deferential tone. 'I exist only to serve the Legion.' A thin smile twisted the Iron Warrior's mouth. 'To do so, I require another sixty thousand slaves. Can you manage that, lord captain?'

'Digging more holes in the desert, sergeant?' Morax snarled.

Ipos kept his voice subservient as he answered the Skylord's displeasure. 'No, now we need to fill them. If the orks gain a foothold this side of the Mare Ossius, it will be the worst mistake of their campaign. I can guarantee it.'

'Sergeant Ipos's plan is sound,' the metallic rasp of Oriax's servitor-proxy intoned. 'With the proper allocation of Flesh, everything can be in readiness. I have already detached three-quarters of my tech-adepts to the project.'

Warsmith Andraaz brought his armoured fist slashing through the air. 'I have already decided on Sergeant Ipos's plan. The debate is closed. Captain Algol, you will provide the sergeant with whatever he requires.'

'The Flesh he asks for was already detailed to reinforce the Witch Wall,' the Skintaker objected.

Andraaz clenched the talons of his power claw, sending a crackle of energy rippling across his forearm. 'Then Captain Gamgin will just have to do without,' he declared.

STRETCHING ACROSS HALF a continent, marking the shoreline of a dead ocean, the black mass of the Witch Wall was a synthetic scar upon the face of Castellax, so immense as to be visible from orbit whenever the planet's pollution levels dropped to sub-toxic levels. A megalithic mass of stone, ferrocrete and plasteel half a kilometre high, the fortress was a monstrosity of guns and assault batteries. Divided every few hundred metres into fortified segments, fed by a network of subterranean railways, workshops, arsenals and troop-kennels, the wall was a world unto itself. Locked within its dungeons, generations of slaves laboured in the darkness to provide ammunition for its guns, to produce synthetic food for its garrison, to supply energy to its generators. Imprisoned within containment-crypts, their bodies immersed in preservative salt-baths, their brains wired into thrall-engines, hundreds of psykers sent their mental screams wailing through the battlements, a psychic clamour to confound the witchery of any enemy.

Four hundred thousand janissaries and mamelukes manned the defences of the Witch Wall, an army equipped with the best munitions to emerge from the factories of Castellax. Only the very best of the millions who passed through the brutal training regimes were allowed to serve here. Captain Gamgin would accept nothing less.

The Iron Warrior prowled along the wind-swept battlements, ignoring the caustic pollutants brushing across his armour as the breeze stirred up the dusty bed of the Mare Ossius. The extinct ocean was at his back, before him yawned the blighted wastes of the desert and the yawning pit of the Convallis Robigo, a great canyon gouged into the surface of Castellax by centuries of indiscriminate strip-mining. The lower depths of the canyon were a poisonous bog of acids and alkalis, toxic waste and industrial run-off. Those who attempted to desert the Witch Wall's garrison, weak-willed cowards unable to endure the constant wailing of the entombed psykers, were often tossed into the canyon where their lingering deaths could be observed by the closest of the forts.

Now a different sort of spectacle was unfolding about the rim of the canyon. Gamgin raised the magnoculars to his helm, staring through the polarised optics to filter out the haze of pollutants and distance. His hearts pounded faster as he saw the magnitude of the ork warhost. It seemed to stretch away to the very horizon, an armada of ramshackle machines and roaring engines, a veritable storm of smog rising from the motley confusion of exhausts. Through the polluted sky, a swarm of alien aircraft soared and hovered, swooped and dived, like angry flies buzzing over an unburied corpse.

Gamgin lowered the magnoculars and glared at the nearest guard post. Even through the filters of his helmet, he fancied he could smell the fear dripping off his troops. Weak, fragile men. For all their training, for all the discipline that had been whipped, beaten and burned into them, they remained pathetic Flesh. This was the foundation the False Emperor had imagined he could build his Imperium upon. It would be amusing if it wasn't so pathetic.

Gamgin marched to the guard post, the janissaries snapping to terrified attention as the hulking Iron Warrior loomed over the fire control of their missile battery. Obedience through fear, so long as the Flesh was more afraid of Gamgin than the orks, they would do their duty. Reaching down to the face of a trembling loader, the Space Marine decided to remind his troops why they should fear. Gripping the man's insect-like rebreather, Gamgin pulled the mask away, exposing the soldier's pale flesh to the toxic dust. At once, the skin began to blister.

'Breathe,' Gamgin ordered. The doomed soldier stared back at him, his eyes imploring the monstrous giant for mercy. 'Breathe,' Gamgin repeated, closing his fingers about the janissary's face, forcing the man's mouth open. The loader struggled in the Space Marine's grip, but at last his starving lungs forced him to draw the unfiltered dust into his lungs.

The Iron Warrior dropped the quivering wretch, leaving him to bleed out as the poisons burned away his lungs. The twitching body would be an object lesson to his comrades, a reminder to them of who they served... and why.

'Soldiers of the Witch Wall,' Gamgin growled into his helmet's vox-bead. His voice boomed out from the thousands of vox-casters stretching across the continent-spanning stronghold, echoing through the endless labyrinth of service tunnels and sub-cellars running beneath the ground. 'The hour of your duty is at hand. The enemy shall set upon you with all his savagery and in all his numbers. He will seek to breach the wall. He will fail. You will drive him back. You will destroy him. You will kill him. You will butcher and annihilate him. Here we exterminate the xenos vermin who have dared trespass upon our world. No quarter shall be given, no mercy shall be shown. Your orders are total annihilation!'

Gamgin's voice dropped into a bestial snarl. 'You will obey your orders. The Iron Warriors demand it of you. Fail your masters and you will wish the orks had taken you...'

All across the wall, Gamgin could see officers hurrying to spur their commands into readiness, lashing out with whips and clubs at those who failed to respond quickly enough. The bark of orders, the shouts of command echoed across the barrier, sometimes interrupted by the groan of shells being loaded or the creak of elevators bringing up missiles from the underground arsenals. The thrum of hundreds of lascannon and plasma batteries cycling over to full charge formed an omnipresent susurrus that silenced even the howls of the buried psykers.

This was the Witch Wall, and the green tide of the invader would be broken upon it. Gamgin already had a freight train waiting on one of the rail bridges to bear evidence of his victory back to Vorago. When the fighting was over, three thousand slaves would be sent into the wastes to collect the heads of slaughtered orks. It would be a fitting tribute to Gamgin's command and the defences he had engineered. One that none of his battle-brothers would be able to deny him.

THE SHRIEKING SIREN of an ork fighter-bomber ripped across the sky, the primitive aircraft swooping so near the battlements that Gamgin could clearly make out the snaggle-toothed squig painted across its nose. Streamers of black smoke belched from the plane's wing, but it was impossible to tell if it was from damage or the crude exhausts of its combustion engine. Whatever its condition, the Iron Warrior watched as the plane's guns opened up, splashing the wreckage of a gun crew across the interior of a weapon pit. An instant later, the bright beam of a lascannon burned a hole through the plane's fuselage, sending it plummeting from the sky to crash in a great fireball against the desert floor.

As far as Gamgin's eyes could see, similar scenes of carnage were being played out. That swarm of ork planes and gyrocopters had struck with the fury of a tempest, blazing across the length of the wall in a firestorm of rocketry and gunfire. Hundreds had been burned from the skies and still there seemed no end to the alien flyers. With reckless abandon, the orks had flown straight into the anti-aircraft batteries and missile defences, negating the efficiency of each strategically positioned emplacement and ruthlessly trained gun crew through sheer weight of numbers. The orks had simply overwhelmed each position, sacrificing dozens of their planes to knock out a single lascannon or missile battery.

It was viciously inefficient, but Gamgin could not deny that the xenos strategy was yielding results. He had been compelled to husband his resources, order entire batteries to stand down and keep quiet so that they might avoid drawing the attentions of the ork flyers. It galled him to allow the aliens any kind of respite, but he knew he had to preserve his strength. For all the malignity of their attack, the ork planes were only a distraction. The real battle would be joined when the xenos ground forces joined the assault.

Out across the desert, the black smog of the ork advance drew closer. Gamgin stalked towards the edge of the battlements, ignoring the chatter of a passing fighter-bomber's boltguns as he peered through the magnoculars at the oncoming horde. Like some thousand-headed beast, the alien army rolled through the dust, implacable and unstoppable.

Or so it might appear. Gamgin smiled coldly as he watched the advance. Soon the xenos vermin would reach the range of the wall's heavy artillery. It was disappointing to allow the alien vanguard to pass unmolested, but it was necessary. There were other defences that would deal with them. He turned the glasses, following the leading rabble of bikes and buggies, trucks and wartraks. He could see some of the ork gunners firing at the wall, ignoring the fact they were still woefully out of range. Pitiful brutes, it was almost embarrassing to slaughter them. They'd never appreciate the skill with which they were exterminated.

A red-painted warbike was the first of the ork machines to hit the minefield. It was thrown into the air in a burst of flame and smoke, spinning end over end until it crashed in a smouldering heap. Other machines soon joined it in destruction, an entire section of desert seeming to blossom into a garden of explosions. Now that the first mine had been struck, the proximity sensors attached to the rest had been activated. The orks didn't need to actually pass over the buried explosives now. Simply coming within five metres of them was enough. It was amusing to watch the xenos trying to veer across the deadly expanse, trying to avoid the death lurking under their tyres.

The entry of the vanguard into the first ring of mines was the signal Gamgin's artillery had been waiting for. Biding their time while the ork flyers raged across the sky, now the wall's heavy guns roared into violent life, hurling tons of explosive across the desert to slam into the oncoming xenos. Tanks were shattered by four-ton shells, their hulls shredded like parchment. Battlewagons vanished in great sheets of flame, the aliens swarming about their decks obliterated in the flash of an eye.

Somehow, the orks refused to break under the onslaught. Every second brought death to hundreds of the aliens, yet still they came, thundering through the artillery barrage, racing across the smoking moonscape of the minefield. Now the alien vanguard was near enough to the wall that the janissaries began opening up with their lasguns and autocannon.

Gamgin watched as the orks hit the next ring of defences, the buried chainwire that leapt up from the sand as the vibrations of the alien machines activated their sensors. He saw ork bikers hit the snarling stretches of wire, their bodies torn into gory cubes by the whirling blades. Dozens of orks hit the wire, cut to ribbons in a burst of blood and gristle, yet still the creatures refused to break. Heavier vehicles lumbered forwards, firing a crazed array of weaponry into the obstructions or simply riding it down beneath their treads.

Ferrocrete tank traps, the jagged obstructions called the Devil's Teeth, delayed the orks only a bit longer than the chainwire. With callous disregard for their own comrades, the orks slapped explosive charges to the obstacles, wrapped chains about them and pulled them free or employed heavy dozer blades to topple them over. All of this while a withering fire poured down on them from the black face of the Witch Wall. The carnage was unspeakable, thousands of greenskin dead lying torn and mangled across the desolation.

Yet still they came.

Gamgin growled into the vox-bead, sending his fury echoing along the wall, enjoining his troops to still greater effort. Guns fired into the orks until their barrels became red-hot, elevators shot up from the arsenals with such rapidity that fresh gangs of slaves had to be sent along to unload the ammunition when it reached the gun emplacements and missile batteries. Hour by hour, the humans strove to repulse the alien invader. Protein-pastes packed with stimulants were dispensed, punishment squads executed those too fatigued to fight, conscripts were drawn from the subterranean workshops and munitions plants.

The orks finally penetrated the Devil's Teeth, sparing no thought for their massed dead. Now the rumble of alien guns slammed against the battlements, pitting and scarring the black walls. The aliens plunged ahead, striking hidden gas projectors and deadfalls, subsidiary pillboxes and fortified blockhouses. Each obstruction was met with the same response – mindless, barbaric violence. There was no hesitation, no pause to consider strategy in the face of a changing battlefield. Nothing, it seemed, would be allowed to blunt the momentum of the ork advance.

Gamgin glared down from the wall, appreciating for the first time the nature of the enemy. He had allowed himself to be deluded, to mistake the individual ork, the crude almost bumbling savage as his real foe. It was not the individual ork he was fighting, but the Waaagh!, the gestalt collective, the millions-strong warhost, an elemental force that could do nothing except advance and attack.

The Iron Warrior snarled into his vox-bead, calling up fresh reserves from the lower bunkers. Swiftly, the soldiers ascended to the battlements, bringing with them massive drums of lead. With practised precision, the janissaries opened the drums, exposing the ash-like contents. Gamgin turned and faced towards the dead sea, evaluating the strength and direction of the wind.

If the orks were an elemental force, then he would use another element to destroy them. 'Seed the wind,' Gamgin ordered. Obediently, the janissaries dug into the barrels of ash with long leaden ladles and cast the shimmering poison into the wind. The corrosive chemical would bond with the toxic dust swirling up from the dry ocean bed. A few moments after being cast into the breeze, it would create an acidic cloud capable of chewing through flesh. The orks might be hardy enough to breathe the polluted fumes of Castellax's atmosphere, but they wouldn't shrug off the Daemon's Breath.

It was a death sentence, of course, for the advance troops down in the bunkers and blockhouses, but Gamgin was pragmatic about such losses. With the orks already swarming about their positions, the isolated men were as good as dead already. Besides, there was plenty of fresh Flesh waiting and eager to replace them. Common humanity needed little encouragement to breed like vermin.

Agonised howls rose from the massed orks as the deadly cloud descended upon them. Through the magnoculars, Gamgin could see the acid corroding their flesh, scorching and blistering as it gnawed its way through the leathery skin. Where an instant before there had been an unstoppable horde, now he stared down upon a twitching morass of suffering. Coldly, he ordered the men on the wall to fire down into the afflicted aliens.

Uncertain of what had beset their vanguard, the main body of the ork column shifted, changing direction. Gamgin sneered at their effort to escape the trap. The aliens might avoid the cloud, but they would soon find themselves beset by an even more primal adversary. Eagerly, Gamgin watched as the first ork tank rumbled out onto the seemingly innocuous stretch of desert on the southern flank. Only a trained eye could see the subtle difference in hue, even the men stationed on the Witch Wall weren't so sharp as to immediately spot the difference. And it was an important difference.

The difference between life and death.

The tank's speedy advance collapsed in a groan of protesting gears and shrieking aliens. The armoured vehicle plunged into the open ground, sinking through the thin scum of dirt and debris which covered the polluted quagmire. Not as impressive as the Convallis Robigo, the canyon was more strategically placed, an implacable barrier to guard the fortress's flank.

Unable to check the momentum of their charge, dozens of other ork machines followed the first tank into destruction. Frantic drivers and crew tried to throw themselves from their doomed machines only to flounder in the toxic mire as they too were sucked down. Once the oily clutch of the mire closed about a victim, no force could drag it free.

Locked between the quagmire and the billowing acid cloud, thousands of orks were abandoned to the mercy of the Iron Warriors. Gamgin would show them none. At his command, a vicious barrage of artillery and missiles slammed into the confusion of buggies and battlewagons.

From the doomed column to the south, Gamgin turned his gaze to the north. A section of the ork assault force had diverted towards the railway, braving the minefields in preference to the acid cloud and the quagmire. The

Iron Warrior glared at the alien machines. They would not escape. Issuing orders into his vox-bead, he started to redirect his artillery against the northern column. It was then that the entire fortress was shaken by a tremendous impact. The janissaries in the gun emplacement closest to him were knocked about like rag dolls, one man splitting his head open against the bore of the gun. Gamgin himself was nearly thrown from his feet. A kilometre away, he could see a great smouldering crater pitting the face of the Witch Wall.

An instant later, the wall was rattled by a second impact, an entire stronghold collapsing in an explosion of ferrocrete and plasteel. Gamgin's mind whirled at the impossible devastation, something he would expect only from a battleship or the largest Titans.

Raising the magnoculars once more, he followed the slender ribbon of railway into the west. There, in the distance, Gamgin saw them: two gigantic lumbering machines. In size, they bore no kinship to any tank or train he had ever seen. They were more like Imperial strike cruisers mounted on carriages, trundling down the railway with sluggish yet inexorable momentum. Gaping in the face of each of the mobile battlefortresses was a mammoth cannon, the sort of thing that would be more properly used to pummel a planet into submission from high orbit.

Gamgin clenched his fist. The Witch Wall would never withstand the approach of these monsters. Their guns would blast open a hole in them through which the entire Waaagh! could pour. There was nothing he could do to stop them. All he could do was inform the Warsmith that he had failed. The Witch Wall was breached. The Mare Ossius lay open before the invaders and perhaps Vorago as well.

CHAPTER VIII
I-Day Plus Sixty-Four

THROUGH THE POISONOUS green mist, the droning crackle of the Lingua-Technis echoed, slithering off the maze of immense pipes and slime-covered conduits. It was the phantom voice of forbidden praise, the shadow worship of the doomed and the damned.

Enginseer Heroditus bowed his head and kept his mechadendrites piously folded as the chant progressed. Only that facet of his brain assigned to reciting binary orisons to confuse the sentinel-implants hidden within his own body was not devoted to the ritual of praise. All bless the Omnissiah!

Gathered within the radioactive sump-pit, the abandoned sub-catacomb far beneath the manufactorums of Vorago, the indentured tech-priests of Castellax resembled a conclave of grotesque ghouls in their robes of synthfibre. The stink of antiseptic unguents and grease-lubricant oozed from one and all, a stench which would have overcome anything still more flesh than machine. With their senses partitioned by automated cogitators or replaced entirely by cybernetic mechanisms, the tech-priests barely perceived the reek, much less reacted to it.

Heroditus cast his gaze across the clandestine gathering. There were nearly a dozen this time, an observation which brought a tremble to his valve-pump. It was dangerous to assemble in such numbers. If the absence of even one of them were to be noticed, if anyone were lax in his orisons or failed to lose a trailing Steel Blood...

Fabricator Oriax's punishment would be a thing of unrivalled horror, of that Heroditus was certain. If the Iron Warrior discovered why his slaves were sneaking through the sewers and catacombs, his vengeance would be more terrible still.

Strangely, that observation brought confidence rather than caution. Heroditus suspected it was organic illogic, but somehow the thought that Oriax would be alarmed if he became aware... That made the enginseer feel pride. It made him feel strong. For the first time since Castellax had fallen to the Iron Warriors, he had a sense of accomplishment.

It was a reckless emotion and Heroditus drove it from his mind as soon as it started to assert itself. Pride and confidence might make a man, even a tech-priest, overbold. With all the evil of the Iron Warriors already ranged against them, they did not need their own foolish mistakes, errors born of hubris, presenting them with still greater obstacles.

As his mind emerged from such ruminations, Heroditus focused upon his fellow tech-priests. More had arrived and there were nearly twenty of them, hunched amid the pipes, perched upon the corroded gantries, skulking against ferrocrete reservoirs and titanium flow valves. Again, he felt an impulse of wariness as he considered such numbers. If even one of his fellows had failed to distract his sentinel-implant...

'Brothers of the Machine!' the voice of Logis Acestes sliced across the binary chant like a rusty razor. The senior adept of the Mechanicus to survive the invasion,

Acestes was a lank apparition, a scarecrow of steel and plasfibre bundles draped in a heavy cloak of synthetic leather. An expert at predictive simulation and mathematical extrapolation, Acestes was the only member of their little cabal who had avoided capture at the fall of Castellax. His robes yet bore the Cog Mechanicus symbol of the Adeptus, a mark not only of his freedom but of his uncompromised servitude to the Machine-God. The Logis had hidden himself away for many decades in the most forsaken depths of Vorago before emerging from the shadows and recruiting his congregation from Oriax's slaves.

The chant fell silent as Acestes raised his arms, slim pistons of steel fitted with an array of hinged servo-limbs, each ending in an esoteric confusion of tools, blades and pincers. The nest of tubes and hoses which protruded from the hood of his robe contracted as the Logis drew air into the archaic circulator attached to his chest. The device hissed and shuddered as it distilled the worst pollutants, expelling them in a black slime which oozed from a vent in its side.

'My brothers,' the Logis spoke. 'Long have we endured the confusion of servitude, of prostituting the rites of the machine-spirit to obscene purposes. But now, the time of forced blasphemy is nearly over. Soon we shall rise and achieve that for which we have struggled!'

Speaking, Acestes pivoted on his ankles, swinging his body around and gesticulating at the jumble of machinery piled atop a brick-work causeway. Pale servitors, their mechanics displaying a frightful state of decay and corrosion, their flesh branded with the Cog Mechanicus, scurried about the seeming scrap-heap, choosing isolated pieces and arranging them in carefully sorted piles.

'We may thank the Omnissiah for providing the xenos incursion, for it has given the heretical oppressors over to distraction. While their eyes are set upon the orks, they allow their vigilance to wane. Opportunity, so long elusive, now provides us with all we require.'

The crimson optics protruding from the nest of hoses that served Acestes as a face whirred on their metal stalks, fixing a lone tech-adept with their mechanical stare. One of the Logis's limbs circled forwards, jabbing a slender plasma-cutter in the adept's direction.

'We cannot allow anything to interfere with our duty,' Acestes declared. 'One among you has become suspect. The Steel Blood are no longer attentive, as though they have lost interest. There can only be one cause for such an adjustment in their calculations.'

The doomed tech-adept did not protest, did not seek to escape. He understood the judgement that had already been reached. Though he was aware of no conscious treachery, the possibility of implanted treachery was too great to permit. He himself had reported the inattentiveness of the Steel Blood towards him. Alone among the conspirators, he did not need to chant the liturgy of distraction to elude the servitor-spies. It was a problem that had perturbed him greatly. Despite his role in the drama, he admired the directness of Acestes's solution.

Stepping around the scorched husk of the tech-adept, Enginseer Heroditus approached Acestes. He bowed his head before addressing the Logis, an act of almost automatic contrition. Acestes had not profaned his knowledge and ability by serving the cause of the traitors; that placed him far closer to the Machine-God than any of them. It was a holiness that made the enginseer feel lowly and unclean. If his synthesised voice was capable of conveying emotion, his words would have been meek and humble as he spoke.

'The heretic Ipos has mobilised nearly a million slaves,' Heroditus reported. 'He works them day and night, without rest or respite. Already the first of the munitions have been disassembled and removed from the city.'

Acestes nodded, digesting the enginseer's words. 'It is a sacrilege to defile such holy armaments,' he sighed. 'The traitors compound their sins without thought of what they do. For all their terrible potential, the vile Traitor Marines yet wallow in the ignorance of their barbarities. We must not repeat their error! Have the machine-spirits been placated? Have the proper supplications been made?'

'Yes, Revered Logis,' Heroditus answered. His mechadendrites curled in upon themselves, grasping the thick loop of power coil protruding from the synthfibre sack he carried. Extending the cybernetic limbs, he offered the heavy loop of electrum to Acestes. The Logis nodded and gestured with one of his steel claws. With another bow, Heroditus deposited the coil on the ground beside the senior tech-priest.

'The heretics continue to allow us to oversee the profanation of the ordnance,' Heroditus explained. 'Their janissaries understand nothing of what we do. With their eyes upon us, we take what we need. It is only when Ipos or one of the other Chaos Marines are around that we must display caution.'

'What of the arch-blasphemer Oriax?' Acestes demanded. 'Are his spies not observing you?'

A curious sensation tugged at Heroditus's mind as he heard the question. It took him a moment to realise his brain was sending out the impulse to make his face smile... as if there was still enough organic flesh for such an expression. 'We have practised the logarithms which will deceive the Steel Blood,' he explained. 'Beneath the purification and pacification litanies to sanctify the blasphemous disassembly, we disseminate the logarithms and confuse the sensors of Oriax's servitors. The Fabricator sees only what we allow him to see. Any of our own whom we suspect of serving him have been deleted. The frantic pace of Ipos's schedule has resulted in many accidents. The traitors have not noticed those we have arranged.'

'It is well,' declaimed Acestes, 'but never allow your vigilance to become complacent. Any of our brothers may become corrupted and lose their spirits to the heretical dogma of the traitors. We cannot allow that. There is too much work yet to be done. We must not fail in this duty which the Omnissiah has bestowed upon us.'

'We will not fail,' Heroditus promised. 'We have been studious in our distasteful labour. Never do we take more than can be concealed. From each of the ten, we take only what will not be noticed. Though it is a profanation of the sacred template, we have bypassed fail-safes and redundancies to ensure the mechanisms remain functional.' The enginseer paused, a sensation of disgust crackling through his neurons as he contemplated the despicable violations he had helped perpetrate. He could only trust that the machine-spirits of the offended ordnance would forgive him for what he had done.

'The problem,' Heroditus continued, 'is with Lartius Maximus. We were compelled to remove systems without redundancies. Revered Logis, the machine-spirit is impaired. The ordnance will not function.'

Acestes considered the grim revelation. He turned and gazed at the mechanisms already assembled atop the causeway, his optics focusing on the immense cylindrical housing taking shape in the shadows. 'When will the traitors be aware of its failing?'

'If the Omnissiah smiles upon our labour, they will not know anything until they try to activate the ordnance,' Heroditus said, his optic senses gazing up reverently at the housing the servitors were building. 'I think only one of our own, or the arch-blasphemer Oriax could understand the omissions in Lartius Maximus. If Oriax does not interfere, by the time the traitors know it will be too late. By then, Lartius Maximus will be lost behind the xenos advance.'

Logis Acestes's voice dipped into a thin whisper. 'Then let us pray that the Omnissiah favours us and keeps Oriax inside his sanctum.'

* * *

HUGE BLOCKS OF ferrocrete exploded into the murky sky, hurled dozens of kilometres by the relentless punishment of the ork artillery. The city of Aboro was burning, entire blocks enveloped in flame as fuel stores and industrial waste caught fire. The conflagration roared like a hungry beast as it devoured the factories and processing plants, devouring the very heart of the city with its crimson fangs.

Captain Rhodaan watched the holocaust unfold from the shelter of a ferrocrete pillbox, one of hundreds lining the streets of Aboro. On his back, Eurydice shivered in bloodthirsty anticipation. The Iron Warriors had poured half a million troops into Aboro, along with attendant artillery and armoured support. Even Morax's diminished Air Cohort had played a role, engaging in fierce aerial skirmishes to deny the enemy control of the skies. Street by street, block by block, the humans had defended their city, blunting the momentum of the ork onslaught, forcing the beasts to fight for every centimetre of ground.

Rhodaan was certain the janissaries fought under some delusion of heroism and accomplishment. Such phantasms were a part of Gamgin's relentless training pogroms, things which became a part of the slave-soldier's psyche. They were always there, lurking in the subconscious, waiting to be exploited.

The Flesh would obey, that was all they were good for. Let them believe the battle was of consequence. Let them remain ignorant that Warsmith Andraaz had decided to concede Aboro to the enemy weeks ago. Knowledge could only dull their efficiency. For all their frailty and weakness, men clung to the belief that their lives had value. If it would make them fight harder, Rhodaan was willing to allow them their little fantasy.

The defence of Aboro was inconsequential in its own right. With the orks across the Mare Ossius, holding the city could only weaken the resources available to the defence of Vorago. But if the Iron Warriors could not hold the southern city, they could still exploit its doom.

By making a powerful stand in Aboro, they had drawn the full attention of the invaders. Columns of enemy had diverted from their incursions in the north to take part in the battle, ignoring soft targets of opportunity in their savage lust for a worthy fight. By the sacrifice of Aboro, dozens of outposts and camps had been granted a reprieve, time to evacuate their resources to Vorago.

Now, the fighting in Aboro was reaching the critical stage. The ork warlord, tiring of the bloody slog to exterminate the human defenders, had finally decided to settle the question in typically brutal fashion. Every cannon in the alien warhost had been turned against Aboro, pounding it in a merciless barrage without respite for the past three days. It didn't seem to bother the ork warlord that thousands of its own troops were still fighting in the ruins. The city had become an annoyance, an impediment to the warlord's grand scheme. As such, it would be obliterated.

Rhodaan smiled within the ceramite casket of his helm. Everything was going according to plan.

Dust rained down from the ceiling as Rhodaan descended the steps leading from the pillbox to the vault-like cavern which formed the terminus of Aboro's main rail-line. A metallic trail of mag-lev plates stretched away into the subterranean vastness, glistening with a greenish gleam in the fitful illumination of suspended flood lamps. With each fresh salvo from the ork artillery, each tremor that groaned down the tunnel, the lights flickered and threw the passage into momentary darkness.

The tunnel was swarming with Flesh, janissaries and slaves frantically loading supplies into the freight cars of a monstrous train. Despite the barrage, the terror which glistened in the eyes of each man, the Flesh operated with discipline and restraint. The crazed desperation of other evacuations had no place here. Because here, in this tunnel, the Flesh were in the presence of their masters. The Raptors of Squad Kyrith marched along the loading ramps, the lenses of their gruesome helmets watching the throng for the first sign of panic. The first hint, the first suspicion, and the Iron Warriors would act, cutting down the malcontent before he could spread his disobedience to those around him. It was a duty the Space Marines had performed several times already, the mangled remains of their victims tossed unceremoniously into the waiting freight cars.

Rhodaan returned Pazuriel's salute as he marched along the ramp. 'The ork barrage is beginning to lessen,' he told his minion. 'We can expect the filthy xenos to launch another assault soon.'

Pazuriel nodded his head. 'We will be ready,' he said, turning his gaze onto the slaves. 'The Flesh will be herded to the prepared positions. Those sections designated to protect the train will be loaded onto the garrison carriages. Everything will follow Captain Gamgin's plan.'

Eurydice twitched as it registered Rhodaan's annoyance. 'No plan is exact,' he reminded Pazuriel. 'It remains perfect only until it has encountered the enemy. Remember that, brother. Always guard against the unexpected. More so when the foe is as unpredictable as orks.'

'But the xenos vermin have acted exactly as predicted,' Pazuriel persisted.

'Yes,' Rhodaan agreed. He spun around, his armoured gauntlet striking out and smashing the face of a janissary who had dared step in the Iron Warrior's shadow. The stricken man collapsed, his burden of protein-paste spilling across the ramp. Empty eyes stared blindly at the trembling roof. Rhodaan's blow had snapped the wretch's neck. The other Flesh in the vicinity hurriedly scattered, pushing against the mass of their fellows until they had widened the perimeter surrounding the Raptor's position.

'The xenos are performing exactly the way Ipos and Oriax said they would,' Rhodaan continued, turning his back on the murdered soldier. 'That is why I want you to be ready for any surprises.' He left unspoken his belief that it wasn't the orks alone they had to be wary of. Over-Captain Vallax and his Squad Vidarna had been a bit too gracious in allowing Squad Kyrith the honour of conducting the Aboro operation. Such beneficence from his commander brought Rhodaan's suspicions to the fore.

Prowling along the ramp, dust and debris clattering from his armour, slaves scrambling to clear his path, Rhodaan approached Captain Gamgin's command centre in the staff carriage just behind the train's enormous mag-engine. The car was a bulky mess of armour plate and gun turrets, a forest of antennas bristling from its roof. One side of the carriage had been swung open, the titanium doors lashed to hooks set into the base of the car's frame. The exposed interior was without partition, a single room stuffed with terminals and workstations. Dozens of pict screens displayed various views of Aboro, scores of cogitators rumbled and chattered as they analyzed the reports streaming in from the vox-casters. Mobs of janissary officers, their shoulders festooned with garish strings of braid and brass, scurried about the command centre, their pace growing ever more frantic as they turned from one work station to another. Every report made it clear that the complete breakdown of the city's defence was imminent.

Through it all, like a primordial god, stalked the huge shape of Captain Gamgin. The Iron Warrior held his helmet beneath his arm, exposing his scarred visage and glowering countenance. His expression remained implacable as he read the reports and studied the image relays. Amid the barely suppressed panic of the Flesh, Gamgin was a rock of calm calculation, digesting each new report before dispensing his orders in a voice as cold as steel.

Rhodaan was not deceived by Gamgin's air of invulnerability, of emotionless logic and careful calculation. He was also a legionary and knew the strange alchemy of duty and honour which governed the mind of an Iron Warrior. Devoid of fear for their own lives, absolutely without empathy for the sacrifices of others, an Iron

Warrior cared about only one thing: the Legion. To fail the Legion, to disgrace the Third Grand Company, this was the secret terror that smouldered deep inside their hearts. Gamgin had failed to hold the Witch Wall, failed to keep the orks isolated on the far shore of the Mare Ossius. That was a shame which burned within him with the intensity of star-fire. Rhodaan could almost see it blazing from Gamgin's eyes. To atone for his failure, to redeem himself, these were the things that mattered to Gamgin now, not the defence of Aboro or the lives of half a million slaves.

'Lord captain,' Rhodaan's voice growled from the vox-casters in his helm. He slammed his fist against his chest plate in salute as Gamgin turned away from a bank of pict screens and faced the Raptor.

'The time is at hand,' Gamgin declared. He waved an armoured hand at the pict screens. 'The Steel Blood maintain their vigil. The orks have ignored thirty-seven per cent of them, leaving many of them transmitting well behind enemy lines.' The Space Marine's face twisted in a derisive sneer. 'Simple brutes, incapable of appreciating the value of intelligence!' He pointed to one of the pict screens, his finger stabbing at the broadcast image as though thrusting a sword into it. For Gamgin, the image was as familiar as it was despised.

'The artillery barrage is being lifted,' Gamgin said. 'This is why. The orks are moving for the final push, bringing up one of their battlefortresses.' The Iron Warrior's eyes took on a cold glint. 'Their warlord wants to be in on the kill personally.'

'They might still use their big cannons,' Rhodaan cautioned as he studied the grotesque ork machine. Bigger than a strike cruiser, the immense vehicle straddled the railway, exploiting the mag-plates to aid its propulsion. The mammoth barrel of an orbital cannon jutted from the front of the machine's hull. It had been such weapons which had broken the Witch Wall and pulverised the

Charybdis Line. With a range of several hundred kilometres, it might still prove an insurmountable obstacle to their plans.

Gamgin nodded in understanding. 'It is time for Squad Kyrith to play their part,' he said. He turned and gestured at a detailed map of Aboro, the underground networks of service tunnels and industrial sewers clearly picked out in neon ribbons of gold and azure. 'The battlefortress is moving through quadrant alpha-seven. When it crosses into alpha-nine, it will be poised fifty metres from this sub-station.' Gamgin's finger pointed to a crimson smudge linked to one of the golden lines.

'The orks have become callously arrogant in their push,' Gamgin said. 'Convinced they have crushed all but a token resistance, they have forgotten even the most rudimentary security protocols.'

Rhodaan clenched his hand into a fist. 'I will give them reason to regret their confidence. The gun will be silenced.'

'Do not compromise the enemy's mobility,' Gamgin warned.

The reminder brought a curl to Rhodaan's lips. 'I am no half-seed,' he hissed back. 'I do not forget my orders. I do not fail in my duty.'

The last barb brought a flash of colour to Gamgin's features. 'Your ability had better equal your boasting,' he snarled, 'because I will be waiting for you in the Eye!'

Rhodaan slammed his fist across his chest in salute. 'A long wait, brother,' he growled as he turned his back on the command carriage. As he marched back along the ramp, he scolded himself for his anger. Gamgin was of no consequence. His career was over.

It was wasteful to squander hate on the dead.

THE NEXUS OF quadrants alpha-seven and alpha-nine was a scene of ruin and desolation. Fires raged unchecked, sewage bubbled from ruptured pipes, waste-gases vented from shattered collection vats. The charred husk of a reclamation tower leaned precariously against the burned-out rubble of an ore-smashing facility. The skeletal framework of a servo-crane lay strewn across the street, its cybernetic operator still pawing mindlessly at the charred control column.

'The xenos have done a good job flattening this sector,' observed Brother Gomorie, his afflicted hand flowing into a cleaver-like appendage in emulation of the image. Strange reflections played across the infected mess of flesh and metal, too suggestive in their resemblance to coherent images to be merely a trick of shadow and flame.

Crouched within the exposed sub-cellar of a shelled warehouse, the Space Marines of Squad Kyrith shifted away from Gomorie, uncomfortable with this reminder of their battle-brother's affliction. The taint was a symbol of the raw, undisciplined nature of Chaos. It was a reminder of the menace that lurked inside each of them, the unfocused power which might rise up to overwhelm them in mind and body. It was a warning of what it meant to fail the Legion, to be consumed by the weakness of mere humanity. Mankind was the prey of such forces, only a Space Marine had the force of will to resist and restrain such power. Chaos was a power to be harnessed by those with the strength and vision to use it. Yet each of them knew that few, even among the Space Marines, had such strength. Gomorie was an example that even among the Iron Warriors there was weakness.

'Inefficient,' Baelfegor grumbled with contempt, keeping his eyes turned from Gomorie's hand. 'With all the ordnance they've fired, we could have smashed an entire world.'

'Perhaps you should offer your services to the xenos as military advisor,' Uzraal sneered. 'They'd probably make you a general, half-seed. If they didn't shoot you outright for your incessant complaining!'

Baelfegor bristled at the insult, his hand clenching tight

about the grip of his meltagun. 'We must discuss this again, brother. At a more appropriate time.'

Uzraal leaned into the other Space Marine's face. 'I welcome it,' he hissed. 'You are little more than a flesh-maggot in my eyes.'

'Don't let the orks shoot you, brother,' Baelfegor growled back, enjoying the way Uzraal grew tense when their kinship was addressed. 'I should hate to be cheated because you were clumsy.'

The whirring edge of Rhodaan's chainsword suddenly sliced down between the two Iron Warriors, missing the masks of their helms by a matter of centimetres. Baelfegor and Uzraal cringed away from the menacing blade.

'Keep your focus on the mission,' Rhodaan snarled at them. 'I will tell you when you have permission to die.' He could feel the hatred of the reprimanded Iron Warriors stabbing at him from behind the optics of their helmets. *Good*, he thought. *Let them hate, so long as they fear.* Fear was obedience, no different for his fellow Space Marines than it was for the miserable Flesh who fed their war machine.

The walls of the pit-like sub-cellar trembled, sending scorched beams and shapeless lumps of heat-blasted ferrocrete tumbling into the depression. Rhodaan focused upon the tiny display of the data-slate he held, the feed from a nearby Steel Blood. The transmission depicted the gigantic ork battlefortress ploughing through the ruins, its enormity far in excess of the trains the tracks had been designed for. Buildings were brushed aside by the oncoming behemoth, its hull pulverising walls into rubble as it forced its way onwards. Rhodaan could almost hear the ground whining in protest as the prodigious weight of the machine pressed down upon it. That the mag-plates could afford any kind of support to such a monstrosity was grim testament to the genius of the Iron Warriors' engineering.

The orks had profited long enough from such genius.

Now the xenos would become victims of it.

'Stand ready!' Rhodaan barked, loosening the catch on his plasma pistol's holster. The other Space Marines followed his example. Soon the pit resounded with the metallic whine of idling turbines as the Raptors activated their jump packs.

The tremor's violence continued to rise, the roar of collapsing buildings becoming a deafening clamour. A smog of dust and debris billowed across the mouth of the pit, blotting out the Space Marines' view of the polluted sky. Now, the groan of pulverised architecture was accompanied by the mechanical shriek of mighty engines, the bellow of driving pistons and the crazed chatter of firing guns.

Rhodaan's horned helm stared straight up into the obscuring dust. 'Iron within! Iron without!' he shouted as his thumb depressed the launch rune and his pack's thrusters launched him into the sky. He could hear the battle cry repeated by the other Raptors as they flew after him.

It took only the blink of an eye to clear the gritty smog of dust and wreckage. One instant, Rhodaan's vision was consumed by a grey oblivion. The next he was hundreds of metres above the burning streets of Aboro, staring down at the Cyclopean enormity of the ork battle-fortress. Turrets and weapon batteries protruded from every corner of the colossus, scattered about in random disarray. Tall towers, ornamented with scrap-metal glyphs and primitive clan heraldry, bristled from the top of the hull, a crazed forest of gun emplacements, observation posts and communication hubs. As the Iron Warriors shot up into the sky, they could see clusters of orks firing their weapons into the ruins, venting their bloodlust in a display of mindless aggression. Those few who were observant enough to notice the Raptors as they rocketed into the sky could only blink in open-mouthed confusion, their savage brains losing precious seconds as they struggled to comprehend what they were seeing.

Before the orks could react, the Iron Warriors were diving down upon them. Pazuriel smashed into the tallest of the towers, pulverising the face of a stunned ork with his boot as he descended. An instant later and the Raptor's chainaxe was transforming the observation post into an abattoir. Gomorie landed upon the flat roof of an anti-aircraft emplacement, his bolt pistol rupturing ork flesh with a steady fusillade of explosive rounds while his afflicted hand lengthened into an eviscerating tendril of flailing bio-steel.

Leaving his battle-brothers to spread alarm among the xenos and keep their focus upon the towers, Rhodaan spread his demi-organic wings and dived upon the yawning mouth of the main gun, its bore a full ten metres wide. Baelfegor and Uzraal followed in his wake. All three Iron Warriors struck their objective at the same moment, the mag-clamps within their boots gripping the surface of the cannon. The three Raptors had only a second to gain their bearings before bullets began ricocheting off the surface of the cannon. From a confusion of gantries and catwalks fixed to the hull of the battlefortress, a swarm of orks appeared. The aliens hooted and howled as they fired down at the Iron Warriors.

Baelfegor returned fire, dropping an ork with each burst from his bolt pistol, the mangled aliens hurtling from the walkways to smash against the street far below. Uzraal withdrew a frag grenade from the dispenser on his belt, throwing it at the centremost of the gantries. The explosive ripped through the packed orks, killing dozens outright and sending the wounded stumbling back inside the fortress. The aliens on the lower gantries took cover as a rain of debris and torn bodies came crashing down on them, while those above the explosion were blinded by an oily cloud of smoke.

'Down,' Rhodaan ordered. Taking advantage of the brief respite, the three Raptors withdrew into the muzzle of the cannon, using their mag-clamps to climb down the bore of the gun. The hearts of each Iron Warrior pounded inside his chest, as they wondered if one of the ork gunners would take it into its mind to fire the cannon while the invaders were inside. Rhodaan was gambling that their communication wasn't that efficient. By the time the xenos relayed such a command, the Space Marines would be at their objective.

Near the base of the barrel, Rhodaan fired his plasma pistol, unleashing a full charge of superheated destruction into the side of the gun. For an instant, the metal turned white hot, then crumbled into blackened ash. The Iron Warriors didn't hesitate. Gripping in both hands, Uzraal deactivated the mag-clamps in his boots. Half falling, half leaping, the Raptor lunged through the smouldering hole Rhodaan had made.

Uzraal found himself in the arming chamber of the immense gun, shells bigger than railway cars stacked and piled throughout the mammoth room. it was occupied by a small army of wiry aliens, wizened little dwarfs barely a quarter the size of their hulking ork masters. Stricken with amazement by the strange injury to the gun, the gretchin were still watching in stupefied awe when Uzraal came lunging into the room. They barely had opportunity to scream before the Iron Warrior's flamer was turned on them, streams of burning promethium engulfing the nearest of the grots and transforming them into living torches.

The survivors scattered, throwing down tools and supplies as they scrambled for cover. The few orks in the arming chamber, brutish runtherds and hulking artillerists, barked jeers and curses at the frightened gretchin, then dragged a motley assortment of pistols and blades from their belts. Before the orks could join the battle, they found themselves beset by new enemies.

Leaping through the gap in the cannon, Baelfegor threw himself into a rolling dive, his bolt pistol firing as he skidded along the floor. A one-legged runtherd, its face a maze of tattoos and hair-squigs, wilted under the barrage. The orks near him ducked behind shells and loading gantries in a desperate effort to avoid their comrade's fate.

From beside the cannon itself, a hulking ork clad in thick layers of flak armour and tool belts took aim at Baelfegor, squinting down the sight of a blocky weapon that appeared to be a confusion of spare parts, muzzle brakes and powercells. The mekboy barked with laughter as its combi-weapon belched into life, hurling a concentrated beam of energy at the Iron Warrior. The brute's own laughter spoiled its shot, giving its target just enough warning to realise his peril. Flinging himself across the room, Baelfegor crashed behind a stack of spent shell casings, the back of one of his boots reduced to molten slag by the glancing shot.

The xenos wasn't to get the opportunity to fire again. Even as it swung around to follow Baelfegor's flight, the mekboy's head evaporated in a sizzling mess of steam. Rhodaan scowled at his overheated plasma pistol, hoping the sensitive power coils hadn't been compromised from over-use. Sliding the smoking weapon into its insulated holster, he activated the thrusters of his jump pack, rocketing across the arming chamber to where the rest of the gun crew had taken shelter.

The orks were just recovering from their initial shock when suddenly Rhodaan was among them, his chainsword lashing out in a vicious dance of dismemberment and death. Pistols, axes, swords and bludgeons, the entire brutal arsenal of the bellowing aliens was unequal to the murderous precision of the Iron Warrior. The howling mob of xenos killers disintegrated into a tangle of severed limbs and mangled bodies, blood and spattered brains.

The massacre of the fearsome orks threw the surviving gretchin into complete panic. Shrieking in terror, the greenskins ran from their hiding places, fleeing in complete disorder down entry hatches and loading bays.

Uzraal and Baelfegor didn't waste their time on the fleeing monsters. The moment Rhodaan engaged the orks, the other Raptors converged upon the gun, removing melta bombs from their belts and slapping the magnetic charges against the breech of the gun.

'Why do we waste time with the gun?' Baelfegor grumbled. 'With a little time we could rig the entire arsenal to detonate. Blow this abomination back to Dirgas!'

'That would stall the ork attack,' Uzraal agreed, stuffing the last of his charges into the shell extractor. 'Give the miserable flesh-maggots more time to run.'

'Follow orders,' Rhodaan told them. He paused a moment, listening to the sound of more orks rushing down the corridors of the battlefortress. From the sound of it, they'd been momentarily blocked by the fleeing herds of gretchin. He didn't expect that obstacle to delay them long.

'Set the charges and get out,' Rhodaan ordered. Leaping from the raised loading platform, his demi-organic wings snapped open, dropping him to the base of the cannon in a twisting glide. He lost no time climbing back into the barrel, or engaging the thrusters of his jump pack once inside. The confined space magnified the force of the engines, shooting him from the cannon with a velocity that would have shattered the bones of a mere human. Even as a legionary, the experience tested his endurance almost to the limit. He could feel blood vessels burst, the softer tissues of ear and nose tearing as he thundered out into the sky. Using his wings, Rhodaan turned his ascent into a spin, allowing him to watch as the rest of his squad came shooting from the cannon one by one.

An instant later, the belly of the battlefortress shuddered. Thick black smoke belched from the cannon and the hull around it. The detonation of the melta bombs was the signal Pazuriel and Gomorie had been waiting for. Rocketing from their positions on the towers, the final members of Squad Kyrith rose from the stricken xenos behemoth.

It would have been easy to destroy it, Rhodaan mused. Baelfegor had been right about that. The ork warhost in Aboro would have been crippled by such a loss. But Gamgin's plan called for the elimination of that warhost, not its temporary debilitation.

The melta bombs provoked a response from the rail terminus, the last stronghold of human resistance in Aboro. Every siege gun and missile battery left in the city opened fire, the barrage crashing down all around the battlefortress. The impossibly thick hull withstood even the worst of the barrage, a field eerily similar to the void shield of a Titan crackling into life and blunting the attack. Ork gun crews returned the barrage and Rhodaan fancied he could hear the ork warlord howling in frustration over the loss of its main cannon.

The orks would be mad now, mad enough to forget anything except revenge. Mad enough to forget what little their primitive minds understood about logic and strategy.

Captain Gamgin's trap was baited. Now all that was left was to reel the prey in.

CHAPTER IX

I-Day Plus Sixty-Five

THE PICT SCREENS turned black one after another as the armoured train sped away from Aboro and beyond the transmission range of the Steel Blood. Captain Gamgin stayed beside the terminals, watching as the last view from the city began to flicker and distort. Through the eyes of the cybernetic skull, he watched as a vast swarm of buggies and battlewagons raced out from the ruins. A cold smile formed as he saw the immense bulk of the battlefortress, smoke still rising from its sabotaged cannon, lumber down the tracks. The core of the ork warhost, every vehicle and piece of armour the xenos could assemble, was tearing across the desert in vengeful pursuit of the humans.

The janissary officers had been horrified by Gamgin's decision to retreat in broad daylight. It had taken four messy executions to silence their pleading. Terror of the ork air supremacy had overwhelmed their discipline. They should have known better than to question an Iron Warrior.

By standard logic, the exodus would have been suicidal. The ork planes would have strafed and bombed
the exposed train into oblivion. It was a sound strategy
any rational commander would adopt. Fortunately an
enraged ork was far from rational. Lifting the artillery
barrage before the city was fully subdued had given Gamgin an understanding of the ork warlord's mentality. The
beast was selfish, it wanted the credit for destroying the
enemy for itself personally. It wouldn't suffer its under-
lings to steal that achievement.

During the first hour out from Aboro, the train had
been bombed and strafed repeatedly. Those attacks had
been barely fended off by the weapon emplacements
mounted on the carriage roofs. Doubt had started to
creep into Gamgin's own mind, for who could say with
any certainty how a xenos brain might think? Then,
through the eyes of the Steel Blood, he had watched that
moment when the ork flyers peeling off from one of
their runs had flown over the alien ground forces. Plane
after plane was blasted from the sky by their own troops
in a vicious storm of rocketry and cannon-fire. The crippled squadrons had fled southwards, keeping well away
from their crazed comrades. The message had been clear
enough even for orks. Since the fratricidal exchange, not
a single ork plane had appeared overhead.

The warlord was going after the bait, but Gamgin was
becoming worried. Only the lightest and fastest elements of the warhost were keeping pace with the train.
He wanted more than that before he sprang his trap.
He needed more than that to atone for his failure at the
Witch Wall. Like the alien warlord, there was revenge to
be satisfied. Only destruction of the battlefortress would
bring that satisfaction.

Gamgin turned away from the pict screen as it finally
went dark. The walls of the command car echoed with the
impact of heavy calibre bullets, the chatter of a stub gun
or large bolter. Human technicians and officers cowered

behind their work stations each time a fresh salvo crackled against the train's heavy armour. The towering Iron Warrior marched past them, his face dripping with contempt. Was there anything in the universe so weak as man?

The Space Marine's gauntlet closed about the shoulder of a technician cringing in his chair. It took the barest exertion to tear the man from his station, his chair's straps and buckles shredding into frayed ribbons beneath the Iron Warrior's strength. The man landed in a screaming heap on the floor, several of his ribs snapped like twigs by Gamgin's assault. The legionary didn't glance at the broken man, the Flesh dismissed from his calculations as soon as he was no longer in the Iron Warrior's way.

The casual mutilation of the janissary turned every eye in the command car to Gamgin. Horrified men watched as the giant lifted a slender communication wand from the terminal, the device looking puny and toy-like in the Space Marine's hand. 'Gamgin to engine,' he snarled. 'Reduce speed.' His face pulled back into an expression of inhuman malevolence. 'Do not question. Obey.'

Gamgin turned away from the terminal, dropping the communication wand. Before the stunned gaze of the officers, the Space Marine strode to the armoured wall and peeled back one of the titanium shutters. Silently, he gazed upon a desert swarming with scrap-work machines and murderous aliens. A stub gun stitched a tattoo of death across the armour, several rounds punching through the armaplas window and deflecting from the inner wall before finally embedding themselves in the floor. Fresh screams sounded from the men unfortunate enough to be caught in the fire.

The Iron Warrior remained at his post, no emotion crossing his features, his attention fixated upon calculations of speed and proximity. He watched the ork buggies and bikes swirling around the train, swarming like angry insects. They were less than vermin to him. It was bigger prey he wanted, prey that had fallen too far behind. The crew in the mag-engine would make the necessary adjustments. He had made that clear to them.

A palpable tension filled the command car, every mind but one gripped by terror. The janissary officers had been under no delusion that their superhuman overlords were beneficent, but until now they hadn't stopped to consider that the Iron Warriors were insane. Digging deep inside himself, drawing upon reserves of courage he hadn't believed possible, a young captain squirmed out from beneath a fire control station. Rising to his feet, he looked into the eyes of his fellow officers, trying to bestow upon them a small part of his own courage.

All he found was fear. The others were too in awe of the Iron Warriors to act, clinging to the fragile belief that through obedience they could earn their own survival. For an instant, the young captain knew the contempt the Iron Warriors felt for lesser humanity. Grimly, he drew his laspistol, holding it behind his back as he approached the comms station and the wand dangling from its tether.

'They are reducing speed, captain. No need to repeat their orders,' Gamgin's booming voice declared, freezing the janissary officer as he reached for the wand. His head snapped around, staring in horror at the armoured giant. The Iron Warrior hadn't moved, his gaze still upon the battle outside.

Superstitious terror closed its icy fingers about the officer's heart, beliefs about the near-divinity of the Space Marines rising unbidden from ancient childhood. It was the gleam of broken armaplas that restored the captain's boldness. There had been no magic in Gamgin's intercession, simply his reflection in the glass.

'The orks will overwhelm us if we slow,' the officer shouted. 'Our troops are barely keeping them off now!' He raised his laspistol, pointing it at the giant. 'I was there at Gamma Five. The only way we can escape is to cut loose the rear cars and leave them to the orks!'

Slowly, the Space Marine turned, his cold eyes boring into those of the captain. 'Who said we are trying to escape?' he snarled.

A beam of sizzling energy leapt from the laspistol, searing across the command car. For a brief moment, the officer dared believe he had accomplished the unthinkable. He dared believe he had achieved that secret dream locked inside the heart of every human on Castellax. He dared to imagine he had struck down an Iron Warrior.

Like all dreams, the captain's was nothing but shadow and fog. He had aimed at Gamgin's unprotected face, and his aim had been true. But he hadn't factored the superhuman reflexes of a Space Marine into his shot. Instead of burning a hole in the Iron Warrior's forehead, the las-beam had seared across the giant's cheek, exposing the gums and teeth beneath the skin. The maimed flesh contorted in a sneer.

In a blinding flash of speed, Gamgin drew his bolt pistol and aimed it at his foe. 'Pain,' he growled as his finger depressed the trigger. The janissary captain shrieked as the explosive round struck him in his gut, detonating with an impact that split his body in two. The screaming torso struck the wall and slid to the floor.

Gamgin's roar of frustration boomed from his armour's vox-casters. He could feel the train picking up speed. The craven little human had countermanded his commands, the cowards manning the engine were going to outpace the ork warhost!

Gamgin marched to the armoured door of the carriage. It took six men to lock the massive doors in place. The Iron Warrior's effort was made even harder by the fact that he was trying to open the doors against the velocity of a speeding train, bypassing locks and safeguards set in place by a dozen security cogitators. Sweat dripped down his forehead, his muscles burned with strain, the servo-motors in his armour groaned in protest, threatening to seize up and freeze his limbs in place.

Pride. Duty. Honour. Like a religious mantra, the three words formed a cadence in Gamgin's mind, refusing to allow him to relent. Gritting his teeth, the Iron Warrior redoubled his effort.

With the scream of broken metal, the armoured door swung open, slamming against the side of the train before it was torn away completely by its own weight. The smoke which had a moment before filled the carriage was sucked away in an instant, consumed by the raging windstorm of the train's passage. Stunned men scrambled for handholds as the wind tore at their uniforms and whipped across their faces. The few who had managed to don their goggles hastily turned to the exposed doorway, searching for some evidence of their murderous overlord.

There was no trace of Gamgin.

Not inside the command car.

GAMGIN'S ARMOURED FINGERS closed about the lip of the command car's roof, the optics of his helm cycling through different magnifications as he alternately directed his gaze at the fast attack swarms circling the train and the heavier ork machines steadily receding further into the distance.

The Iron Warrior ducked his head against the roof as the gunner in the back of a scarlet war buggy sent a barrage of metal flechettes clattering against the command car. Screams rose from the carriage beneath him, telling Gamgin that the orks had disposed of at least a few of the simpering Flesh.

Dismissing the officers and the orks from his thoughts, Gamgin focused instead upon the mag-engine ahead of him. At the train's present velocity, the slightest misstep would smear him across the desert, his body smashed to pulp inside his armour. It was not the sort of death an Iron Warrior would seek. Gamgin knew of a far better one, one that would blot out the shame of his failure and make his name a legend.

Mustering his superhuman body's tremendous strength, Gamgin flung himself from the roof, clearing the five metres between the car and the mag-engine. The Iron Warrior's gauntlets scraped against the curved surface of the engine roof as the train's momentum dragged him backwards. For a moment, it appeared to be a vain effort, but at the last instant the Space Marine's fingers closed about the leaden nub of a purity seal. Years of exposure to the pollutants of Castellax had hardened the seal and endowed it with incredible tensile strength. For a second, it was able to arrest Gamgin's momentum. It was all the time a Space Marine needed.

Using the seal to pivot, exploiting the momentum of his own body, Gamgin swung down into the bed of the mag-engine, landing amid the pulsating power coils and shuddering piston-drives.

Smashing his boot against the door separating the bed from the control booth, Gamgin burst in upon his objective. The horrified crew gawked at the giant, their faces drawn into almost comical masks of shock. The Iron Warrior chose the closest of the men, splattering his brains across the booth with a shot from his pistol.

'Who else wants to question my orders?' he growled at the other crewmen. With obscene haste, the slaves leapt to the controls, drawing down the magnetic pulse. At once Gamgin could feel the train reducing speed.

'Survival is the reward for obedience,' the Iron Warrior told the ashen-faced men, savouring each word of the lie.

Shots slammed into the sides of the engine, the stutter of automatic fire, the crack of plasma bolts, the shriek of spear-launchers and grapnels. Gamgin peered through the armaplas window, watching as ork buggies swarmed around the slowing train. He saw two of the scrap metal constructs bowled over by the hurtling train, dragged along in its path by the cables their gunners had unwisely fired into the engine. Janissaries on the rear cars increased their desperate efforts to fend off the attacks, directing a withering stream of bolt-shells and las-beams into the alien horde. Each casualty only seemed to increase the orks' determination, goading them closer to the hurtling train, urging them to step up the rate of their own fire.

The heavier ork machines were drawing close now. Battlewagons and trucks kept pace with the train, casting ropes and chains onto the roofs so that alien warriors might board the carriages. The janissaries were frantic in their efforts to stop the boarding actions, but at every turn the fierce vitality of the greenskins defied their efforts. Only a concentration of fire could drop the monsters and while focusing on one attacker, others were able to scramble up the ropes and onto the roofs.

Gamgin dismissed the doomed Flesh, staring instead at the immense bulk of the battlefortress. At its present speed, the mobile stronghold would be right where he needed it to be. The Iron Warrior smiled as he stared at the little counter displayed in the corner of his optics. Only a few more kilometres and everything would be in place.

A violent impact against the roof of the engine brought Gamgin spinning away from the window. Snarling his annoyance, the Space Marine fired his bolt pistol into the ceiling, his shots rewarded with the pained howls of orks. From the opposite window, he could see the black mass of a battlewagon, its body swarming with roaring aliens. A tall mast equipped with a spiked gangplank told the rest of the story. Blood-hungry orks surged along the rickety walkway, shoving their own comrades off in their eagerness to do battle. Gamgin saw one ork pitch into oblivion, a second dangling precariously from a hand-hold on the plank's steel side.

The Space Marine decided he had seen enough. Bringing his bolt pistol against the face of the window, he blasted a hole in the armaplas. Wind howled through the control booth as the room lost pressure. Gamgin ignored the tempest and thumbed another grenade from his belt.

Without hesitation, he dropped the explosive through the window and into the bed of the battlewagon.

The engine shook as the grenade detonated, peppering the side of the train with shrapnel. The stricken vehicle disintegrated as its hull lost its integrity, bursting into a shower of metal scrap and mangled bodies. Warbikes veered away from the debris, some of the riders shaking leathery fists at the wreckage as they passed it.

The crump of heavy boots on the roof was a reminder that some of the orks had managed to disembark before the explosion and survive the resulting shrapnel. A bright crimson glow began to eat through the ceiling, the burn of a meltagun. Gamgin directed another burst from his pistol overhead and the glow began to fade.

'I'll be back,' the Space Marine hissed, glaring at the terrified slaves. His gauntlet closed about the control booth's door, wrenching it open in a vicious tug. An ork, its body peppered with oozing wounds and slivers of metal, stood on the other side, an immense hammer gripped in its paws. Gamgin drove the muzzle of his pistol under the brute's chin and exploded its skull.

Shoving the shuddering corpse aside, the Iron Warrior threw himself at the half-dozen greenskins trying to tear apart the mag-drives. As he ruptured organs with bolt-shells and split bone with his combat knife, Gamgin was struck by the immense weight of an ork warrior dropping down from the roof of the engine. The Space Marine flattened beneath the murderous ambusher, smashed against the metal floor of the platform.

The massive ork, one of the hulking brutes that served as bosses among their kind, brought the talons of a crude power claw shearing through the fingers of Gamgin's right hand, slashing through the ceramite plates and the reinforced bones of the legionary's fingers. A fist the size of a human head slammed into the side of the Iron Warrior's helmet, the ork's tremendous strength further magnified by bulky piston-motors fitted to its scrap-work armour. Gamgin's right side optic display burst into a crackle of static.

The fungal stink of the ork's breath washed over Gamgin as the alien leaned over him. Through his still functional optic, the Space Marine could see the brute's shadow falling across the platform. Judging the ork's position, exploiting the power of his vat-grown muscles and the servo-motors in his armour, Gamgin arched his body and brought the back of his helmet smashing into the ork's face.

The brute reared back, blood raining from its pulverised nose, a cracked tusk hanging from the corner of its mouth. Gamgin rolled out from under the monster, taking advantage of its momentary confusion. The Iron Warrior's knife came slashing down, tearing through the cables looped about the ork's hip.

Roaring, the ork was swinging around to avenge itself on the Iron Warrior when he made his attack. Sparks exploded from the broken cables, oil spurted from severed hoses. The alien's leg froze in place as the mechanics of its scrap-work armour seized. The resulting loss of leverage spilled the huge ork to the floor of the platform.

Gamgin tore a fat-mouthed plasma pistol from one of the orks he had killed. Coldly he pointed the weapon at the crippled alien. It glared back at him, its beady eyes filled with frustrated rage.

Slowly, Gamgin lowered the pistol.

'You were almost early to your own funeral,' he told the ork.

FROM THE AIR Cohort gunship that extracted them from the ruins of Aboro, Rhodaan and his squad had a perfect view when a ten kilometre-wide section of desert suddenly vanished. One instant they could see Gamgin's troop train speeding down the tracks, flanked on all sides by a numberless swarm of ork buggies and battlewagons, the gigantic bulk of the battlefortress lumbering several kilometres behind. The next instant, that vista was obliterated in a burst of fiery annihilation. It seemed as though a talon of fire had reached up from the flaming core of Castellax to visit a vengeful judgement upon the puny creatures who capered about its surface. For hundreds of kilometres, the desert became a mass of dust and debris, smashed flat by the holocaust's murderous might.

The shock wave of that blast sent earthquakes coursing through the continent, gouging new faults in the substrata of Castellax. Air currents shifted wildly, sending storms raging across the planet as its desiccated atmosphere tried to adjust to the sudden vacuum from the hole that had burned clear to its stratosphere. A wall of dust and sand three kilometres high spilled across the desert, smothering entire outposts lying in their path.

The gunship pitched and rolled, its crew fighting wildly to maintain control. Rhodaan forced his way into the cockpit, brushing the men aside. The Space Marine forced the gunship higher, trying to rise above the cataclysm.

Even for Iron Warriors, there was a feeling of awe at the incredible power that they had witnessed. Captain Gamgin had sought to redeem the legacy of his service, to make his name a thing of honour in the sagas of the Legion. Rhodaan didn't know if Gamgin would be remembered by the Legion, but as he gazed down at the glass-lined scar gouged into the desert, he was certain of one thing.

Castellax would forever bear the mark of Gamgin's passing.

ONE SURFACE-TO-ORBIT MISSILE had caused such carnage. Unable to employ the weapons against the ork ships circling Castellax due to the debris field, Sergeant Ipos had proposed a different use for the ordnance. Detaching the mammoth warheads from the missiles, thousands of slaves had buried them across the desert in a ring of annihilation that no force could defy. Seeking to redeem himself for failing to hold the Witch Wall, Captain Gamgin had offered to goad an entire ork army within range of the trap, turning a defensive position into a weapon of offence.

The gambit had been a vicious success. Drawing the orks after him, a transmitter inside his own armour sending the detonation signal to the bomb, Gamgin had claimed over a million aliens in his final moment. Even the xenos had been taken aback by such devastation. For three weeks, they were silent, keeping to their scattered strongholds, regathering their strength.

When the orks did start to move again, however, it became clear that their objective was now Vorago itself. The annihilation of an entire army group had done something to the aliens, given them a focus and drive that had been absent before. No longer did they range pell-mell across the wastes, assaulting every outpost and settlement in their way. It was as though some fiendish hand had reached out and brought the beasts to heel. In the councils of the Warsmith, discussion began to turn to the supreme warboss, the focus of the Waaagh! itself.

Biglug. It was a name that had become increasingly prominent in the ork vox signals blanketing the planet, a name that had been echoed in the feral war cries of the invader. Oriax interpreted it as evidence that the warlord was taking a more direct hand in the campaign.

The ork advance on Vorago, for instance, displayed a care and caution no one had expected from the aliens. Their solution to the threat of more buried warheads had been at once brilliant and simple. Rather than scour the desert trying to detect the hidden traps, the orks focused their attention on the one spot where they could be certain the ground was clear. A vast alien horde descended on the gaping pit where Gamgin had sprung his trap. With amazing industry, the orks began to construct a bridge across the crater, concentrating such an immense number of flakwagons and crude fighter planes at the site that Morax's Air Cohort was incapable of attacking the construction.

Once the orks were across the pit, they would be within the ring of warheads Ipos had buried. By deploying the traps in a manner that would maximise their breadth, the Iron Warriors had thought to construct a wall of death far beyond the environs of their stronghold. It was a tactic that would have stalled Imperial ground forces for months. They had expected the orks to be similarly delayed. The very simplicity of the alien mindset was again proving a foil to their plans.

As it stood, they could expect the orks to reach the outer defences of Vorago within one month.

Already pushed to their limits, the millions of slaves toiling beneath the lashes of the Iron Warriors would have to increase their productivity.

There was no choice if Castellax were to withstand the siege.

A GREEN HAZE drifted through the skies of Vorago, crawling around the smoke stacks and spoil heaps as though possessed of some loathsome life of its own. There had been many strange colours and clouds in the skies since the detonation of the orbital warhead. The explosion had thrown clouds of dust and debris into the atmosphere, elements ripped from deep within the planet's strata. Some of the displays had been amazingly beautiful, illuminating the sky with hues of surpassing wonder and vibrancy. Others had been dark smudges, aerial blots that made the normal shades of smog and pollution seem clean and cheerful.

As he stared up at the green haze, Yuxiang was struck by its ghastly gyrations. He could almost feel the thing dripping its poison into the streets, corroding the metal siding of hab-pens and the brickwork of storehouses. What it was doing to mere flesh, that was something he tried very hard not to think about.

'Next.' The word was pronounced like a death sentence, which in a very real way it was. Yuxiang turned his gaze from the ghastly sky to the even more hideous vista of Vorago proper, or at least that section of the city he could see from his place atop the firebreak.

Firebreak. A typically deceptive turn of phrase. Yuxiang doubted if the megalithic ferrocrete wall had ever been intended to confine industrial fires to a single section of the city. No, from the very start the Iron Warriors had engineered their cities with an eye towards battle. Each street was a nest of hidden pillboxes and bunkers, fortified blockhouses and flak towers loomed above each district. The firebreaks were arranged in strategic patterns, positioned to support the other fortifications. Staggered along their faces were gun emplacements and missile batteries.

As final proof of their purpose, the surface of each firebreak was scored with two-metre-deep holes. One wall in each of these pits looked out over the city, a narrow slit cut into the ferrocrete. There was just enough room in the pit for a man to be posted with some measure of accommodation and comfort.

Naturally, the Iron Warriors expected two men to a pit.

The long line of slaves gradually dwindled as men were detached and lowered into the pits. Overseers from bombed out factories and janissaries from disbanded regiments supervised the positioning of men and the distribution of equipment. The slaves who had been pressed into the Vorago militia were similarly dispossessed, men from conquered outposts, destroyed settlements or, like Yuxiang, from decimated districts within the city itself.

'Next,' the tired growl came. The man ahead of Yuxiang shuffled forwards, raising his arms as a uniformed janissary inspected him, checking for any sharp objects that might allow the slave to cause mischief. When he was satisfied, the soldier nodded to the officer in charge. He was a dark-skinned colonel, his hair beginning to turn grey, his eyes lifeless and doll-like, utterly devoid of compassion or empathy.

At a gesture from the colonel, the slave was directed into the pit. When the man didn't move fast enough, a burly overseer stepped forwards and jabbed the glowing end of a shock baton into his ribs. With a yelp of pain, the slave dropped down into the hole.

'Next,' the colonel snarled. Yuxiang stepped forwards again, submitting himself to the humiliating inspection. Then it was his turn to march to the pit. Tired as he was, he forced himself to move quickly and deny the thug with the shock baton his sadistic pleasure.

Dropping down into the pit was made harder for Yuxiang by his efforts to avoid the slave already down there. Somehow, he managed to prevent himself hitting anything more important than a toe. The other man was too exhausted even to curse at him.

'Chains,' the colonel's growl echoed down from the mouth of the pit. Yuxiang and his companion glanced at the wall, finding the thick loops of chain bolted into the ferrocrete. Reluctantly, they brought the iron links into contact with the manacle locked around their left wrist. As the chain made contact, an automated clasp clicked open and closed about the striated edge of the manacle. The slaves raised their arms, tugging at the chain to show the colonel that the manacles had been secured.

'Weapon,' the colonel called out, turning away from the pit. A janissary appeared at the opening and lowered a weathered lasgun down to the slaves. One weapon to a pit, that was also the Iron Warriors' decree. The expectation was that when the armed man died, the unarmed man would take up his weapon. With barely enough room in the pit to aim one gun, anything more would be excessive.

Yuxiang took the lasgun, noting how light it felt in his hands. The slaves who had been dragooned into the militia had received an entire twenty minutes of training. In that time, Yuxiang had been allowed to handle a lasgun twice. It took him only a moment to appreciate the reason the weapon was so light. There was no power pack. The slight detail of ammunition was something the Iron Warriors would delay until the last possible moment.

When the orks were within firing range of the wall, then would be the time to distribute ammunition.

Any sooner and the slaves might take it in their minds to shoot at someone else.

ROUNDING HIS CRYSTALLINE throne, Warsmith Andraaz gestured with the talons of his power claw, using the razored fingers to emphasise his statements.

'The loss of Captain Gamgin has not bought us the time we had anticipated,' Andraaz said, accusation in his tone. Several eyes turned towards Sergeant Ipos, one of the Rending Guard even shifted his position slightly to face him, but the Iron Bastion's seneschal seemed oblivious to the unspoken recriminations.

The massive table at the centre of the war room came alive with a three-dimensional image of Vorago and its environs. While the assembled Iron Warriors watched, the glowing lines representing railways and roads began to darken and wink out. 'According to Fabricator Oriax's predictions, we can expect all ground transport to be cut off within two months,' Andraaz stated. His gaze shifted to Skylord Morax. 'Less if the xenos gain air supremacy.'

Morax was quick to reassure the Warsmith. 'The Air Cohort will be able to resupply Vorago as long as we can assemble resources at the northern outposts. If the humans cannot maintain those positions, then I make no guarantees.'

'It sounds like you are already excusing failure,' Admiral Nostraz hissed. 'I think the Air Cohort would benefit from new leadership.'

Morax fixed his rival with a menacing glare. 'You would do better? The man who allowed the orks to make planetfall? I think Gamgin lacked perspective. There are some who have done far more to disgrace the Third Grand Company.'

Nostraz rose to the Skylord's challenge. 'You are too concerned with damaging infrastructure and destroying resources,' the admiral sneered. 'You are too worried about preserving a non-existent production quota. You prosecute this war like an accountant, not a soldier!'

'Enough,' Andraaz snarled. 'This bickering achieves nothing. If we are to drive back the invader, we must focus only on that task. Ambition, glory, hate, all of these are distraction!' The Warsmith's talons closed into a cage of crackling steel. 'Destruction! Extermination! Annihilation! These are the only things which shall find a place in your hearts. These are the only pursuits worthy of an Iron Warrior.' Andraaz gestured at the illuminated display of Vorago. 'So long as we hold Vorago, we hold Castellax!'

'Grim Lord,' Skintaker Algol said, pulling away from the pallid slaves mending his grisly cloak. 'The defence of Vorago will be difficult. We have supplies of food and water for the Flesh that will maintain them for six weeks. No more.'

Andraaz rounded on the slavemaster. 'How many slaves have you taken into your calculations?'

The Skintaker's eyes narrowed with understanding. 'The full supply of Flesh available, the current population of Vorago. Fifty million.' Algol paused, warming to the idea the Warsmith's objection had aroused. 'I will begin sending disposal crews to eliminate the excess and begin establishing protocols for the reduction of reserves. The useless eaters will be eliminated, Grim Lord.'

Morax's eyes bulged as he heard the callous extermination of millions of slaves being bandied about. 'It will take years to cultivate a new workforce from the embryo vaults!' he cried. 'Even when the orks are forced from Castellax, it will take us decades to resume production. We will fall behind in our tithe to Medrengard!'

Andraaz scowled at the angry Skylord. 'Medrengard will not investigate our shipments for much longer than that,' he declared. 'Warp travel being what it is. By the time it becomes an immediate concern, my raider fleets will have collected fresh slaves for my factories.' He waved his hand towards Admiral Nostraz. 'That fleet is still available to us through the cautious tactics of your brother-captain.

'No,' Andraaz mused, pacing back towards his throne. 'The question of supplies and Flesh is a concern for the future. For now, we must rid ourselves of the xenos menace. To do that, we must draw upon all resources that are available to us.'

As he made the last statement, the Warsmith fixed his gaze upon the ghoulish servitor acting as Fabricator Oriax's surrogate. The half-machine folded its arms together in a gesture of genuflection.

'All shall be in readiness, Grim Lord,' the fleshless voice hissed from the servitor's vox-caster.

Andraaz shifted his gaze to Over-Captain Vallax. 'The loss of Captain Gamgin has impaired the prowess of the Third Grand Company. It compels me to commit the most extreme of the resources available to us.' The Warsmith's eyes became like chips of steel as they stared into Vallax's face. 'You will fetch Brother Merihem from the Oubliette,' the Warsmith declared. 'It is time he rejoined his brothers.'

Vallax's hair turned an icy blue as he heard what the Warsmith asked of him, a visible manifestation of the repugnance boiling inside him. He hesitated before speaking, trying to conceal the distaste he felt. It would do no good to object, the orders of the Warsmith were not open to question.

'It shall be done, Grim Lord,' Vallax declared. As he spoke, he turned his head, staring across the table to where Captain Rhodaan stood. A frigid smile crawled across Vallax's lips.

It was as well that Rhodaan had returned from Aboro.

Vallax's subordinate hadn't quite outlived his usefulness, it seemed.

CHAPTER X

I-Day Plus Eighty-Seven

THE HOWLING VIOLENCE of an ash-storm swirled about the lone assault boat as it sped above the desert wastes. The squadron of fighters which had started out as the transport's escort had fallen back some time ago, unwilling to brave the ravages of the storm. The crew of the assault boat would have done the same but for the insistence of their passengers. Between the fury of the storm and the fury of the Iron Warriors, the men wisely chose to defy the elements.

Rhodaan stared from the window, the optics in his helm shifting through visual frequencies in an effort to pierce the clouds of toxic ash. It was an effort beyond even the artifices of pre-Heresy engineering.

'Do you see anything, captain?' The question came from Brother Gomorie. Like Rhodaan, the Raptor was leaning against one of the windows trying to see through the howling storm.

'The impurities in the ash are confounding the optic filters,' Rhodaan said. 'They don't present a unified visual frequency for exclusion.' He shrugged, the gesture exaggerated by his unimpeded shoulders. After days of continuously bearing the weight of a jump pack, it would take time to adjust to that burden's absence. By then, of course, they would probably be redeployed in their capacity as Raptors and wearing the heavy packs once more.

'The storm will confine itself to the hot air over the desert,' Rhodaan told Gomorie. 'Once we drop down into the crevasse, the air will clear.' He stared hard at the other Space Marine, reading the agitation in his posture. 'We will be able to see the Oubliette before we land.'

Rhodaan saw the way Gomorie's infected hand twitched in a spasm of bio-steel at the very mention of the prison-hermitage. A journey to the Oubliette was distasteful enough for the rest of them, but he could appreciate how much worse it must be for Gomorie. For Rhodaan and the majority of his brothers, the state of Brother Merihem was repugnant, but at the same time distant. His corruption was like the rumble of artillery on the horizon, menacing but not immediate.

To Gomorie, however, the fallen Iron Warrior's fate was deeply personal. The same contagion that had overwhelmed and consumed Merihem had set its foul seed in his flesh. It was a daily struggle to restrain it, to force the infection into abeyance, to prevent it from raging through his mind and soul. So far, Gomorie's force of will had been strong enough, his sense of identity proud enough to resist. Yet always, at the back of his mind, lurked the knowledge that one day the virus would win out. One day he would become like Merihem, all the gifts of the Legion devoured by the warp-taint until the superhuman degenerated into the subhuman.

'Do you think any good will come of seeking out the abomination?' Uzraal asked. Like the rest of Squad Kyrith, he was visibly anxious. Before leaving Vorago, the Raptor had removed a meltagun from the stores. He was now stripping it down and cleaning its components for the sixteenth time.

Rhodaan considered the question for a moment before answering. 'Whatever else he is, Brother Merihem is an Iron Warrior. Warsmith Andraaz believes that will be enough to bind him to our cause.'

'But what do you believe, lord captain?' Gomorie asked.

Unconsciously, Rhodaan reached down to his left leg. Despite the heavy layers of ceramite and plasteel, the neurofibres and servo-motors, the mesh of insulation and padding, he imagined he could feel the ugly scars beneath his fingers. Merihem had given him those scars when he was being subdued and entombed within the Oubliette.

He shook his head and returned his gaze to the window. 'I would not question the Warsmith,' Rhodaan said. 'Even if I did believe him wrong,' he added in a bitter undertone.

THE LONG, JAGGED crevasse marked the easternmost limit of the Ossuarium, the vast desert which dominated Castellax's eastern continent. Hundreds of metres deep, its floor choked with a slurry of ore waste and acidic runoff from the strip mines pitting the walls of the canyon, the trench was dark and shadowy, all sunlight smothered by the ash-storm raging above it. Frost, brown from the polluted air, began to gather on the windows in defiance of the assault boat's heat shield.

Before the frost could completely obscure his view, Rhodaan saw an immense shape rising from the sludge of the canyon floor, a monstrous tower of stone and plasteel. Its sides bristled with gun turrets and sentinel relays, flood lamps and vigil monitors. As the assault boat neared the tower, the weapon emplacements rotated, locking the craft in their aiming reticules.

'Approaching aircraft,' a stern voice growled across the boat's vox-channel. 'Identify or be destroyed.'

'Assault boat delta-nine-seven, Castellax Air Cohort,' one of the pilots stammered, his voice quaking with fear.

Rhodaan switched over his vox-bead to transmit across the localised frequency. 'We are Iron Warriors,' he snarled. 'You have been warned to expect our arrival. Fire on us at your peril.'

There was a moment of silence. Rhodaan could almost see the human officer at the other end of the transmission trying to make his courage equal to his duty. 'What... Give the code word.'

'The word is "Carnage". If you would not learn the full meaning of that word, you will transmit landing instructions.' Rhodaan watched the gun turrets rotate back into their original positions and a pattern of blinking lights blaze into brilliance on the flattened roof of the tower.

'Brothers,' he called out to his squad. 'Welcome to the Oubliette.'

The assault boat was still settling onto the landing pad when Baelfegor swung open the door and lowered the boarding ramp. The edge of the titanium ramp scraped across the ferrocrete surface, gouging a long scratch across the ground. The Space Marines seemed oblivious to the precipice yawning to either side of them as they tromped down the trembling ramp.

A score of janissary troopers, their faces locked behind the insect-like frames of rebreathers, their bodies bulky beneath heavy flak armour, snapped to attention as the first of the Iron Warriors descended to the platform. Behind the goggles of their masks, their eyes were wide with awe. For most of them, this was their first view of a Space Marine. It was a moment of wonder and terror that would stay with them always.

Rhodaan marched between the columns of humans, towering over them as he passed. Ahead of him, a heavy-set woman stood at the end of the janissary ranks. Features accustomed to imperious command wilted into timid obedience as the armoured giant drew closer. Her gloved fingers closed a bit tighter about the grip of her rune-crusted command rod, as though trying to draw some measure of reassurance from the badge of her office.

'Warden Geena Zhroah, at your command, my lord,' the woman said, bowing her head as Rhodaan stood before her.

The Raptor turned his head, staring down at the warden as though noticing her for the first time. 'We have come for our battle-brother,' Rhodaan stated. 'Bring him to us.'

The warden's complexion became pale. 'There have been… complications, my lord. The abom– Your brother-lord has failed to respond to the pacification vapours.'

Rhodaan's tone hardened. 'You have only one duty here,' he warned, pointing at the baton clenched in her fist, reminding her that with her authority came responsibility. 'Attend to it,' he added in a low hiss before continuing his march down the landing pad, the rest of Squad Kyrith following behind him.

The warden's body trembled as she stared after the Iron Warriors. Slowly, she raised the command rod to her lips, pressing the rune which would broadcast her voice to the tower control room. 'This is Warden Zhroah,' she announced. 'The inmate is to be exhumed from the Reclusiam.' She licked her lips, feeling sick as the next words formed in her mind. 'Pacification protocols are suspended. Open the crypt. The masters will tolerate no delay.'

Grimly, the warden powered down the volume of her vox-unit. She didn't want to hear the horrified protests from her officers. She knew what her orders meant but there was nothing that could be done.

Even so, she wondered how many men she had just sent to their deaths.

THE LIEUTENANT KEYED the final runes into the control slate embedded in the crypt's door. Before the first adamantine tumbler began cycling into its disengaged pattern, the officer was scrambling down the long corridor, dashing past the brigade of janissaries lining the hall. The soldiers closed ranks as the officer passed them, raising their shot-guns and lasguns, aiming the weapons at the groaning door. Sweat dripped from each man's brow as he listened to the tumblers rotate.

At the end of the hall, the major in command of the extraction struggled for composure. He might be the only man in the Oubliette who had any real understanding of what was behind that door. Aside from the warden herself, he didn't think anyone had clearance to view the old holo-recordings of the entombed Iron Warrior. It was felt that ignorance of what they were guarding would be beneficial to the mental condition of the garrison. Being privy to the secret himself, the major had to sympathise with the logic behind such a decision.

'Lasguns at full charge,' the major reminded his troops, his voice crackling through the vox-casters lining the hall. He listened as the last of the tumblers cycled into its open phase, watched as a burst of steam gushed from the vents in the hydraulic locks. Three janissaries bearing enormous bronze keys advanced down the hall. They would need them to unlock the chains which restrained the captive. The major wasn't especially looking forward to that moment. He felt it was better for all concerned if the Iron Warrior remained shackled. Even Merihem would be slowed down by a few tons of titanium lashed about his limbs.

Like the segments of some metallic flower, the layers of the immense door peeled away. The janissaries in the hall shielded their eyes against the bright glare emanating from the tomb beyond the door. As their eyes adjusted to the light, their pulses quickened. Framed in the doorway was a gigantic shape, a figure of colossal propor-tions, immense beyond even the standards of the Space Marines. Three metres tall, at least half as wide across its hunched shoulders, the dark shape all but filled the entrance to the crypt.

For a long time, silence gripped the corridor. The

janissaries barely dared to breathe, their eyes riveted to the hulking shape of the Oubliette's lone prisoner. Framed by the glare of its cell, the shape was only a black shadow to the men in the hallway, utterly without detail or distinction. It was there – that was all the soldiers knew.

The major watched along with his troops as the shape contemplated them. The chains, those restraints the warden placed so much faith in, were still locked about the monster's body. Immense coils of titanium, each link as big around as a man's chest, the Iron Warrior was still restrained. Why then did the major's heart quake in fear? His hand shook as though afflicted with palsy as he raised the vox-bead to his lips. 'Lord Merihem,' he said, his words echoing from the vox-casters. 'We have been appointed your honour guard, to conduct you to your battle-brothers. They have…'

The officer's voice faltered as the hulking shape began to move. With ponderous steps that sent a shudder through the floor, Merihem descended from his cell. As the Iron Warrior emerged from the light, moans of terror rose from the watching janissaries. They had suspected that the Oubliette's inmate was something monstrous and horrible. In their worst nightmares, however, they had never imagined such a walking atrocity.

Veins of wire and cable rippled about Merihem's huge body, pulsating and writhing with fecund gyrations. Slabs of metal oozed along his limbs, slithering and rippling with loathsome vitality. Plates of armour bubbled and boiled, shifting shape and substance with each step, flowing in a cascade of obscenity. Streams of raw, glistening meat burst from between the metallic chaos, exuding the charnel stink of putrescent decay. Amid the formless madness of his body, buried atop a steel stump of a neck, the face of Merihem contemplated the terror around him. Small and dwarfish beside the ghastly enormity of the body beneath it, the face was devoid of colour, almost transparent in its pallor. It was utterly perfect in its cast, almost ethereal in its terrible beauty. The black eyes set amid the pallid flesh gleamed with abhorrent wisdom and forbidden knowledge.

With another step, the chains wrapped about the monster grew taut, then fell away, crashing to the floor in a confusion of twisted metal. At some point, perhaps hundreds of years past, the Iron Warrior had burst his bonds all on his own, without the need for rune-encrusted keys and the pardon of his Warsmith.

The major was gripped by the same horror that froze his men. It was one thing to observe such an abomination on a holo-recording. It was something else entirely to stand before it in the flesh, free and unfettered. His lips fluttered impotently as he tried to frame a command, an order that would arrest the monster's advance.

An instant later, the opportunity was gone. One of the janissaries, unable to restrain his fear in the face of Merihem's thunderous steps, opened fire with his lasgun. The beam seared down the hallway, sizzling against the oozing morass of the Iron Warrior's breast. The monster paused, his black eyes fixing upon the soldier. Merihem's mouth peeled back in a malicious grin, exposing a nest of glistening metal fangs.

All restraint collapsed. Fingers pulled at triggers and activation studs, loosing a withering hail of fire down the hallway. The walls trembled from the roar of guns, the air grew thick with smoke. A wave of energy beams and solid shot wailed along the corridor, one hundred guns all trained upon a single target. It should have been murder.

It was.

Screams reverberated along the hallway as janissaries pitched and fell, their bodies ripped and torn, organs burst and limbs exploded. Beneath the steady crack of guns, the thunderous steps of Merihem formed a ghoulish beat. Through the gun smoke the hideous giant loomed, his arm raised. The sludge of metal and meat which formed his body knitted itself into distinct shapes, flowing into the semblance of autocannons. More than a semblance, Merihem's arm became the weapon itself, loosing shot after shot into the soldiers. Through the slush of ruined bodies, the Iron Warrior marched, almost oblivious to the havoc around him.

Almost, for sometimes the Space Marine would pause before a wounded man or linger over a trembling wretch who had somehow survived a burst from his guns. Then the monster's pallid face would smile and the claws of his other arm would descend.

The remaining janissaries took advantage of such pauses, retreating down the hallway. In an act of duty he knew to be futile, the major drew his laspistol and fired into the controls for the elevator behind him, desperately hoping to contain the escaped monster on this level of the tower. An instant later, one of his own soldiers, horrified to see their only hope of retreat destroyed, exploded the officer's skull with a burst from his shotgun.

With nothing left to lose, the men trapped at the end of the corridor threw grenades at the oncoming giant. The concussion wave from the confined blast dropped a dozen men, their ears burst by the fury of the explosion. Their comrades didn't spare them any attention, focusing instead on the smoke-filled hallway, desperately trying to see if their ploy had worked. Their hearts sickened after a moment as they heard Merihem's ponderous tread once more. Through the smoke, the hideous giant appeared, the corrupt substance of his body already flowing back into the wounds inflicted by the grenades.

The last fifty janissaries opened fire. Merihem waded through the barrage as though it were no more threatening than a light rain. The Iron Warrior's left arm lengthened, shaping itself into whirring blades not unlike the industrial saws in a manufactorum. The pallid face was soon darkened by spattered blood, but the vicious smirk remained.

It took the Obliterator only a moment to wrench open

the armoured door to the elevator, a moment more to fuse his palm to the interior controls and allow his will to dominate the simple cogitator within. Something the little Flesh had said about his battle-brothers coming for him governed the command Merihem sent racing through the wires.

If Iron Warriors had come to the Oubliette, they would be on the roof. Merihem sent the lift speeding upwards. After so many years, he was eager to see his battle-brothers again.

'IT IS FREE!' Warden Zhroah shrieked. Desperately she tried to form her janissaries into a battle line, but even her threats were having a hard time overcoming their terror. Some fool in the command centre had broadcast images from the hallway to the pict screens on the landing pad. Every man on the roof had seen them before the warden cut off the transmission. Rather than face what was coming, seven of them had jumped off the tower. One of Rhodaan's Raptors had been compelled to guard their assault boat and prevent the frightened men from stealing it.

The warden turned towards Rhodaan, falling to her knees as she begged the armoured giant for help. 'You can stop him!' she pleaded, trying to make herself believe her own words. 'You have to stop him!' she added when the Space Marine failed to take notice of her.

Rhodaan's horned head turned, his optics glaring down at the woman. 'We came here to bring back our battle-brother, not to destroy him.'

'But he will kill us all!' Zhroah cried.

The Iron Warrior stared back at the elevator, watching as the indicator sped towards the roof. 'All Flesh dies,' he said.

The heavy steel doors slid open as the carriage reached the top of the shaft. Zhroah's janissaries sighted down the barrels of their weapons, each man tense and ready for action. The warden crept behind the soldiers, biting her lip to keep from giving the command to fire. The Iron Warriors wanted their corrupt brother alive, to take any action against Merihem would be to sign her own death warrant. Besides, she had seen the transmission. She knew how hopeless it was for mere men to defy something like the Obliterator. Rhodaan and his Space Marines were their only chance.

'Brother Merihem,' Rhodaan called out, his empty hands held away from his body in a non-threatening display. 'We have come to bring you back to Vorago.'

The immense bulk of Merihem stalked out onto the landing pad, his movements wary as those of a wild beast. The Obliterator towered over the other Iron Warrior, neck sinking into his viscous body so that the lowered head might stare more easily at the Raptor. For an instant, as he advanced, Merihem's body jerked backwards, his arm extending back towards the elevator. There was a sound of tearing metal. In the next instant, the extended arm was slithering back towards the Obliterator, the hand encased in the twisted remains of the control panel. Before the eyes of the onlookers, the debris began to corrode, bubbling into a molten mess that seeped into the monster's body. Torn wires whipped away from the shaft, sinking into Merihem's wrist.

The pallid face smiled coldly at Rhodaan. 'It has been a long time,' the Obliterator said, his voice sounding like slime sloshing in a sump pit. The black eyes narrowed. 'I have not forgotten you, Rhodaan.' Colourless lips peeled back, metal teeth gleamed. 'This time, I will not leave enough of a leg for them to stitch back on.'

Rhodaan felt his hearts go cold at the reminder of what he had suffered the last time he had encountered the Obliterator. The abomination should have been destroyed then, but the Warsmith had dictated otherwise. The monster should have been left to rot in his cell regardless of the orks, but again, the Warsmith had decreed otherwise.

Seldom had Rhodaan been more tempted to disobey an order, but his sense of duty held him back. Whatever his feelings, he had to obey Andraaz's commands.

'The Warsmith sent us,' Rhodaan said, maintaining his composure as the hulking Merihem loomed over him.

'Kind of him to remember me,' Merihem sneered. 'When I am finished with you, it will be his turn.'

Rhodaan shook his head and sighed with mock disappointment. 'I had hoped you would be cooperative,' he said.

While Merihem was still focused upon Rhodaan, Baelfegor and Pazuriel sprang into action. With incredible speed, the two Iron Warriors dived at the monster, their armoured fists pounding against the viscous morass of metal and wire. As they dashed away, they left behind fist-sized bombs magnetically clamped to the Obliterator's body. Before the giant could react, the bombs detonated, engulfing Merihem in a blaze of crackling energy.

'Haywire grenades,' Rhodaan explained. 'You might remember them from the last time you defied the Warsmith.'

The pallid face wailed in pain, the Obliterator's huge bulk reared back as electricity crackled about it, sizzling along wires and dancing across plates. An ozone reek rolled across the roof.

Rhodaan stared up at the screaming monster. Haywire grenades were designed to disrupt energy transmissions, to shut down the electrical circulation within any machine, even one infested with the techno-organic Obliterator virus. 'I am disappointed in you, brother,' he told the writhing giant. 'I had expected more of a fight.'

Merihem's arm came whipping around, smashing into Rhodaan and flinging him across the roof. A half-dozen janissaries collapsed beneath the hurtling Space Marine, cushioning his fall and preventing him from pitching over the edge.

Electricity continued to crackle about the monster's

body, but the pallid face was no longer screaming. Instead, there was an expression of daemonic delight. Lurching forwards, the Obliterator started after Rhodaan, pausing only when Pazuriel and Baelfegor rushed at him, another set of bombs clenched in their fists. Merihem's arm contracted into a muzzle and series of energy coils. As the two Iron Warriors ran at him, he sent a sonic concentration smashing into them. The Obliterator's body had partially absorbed the first set of bombs, allowing him to understand their mechanism and the frequency by which they were armed. The sonic projection detonated the bombs the Raptors held, felling both of them as the servo-motors inside their power armour shorted out.

The delay was enough for Rhodaan to regain his feet. Grimly, he drew his chainsword and plasma pistol. 'The Warsmith wants him alive,' he called out. The reminder was for Uzraal, creeping around Merihem's flank with a meltagun rather than the terrified janissaries and their puny efforts to bring down the monster.

'Your concern is touching,' Merihem growled, crushing the head of a janissary in one hand while raking three more with the autocannon that had formed at the end of his other arm. Energy still crackled around the monster's body, as though the haywire grenades were still trying to bring him down.

'Alive doesn't mean unharmed,' Rhodaan growled back. With a fierce cry, he lunged at the Obliterator, a superheated shot from his pistol sizzling across the beast's knee. Wires bubbled, metal burned as the star-fire scorched its way through Merihem's leg. The Obliterator wobbled uneasily for a moment, then the two halves of his leg knitted back together. While Rhodaan's pistol was still cooling down, the monster struck at him with his claw.

'That might have worked before,' Merihem jeered, not entirely surprised when Rhodaan dodged beneath the sweep of his claw. 'But the gift has had a long time to work on me since last we met.' The Obliterator's chest bulged outwards in a cage of wire as Rhodaan chopped at him with the edge of his sword. The Raptor pulled back before he could become snared in the nest of metal, springing away as the monster's left hand slashed at him.

'The old tricks won't work,' Merihem scoffed. The Obliterator drew back, the metal of his arm parting to expose a mush of raw, pulsating flesh. 'I have insulated myself, bundled my core within living flesh. So much for your disruptors!' The monster's smile became even more malignant. His arm bulged into a ring of autocannon muzzles. 'So much for you!'

'Brother Merihem! Remember you are an Iron Warrior. Remember your duty and your honour!'

The Obliterator's head swung around, oozing along his neck until it faced backwards. The black eyes narrowed with scorn as he saw a lone Iron Warrior rushing towards him. The fool's hands were empty, he hadn't even remembered his weapon.

Just as Merihem was shifting his autocannon to address the interloper, the Obliterator noted one of the Space Marine's hands. His smile collapsed as he recognised the infection. He froze, his gaze locked on to Gomorie's hand. It was like looking into his own past, at the man he had once been. Duty, honour, the things that had once been the core of his identity, the things that had been so important before the virus had consumed him.

Rhodaan hesitated, studying Merihem's reaction to Gomorie. He could almost see the training and hypno-conditioning reasserting themselves. There was a chance, just a chance, the monster would listen now.

'Brother Merihem,' Rhodaan called out, lowering his sword. 'Castellax is besieged by xenos hordes. The abominable orks think to steal this world from the Iron Warriors. We will not allow that. We will slaughter every last one of them. Your place is with us, brother, fighting at our side. Reclaim the honour that is your right as an Iron Warrior!'

Merihem was silent for a moment, his gaze shifting between Rhodaan and Gomorie. At last, the monster relented, the autocannon disintegrating, melting back into the morass of his body. 'I remember my duty. I will see the xenos driven from Castellax.' The black eyes grew sharp, stabbing into Rhodaan's optics. 'But afterwards there will be a reckoning,' the Obliterator promised. His head twisted around, staring across the roof. His little face curled into a malicious smile. From the end of his hand, a spear of metal shot forth, hurtling across the landing pad.

Warden Zhroah writhed on the end of the harpoon, blood bubbling across her lips as Merihem dragged her to him. Callously, he ripped the metal spike from her chest, studying her as she tried to suck air into ruptured lungs. As the warden expired, Merihem fixed Rhodaan with a menacing stare.

'A reckoning, brother,' the monster hissed.

CHAPTER XI

I-Day Plus Ninety

IN THE EARLY dawn, as the sun's rays struggled through the murk of Castellax's diseased sky, the ork assault on Vorago began. For days the city had watched the aliens assemble on the polluted plains, a numberless horde that boiled up out of the desert like a hurricane. At first, small mobs of the invaders had charged directly for the gigantic perimeter wall which surrounded the city, throwing themselves upon the rings of defences that guarded Vorago in a display of brute aggression. Chain-wire, minefields, pits of industrial acid, trenches lined with razored shards of scrap-metal, concealed deadfalls, ferrocrete barriers – all of them took their toll upon the impetuous attackers. In only a few hours, the outskirts of Vorago came to resemble a junkyard strewn with the broken wrecks of alien machines and the mangled shapes of alien carrion.

There was little real fighting in those first reckless attacks. From their positions on the walls, the Flesh could fire down into the orks with relative impunity. The few ork aircraft that put in an appearance were quickly shot down by the Castellax Air Cohort and the anti-air batteries strewn across the roofs of Vorago.

Algol knew that there would come a time when the Flesh of Vorago would look back upon those initial attacks as the 'happy times'. If the aliens had been capable of deliberate strategy, he would have called those first charges probing attacks, but the reality was they were simple blind aggression, the wildest of the orks expending themselves in a reckless advance without plan or purpose. The result wasn't a battle. Upon the formidable rings of traps and barriers the Iron Warriors had erected, the aliens died in their thousands.

Yet the defenders could take small comfort from the slaughter, for beyond the waves of ork buggies and trucks, the mobs of infantry and armour throwing themselves against the walls, Algol could see the real storm gathering. A vast encampment was taking shape, a great sprawling mass of orks that stretched across the horizon. Not in their hundreds or their thousands, but in their millions. It was almost like watching another city sprouting up from the parched dirt of the plain, a city peopled with giant monsters devoted to razing Vorago and killing everyone within its walls.

Distinct amid the sprawl of machines, tents, trenches and bivouacs, the grotesque bulk of the battlefortress towered. The second of the immense behemoths that had broken through the Witch Wall, the gargantuan machine formed the core of the ork encampment. An effort by the Air Cohort to bomb the thing had proven futile, only two planes had escaped from the murderous anti-air fire concentrated around the fortress. A Deathstrike missile had been launched from the Iron Bastion itself, but the weapon had detonated without effect against the crackling void fields protecting the battlefortress.

For three days, the orks waited and gathered their strength. On the third night, the darkness was violated by the fierce war cries rising from the alien camp, primitive howls and chants that were punctuated by the sound of weapons being discharged into the sky. All through the hours of darkness, the clamour continued unabated, sometimes growing louder, sometimes dropping to a dull roar, but always the noise was there. Until just before dawn, when an eerie quiet descended upon the ork camp, a brooding stillness that sent a chill into the weak hearts of the Flesh.

The stillness shattered as the first rays of dawn stabbed down onto the roofs of Vorago. From the ork camp came the deafening bellow of thousands of guns. The sky was torn by the shriek of shells as the titanic artillery barrage hurtled overhead. The city shook as death rained down upon it, tons of ferrocrete and stone flung into the air as explosions erupted throughout Vorago. Streets became choked with rubble, factories and hab-pens collapsed, fires raged unchecked.

Billowing outwards from the ork camp, rushing forwards beneath the roar of artillery, the xenos came. Tens of thousands of machines, advancing in a great mass of snarling engines and black promethium-smoke. After them came millions of infantry, mobs of hulking green warriors howling and bellowing, sometimes firing their weapons at the distant walls despite the extreme range. Vicious ork aircraft flew into the sky, not the handfuls that had been so easily dispatched before, but in their hundreds, entire squadrons of bombers and fighters, whole wings of box-like gunships and transports.

Algol felt a sense of exhilaration rush through him as he watched the battle begin. Simple, brutal creatures, the orks nevertheless possessed a degree of cunning. With callous opportunism, they concentrated their attack on those sections of the perimeter where the wreckage of their own comrades was thickest. In these regions, the traps laid by the Iron Warriors had already been expended, claiming their toll in casualties. By driving over the very bones of their own dead, the orks eased their passage through the outer defences.

Steadily, relentlessly, heedless of the fire being hurled down upon them from the walls, the orks ploughed closer and closer to Vorago.

The Skintaker smiled. It was going to be a good fight.

TAOFANG'S VIEW OF the attack abruptly became far more personal. A trio of ork gunships swept along the length of the perimeter wall, spitting death across the parapets with boltguns and heavy stubbers. Janissaries and conscripted slaves returned fire, peppering the bulky aircraft with a desperate fusillade of solid-shot and las-beams. The rattle of bullets and shells against the heavily armoured fuse-lages crackled down the length of the wall, mocking the horrified men below.

Contemptuously, the orks refused to withdraw in the face of the effort to repulse them. Instead, the doors set into the sides of the gunships rolled back, exposing compartments crammed with hulking green monsters. Barking their savage glee, the ork troops didn't even wait for the gunships to descend to the parapets. Firing their weapons as they fell, the brutes dropped the four metres between gunship and wall. Their powerful bodies absorbed the shock of the impact, for the most part. Even those who suffered injury clung to a stubborn urge to fight. Taofang saw one ork, his body draped in plates of metal wired together in the crudest semblance of armour, land in such a way that its legs snapped like twigs beneath it. Rather than consider its hurt, however, the alien dug a big pistol from its belt and began shooting at a squad of janissaries. His last sight of the monster was watching it crawl after the squad, its broken legs dragging behind it.

Another of the gunships hovered only twenty metres from where Taofang and his platoon were positioned. The gunship was venting smoke and flame from a huge rent in its hull, the result of a missile fired at it from one of the flak towers inside the city. The pilot seemed to be making a concentrated effort to keep its ship airborne, its bloodied face visible through the glass cowling over the cockpit.

Taofang watched with horror as the door in the side of the gunship slid back. Smoke billowed from the compartment, the orks inside were black with burns and many were scarred with slivers of shrapnel. The janissary could imagine the carnage that had taken place within the gunship when it had been struck. By rights, these creatures should be counting themselves lucky and slinking back home to tend their wounds. Instead, their beady eyes were glowing with hate and a primal lust to destroy.

'Don't let them reach the wall!' The order came from a young major, his face a mess of grey scars, the legacy of a slave riot at a strip mine long ago. Major Kuantai was matching words to actions, firing a long-barrelled stub pistol into the ork ship as he shouted commands.

Since the fiasco at Gamma Five, Taofang's mauled regiment had been broken up, the survivors deployed in irregular formations cobbled together from janissaries, overseers, rail guards and even Air Cohort ground crew. In his current platoon, there were only five Scorpions. The only other soldier he knew was Mingzhou, the Jackal sniper. It was an eerie thing, fighting alongside men who you didn't know, wondering whether they could be counted upon when things became desperate.

The leadership of an officer like Kuantai made the difference. The major led by bold example, demanding nothing from his troops he wouldn't demand of himself. Where officers like Colonel Nehring would slink off and leave the men under his command to risk all the danger, Kuantai was there with them, sharing every hazard.

Emboldened by the major's bravado, Taofang leaned out from behind the ferrocrete embrasure he was using for shelter. Steadying his grip on his lasgun, he fired into the gunship, targeting one of the blackened brutes standing in the doorway. The ork howled back at him, brandishing a huge axe with an electrified blade. Grinning murderously, the alien leapt down onto the parapet. It lunged up from its crouch as it landed, storming across the wall, its beady eyes locked on Taofang.

The janissary fired shot after shot into the charging ork, but the las-beams failed to strike any of the alien's vitals, or else the beast was too stupid to recognise its injuries. Roaring like some prehistoric leviathan, it closed upon Taofang. Reeling back, he cringed as the ork's axe sheared through the side of the embrasure, sending a sliver of ferrocrete crashing to the ground.

Before the monster could strike again, its face was split by a crimson beam of light. The ork blinked in confusion, stumbled back. It dropped the axe and jabbed a fat finger into the smouldering hole in its forehead. There was a confused look on its face as it probed the wound. A glob of greasy material hung from its finger as it withdrew. The ork sniffed curiously at the stuff, then, finally acknowledging that it should be dead, slammed against the side of the embrasure.

Taofang looked around, waving his thanks to Mingzhou. The flame-haired wastelander was lying prone across the roof of a pillbox, already seeking another victim for her lasrifle. He chastised himself for the absurdity of his emotions. A battlefield was no place for frivolities like gratitude.

Firming his grip on his lasgun, Taofang dashed across the wall towards the low barricade where a dozen janissaries were trying to hold their position. Ranged against them were only a handful of orks, but the odds went beyond mere numbers. Each of the orks was the equal of three men when it came to raw muscle and strength, and the weapons they carried were similarly powerful. While the humans fired their las-beams into the monsters, charring their armour or sometimes scorching their leathery flesh, the high-calibre rounds flying from the ork's boltguns and stubbers were chewing chunks from the barricade. Only the slovenly aim of the charging aliens gave the humans any chance at all.

Taofang rushed into the embattled position, pressing himself against the barricade. He could feel the vibrations of the ork bullets slamming into the ferrocrete, a steady tattoo like the pounding of a drum. One janissary, rising to take his shot at the aliens, fell in a twitching mash of pulverised flesh, his chest exploded by a burst from a stubber. Taofang could see panic spreading among the others as they watched the wreckage of their comrade writhe. He could feel the same panic blazing up inside his own body.

Just as fear began to overwhelm them, Major Kuantai rose from behind the barricade and lobbed a fistful of grenades into the orks. The aliens vanished in a brilliant blaze of fire and smoke. Even before the smoke started to clear, Kuantai had his pistol drawn and was vaulting over the barricade.

'Come on!' the officer shouted to his men. 'We finish them, or I promise you they will finish us!' Kuantai didn't wait to see if the janissaries were following him, but ran across the scarred surface of the wall to loom over the bleeding bulk of an ork that had been caught in the explosion. Vengefully, Kuantai brought his pistol against the beast's skull and blew its brains out. Wiping the gore from his tunic, the major looked up to see his soldiers executing the other injured aliens.

Taofang saw the grim smile that appeared on Kuantai's face. It was an expression of defiant fatalism. The men under Kuantai's command might be annihilated by the orks, but they would not be broken. Such was the major's determination. Strangely, it gave Taofang a feeling of pride.

For more than half an hour, the fighting on the parapets continued. In the end, the defenders were neither annihilated nor beaten. Exhausted, shivering as the repressed horror of the close-quarter fighting returned to them, tending a catalogue of wounds that ranged from cuts and scrapes to broken bones and severed limbs, the janissaries were strewn along the wall, too weary even to separate the living, the dead and the dying. They had paid a desperate price to hold their position, but under Major Kuantai's leadership, hold it they had.

His back against the cold bulk of an embrasure, Taofang tried to bind the gash across his forearm by pulling at the bandage with his clenched teeth. Despite the pain, he counted himself lucky. A few centimetres more and the ork's knife would have taken the whole limb. Just the same, it was hard to feel fortunate with his arm feeling like it was on fire.

'Let me do that.' Mingzhou didn't give him a chance to protest. Crouching beside him, leaning the lethal length of her lasrifle against the embrasure, the sniper inspected the crude bandage. Her face twisted in a scowl of disapproval. Taofang bit his lip as she undid the wrapping and a wave of raw agony coursed through his body.

'You're lucky you didn't lose this,' Mingzhou observed as she redid the bandage.

Taofang winced, trying not to squirm while she worked. 'I… I guess my… protector had other things… to do.' He cried out as the woman gave a sharp pull and the bandage tightened.

'You should have kept your head down,' Mingzhou reprimanded him. She gestured irritably at the bloody bandage. 'Only a fool lets himself get that close to an ork.'

Somehow, through the pain, Taofang managed a smile. 'We had to get the orks off the wall,' he said, then shook his head. 'I suppose you could say I let myself get caught up in the moment.' His gaze strayed from the sniper to a cluster of men prowling along the wall, inspecting the bodies strewn about the parapets. Centremost among them was the figure of Major Kuantai, his tunic spattered with blood, his side bandaged where an ork bullet had nearly broken his ribs.

'A brave man,' Mingzhou conceded, her tone bitter.

Taofang shifted his body, eliciting a sullen groan as his arm brushed against his belt. 'If not for him, we could never have held the wall.'

'A brave man,' Mingzhou repeated. She might have said more, but whatever words were forming themselves stayed unspoken. Her eyes became wide with alarm, pallor crept into her face. Taofang could see her body grow tense beneath her uniform and he wondered what could make this bold, almost callous woman, display such fear.

Turning his gaze back towards the officers, Taofang found his answer. His own pulse quickened as he watched a gigantic figure stalk along the parapet. It was something he had last seen in Dirgas, the ghoulish shape of Skintaker Algol.

THE SKINTAKER DID not spare a glance for the dead and dying men strewn around him, indeed it was left to the wounded to drag themselves from his path. Algol's attention was fixed entirely upon the officers. As these men became aware of the Space Marine's approach, their conclave broke apart, each man snapping to attention and sketching a hasty salute.

Algol glowered down at them, the optics in his skull-like helm seeming to smoulder with rage. 'Which Flesh is in command here?' the Iron Warrior demanded.

Paling visibly, a tremor in his step that hadn't been there even in the thickest of the fighting, Major Kuantai advanced and bowed before the armoured giant. 'Major Kuantai of the 4/5 Rosicracian Tigers...'

Algol closed the distance between them in a single step, his cloak of human skin snapping in the wind. The Iron Warrior paused a moment, as though listening to the sounds of battle raging in other parts of the city, then his attention reverted to the puny human trembling before him.

'Casualties: one hundred and fifty-four,' the Iron Warrior growled. 'Xenos losses: seventy-five.' Algol raised his hand, the talons of his gauntlet pointing into Kuantai's face. 'This action took forty-two minutes.' The statement ended in a grunt of contempt. 'One Iron Warrior could have accomplished this much in three.'

Kuantai bowed again. 'Forgive me, lord captain,' he begged. 'I shall do better.'

'Your successor will,' Algol hissed. His armoured hand smashed down, punching through the back of the bowed officer. Kuantai screamed as steel fingers ripped into his flesh and pulled several centimetres of spine from his body.

'It seems you *did* have a backbone,' Algol spat, tossing the gory talisman onto Kuantai's quivering body. The Iron Warrior wiped the man's blood on the hem of his grisly cloak, then turned to regard the other officers. 'One of you is now major,' he declared.

The Space Marine turned, started to walk away, then stopped. 'Leave that for disposal,' he said, pointing at Kuantai's body. 'And remember what is expected of you.'

The skull-faced helm glared across the horrified janissaries. 'The eyes of the Legion are everywhere,' he warned. 'If you are weak, we will know. There is no room for weakness on the battlefield. Remember that too.'

The Skintaker whipped his cloak about him and marched away, savouring the stink of terror. Let them fear, he thought. Fear is the seed of obedience. If it would not take root, then there was always room for a fresh face on the raiment of Algol.

YUXIANG ROLLED HIS shoulders, the only effort the narrow confines of the pit allowed him when it came to stretching his cramped body. His fellow inmate, a burly welder named Shenlau, gave him an ugly look as his arm brushed against the man's chest.

'Enough of that,' Shenlau cursed. 'There's not enough

room already.' He slapped his calloused palm against the stock of the lasgun. 'You want to spoil my aim?'

Yuxiang matched the other man's angry stare. 'What do you expect to shoot from way back here?' he demanded. Despite the thunder of artillery and the las-pack a janissary had tossed down into the pit some hours before, he found it inconceivable to think anything could penetrate the perimeter of Vorago, much less drive so deep as to reach the firebreak.

With short, scuffling steps, Shenlau pulled away from the narrow slit in the side of the pit. Extending the lasgun, he motioned for Yuxiang to take a look for himself.

The firebreak towered over the adjacent buildings, offering a panoramic view of Vorago that was interrupted only by the still more immense flak towers. Yuxiang could see the entire district laid out below, the streets slashing their way through the maze of factories and processing plants. For the first time, he was confronted by the deranged layout of the city. Streets and roads, even railways, twisted and twined around the buildings, seldom allowing themselves more than a few blocks for any straightaway before resuming their meandering habits. Seen from above, the effect was a confusing labyrinth. It didn't take much imagination to picture the effect the maze would have on someone actually down in the streets.

The bright blaze of an explosion drew Yuxiang's eyes to the immense perimeter wall. He could see ork gunships, resembling gigantic scrap metal bloat-flies, buzzing about the parapets, unleashing a murderous fire into the defenders. Alien warriors, disembarking from the hovering aircraft, ran amok along the wall, slaughtering any human unfortunate enough to cross their path. It was a scene at once fascinating and horrifying. But it was soon eclipsed by an even more awesome vision.

The city was rocked by a tremendous explosion, even the walls of the pit rained ferrocrete dust as the tremor rolled through the firebreak. A boom like the cracking of the planet roared through the air. Yuxiang felt Shenlau's hand clawing at him with sweaty fingers.

'What is it?' the man pleaded. 'What is happening? What do you see?'

Yuxiang hesitated, wondering how mere words could describe the holocaust of destruction he had just witnessed. An entire section of the perimeter wall had blown up, ripped from the earth as though by some giant hand and then dashed across the landscape. The force of the explosion had flattened nearby buildings and toppled distant smoke stacks. Where the section had been there was now only a thick haze of smoke and a blackened crater marred by the odd ferrocrete block or twisted titanium girder.

'The wall… The orks blew up the wall...' Yuxiang managed to gasp. He pressed closer to the slit, trying to will his eyes to pierce the smoke. It might be his imagination, but he thought he saw shapes moving in the smoke. Had someone survived the explosion? It seemed impossible.

The next instant dissolved the naïve idea that anything human had survived the breaching of the wall. The shapes moving through the smoke were orks, their squat, apish builds clearly distinct even from such a distance. At first only in small mobs, but then in increasing numbers, the aliens rushed across the destruction, their savage brains showing no hesitation, no fear of crossing the scene of such recent havoc.

The trickle of xenos warriors soon became a swarm, numbers greater than Yuxiang could calculate. Roaring and shooting, the orks rushed into the winding streets, eager to find something to kill.

It was only when they were deep within the labyrinth that the orks discovered the trap they had rushed so recklessly into. From his vantage on the firebreak, Yuxiang watched as the hidden defences of the district swung into operation. Automated death traps hidden in every factory, each sewer and workshop; traps that exploited the hazards of Vorago's production plants and processing centres. Reclamation towers sprayed showers of molten slag onto the heads of the oncoming orks. Toxic vapours vented from the air recyclers built into the walls of factories. Raw industrial waste was pumped into the streets, spilling from the sewer lines and flow trenches. Entire buildings shuddered and collapsed, broken by charges planted against their very foundations, the rubble burying whole mobs of orks and blocking the paths of those who followed.

As he watched trap after trap deployed against the orks, a sickening thought occurred to Yuxiang. The Iron Warriors had planned for this. These traps had been built when the structures were first being constructed. From the start, they had been prepared for an enemy to attack Vorago, to breach the perimeter and fall prey to the deadly maze within. More than prepared, perhaps the Space Marines had even goaded the xenos horde into the labyrinth, drawn them in like a rat catcher baiting his snares. Had it been an uncannily accurate ork barrage which broke the perimeter wall, or had it been some ruthless machination of the Iron Warriors themselves?

'Let me see!' Shenlau demanded, clamping his hand on Yuxiang's shoulder. 'Let me see,' he repeated in a low growl when the slave didn't move. 'I've got the gun,' he hissed. 'My place is at the window!'

Yuxiang turned his head and glared at the other man. 'What will you do? Shoot me?'

Shenlau smiled coldly. 'If I thought a disposal team would fish you out of here before you started to stink, I'd consider it.' His finger tightened about the trigger, his eyes like chips of ice. 'I still might.'

'Go ahead,' Yuxiang said, calling the other slave's bluff. He jabbed his thumb at the slit behind him. 'From what I can see, we'll both be dead soon.'

Shenlau's eyes went wide. 'The orks are winning?' he cried.

Yuxiang shook his head as he awkwardly drew away from the window.

'Orks or Iron Warriors, it makes no difference,' he said. 'Either way, whichever wins, we lose.'

'THE ORKS HAVE taken the bait. They are rushing into the breach in Omicron-Sigma. From the information being relayed by Oriax's Steel Blood, we can expect to exterminate upwards of fifty thousand of the filth.'

Warsmith Andraaz digested Sergeant Ipos's report, the talons of his power claw drumming against the arm of his diamond throne. Though the death toll was impressive, it hardly justified the demolition of their own perimeter wall and the sacrifice of an entire district. No, the slaughter of so many orks was inconsequential, a drop in the bucket beside the vast number of aliens still laying siege to the city.

The real purpose of the ploy was more subtle. The Warsmith turned his attention away from Ipos, fixing his imperious gaze upon the cadaverous shape of Oriax's servitor. 'Fabricator, you have heard Ipos's summary of the situation. How soon can we expect results?'

The servitor stared blankly at the massive Warsmith, its dead features displaying only the same silent agony they always bore. After a brief space, the metallic voice of Oriax crackled from the cyborg's vox-caster. 'The death of so many orks in such a short period will cause a disruption in the gestalt consciousness of the horde. They will become confused, unfocused. We can expect them to break off their attack while their individual psyches adjust.'

'Your Steel Blood are in position,' Andraaz did not phrase it as a question, but rather as a vocalization of what he expected the Fabricator to have already accomplished.

'Yes, Grim Lord,' the vox-caster crackled. 'I am able to monitor more than thirty-nine per cent of the xenos camp. My spies will maintain visual observation of the orks throughout this crisis.'

'They will look for leadership,' Ipos stated. 'In that, they are no different than any thinking creature of limited ability. When beset by calamity, they look to something better than themselves to tell them what to do.' The Iron Warrior shook his head, his features dripping with disdain. 'That has been the foundation of societies primitive and modern, the basis of every religion, government and tyranny. The weak look to the strong. They desire to be dominated.'

Andraaz continued to regard Oriax's ghoulish proxy. 'Tell me, Fabricator, where do the orks look for guidance? Where is their leader?'

Again, the servitor was silent for a space. Deep within his sanctum, Oriax was consulting the data being fed to him by his grisly spies. It was almost a minute before the servitor answered.

'There is evidence of a convergence of xenos around the battlefortress,' Oriax pronounced. 'Data gathered by Captain Rhodaan and our martyred battle-brother Captain Gamgin suggest that the warboss of the attack against Aboro was headquartered within a similar battlefortress. It would be unlike an ork to stray too far from custom.'

The Warsmith digested the information, nodding his head as he pondered the situation. His cold gaze swept across the assembled commanders of the Third Grand Company, finally settling on Over-Captain Vallax.

'Recall your squads from the walls,' Andraaz commanded. 'I have a mission for my Raptors.' His gaze hardened and an edge crept into his tone. 'All of them, this time, Over-Captain.'

Vallax bristled under the reprimand, crimson streaks shifting through his mutated hair. 'I obey, Grim Lord,' he replied, adding another humiliation to the growing list of offences Rhodaan had perpetrated. The upstart's luck couldn't last forever. It was a prediction that eased Vallax's pride.

Especially since he intended to take a hand in bringing that prediction to fruition.

CHAPTER XII

I-Day Plus Ninety-Two

ENGINSEER HERODITUS CAREFULLY made his way around the hulking atmosphere generator, reciting a binary mantra of serenity as the machine shuddered and wheezed erratically. He set a slender appeasement seal against the device's power plant, a long strip of aluminium lined with letters etched in acid. The generator seemed to accept the offering, subsiding with a shudder into a lesser degree of agitation.

The generator's machine-spirit had every right to take offence, Heroditus reflected, feeling a twinge of guilt transmit through the neurofibres of his nervous system. It had been woefully abused in its hurried disassembly and clandestine removal to the depths beneath Vorago. Necessity had demanded that the customary rituals of approbation be dispensed with. Only the most cursory of placations had been attempted and there had been no time to wait for the generator's acquiescence to its relocation. Heroditus felt like an atavistic techno-barbarian defiling such a complex mechanism in so crude and deliberate a fashion.

Still, he had to defer to the wisdom of Logis Acestes. Since the beginning of the ork assault on Vorago, the vaults beneath the city had become compromised. Packs of escaped slaves from the factories, deserters from the janissaries, renegade overseers and slavedrivers; all of these and more had fled the besieged city to take refuge in the forgotten tunnels and catacombs. It was a situation that could not be tolerated by Acestes and his disciples. Their work was too important to allow any risk of exposure.

Precious labour had been expended constructing combat-servitors to patrol the passages connecting to the assembly chamber. Nothing so ostentatious as a Praetorian, but rather an assemblage of cyborgs that would appear quite mundane until their murderous directives asserted themselves. Meticulous care had been taken with their neurologic protocols so that should one of the combat-servitors be disassembled it would appear to be the subject of malfunction rather than deliberately pernicious programming.

Such crude measures of dealing with intruders was too uncertain to satisfy Acestes, however. His plan was to employ the atmosphere generator from one of the smelting plants to ensure the conspirators would be undisturbed. The atmosphere in the tunnels was poisonous, but its lethality might be bypassed by taking certain precautions. Death was certain for any organism exposed to the air in the tunnels for a prolonged period, but there was a big difference between a matter of minutes and a slow decline over several decades from trace carcinogens.

It made Heroditus ashamed the way the generator had been adjusted, its function deliberately violated to transform it from a source of clean, sustaining air to a purveyor of death. Instead of removing toxins from the air, the generator was now pumping them into it, a vicious cocktail of proticide that would bond with its victims on a molecular level, rendering the protons within the atoms unstable. Death would be almost instant and within an hour, even the evidence of a corpse would be obliterated as the body reduced itself to a sort of protean goo.

Heroditus had passed several of these puddles of organic mash on his descent into the catacombs. It was a pity that the dead were unaware they were martyrs to the Omnissiah, that their passing was necessary to ending the heretical dominion of the Iron Warriors on Castellax and ending the blasphemies being churned out from their factories. Of course, their deaths had been so quick they really hadn't had the opportunity to reflect on such blessed dissolution even if they had known what was killing them and why.

As the enginseer stepped around the shuddering generator, he removed the complicated array of anti-toxin injectors from his chassis. He stared at them for a moment, evaluating how much of the chemicals remained. Enough for another journey through the tunnels? Perhaps for two? It was beneficial that so much of his flesh had been sacrificed to the Machine-God already, even to sustain what little remained against the effects of proticide took a distressingly high proportion of anti-toxin.

It was even more distressing that there were insufficient resources at hand to manufacture the poison in volume. *Had there been, Castellax could be scoured of both its infectious presences!* Heroditus quietly reprimanded himself for such a flagrantly emotional thought. There were too many orks to simply poison into extermination and, even if they could, there were the Iron Warriors themselves to consider. Against a normal human, the poison was invariably lethal, but the holy Adeptus Astartes and their fallen kin were a different matter. Proticide had proven incapable of defiling the enhanced genetics of a Space Marine, the advanced healing and regenerative properties of their cells nullifying the poison almost instantaneously. The best that exposure could inflict on an Iron Warrior would be a sensation of nausea. Even that was something of a triumph for the unknown geneseer who had created the poison.

No, even with the tunnels around the assembly chamber filled with proticide, the conspirators still had to fear discovery by the Iron Warriors. The blasphemous Chaos Marines would have nothing to fear from the poison, they could march through it at their leisure to reach the rebel tech-priests.

This was the subject of Heroditus's recent foray into the city. Every opportunity had to be exploited to prevent the Iron Warriors from becoming aware of the hidden cabal dedicated to their annihilation. The enginseer had met with other tech-priests, those who had remained at their posts in the factories and power plants, armouries and assembly centres. If things were too quiet, the Iron Warriors would become suspicious. For this reason, the tech-priests had arranged small acts of sabotage and inefficiency in the factories ever since the beginning of the campaign. Now, however, logic dictated that they should step up their efforts, become almost openly overt in their sabotage. It was the natural evolution demanded by the changing situation and the seeming vulnerability of the Iron Warriors in the face of their xenos attackers.

Heroditus knew what he was asking of his brothers. The Iron Warriors would be severe in their retaliation. Where before the production had been sabotaged in subtle ways so as not to draw too much attention or too close a scrutiny, now they had to be almost blatant. Guns would be produced with dramatic proclivities towards inaccuracy. Explosives would be rendered half as destructive. Ammunition would be altered from their design to increase swelling and warpage after use to increase jamming and blockage.

While the Iron Warriors concentrated upon a thousand fiascos throughout Vorago, they would be oblivious to the great menace growing under their very feet.

The pumps in the enginseer's chest increased their rhythm as he contemplated the tremendous blast which had shook the city when the Iron Warriors demolished the perimeter wall and invited the orks into their trap. The ordnance Acestes was assembling would make the earlier blast seem insignificant, it would be like the fist of the Omnissiah crashing down upon the foul violators of holy standard template constructs.

Heroditus focused his optic senses from the murk of the chamber floor to the causeway where the warhead housing was reaching completion. He could see Logis Acestes kneeling before the weapon, his vox-speaker crackling with a Lingua-Technis mantra of baptism.

After careful evaluation, it had been decided to christen the machine-spirit of the new ordnance after its defiled predecessor. Vindex Lartius. When it was complete, it would fulfil its purpose in a cataclysm of destruction.

Vindex Lartius would avenge not only Lartius Maximus, but all of Castellax.

Heroditus paused, an incongruous thought occurring to him. Even at this late stage, there was still the potential for failure. Everything depended upon the barbaric xenos maintaining their assault, pressing their attack against Vorago. If that attack should falter, then the opportunity would be lost. The deployment of Vindex Lartius would be inconsequential.

The hour of vengeance must await the onslaught of the orks.

THE THUNDER OF anti-aircraft shells burst all around the assault boat as it hurtled above the wasteland. The rattle of shrapnel against the hull formed a persistent clamour, echoing and re-echoing through the craft. The serf-slaves tending the craft looked more like frightened vermin as they tended to their duties.

'What's wrong, flesh-maggot?' Brother Uzraal growled through his helmet at the human he had selected as his current irritation. 'Did you think you would live forever?' The human, shivering from head to toe, tried to ignore the giant's taunts, burying himself in his study of a proximity terminal. It was the worst thing he could have done. Uzraal, feeling slighted, rose from his crash-couch and began to walk towards the man.

'Answer your betters when they speak to you,' Uzraal hissed. The assault boat rocked wildly as flak burst directly below it, but the mag-clamps in the Space Marine's boots made him barely react to the craft's motion.

'Leave it alone, brother,' Pazuriel advised. 'The Flesh isn't worth the effort.'

Uzraal turned and favoured the other Raptor with an icy stare. 'It has forgotten its place. It needs a lesson.'

Pazuriel glanced aside at Baelfegor and Gomorie before replying. 'I was unaware you had taken up slave indoctrination as a vocation,' he said. 'A peculiar secondary specialty for an Iron Warrior. It is fine for Captain Algol, he's a degenerate homicidal sadist with delusions of godhood.' He paused, leaning back as though pondering a sudden revelation. 'Actually, Uzraal, it probably suits you.'

The other Raptors laughed at Uzraal's expense. Uzraal glared back at them as he stalked back to his crash-couch. Battle-brothers bound by duty and obligation, shackled to one another by chains of honour and loyalty. That didn't make them despise each other any less. When he looked at another Iron Warrior, he saw a reflection of himself and there were few in the Legion who liked what he saw.

Captain Rhodaan left his squad to vent their agitation. After a tour along the walls, supporting pathetic contingents of Flesh, they were all eager for real action, a proper deployment that would allow them to use the skills they had been taught. A tactical strike against the enemy, that was the purpose of Raptors, not a demeaning role as nurse-maids to a rabble of puny humans who couldn't even manage a defensive role without help. There was no glory to be had there!

Rhodaan smiled. That was over now. Warsmith Andraaz was unleashing the sword of the Third Grand Company at last! A swift thrust straight into the ork headquarters, and the extermination of the ork warboss. With the head struck from the body, the rest of the xenos horde would collapse, riven by infighting as thousands of petty war-lords vied with one another for control. The death of the warboss would shatter the alien juggernaut and allow the Iron Warriors to pick it apart at their leisure.

There would be no moment of greater import in the entire campaign. Only the thought that he must share the glory with Over-Captain Vallax and his Faceless bothered Rhodaan, though he supposed Skylord Morax would be there too, to try and steal some of the thunder. The Cas-tellax Air Cohort was being deployed in a diversionary assault, attacking the battlefortress from the north while the assault boats struck from the south.

Far below the assault boat, the great swamps of indus-trial sewage beyond Vorago's walls were giving way to the desolation of the desert. Orange dirt, riddled with pollutants and baked into a consistency as tough and unforgiving as cement, stretched away in a great sweep of waste, broken here and there by the blackened smudge of a fallen aircraft. Ork or human, the debris shared a kindred expression of forlorn abandonment. Even the scavenging xenos were unwilling to trek across the bleak wastes for so meagre a prize. The wrecks would linger there for months until wind and pollution broke them apart and added their rusty residue to the dirt.

Beyond the desolation, the sprawl of the alien encamp-ment loomed like the shore of some tainted ocean. A smudge of smog and smoke rose from the camp, defiling even the polluted sky of Castellax. At this distance, the camp was just an indistinct blackness on the horizon, but here and there bright flashes winked amidst the darkness.

The discharge of missile launchers and cannon, the chatter of flak guns and plasma batteries. The orks had noticed the raiders flying towards them across the desert.

As the assault boat was shaken by a nearby burst of flak, Rhodaan considered that Morax's pilots were managing a commendable performance. He could almost picture the Skylord briefing his crews, laying out the parameters of their mission before enjoining them about taking extreme care not to lose any planes in the execution of that mission.

'Distance to target,' Rhodaan snapped at the serf-slave tending the proximity terminal.

'Fi-five kilometres, lord captain,' the human stammered, casting a wary glance in Uzraal's direction as he answered.

Rhodaan turned towards the door in the side of the assault boat, the demi-organic wings of his jump pack unfolding expectantly, knowing that soon the Raptor would again be soaring through the sky. The other members of Squad Kyrith made last minute inspections of their armour and gear, Pazuriel and Baelfegor tending one another's jump packs to ensure the intakes were free of dirt. Uzraal hefted the bulk of his meltagun, conspicuously pointing it in the direction of the human irritation. Gomorie knelt on the deck, scrubbing his tainted hand. The serf-slaves watched the water drip into the metalised flesh, smacking their lips in longing. It had been three months since any of them had tasted real water, forced to subsist off rations of liquid reclamations that had been processed and recycled dozens of times.

'It won't help,' the rolling bellow sounded from deep within the cargo hold. Gomorie looked up to stare at the grotesque hulk of Merihem.

'The virus will win out,' Merihem explained. 'You should embrace your doom. Defying it will only bring you pain.'

Gomorie stood and turned towards the monstrous Obliterator. 'My honour and my duty will sustain me,' he declared.

Merihem laughed, his pallid face exposing its steel teeth. 'So I thought... once.' His body flowed in an undulation of liquefied metal, ropes of raw meat gleaming behind the confusion of plates and wires. 'Accept what is and what will be. All else is... delusion.'

Captain Rhodaan listened to the exchange between the Space Marine and the monster. It was the first time Merihem had spoken since embarking and Rhodaan wasn't sure if that was a good thing. He had read the reports detailing the Obliterator's performance in the ork attack on the perimeter wall. Merihem had single-handedly held a three-kilometre section, accounting for some five hundred xenos casualties. Of course, the reason the abomination had defended his post alone was because he'd also accounted for three hundred janissaries and slave-militia, going so far as to dig the latter from their firing pits.

More and more, Rhodaan was coming to appreciate the kind of beast Merihem was. The virus had wiped out all sense of kinship to the Legion. He suspected that the only thing motivating the Obliterator was some perverse fascination with Gomorie's infection and the Raptor's efforts to overcome it. What would happen if that fascination were to lose its hold was something Rhodaan hoped he wouldn't have to find out. The orks and the schemes of Vallax were enough to worry about, he didn't need the prospect of a blood-mad Obliterator at his back.

'Two kilometres, lord captain,' the serf-slave announced. The assault boat shuddered violently as a flak shell exploded against the fuselage, sending slivers of metal slashing across the cabin. Two humans wilted under the debris, their bodies torn and mangled. Baelfegor grunted in irritation, plucking a six-centimetre chunk of steel from his vambrace. The coagulants in his blood sealed the wound almost immediately.

'Squad Kyrith,' Captain Rhodaan growled, reaching to the door and flinging it open. Wind whipped about him, smoke from the damaged fuselage streaming into the ship. He could see the confused sprawl of the ork encampment whizzing by far below, a jumble of scrap-heaps, bonfires and sheet metal shanties. Here and there, patches of desert burned a rusty orange by the pollutants in the air gaped between the ork bivouacs. Beyond the junkyard sea, like a great island of darkness, towered the enormity of the battlefortress. Rhodaan felt the faintest flicker of doubt as he stared at the cyclopean machine. Grimly, he crushed his uncertainty. He was an Iron Warrior. He would not fail in his duty, whatever obstacles the xenos might put in his way. His voice was an angry snarl as he hissed into his vox-bead. 'Ready for battle.'

'Iron within! Iron without!' the other Raptors roared, marching towards the doorway. One by one, the Space Marines leapt from the assault boat, hurtling into a sky blackened by clouds of flak, plummeting hundreds of metres before igniting their jump packs and launching themselves at the gigantic hull of the battlefortress.

Rhodaan waited until each Iron Warrior was deployed. He hesitated in the doorway, glancing back at Merihem's imposing bulk. 'If the transport can land close enough, I will see you inside, brother.'

'You will see me inside,' Merihem assured him. 'Flesh will not fail Iron,' he assured, his face peeling back in a daemonic leer.

Rhodaan turned his back on the monster, flinging himself out into the polluted sky. As he descended, he felt an uncharacteristic twinge of pity for the crew of the assault boat.

If the orks killed them, they would be lucky men indeed.

WITHOUT WARNING, THE orks resumed their artillery barrage, pounding Vorago even more viciously than before. It was wild, erratic fire, spread throughout the city without any strategy or concentration. Shells exploded in the destroyed Omicron-Sigma with as much frequency as they did within the 'secure' districts beyond the firebreaks. Even the Iron Bastion was victimized, the megalithic tower's void shields crackling with a spectral glow as xenos ordnance detonated against the force field.

Yuxiang covered his ears and opened his mouth as he crouched in the bottom of the firing pit, aping the actions of some janissaries he had seen caught beneath the fury of an artillery strike. He kept his eyes open, however, stubbornly refusing to close them even when smoke and dust skittered through the narrow slit in the wall, coating the slaves inside with a layer of gritty filth. All but deaf from the thundering guns, he was determined he would at least see death when it came for him.

Shenlau, displaying even more stubbornness, kept himself at the firing slit, the lasgun thrust through the opening. The man exhibited such unwavering commitment and resolve that even the Iron Warriors could have found no fault in the slave's courage. With the firebreak itself shaking and trembling under the fury of the barrage, Shenlau maintained his vigil, immovable as a statue, as steadfast as a mountain.

It took Yuxiang several minutes to realise the reason for his companion's composure was that the man was dead. Little beads of blood dripping down the wall, that was his clue. Timidly, he reached out a hand and tugged at Shenlau's leg. When there was no response, he recoiled in disgust. Yuxiang was no stranger to death, no man of Castellax was ever far from its shadow, but to be trapped alone, within the narrow confines of the pit... It was a thing that awakened horror in his mind.

As though sensing Yuxiang's fear, the corpse abruptly lost its poise and toppled from where it had been standing, spilling across the pit and trapping Yuxiang beneath it.

The slave shrieked in terror, squirming under the morbid weight, trying to push it off of him. Every effort was thwarted by the confines of the pit, the corpse invariably striking a wall and sliding back down upon him. Yuxiang could see the grisly gash in Shenlau's forehead where a sliver of shrapnel had split open his skull. A greasy slime of brains and blood oozed from the wound, turning black as it absorbed the ferrocrete dust coating the cadaver's face.

Many horrible minutes passed as Yuxiang struggled with a dead man. It was only by squeezing himself against the back of the wall and using his legs to lever Shenlau to one side that he was finally able to extricate himself from the abhorrent weight. More minutes passed as Yuxiang stared in loathing at the body, trying to force his brain to accept its disgusting presence and closeness.

The violence of the ork artillery began to slacken, dropping from a deafening thunder to a sporadic rumble. The comparative silence came almost as a shock to Yuxiang. Suddenly, it seemed, he could hear again. Faintly, dimly, voices drifted down to him from above. There was another sound as well, a wet, meaty sound that he couldn't account for, but which sent a chill down his spine all the same.

Frightened into action, Yuxiang forgot his loathing of the corpse and instead crouched over it, trying to roll it away from the wall in a frantic search for the lasgun. Shenlau was already starting to grow stiff, making the effort doubly difficult. Only by pressing his entire weight against each leg and breaking it at the knee was Yuxiang finally able to move the corpse and slip past it towards the firing slit.

The lasgun was there! Eagerly Yuxiang grabbed the weapon, his fingers wrapping about its grip with the desperate gentleness of a lover. The sounds drifting down into the pit were closer now, resolving themselves into words.

'Post three-forty-two,' a nasally pitched voice cried out. 'Two conscripts.' There was a pause, then the voice continued. 'Two subjects for disposal. Forward a claim for replacements to central processing.'

Disposal. The word made Yuxiang's stomach lurch. The voice he was hearing belonged to corpse-collectors, making their rounds and fishing the dead from the firing pits.

He looked aside at Shenlau. At least he would soon be spared the noxious company of a corpse. The disposal team would pull him out and then a new conscript would be sent to replace him.

How will that help me? Yuxiang wondered. He stared up at the lip of the pit, watching as shadows began to play across the surface. He hefted the lasgun, aiming upwards. Quickly he lowered the weapon, disabusing himself of the reckless and suicidal impulse. Even if he killed the men in the disposal team, it wouldn't get him out of the pit. Janissaries would just come along and shoot him like a rat for daring to rebel. The most bitter irony was that such a small act of defiance wouldn't even be noticed by the Iron Warriors, rendering the very gesture worthless.

No, the only way Yuxiang could make his life count for something was to survive. To do that, he had to get out of the pit.

Staring at the body of Shenlau, a daring idea came to him. Fighting down his repugnance, he brought his hand sweeping down the corpse's forehead, coating his palm in the dead man's gore. Yuxiang hesitated a moment, staring in disgust at the filth, but the sound of the disposal team marching away from the nearest pit settled his repugnance. In one quick motion, he wiped the crud across his face, then threw himself to the ground.

'Post two-forty-two,' the voice called down. 'Two conscripts.' The corpse-collector peered down into the pit, his features obscured by a brutish gas mask and rebreather. 'Anyone alive down there?' he shouted. He paused a moment, then spoke to his comrades who were just out of sight. 'Two subjects for disposal. Forward a claim for replacements to central processing.'

Behind his mask of gore, Yuxiang watched as a pair of burly, thuggish looking men wearing plastic dusters and ugly breath masks peered down into the pit. In the next moment, one of them produced a long, hook-headed spear. Yuxiang watched in silent horror as the men stabbed the weapon downwards, scraping it along the floor of the pit. He felt the cold steel rasp along his leg, cutting the skin as it progressed towards Shenlau. When the hook was close to the corpse, the man wielding it gave it a deft twist, slipping the barbed curve of the hook up and under the body's arm. There was a revolting, meaty sound as the hook stabbed into the flesh. The next instant, both men were struggling with the spear, pulling it upwards hand-over-hand and dragging the body skewered on the end of the hook out of the pit.

Yuxiang's insides went cold. They were going to do the same to him! He was committed now, he hadn't called out when the overseer asked if anyone was alive. If they found out he was alive, he'd be shot as a coward. Yet if he tried to play dead, the terrible hook would come for him, sticking him like an insect on a pin. Hungry steel would tear his flesh…

There was no other way. He had to escape the pit. What he would do after that, Yuxiang didn't know. All the mattered right now was getting out. Biting down on his own tongue, he waited for the bruisers to return. Now that he had resigned himself to the ordeal, everything seemed to move with excruciating slowness. The hook descended at a slothful rate, sliding clumsily along the floor in its advance. The disposer missed him on the first pass, compelling him to repeat the procedure. Yuxiang braced himself for the agony when the–

It was all he could do to keep from screaming when the blade stabbed into his body, slashing through skin and muscle, lodging itself against bone and sinew. Spots flashed before his eyes, he could hear his own blood pounding in his ears. Consciousness flickered; it was a fight to retain his awareness. If he submitted to the lure of oblivion, he might give himself away by some unconscious action, alerting the disposers that he was alive.

He had to stay awake. He had to stay aware and alert. It was the only way he could be certain.

Then the disposers began to extract him from the pit and all of Yuxiang's weight came to bear on the hook embedded in his body. He thought he knew what pain was, but until that moment, he didn't even have a clue.

His last conscious act was to clench his teeth against the scream he so desperately wanted to utter. Then the red agony overwhelmed him and awareness fled into some dark corner of his being.

Yuxiang didn't see the overseer give him a cursory inspection as he was lifted from the pit. The man saw nothing different about Yuxiang than any of the hundreds of other corpses he had hauled away. With a shrill command, he led the two bruisers to a small, tank-like tractor, its bed piled with human carrion.

'Those last two make a full weight quota,' the overseer said.

The larger of the two disposers dumped Yuxiang unceremoniously on the top of the heap. 'Back to processing?' he asked, his tone making it clear the prospect didn't please him.

'Unless you want to stay around here and wait for the next ork attack,' the overseer said.

That prospect seemed to disturb the disposers even more. Without a glance at their macabre cargo, they closed the gate at the rear of the tractor's bed and scrambled around to the driver's cabin. The combustion engine sputtered noisily into life and the tractor began its long journey into the bowels of Vorago.

An immense cliff of rusted metal, exposed wires, dangling chains and apparently random jumbles of scrap, the hull of the ork battlefortress towered before Captain Rhodaan as he dropped through the smoky sky. It was like a small city, if that city had been designed by an inattentive child with an overabundance of sadistic imagination and a little aptitude for symmetrical construction. Towers rose from slab-like masses of metal in seemingly random disorder, their sides bristling with spikes, guns and pipework gantries. Massive glyphs cut from sheet metal were bolted to every available surface, grinning in brutal glee at the destruction wrought by the aliens. From stem to stern, the battlefortress was nearly five kilometres long, its tallest towers and communication masts reaching at least a kilometre into the sky. Rhodaan could almost weep for the opportunity such a target would have offered their now vanquished orbital defence stations. Something so colossal could have been targeted from orbit with the naked eye and obliterated in a single bombardment.

A veritable curtain of firepower sizzled through the air around Rhodaan; occasionally a lucky shot would strike his power armour, glancing off the thick ceramite plates. It was as well for the Iron Warriors that the heaviest ordnance invariably found its way into the paws of the biggest orks. They were apt to be the most arrogant and belligerent, their vicious enthusiasm rendering their accuracy wild and erratic. Precision was left to the smaller breeds and these were forced to make do with whatever weaponry they could steal or scavenge.

Still, there was always the possibility of some xenos having the wit to take advantage of a human-crafted targeter system. Certain elements within the ork horde had displayed a propensity for aping human strategy and armament. An Iron Warrior did not march through millennia of unending warfare by leaving anything to chance if he could avoid it. As he hurtled through the sky, Rhodaan reached to his belt, thumbing small coin-like discs from the grenade dispenser. Touching their surface, he powered the tiny bombs into action, tossing them into the air around him. Instantly, thick black smoke billowed

SLURRY
PIT

ORAMIS

CHALYBYBIS

MARE
OSSIUS

ISUADIBILIS

CONVALLIS
ROBIGO

A
A A
A
A A

DIRGAS

SLURRY
PIT

VORAGO

OSSA-RIUM

ABORO

OUBLIETTE

CASTELLAX MAP

- ● OUTPOST
- ◉ TOWN
- ● CITY
- ◯ AERODROME

- ▲ MOUNTAINS
- ▬ HILLS
- ⌃ MISSILE MINES
- A SPOIL HEAP
- +++ RAIL TRACKS
- ▭ FORTIFICATIONS

IRON WARRIORS OBLITERATOR

from the discs, choking the sky in inky darkness, further obscuring him from the deranged marksmanship of the orks.

Judging the distance between himself and the battle-fortress, Rhodaan estimated he would need to repeat the procedure one more time. The Space Marine's armoured bulk was dropping much faster than the grenades spewing his smoke screen. In a few seconds he would fall beyond the inky cloud and be exposed to the vision of his enemies.

Within his helmet, Rhodaan smiled coldly. The orks wouldn't take advantage of that brief opportunity. Most of their fire was concentrated on the assault boat. It was typical of the xenos mentality to concentrate their attack on the biggest target, ignoring any other menace until it was too late. Through gaps in the smoke, Rhodaan could see the transport ship, its fuselage aflame, its nose a mass of twisted wreckage. While he watched, the ship smashed into the side of the battlefortress, its wings shorn away instantly by the impact, a great ball of fire welling up around it.

Nothing human could have survived the impact. The thought came to Rhodaan with a mixture of worry and relief, his feelings conflicting with his determination to carry out his mission and achieve his objective.

'Brother Merihem?' Rhodaan transmitted across the inter-squad vox-channel.

There was a moment of silence, then the gruesome crackle of Merihem's voice slithered across the vox. 'I... function,' the Obliterator said.

Rhodaan deployed the second bunch of smoke grenades, exploiting his moment of exposure to orient himself with the layout of the hull. This close to it, he was again reminded of an Imperial cruiser dragged from orbit and cast adrift upon the desert. The similarity gave him inspiration. Before the smoke engulfed him once more, he used his demi-organic wings to steer towards a gun emplacement high upon the machine's central superstructure.

'Hone in on Squad Kyrith's identifier,' Rhodaan ordered. 'Rendezvous with us at your first opportunity.'

Rhodaan could hear the chatter of gunfire across the vox-channel. 'I obey,' Merihem replied, his words almost drowned out by screaming aliens in the background.

No need to tell the Obliterator to kill everything in his way, telling the monster to do anything else would have been the problem. If they had sent a rabid tyranid hive tyrant rampaging through the belly of the battlefortress, the Raptors could have asked for no better diversion. Merihem would march through the orks like some primordial devil, flinging death at anything that dared show its face. The orks, with that wonderfully simple, savage lust for combat, would converge upon the marauding monster by the hundreds.

While the xenos were trying to stop Merihem, they would expose and neglect other sections of the battlefortress, easing the progress of the Raptors. In the long run, it was of no consequence if the orks destroyed Merihem or not, by drawing the aliens to him, the Obliterator would have served his purpose.

Rhodaan's diving form ploughed through the last stretch of smoke. The Iron Warrior's wings unfurled, arresting his descent almost instantaneously. He found himself directly above his objective, the flattened paddock where the orks had slapped together a flak battery. Leathery green faces gawped at him in surprise.

The armoured giant didn't give the aliens a chance to recover from their shock. His plasma pistol blazed in his hand as he fired into the ork gunners, the super-heated gas melting through organ and bone with the ferocity of an enraged sun. Mortally wounded aliens collapsed in shuddering heaps, upsetting the belts of ammunition strewn about the platform.

Descending the final few metres to the deck in a

graceful dip, Rhodaan's boot crunched down on the skull of a mangled ork, grinding it into pulp. Folding his wings, Rhodaan fired his pistol at an ork huddled behind one of the flak guns, spraying the alien's face with molten metal as the shot scorched along the creature's cover. The injured ork hopped away, one paw covering its melted face while it fired blindly with the massive stub-pistol clenched in its other hand. A second shot of plasma settled the alien, dropping its steaming carcass over the railing which bounded the platform on three sides. Rhodaan could hear its coarse scream as it plunged down the side of the battlefortress to the desert far below.

'Squad Kyrith, report,' Rhodaan snarled over the vox, spinning as another lurking ork came rushing at him from behind a flat-bedded ammo cart. The alien's momentum kept its body plunging towards the Iron Warrior even after a ball of plasma evaporated most of its head. Rhodaan side-stepped as the ork neared him, letting the corpse pitch over the side and hurtle after its comrade.

'Brother Pazuriel. Have effected entry at missile emplacement one hundred metres east of your position.'

'Brother Gomorie. Securing maintenance corridor fifty metres west.'

One after another, the other members of his squad reported to him across the vox. Rhodaan fitted each of their positions to the map he was drawing inside his brain. The cogitator inside his data-slate would perform the same function, but he knew no machine could ever match the mentality of a legionary. Cogitators could provide logistics and summations but they did not possess a Space Marine's experience or the intuition born from the cauldron of war.

A hoarse bellow of rage brought Rhodaan sweeping towards the side of the gun emplacement. The egress hacked into the side of the hull opened with a hiss, exposing a massive ork with steel-capped tusks and an enormous steam-driven spanner clutched in its paws.

Coldly, the Iron Warrior fired his pistol full into the alien's face, then pushed the twitching body to one side. Beyond the dead ork was a long corridor, its deck uneven, a motley confusion of doors and stairs opening into it almost at random.

Almost, but not quite. Rhodaan could see the echo of a familiar pattern, as though he was peeling away layers of vandalism to peer at the defiled original. He felt no fear as a rabble of aliens came rushing down the corridor, barking and shooting as they came. Calmly, he aimed his pistol and began picking off the maddened brutes.

'Squad Kyrith,' Rhodaan growled into his vox. 'Make your way into the central superstructure. This machine is based on the deckplan of a Dictator-class cruiser. Our objective will likely have established itself in the section analogous to the command deck.'

Rhodaan ducked back through the egress as a howling ork tried to incinerate him with a blast from a flamer. Sheets of fire exploded through the doorway as he pressed himself against the hull. As soon as the flames subsided, he thumbed a grenade from his belt and tossed it down the corridor. No smoke grenade this time but a deadly explosive designed to send tiny shrapnel fragments into the enemy. In the aftermath of the ensuing explosion, pained shrieks sounded from the corridor.

'Converge upon the wardroom,' Rhodaan ordered as he strode back into the hallway, marching through the dead and dying wreckage of orks. 'We will assemble there before making our attack on the command deck.'

A wounded ork clawed at Rhodaan's boot, its fanged face leering at him vengefully. The Iron Warrior glared down at the alien. Viciously, he pressed the barrel of his plasma pistol against its forehead, using the white-hot heat of the gun itself to burn a hole through the ork's head.

'Keep a watch for Squad Vidarna,' he hissed, watching with satisfaction as the ork thrashed beneath him, struggling to remove the heated gun barrel searing through its skull. 'This objective belongs to us. I will not share the glory with anyone.' The tortured ork at last became still beneath Rhodaan's grip. The Iron Warrior rose, staring at its bleeding husk.

How much more satisfying, he thought, if he could do the same to Over-Captain Vallax.

After the mission was accomplished, of course. Anything before then would be more than premature.

It could be construed as treacherous.

CHAPTER XIII
I-Day Plus Ninety-Three

WITH A DEAFENING roar, the massive ork charged across the debris-littered 'wardroom' of the battlefortress. The huge alien was easily head and shoulders above any of the Iron Warriors, its bulky build making it vastly more massive as well. Despite the crudity of the mega-armour which encased its body, there was a sensation of power behind it that was undeniable. The brute smashed its way through the bullet-scarred wreckage of a steel-plated workbench and machinist's shop, sending a weird assembly of tools clattering about the chamber.

Bolt-shells smacked into the onrushing juggernaut, gouging craters in its heavy armour and sending a spray of molten metal blobs flying in every direction. The brute simply grunted, its face locked behind the fanged mask of its helmet, speakers mounted in its shoulder plates magnifying the sound into a pulsating bellow. Lifting one of its enormous arms, the ork sent a withering stream of fire crashing across the room, blasting apart piles of scrap metal and coils of wire, pulverising heaps of scavenged machinery and the husks of half-formed armaments.

The Iron Warriors of Squad Vidarna were there, amid the junkyard confusion, seizing whatever cover they could to protect themselves from the crazed ork's barrage. For once, Vallax and his Faceless didn't dare show their own faces.

From the doorway, Captain Rhodaan watched as the chaotic mixture of bullets, shells and slugs erupting from the ork's combi-weapon chewed away Vallax's cover. The Over-Captain had chosen a solid refuge, a jumble of armour plate looted by the orks from a mag-lev train. The solidity of his shelter, however, wasn't doing him much good as the seemingly inexhaustible barrage sent slivers of metal flying in every direction. The other Raptors of Squad Vidarna were likewise pinned down, kept in check by the ork warriors supporting their massive champion, chief among them a cigar-chomping creature with a heavy bolter clutched in its paws, a hopper lashed to its side feeding a continuous belt of ammunition into the gun.

It was a sore temptation to leave Vallax and his Raptors to their fate. The Over-Captain or one of his henchmen had listened in on Squad Kyrith's frequency and attempted to beat them to the prize. Rhodaan wondered how they were enjoying their stolen glory now. Vallax had made one severe error in his calculations. He'd taken the reference to a wardroom too literally. Instead of finding a bivouac for the ork warboss and its lieutenants, he'd instead stumbled onto a makeshift machine shop, a catch-all armoury and repair centre for the clique of alien mekaniks who maintained the battlefortress.

There was always a danger of underestimating the ork as an enemy. Crude, primitive, often near mindless in its brutality, there existed within the hordes aberrant individuals of terrible potency. Some of these orks exhibited their advanced mentality through use of specialised tactics, others were potent psykers who tapped into the gestalt consciousness of their breed to manifest hideous exhibitions of witchery. The mekboyz were another example of the same aberrancy, cobbling together machines and weapons of astounding capability from nothing but scraps and oddments. Their weaponry might be laughably slapdash in appearance, but at the same time exhibit qualities unrivalled by anything to emerge from the manufactorum of a tech-priest.

Vallax was finding that out now. So eager to prevent his rival from accomplishing the objective, he was now faced with a bigger fight than he had anticipated.

Rhodaan thumbed the intensity setting on his plasma pistol to its highest node, then glanced back at the other members of Squad Kyrith. Brother Uzraal had yet to rendezvous with them, but had encountered the others while making his way to the wardroom. He could feel their eyes studying him, could almost read the thoughts stirring in their heads. They would stand beside him if he chose to abandon Squad Vidarna, he knew that, it would be their secret. But that secret would become a taint from which there could be no recovery. He would lose their respect, and with that respect his squad would lose its discipline and cohesiveness. It would become like Squad Vidarna, a pack of cut-throat opportunists always on the lookout for some advantage to exploit for their own personal benefit. Which of them, he wondered, would be the first to plot against him the way the half-breed Uhlan intrigued against Vallax.

'On my mark,' Rhodaan told his Raptors. 'Gomorie, your initial target is the ork with the heavy bolter. Pazuriel, you take the one in red flak armour with the stubber. Baelfegor, the one with the flamer. After you eliminate your initial targets, employ your own discretion.' He glanced back into the room. 'Leave the big one to me.'

Without further preamble, the Iron Warriors of Squad Kyrith exploded into the room. Focused upon the Space Marines they had pinned down, the xenos were taken by surprise, their shock further increased when explosive bolt-shells detonated the bodies of their comrades. Rhodaan's Raptors did not linger over their triumphs, but immediately dived for cover, firing as they went. Assaulting the alien flank, they caught many of the orks in the open, cutting them down before they had a chance to react.

Captain Rhodaan had only a dim impression of Squad Vidarna rallying to the changing situation, leaping from their own cover to charge the embattled xenos. In that initial burst of violence, his attention was focused on the hulking ork mekboy in the mega-armour. The supercharged shot from his plasma pistol seared across the room, sending a heat-haze ripple in its wake. At its highest intensity, Rhodaan had used his weapon to burn through the hatches of a battleship. However thick the ork's armour, he knew it would make short work of the metal plates and quickly incinerate the alien inside.

It was the Iron Warrior's turn to be surprised and curse himself for underestimating his foe. The shot from his plasma pistol struck true, directly into the ork's side. At least the shot would have struck true, if not for the coruscating blue sheen that suddenly surrounded the creature, distorting the ball of energy and draining away much of its impetus. Instead of burning clean through the ork, by the time the shot passed through the force field, all it could manage was to blacken the garishly painted plates and melt a few exposed tubes.

The mekboy swung around, bellowing its war cry. Rhodaan threw himself flat as the brute opened fire, the deadly assortment of bullets and shells smacking into the floor around him. As he rolled behind the momentary shelter of a metal crate stuffed with scrap, he holstered his expended pistol. It would take the weapon nearly a minute to build another charge in its power coil. Until then, he would have to make do with his chainsword.

Slugs tore apart Rhodaan's shelter, shredding the crate

as though it had been cobbled together from sheet-tin. Instead of dodging around the side of the crate, The Raptor leapt over the top, using his demi-organic wings to hurl himself at the mekboy in a sudden pounce. His chainsword came whirling down at the ork's head before the alien could react.

Again, the ork's force field saved it. As the chainsword's whirring edge descended along with Rhodaan's lunge, its momentum was foiled by the resistance of the field. It was like trying to cleave through water, the crackling energy trying to throw back the blade. Only the tremendous strength of a Space Marine and the powerful servo-motors in Rhodaan's armour could have prevailed. Even then the reward was scant. The edge of the chainsword clove through the mask of the ork's helmet, exposing the alien's scarred face and fanged leer.

The next instant, the mekboy struck back, swatting Rhodaan with the enormous hammer clenched in its fist. The Raptor was dashed to the floor by the savage blow, his body shuddering from the impact despite the protective layers of plasteel and ceramite. Instantly, he tried to roll away, but before he could move, the mekboy's steel-shod boot was pressing down on him.

A grotesque grin split the beast's face as it aimed its combi-weapon at the Space Marine trapped under its heel.

It was the moment of a heartbeat before the ork's expression changed. From sadistic triumph, the mekboy's face collapsed into confused agony. Deep red blood oozed from the corners of its mouth, the hand holding the ponderous combi-weapon fell limp at its side. With a groan, the huge ork slumped to its knees, then crashed onto its face.

Over-Captain Vallax stood above the slaughtered ork, strips of shredded metal and green flesh clinging to the teeth of his chainaxe. For a moment, he stared down at Rhodaan.

Rhodaan stared back at his commander. There was no gratitude in his hearts for the other Iron Warrior's assistance. He had come to Vallax's aid out of a sense of duty and to maintain control over his squad. Vallax had helped him out of something even less noble. The Over-Captain simply wanted to show Rhodaan that he was still the better warrior.

The moment passed. Rhodaan regained his feet. The swift intervention of Squad Kyrith and the charge of Squad Vidarna had been too much for the orks to overcome. In short order, the room had been secured. Before Vallax's chainaxe settled the mekboy, the lesser xenos were already being mopped up.

'Our target should be behind that bulkhead,' Vallax announced, gesturing with the still buzzing head of his axe at the left wall. 'At least if your interpretation of the design of this place is correct.'

Inwardly, Rhodaan bristled under the hostile remark. There was no mistaking Vallax's intention. If the warboss was on the other side, then the Over-Captain would take credit for its extermination. If the target wasn't there, then he would lay the blame squarely on Rhodaan's shoulders. Whichever way things turned out, he would be the loser.

Brother Uhlan stepped forwards, making a cursory examination of the bulkhead door. The half-breed shook his head in disgust as he inspected the crude locking mechanism, a deranged network of analogue locks requiring an equally deranged confusion of keys.

'Step aside, half-seed,' Uzraal's voice snarled across the inter-squad channel. Uhlan didn't hesitate, diving aside as the other Iron Warrior fired into the locks with a blast from his meltagun. In the blink of an eye, the mechanism was dripping down the face of the door.

Rhodaan turned and regarded the last member of his squad. Uzraal's armour was spattered in gore, one of his pauldrons twisted and crumpled from some terrific impact. The Raptor favoured his left leg, displaying a noticeable limp as he marched across the chamber.

'You are late, brother,' Rhodaan reprimanded him.

Uzraal hesitated, glancing from Rhodaan to Vallax and back again. 'I apologise, lord captain. I encountered more resistance in my descent than anticipated.'

'An Iron Warrior makes no excuses,' Vallax sneered. 'Captain Rhodaan, you and this man will maintain this position and safeguard our withdrawal. The rest of Squad Kyrith will provide support for my assault against the command deck.' The Over-Captain's fingers tightened ever so slightly around the grip of his chainaxe.

Rhodaan bit down on his offended pride. 'I obey,' he stated. 'This position will be held.'

There was a slight swagger in Vallax's motion as he turned away, the only hint of the victorious gloating that must be dominating the Over-Captain's thoughts.

'Malfas! Nazdrav!' Vallax shouted. Two of his squad snapped to attention, rushing to the bulkhead when their commander gestured at it with his axe. 'Help Uhlan get that door open!'

Before the Space Marines could converge upon the door and drag it open with their combined strength, the portal burst inwards in a shower of sparks and smoke. The mangled body of an ork crumpled across the fallen door.

Both squads drew back in alarm, levelling their weapons at the doorway, uncertain of what they should expect. Something immense and monstrous loomed out from the smoke.

'Mission accomplished... brothers,' the grisly tones of Merihem oozed across the vox. The Obliterator emerged from the smoke, his hideous body rippling with unclean life at each step. Arrogantly, the monster lifted his hand, displaying the decapitated head of a truly gigantic ork. 'You may tell Andraaz that his opposite number has been subtracted.' The black eyes in the little pallid face narrowed, lips exposing steel fangs. 'I have honoured my obligations to the Legion.'

Vallax advanced towards the Obliterator. 'You are under my command, abomination,' he said. 'While you are, you will show Warsmith Andraaz proper respect.'

Merihem stalked forwards, his arm lengthening into a cluster of missile tubes. 'Respect is earned... not given,' the monster snarled.

'Your obligations to the Legion have yet to be satisfied,' Rhodaan declared. Vallax seemed oblivious to how close Merihem really was to completely losing control. In such close quarters, it was quite possible the Obliterator could kill all of them before the monster could be brought down.

Merihem transferred his angry glare from Vallax to Rhodaan. He hefted the ork head in his hand. 'The warlord is dead,' he stated.

'But the Waaagh! itself has not been broken,' Rhodaan pointed out. 'While the aliens yet infest Castellax, it is your duty to destroy them.'

The Obliterator's armoured body writhed in angry agitation, its hand lengthening into talons that pierced the ork's head, then split it into sections with a twitch of his fingers. The gory fragments plopped to the floor, smashed into pulp as Merihem marched across them.

'I can bide my time,' Merihem promised. He paused beside the body of the mekboy. The missile launcher melted back into the substance of his arm as he reached down to the corpse. There was a cruel grin on the Obliterator's face as he caressed the confused mess of the ork's combi-weapon. Before the amazed eyes of the other Iron Warriors, the weapon began to disintegrate under Merihem's touch, its every particle being absorbed back into the monster's body. In less than a minute, the combi-weapon was gone. A few seconds later, something very much like it was taking shape on the Obliterator's forearm.

Vallax stormed past the hulking Merihem, the rest of Squad Vidarna following close behind him. 'Keep that abomination away from me, Rhodaan,' he snarled.

Rhodaan smiled at the order. Even if he knew how, he didn't think he would.

Some opportunities were too good to squander.

WHAT LITTLE LIGHT filtered down into the cargo bed of the tractor was coloured a dull crimson by the blood dripping into Yuxiang's eyes. It was the blood of dead men, stacked twelve high and five deep, a mangled monument to the savagery of the orks and the callousness of the Iron Warriors. The stink of mortification threatened to choke the slave, turning each breath into an agony of nausea and disgust. The weight of the bodies piled above him threatened to crush him like a slag-roach.

Squirming through the carrion heap, worming his body between torn fragments of flesh, Yuxiang worked his way towards the light. His passage was eased somewhat by the knife he had discovered hidden in the boot of a dead janissary. One stroke of luck weighed against the hours of horror since his ordeal began.

The light became more vivid as Yuxiang thrust his head from the corpses. Immediately he drew a deep breath, filling his lungs with air that hadn't been filtered through the stinking wreckage of men. Even the polluted taint of Vorago's atmosphere was a welcome relief. He closed his eyes, savouring the moment, then drew a second breath. An anxious giggle slipped between his teeth as his mind joined his body in the indulgence.

It was the sound of the disposal crew that snapped Yuxiang back from his idyll, the first tentacles of madness slithering back into the depths of his brain. Quickly he lowered his head and tightened his grip on the knife, watching as the masked corpse-collectors came marching around the back of the slow-moving tractor.

Raising a face made monstrous by his gas mask, one of the disposers made a hurried examination of their surroundings. The tractor had trundled its way deep into the subterranean bowels of Vorago, driving along one of the massive underground roads that connected all of the city's principal buildings. A great tunnel, fifty metres wide and half again as tall, the passage was formed from great slabs of ferrocrete reinforced with steel columns and braces. Light came from chemical lamps bolted into the ceiling at regular intervals, their illumination flickering in sympathy to the ork barrage, which could be felt even at this depth.

The disposer made his inspection, then raised a gloved hand. 'All clear,' he announced, his voice muffled by the mask. 'No sign of Steel Blood.'

Mention of the gruesome skull-spies of the Iron Warriors caused the other disposer to shudder visibly beneath his plastic duster. He cast a nervous glance over his shoulder, then stared at his comrade. 'Let's be quick,' he said, anxiety robbing his voice of all authority.

The first disposer didn't answer, instead grabbing hold of a metal handgrip and climbing onto the back step of the slow-moving transport. As soon as he was aboard, he began prodding and poking the heap of bodies, shifting them around as best he could with a length of pipe. As the black boot of a janissary emerged from beneath the pile, he gave a grunt of pleasure. Immediately he fell upon the boot, savagely pulling at it, trying to wrench it free.

'Body's gone stiff!' the ghoul complained.

'Then break the bones,' the overseer snarled back, again glancing nervously at the tunnel behind them. 'Don't be squeamish.'

The ghoul muttered a curse beneath his breath, then began to viciously pound the corpse's foot with his pipe. Yuxiang wasn't sure if it was imagination, but he seemed to hear a dull crunch accompany each blow.

'This would be easier if you'd let us stop,' the ghoul snapped, continuing to hammer the foot.

'You explain why we're stopped if somebody from processing comes along,' the overseer growled at him. 'Now just focus on what you're doing!'

A cry of triumph came from the scavenger as the boot finally slipped free from the shattered foot. Tucking his trophy under one arm, he began shoving bodies aside to reach the corpse's other leg. Jubilation turned to rage as he found himself staring at a charred stump that ended well above the knee.

'Deacon!' the ghoul cried out. 'Did you notice any loose legs when we were loading up?'

The overseer spun around, distracted from another of his paranoid inspections of the tunnel. 'No,' came the curt answer. 'Only big bits. No pieces. You should know, you lugged them onto the tractor.'

'I thought maybe somebody might have chipped in and tossed the small stuff on while I was busy,' the scavenger cursed.

Deacon's shrill voice became thin and sharp. 'Nobody helps disposal. You know that.'

Angrily, the ghoul took the lone boot from beneath his arm and hurled it into the darkness.

'You shouldn't have done that,' Deacon scolded him. 'Processing Omega could have used that.'

'To the warp with Processing Omega!' the scavenger growled back. He raised the heavy pipe, bringing it crashing down into the skull of a body only a few centimetres from Yuxiang. This time there was no imagination when the hidden slave heard bones shatter. 'I'd like to do that to every one of those sump-vermin!'

Deacon's expression became frightened behind his mask. Nervously, he spun around, watching the tunnel. 'Talk like that and they'll take you to Processing Omega,' he hissed. 'The rest of us too, just for being associated with you.'

The ghoul chuckled, the sound made even more inhuman by his mask. 'Maybe we could all share the same paste-tube,' he joked.

The blood seemed to drain out of Yuxiang's body as he heard the two disposers talk, his mind refusing to accept the obscenity the ghouls were discussing. It couldn't be possible! It was too vile to believe, even of the most monstrous tyrants!

Paste. Processing. No, it couldn't happen, couldn't be real! Even the Iron Warriors wouldn't do such a thing!

Yet with every word that passed between the bickering scavengers, Yuxiang felt his resistance crumble. The monstrosity was true, the Iron Warriors were that inhuman. The fiendish reality was that the lords of Castellax viewed their human slaves as nothing but cattle and, like cattle, they thought nothing of harvesting their flesh. A staple of the rations being issued to the defenders of Vorago, the tubes of protein-paste were created from the bodies of their own dead!

With acceptance of that abominable fact, an even more terrifying realisation seized Yuxiang. The tractor, the cargo he had allowed himself to become a part of, it was on its way to Processing Omega. These weren't bodies piled around him but slabs of meat destined to be rendered down into core nutrients and proteins, dissolved into shapeless mush to be injected into foil tubes and issued to millions of starving wretches!

Horror overwhelmed fatigue, injury, caution – every handicap that might have restrained Yuxiang in that moment. Like a maddened berserker, the slave thrust himself from the pile of corpses, exploding upon the disposers in a burst of violence that might have impressed an ork. The scavenger on the cargo bed was just turning around when Yuxiang's knife licked out, raking across his face with an almost psychotic strength. The ghoul shrieked, clutching at his slashed mask and the gory debris bubbling up from behind it. Yuxiang eviscerated him with a backhanded slash and kicked the body from the bed.

The mutilated man slammed into the trailing Deacon, smashing the overseer to the ground. Yuxiang leapt down after his first victim, intent upon claiming his second when the tractor suddenly lurched to a halt.

Spinning around, the slave saw the driver come charging back from the cab, a cudgel-like maintenance tool clenched in his fist. Yuxiang didn't give the man time to close with him, but instead rushed forwards to meet him. Long accustomed to the brutality of Prefect Wyre and his slavemasters, Yuxiang barely reacted to the blow that crashed against his shoulder as the driver struck at him. It was the only blow the man would strike and he had wasted it.

Again, the knife flashed in Yuxiang's hand, ripping through the disposer's duster and stabbing deep between his ribs. The driver screamed into his mask, flailing on the point of the blade. Throwing an arm about the struggling man, Yuxiang drew him closer, burying the blade still deeper in the man's body.

As soon as he felt the man's struggles falter, Yuxiang tore his blade free and let the driver collapse. Immediately, he turned and sprinted towards the back of the tractor, intent on finishing the third disposer.

The last of the corpse collectors had finally freed himself from the dying weight of his comrade. The eyes above Deacon's gas mask became wide with fright as he saw Yuxiang's blood-coated form looming above him. Desperately, he lifted his hands to ward off the murderous apparition.

'No! Don't do it!' the disposer wailed.

Yuxiang glared down at him, the slave's face pulling back in merciless contempt. 'You help them feed us our own dead!' he shrieked, raising the knife and pouncing on the man.

Displaying unanticipated agility, Deacon rolled away from the maddened slave, darting beneath the bed of the tractor. Cringing against the treads, he shouted at Yuxiang. 'I was only following orders. I was just doing what I was told to do!'

Yuxiang reached beneath the tractor, slashing at the disposer with his knife. 'Now I'm telling you to die!' he yelled.

Deacon recoiled from his attacker, manoeuvring to keep the treads between himself and Yuxiang. 'I'm sorry!' he shrieked. 'We didn't know you were alive.' He squirmed away from a savage lunge, retreating towards the underside of the cab. 'Don't kill me, I can help you! Stop! Listen to me!'

Yuxiang hesitated, staring hard into the disposer's eyes. There was no guile there, only raw terror. Nor was that fear directed solely at the man trying to knife him. Even now, Deacon kept glancing anxiously at the tunnel around them. Yuxiang remembered what the man had said about the Steel Blood. Almost against his will, he felt sympathy for the disposer. Even if the man appreciated the horror of what he was doing, there was nothing he could do about it. If he tried, the Iron Warriors would just kill him and put someone else in his place.

Noticing his attacker falter, Deacon continued to plead with him. 'I can help you,' he insisted. 'If you kill me and run off, they'll look for you. I can keep that from happening.'

'How?' Yuxiang asked, suspicion in his tone.

Deacon gestured towards the back of the tractor where one of the dead disposers lay. 'Put on Zhang's gear. They'll think you are him down at Processing Omega.' Even through the blood coating his features, Deacon could see Yuxiang's doubtful scowl. 'It's the only way,' he declared. 'They won't notice and I won't tell them. If they found out, I'd be shot for lying to them.'

'You wouldn't have a chance to get shot,' Yuxiang promised, fingering his knife.

Deacon nodded in understanding. 'However you want it,' he said. 'But we have to hurry. The Steel Blood might be around any time. Get into Zhang's gear.'

'What about the other man?' Yuxiang said, gesturing with his knife at the driver.

'I'll hide his gear and we can dump the body into the tractor along with Zhang,' Deacon sighed as he saw the horror that flashed through Yuxiang's eyes. 'If they find bodies in the tunnel, they'll know something happened. Nobody will question a few more kilograms delivered to Processing.'

Feeling sick to his stomach, Yuxiang had to bend to Deacon's logic. Keeping his eyes on the disposer, he made his way back to the first man he had killed and started to strip the corpse. 'How will you explain the driver?'

Deacon was already out from under the tractor, frantically unlacing the driver's boots. 'I can drive the tractor,' he said. 'We'll report that Wang had a breakdown and fled into the tunnels.' He paused, shaking his head. 'It happens a lot to disposers. Takes a certain mentality to do this sort of work. They'll send a patrol to look for him, but of course they won't find anything.' He hesitated again as another thought occurred to him. 'What will you do after we reach Processing Omega?'

Yuxiang smiled grimly. 'I'll stick with you,' he promised. 'Just to make sure you stay honest.'

'You'll have to see some horrible things,' Deacon warned. 'Nobody knows how bad the Iron Warriors are until they've seen Processing Omega.'

The comment sent a chill down Yuxiang's spine, a chill that seemed to spread to his heart. Instead of making him shudder, however, it seemed to pour strength into his veins. 'Maybe the orks will destroy those monsters,' he said, then looked up and stared into Deacon's eyes. 'Or maybe that job is up to us.'

Deacon froze, a haunted look creeping into his eyes. He wondered if Yuxiang was slipping from lucidity back into madness.

Yuxiang was oblivious to the disposer's scrutiny. 'Tell me,' he said, 'how well do you know these tunnels?'

THE SUN'S POLLUTED rays glared down upon the scrap yard wasteland of the ork encampment, seemingly eager to illuminate the carnage unfolding amidst the wreckage.

Over-Captain Vallax's chainaxe screamed as he brought it cleaving through the metre-long blades reaching out for him. In a shower of sparks and smoke, the savaged metal was cleft asunder, falling into the toxic desert sand. The arm behind the industrial shears recoiled as though in pain.

Vallax rounded upon his adversary, a hulking cylinder of steel mounted on a pair of piston-driven hydraulic legs. From either side of the cylinder, a mechanised arm protruded, the left mounting a massive cannon, the right equipped with the torn remains of a set of power shears. The crude semblance of a snarling face had been painted across the cylindrical hull, a long visor-like gash serving as its eyes. Behind the gash, real eyes, beady yellow orbs, stared.

There had been four of the 'killa kans' when the Iron Warriors were first ambushed. The machines had been lurking behind a pile of scrap within the ork encampment, seemingly just another jumble of junk. At least until they had lurched upwards in obscene life and started firing on the Space Marines.

That had been their first mistake. With their cannons, the killa kans could have kept the Raptors at a distance, denying them the close-quarters combat at which they excelled. By waiting until their enemies were right on top of them, the xenos had woefully overestimated their own strength.

Malfas had claimed the first of the machines, blowing off one of its legs with a krak grenade and then ripping open its hull with his power fist. The alien operator, a wizened little gretchin that had been hard-wired into the killa kan, shrieked as it was forcibly removed from the cockpit. Its shrieks grew louder when Malfas dashed its brains out against the cylindrical hull.

Uzraal took the second killa kan, his meltagun scorching a hole clean through the hull and causing its promethium-fuelled engine to explode. The wreckage had staggered for a few moments, even managing to fire a few wild shots into the air before it finally slumped over and was still.

The third and fourth machines had become the objectives of Vallax and Rhodaan, the two commanders taking it as a matter of pride to outdo each other. Both of them had warned away the other Iron Warriors, determined to tackle the enemy alone. While Vallax duelled with his foe, picking it apart piecemeal with his chainaxe, Rhodaan scored the hull of his adversary with quick shots from his plasma pistol, trying to angle around to the killa kan's engine.

Since their withdrawal from the battlefortress, the Iron Warriors had been subjected to almost constant attack. The anticipated confusion and disorder from the death of their warlord had yet to manifest among the orks. Vallax laid it down to a simple cause – the presence of Space Marines in the alien camp. With an enemy in their midst, the orks had a common cause to provide them with cohesion and unity of purpose. Once that cause was eliminated, then the brutes would fall to fighting among themselves to determine the new warboss.

It was a theory that supported the facts, though Rhodaan wasn't going to let himself and his men be slaughtered just to prove Vallax right. The only course of action was a speedy extraction from the ork camp, but with air supremacy questionable, extraction was something the Raptors would have to attend to on their own. Short, controlled jumps across the ork camp had drained their packs of fuel, forcing them to make the last leg of their retreat on foot, repelling enraged aliens every step of the way.

Rhodaan dived as his enemy finally opened fire with its cannon. The gretchin inside the killa kan was panicking now that half its comrades were destroyed. In that panic, it could only focus on a limited range of action. By finally goading it into using the cannon, Rhodaan could ignore the menace of the power shears, at least for a few seconds.

A few seconds were all he needed. Throwing himself in a long slide that carried him between the killa kan's stomping legs, Rhodaan fired a blast from his plasma pistol into the underside of the machine's engine. The point-blank shot quickly bore results, thick black smoke billowing from the engine and little flames flickering from rents in the hull. The killa kan swung around, its shears snapping at Rhodaan as the Iron Warrior withdrew. Blasting a vicious bellow across its loudspeakers, the machine started to pursue him. After a few steps however, the bellows turned to squeals. Flames were now spewing from all over the hull, fires raging inside the killa kan. Pursuit degenerated into frantic flight as the gretchin cooked within its own machine. Its blind panic drove it into a stack of ruined battlewagons which toppled on top of the killa kan, burying it completely.

Rhodaan turned away from his victory to see Vallax bringing down his own enemy, sawing through a hatch on its hull, then driving the blade of the axe deep inside to pulp the gretchin within. Greasy blood and gobs of flesh churned from the exposed hatchway, spattering Vallax's armour.

The Over-Captain stared across the wreckage, observing the smoke rising from where Rhodaan's own foe was buried. With an angry shift of his shoulder, he pulled the chainaxe away, glaring sullenly at the whirring blade. 'Brother Nazdrav,' he growled across the vox. 'This weapon is no longer functioning at peak efficiency. You will provide me with yours.'

Rhodaan could see Nazdrav's hand clench into a fist as his commander issued the order, but the Raptor knew better than to question Vallax. Dutifully, he marched to the Over-Captain's side and exchanged his sword for the gore-crusted axe.

'Our ingress to Vorago is two kilometres east,' Vallax announced across the inter-squad channel, gesturing past the piled wreckage with his new sword. 'There is an old drainage pipe. We will cut our way in and employ it to re-enter the city.' The Over-Captain paused, turning to stare at Rhodaan.

'Captain,' Vallax resumed. 'Without the benefit of a jump pack, it seems Brother Merihem has fallen behind. You will provide a rearguard to lead him to the extraction point.'

Rhodaan glared at the Over-Captain, visualising the smirk on Vallax's scarred face. 'Warsmith Andraaz will require every Iron Warrior he can get when he goes on the offensive,' he pointed out.

Vallax nodded. 'Precisely why I want you to recover Brother Merihem. If you do not feel up to the task, however, I am certain we can explain your failure to the Warsmith.'

'There will be no need, Over-Captain,' Rhodaan announced. 'I will stay here and await Merihem.'

'Excellent, captain,' Vallax declared. He waved his arm, motioning the Raptors of Squad Kyrith and Squad Vidarna forwards. 'When you rendezvous with Merihem, lead him back to the drainage pipe. Unless there is danger of the orks exploiting the breach, we will leave the way open for you.'

Rhodaan watched as the Iron Warriors withdrew beyond the scrap yard, listening to the sounds of gunfire as they fended off isolated pockets of aliens. Vallax's last words echoed in his mind, taunting him with their barely disguised malice.

Whatever else happened, he was certain of one thing. He was going to need to find his own way back inside Vorago.

CHAPTER XIV

I-Day Plus Ninety-Four

TAOFANG SCRAMBLED FOR shelter as the clunky ork fighter swept along the wall, strafing anything that moved. The deranged xenos pilot flew its craft so low that he could see its fanged face leering from behind the glass cowling, its mouth gaping in raucous laughter. Heavy bolters, secured to the fighter's wings with loops of chain, chattered incessantly, their vibrations making the plane wobble ridiculously as it streaked overhead. By all the rules of logic, there was no way such a crude patchwork of scrap should be able to fly, yet fly it did, well enough to slaughter the men posted along the firebreak.

'Taofang! Here!'

The janissary spun as he heard Mingzhou call him. He could just see the wild cascade of her crimson hair peaking above the lip of a firing pit. He gave one last desultory glance at the embrasure he had been sprinting towards, then dashed towards the pit. There was a lot a Scorpion could learn from a Jackal, it seemed. Not least of which was that in a crisis it paid to think beyond one's training.

A second ork fighter came screaming down from the sky, stitching the surface of the firebreak with high-impact rounds. Flecks of ferrocrete exploded from the wall. The effect upon the men caught in the path of the automatic fire was more dramatic. Soldiers jerked and writhed like puppets, flailing obscenely before sprawling across the ground like heaps of bloodied rags.

Bullets smacked at his very heels as Taofang rushed to the pit. Without bothering to even look at what he was doing, he threw himself down into the hole, somehow twisting around in his descent so that he found himself staring upwards when the xenos plane went sailing above the mouth of the pit.

'If I knew you were going to kick me in the eye, I would have let the orks shoot you,' Mingzhou complained. 'And if you want to keep that hand, then you'd better move it.'

Experiencing a pang of guilt, which he recognised as absurd given the situation, Taofang pulled away from the sniper, extracting himself from where he had become tangled in her tunic. The motion brought a gasp of pain from him, a stabbing sensation racing down his arm. It seemed he hadn't cleared the lip of the pit as smoothly as he had thought.

Reeling back, Taofang felt the cold wall of the firing pit press against him. Through the ferrocrete he could feel the vibrations of a renewed ork barrage, the most vicious to yet assail Vorago. Each tremor sent a fresh twinge of agony rushing down his arm.

Mingzhou was beside him almost at once, her face pinched with concern. She did the incredible, setting down her lasrifle so she could inspect his arm. It was the first time he'd ever seen her out of contact with the weapon. 'I thought you slept with that thing,' he joked, but the effort brought his teeth snapping together against a fresh surge of misery.

The sniper scowled at him. 'Exactly how much *do* you want this to hurt?' Her hands closed about his arm, one behind and one above his elbow. An icy chill of anticipation crawled through Taofang's flesh.

'Is there a painless option?' he asked, the last word barely leaving his lips before a blast of excruciation thundered through him. His eyes snapped shut, his mouth clamped tight, biting his tongue. His arm felt like it had been set on fire and then smashed under the treads of a tank.

'It's broken,' Mingzhou announced, her voice a grim whisper. 'We might be able to fool Nehring, if we're careful.'

'Why...' Taofang shuddered as he opened his eyes, a wave of nausea almost overwhelming him. He closed his eyes and started over. 'Why fool anybody? I can go to the aid section'

'Broken bones aren't tended at the aid section,' Mingzhou said, dread creeping into her voice. 'Serious injuries are taken care of at Processing Omega.'

Taofang started to shrug, then thought better of it. 'So I go to Processing–'

The sniper pressed her hand against his lips, smothering the rest of his words. Her eyes were like chips of steel as she locked him in an intense gaze. 'Have you ever heard of anyone coming back from Processing?' she demanded.

Smiling, Taofang pulled Mingzhou's hand away. 'Of course they come back. Probably reassigned to whatever units...'

His gaze strayed from the sniper to the other occupants of the firing pit. He suddenly felt cold all over, staring down at the two dead men, factory slaves who had been chained to the walls of the pit. He only had a good view of one of them, a big black hole burned through his forehead. It was more than he wanted to see. He lifted his gaze back to Mingzhou.

No, Taofang decided, he wasn't going to ask her how these men died. Knowing wouldn't do anybody any good.

Castellax bled compassion from men. It was a weakness

that could kill quicker than an ash-storm. Survival was the only thing a man had to cling to, survival at any cost. Whatever didn't help him survive, it was something he had to teach himself to ignore. What good to wonder if someone he didn't know had been murdered? This was a planet of murder; hundreds died each day just to placate the whims of the Iron Warriors. Who would care about two nameless slaves in a firing pit?

Taofang knew the answer to that question even as he asked it. The Iron Warriors were vicious, brutal monsters who thought nothing of slaughtering their own slaves, but they had very different standards for the human cattle who served them. If one slave killed another, then that was a crime against the property of their masters.

'Mingzhou,' Taofang gestured at the dead slaves. 'We have to get rid of them. Make it look like the orks got them.' He pushed himself away from the wall. Drawing his knife, he began to attack the chain binding the closest slave to the wall. In his mind, he kept seeing Colonel Nehring and his shock troops appearing and dragging Mingzhou away.

He couldn't let that happen. Ignoring the pain from his arm, Taofang tried to pry the links apart, to free the corpse from its fastening.

Almost gently, Mingzhou pressed her hands against his chest and pushed him back. 'They won't know,' she assured him. His panic had touched her more profoundly than any words could have. On Castellax, where life was cheap, the rarest thing of all was to fear for any life that wasn't your own. 'We'll be gone before the disposers show up.'

A feeling of intense relief gripped Taofang as he bowed to the woman's logic. The disposal teams weren't the sort to brave ork guns. They'd wait until the worst of the barrage was over before sallying from the tunnels to gather the dead. By then, as Mingzhou said, they would be safely away, neither Nehring nor his monstrous masters any the wiser.

'Post one-thirty-five,' a nasal voice cried out from above, its words almost drowned out by the roar of artillery and the scream of ork planes. 'Anyone alive down there?'

Taofang retrieved his lasgun from where he had dropped it, frantically swinging the weapon towards the mouth of the pit. His moment of relief tasted bitter now. Against all precedent, the disposers were ranging along the firebreak in the midst of the barrage. A fine time for the corpse-collectors to grow a spine!

The weight of the lasgun was too much for Taofang to manage with one arm. Unwisely he set the muzzle against his broken arm. Instantly a surge of pain swept through him, the weapon slipping from fingers shocked into helplessness. Mingzhou tried to squirm past him to reach her lasrifle, but between the janissary and the dead slaves, the space was too tight.

A muffled gasp drifted down from the mouth of the pit. A masked face quickly withdrew, darting away before Taofang could try to recover his lasgun. The faintest suggestion of a hurried exchange filtered down into the pit, then another masked figure stared down at them from above, a long hook clenched in his gloved fists.

'Janissaries,' the man said, making the word sound like a curse. Before the crippled Taofang could move, the disposer lashed out with the hook, swatting his hand and knocking the lasgun from his fingers. Mingzhou lunged for the hook, but with a twisting motion, the disposer pulled it free from her grip.

'Did you kill them?' the disposer demanded, gesturing at the dead slaves.

Taofang glared up at the masked man. 'Does it matter? You'll tell Nehring we did and earn yourself a reward. Maybe an extra ration of protein-paste.'

The disposer flinched as Taofang said the last words, lurching back almost as though he had been struck. The eyes behind the lenses of his mask narrowed. 'What would you do if I didn't turn you in? Would you go back to your regiment, or would you try to escape?'

Mingzhou sneered up at the disposer. 'There is no escape.'

The masked man nodded his head. 'Maybe not, but at least there is a chance to fight back. To die like men, not dogs.'

A cynical laugh hissed through Taofang's teeth. 'No revolt succeeds. I've put down enough of them to know that.'

'Success or failure,' the disposer said. 'They don't matter. All that matters is fighting against... *them*.'

Taofang turned his head, staring into Mingzhou's eyes. He could read the same thought in her mind. The man wasn't just a rebel, he was mad. Fighting the Iron Warriors was suicide. No mere mortal could hope to oppose the Space Marines.

'I can get you away from here,' the disposer was saying. 'Load you onto the tractor as though you were dead, take you away into the tunnels.'

Mingzhou nodded slowly, still staring at Taofang. 'It is better than being turned over to Nehring,' she said. 'And we can sneak away as soon as we reach the tunnels,' she added in a whisper. The suggestion pleased Taofang. He wanted no part in this madman's impossible crusade and was grateful that Mingzhou shared his sentiment.

'All right,' Taofang called up to the disposer. 'Get us off the firebreak.'

The masked man nodded, lowering the hook back down into the pit. 'Loop the straps of your weapons over the point. Get the one from the dead men too.'

Taofang laughed at the order. 'You ask us to trust you, disposer. You ask us to believe in your fight.' His fingers wrapped about the muzzle of his lasgun as he lifted it from the floor. 'That is asking a lot. So I think we'll be keeping our weapons.'

The disposer shrugged. 'You'll have to hide them,'

he said. 'An armed corpse might attract attention.' He dropped flat as a shell burst somewhere overhead, the firebreak trembling with the impact. 'No more discussion,' he snarled. 'Are you coming or not?'

Taofang hefted his lasgun, shaking it at the masked man. 'We're coming,' he said. He hesitated, wondering if it was wise to continue. The rebel had obviously expected to find only slaves in the pit. Taofang didn't want him getting any crazy ideas now that he had two armed janissaries under his wing. 'But we make no promises about fighting the Iron Warriors, disposer.'

'Yuxiang,' the masked man introduced himself. 'And I won't ask you to fight the Iron Warriors.' He paused, his body shuddering beneath the slimy sheen of his plastic duster. 'I won't need to after you have seen Processing Omega for yourself.

'After you have been there, you will know the kind of monsters they are. You will know that they must be destroyed.'

THE HULKING ORK chief thumped its chest with the armoured backs of its power claws. The immense masses of cable and steel were surgically attached to the alien's body at the shoulder, replacing its natural arms entirely. Painted in a bloody shade broken up by rings of black and white checks, the brutal weapons presented a garish contrast to the tattered leather cloak and leggings the beast wore. A bowl-like helmet fitted with massive black horns was crushed down around the brute's scalp, casting its pushed-in face into shadow.

Rhodaan pressed the activation stud on his chainsword and favoured the ork with a grandiose flourish of his blade. His plasma pistol was dangerously close to overheating after fending off incessant waves of orks for the past two hours. It was becoming dangerously unpredictable. Gazing at the ork chief, he didn't think he'd trust anything less than a full charge to burn through the brute's thick skull. Less than that would probably just piss it off.

Killing the warlord hadn't done much to throw the xenos into confusion. The monsters had been fully capable of mounting another assault against Vorago even as the Raptors were extracting themselves from the battle-fortress. Ork artillery thundered through the sky, ork planes ruled the air, ork warriors rampaged across the desert and assailed the perimeter walls. Alien mobs patrolled the wastes, hunting for the enemies who had penetrated into their headquarters.

How many had Rhodaan killed since Vallax and the others had withdrawn into the pipe? The tabulation icon in his helmet registered two hundred and forty-seven confirmations and another twenty-three probables. To the Iron Warrior, the numbers were unimpressive, mere drops in the bucket. There were millions of orks infesting Castellax, the deaths of a few hundred were nothing. There were only sixty-four Iron Warriors on the entire planet – their deaths had to be sold at only the highest price. Killing the warlord would have had consequence. Dying here, in a scrap yard of scavenged junk, would account for nothing. It would be shameful, a disgrace.

Rhodaan would not die in disgrace. When his spirit was cast into the warp, he would stare at the Great Powers and spit at them. They would know he had died as an Iron Warrior, not Flesh grovelling on its knees in the dirt.

The ork chief clambered down from its perch atop the smashed chassis of a tank, barking its savage laughter as it answered Rhodaan's challenge. Weedy little gretchin attendants scurried out from hiding to assist the ork as it advanced, activating a crazed array of drives and gears fitted to the shell of its claws. Streamers of golden lightning crackled around the brute's steel paws, dripping from each chequered talon in rivulets of molten fire.

The Space Marine took one step, then his body jerked back as a high-calibre round smashed into his cuirass. Rhodaan pitched, almost falling, but his psycho-conditioned reflexes turned his sprawl into a roll, throwing him behind cover. A barrage of enthusiastic but erratic fire pelted the ground around him.

Raucous bellows roared from the ork chief's fanged maw. On the scrap-heaps around it, a pack of grimy aliens bedecked in blue paint and wearing human skulls as trophies maintained a steady rate of fire against Rhodaan's refuge. The Space Marine chided himself for underestimating the ork chief. The brainless brutes were so often unable to resist the promise of a fight that it was easy to forget that sometimes the monsters could display a crude intelligence.

Rhodaan thumbed a grenade from his belt. Three more and then he would be empty. The Iron Warrior nodded grimly. He would just have to make each one count. Reaching out, he wrenched a piece of pipe from the broken railcar he was using for cover. With deliberate precision, he threw the piece of debris into the darkest path of shadow he could find.

Ork eyesight was notoriously poor and the aliens reacted on instinct rather than strategy. The sound of the pipe clattering across the shadowy ground brought a withering fire chopping down at it, every xenos gun shifting to annihilate the unexpected sound.

It was a momentary distraction, but a moment was all Rhodaan needed. Darting from around the opposite side of the railcar, he braved the fire of the few orks who still had the presence of mind not to forget their original enemy. The thin grenade sailed from the Space Marine's hand, flying not towards the ork warriors atop the scrap-heaps, but at the base of the junk pile itself.

Rhodaan dove back behind cover, crouching low against the railcar as the grenade detonated. The deafening shriek of tons of metal sliding and scraping together scratched across the scrap yard. There was a dull rumble, the panicked barks of orks, then the upset scrap-heaps came smashing down in a rattling avalanche of rusted metal and shredded steel.

The rolling junk heap smashed against Rhodaan's shelter, pushing it back a dozen metres, threatening to upset it and smash him into paste beneath the mass of the railcar. Bits and oddments went sailing over the top of the vehicle, crashing to the ground in a clamour of dislodged wreckage. Rhodaan held fast to the side of his refuge, braving the cataclysm he had set into motion.

When the clamour fell still, the Raptor lunged to the top of the railcar, using his demi-organic wings to aid his leap. He scowled down at the sprawling mess of twisted metal, the torn bodies of orks strewn about the jumble. A few of the aliens moved feebly, trying to drag their mangled remains free. Rhodaan clenched his fist tighter about his chainsword and drove down upon the torn survivors.

As he hacked the head from one ork and kicked in the face of another, Rhodaan was suddenly bowled over by a tremendous impact. Thrown across the scrap yard, he landed in an agonised heap, only his superhuman constitution and the amazing durability of his power armour protecting him from immediate death. The object that had smashed into him rolled away, the burned-out hulk of a warbike.

Monstrous, familiar laughter roared at him from across the debris-field. The ork chief wrenched its leg free from a tangle of wires and pipe, glaring at the Space Marine with its beady eyes. Its face was a mash of torn flesh and shrapnel, one power claw sparking and hanging obscenely from its torn shoulder. The ork reached out with its good claw, scooping the drive-shaft of a truck from the ground and hurling it like a javelin at the prostrate Rhodaan.

The Iron Warrior had underestimated this brute, but it had done the same in turn. The ork hadn't reckoned upon the agility and speed of a legionary. Rhodaan threw himself flat as the drive-shaft went sailing over his head. As soon as it was past, he sprang into a vicious charge, rushing at the hulking alien beast. He could see the savage anticipation in the ork's eyes, the excitement as it clenched and unclenched its power claw.

At the last instant, before he closed with the ork, Rhodaan activated his jump pack, launching himself over the alien's head. 'You had your chance,' he hissed at the brute. 'Now you can burn.'

As though understanding Rhodaan's words, the ork chief didn't turn to see where the Space Marine was going, but instead stared at the little discs the Raptor had dropped on the ground at its feet. A heartbeat later the incendiary grenades detonated, engulfing the ork in flame.

Screaming, its flesh cooking beneath its skin, the ork chief stubbornly clung to life, staggering blindly around the wreckage in a futile attempt to close upon its killer. The living torch raged and bellowed for more than a minute before a sharp whine whistled across the scrap yard and smacked into the ork's burning body. Rhodaan was forced to shield his eyes as a brilliant explosion consumed the ork.

Spinning around, clutching the doubtful plasma pistol in his fist, Rhodaan tried to find the location of the shooter who had finished the ork. It was a simple task, the shooter made no effort to hide himself. Lumbering across the scrap yard, the missile launcher gradually flowing back into the substance of his arm, Brother Merihem smiled his steel smile at Rhodaan.

'A magnificent battle,' the Obliterator congratulated. 'A good display of tactics against a more numerical foe and with woefully limited resources.'

Rhodaan glanced at the steaming ruin of the ork chief, then glared into Merihem's pallid face. 'How long have you been standing out there watching?'

The Obliterator chuckled, a throaty sound like the gurgle of fuel in a sputtering engine. 'Long enough,' he answered. 'The Legion does not tolerate weakness. It is corruption and corruption must be cut away... or buried somewhere it can be forgotten. Is not that the axiom of the Iron Warriors?'

If his pistol had a full charge, Rhodaan believed he would have melted the smirk from Merihem's face. It was as well the weapon was compromised. The Obliterator might still prove useful to him.

'You were left behind,' Rhodaan said. 'Over-Captain Vallax thought *you* were weak.'

Merihem chuckled again, raising an immense talon of metal and meat. 'And he left you behind, Captain Rhodaan.'

Rhodaan shook his head. 'I disagreed with him. I stayed to wait for you, to lead you back.'

The Obliterator's steel smile grew. 'He left you behind,' the monster repeated. 'You were meant to die out here with the abomination.' Merihem's chest bubbled and flowed, pulling back until it exposed the corroded remains of a cybernetic skull. A pseudopod of meat and plasteel extruded from the Obliterator, extending the skull towards Rhodaan.

'One of Oriax's Steel Blood,' Merihem explained. 'The Fabricator builds such amusing things. He calls these "Steel Blood" because there is a little of himself in each one. I found slaughtering orks tedious, so when I chanced upon this little spy, I distracted a segment of my consciousness by dissecting it. You won't believe the things it has seen.'

To prove his words, the Obliterator reached his talon over and activated the Steel Blood. The crystal eyes in its sockets glowed back into life, its jaws clacking together. From one of the eyes, a beam of light shone, projecting a holographic image onto the ground. Rhodaan watched in fascination as the skull's recording played out, displaying Vallax and the other Raptors creeping down the pipe.

At the first junction, the Iron Warriors stopped. Vallax began issuing instructions to the others. Brother

Baelfegor started to protest, but some sharp reprimand brought him back in line. As Rhodaan watched the Space Marines start planting melta-charges against the walls of the pipe, he could well imagine the argument Vallax had used. There was a chance the orks could use the pipe to infiltrate Vorago and bypass the defences. Therefore, the way had to be shut. The men of Squad Kyrith had no choice but to obey.

The Steel Blood withdrew before the final, fiery detonation collapsed the pipe and brought the street above crashing down. It didn't matter at that point. Rhodaan had seen enough.

'You see, captain,' Merihem laughed. 'We are both orphans, cast aside to die in disgrace and shame. How does that make you feel? Does it make you feel like your existence is a lie? Does it make you feel like an outcast? An abomination?'

Rhodaan clenched his fist. 'Vallax will pay,' he vowed.

Merihem's oily chuckle bubbled from the speakers in his armour. 'Revenge? What a delicious thought, captain. It can sustain a man when all else has crumbled into ash...'

'Let me be, monster,' Rhodaan snarled at the Obliterator. He hefted his chainsword, but before he could strike an undulating coil of metal whipped out from Merihem's wrist and wound itself around his arm.

'I had considered killing you, captain,' Merihem said, tightening the coil until Rhodaan could feel ceramite plates begin to crack. 'But you have persuaded me to let you live. Revenge is too rare a delicacy to let go to waste. It is something we share in common.' The coil of metal retracted back into Merihem's body, releasing the Raptor.

'Shall we go?' the Obliterator asked, extending his talon.

'Where?' Rhodaan demanded, rubbing at his arm, trying to feel if any of the armour plates had indeed cracked.

'Back to Vorago,' Merihem said. His chest bubbled and boiled, withdrawing the crushed Steel Blood back into his body. 'There's another way in. As I told you, you wouldn't believe the things Oriax's spy has seen.'

Rhodaan's eyes narrowed behind the lenses of his helmet. 'You also said we share a need for revenge,' he said, his tone full of challenge. 'Who do you want revenge against?'

The Obliterator turned towards him, all joviality draining from his tiny face. Merihem's eyes were pits of blackness as he stared down at Rhodaan and answered the Iron Warrior's question.

'I haven't decided yet.'

WARSMITH ANDRAAZ LEANED against the back of his crystalline throne, his armoured fingers drumming against the arms in a steady tattoo of brooding malignance. His gaze lingered over the projected image of Vorago and the alien army laying siege to the city, studying the tallies and figures scrolling alongside the image. Casualties among the Flesh were becoming critical, draining manpower from the remaining production lines nuzzled close to the Iron Bastion in the heart of the city. Ammunition stores were being depleted at an unacceptable rate. Food stores were in such a decline that quarter rations would soon be imposed on all non-specialised personnel. Water, however, was even scarcer. Reclamation procedures had been intensified, but there was only so much that could be done to recycle the existing supply.

Most troubling to Andraaz, however, had been the losses to the Iron Warriors. The sacrifice of a million Flesh was nothing to him, but the loss of a single legionary represented a slight against his own prestige and that of the Third Grand Company. So far, two Space Marines had been lost fighting on the walls, Captain Gamgin had executed a suicide attack and Admiral Nostraz had fallen victim to an accident in one of the flak towers while inspecting the missile batteries embedded in the roof. Each was a loss the lords of Castellax could ill afford.

Now, to the list of casualties, Andraaz was forced to add Captain Rhodaan and Brother Merihem. Lost in the fruitless attack against the ork battlefortress, an assault that was supposed to buy the Iron Warriors the time they needed to recover from the rapid ork advance and marshal the resources necessary to go back on the offensive.

'At the current rate of attrition, what are the best estimates for resistance?' Andraaz growled, his eyes never leaving the holographic projection.

Sergeant Ipos didn't need the Warsmith to look at him to know the question belonged to him. 'If losses are maintained at present levels, the Flesh will endure for another three months,' Ipos stated. 'However, Dread Lord, we must anticipate increased casualties from fatigue and distress when we reduce rations.'

'What do you anticipate?' Skintaker Algol asked. The slavemaster's cloak had grown frayed and tattered in the fighting, his cringing retinue scurrying about him trying to mend the gruesome raiment.

'Between a ten and twenty-five per cent increase,' Ipos declared. 'Those are losses strictly from debility and illness. There is no ready formula for determining how many will be lost to enemy fire from reduced alertness and stamina.'

Vallax's hair darkened into an almost black hue, his face curling in contempt. 'If we depend on the Flesh, then we deserve to be defeated,' he said. 'Victory will not come from them. It will come from us. We have to strike at the enemy!'

'We have heard this argument before,' Morax protested, pointing a thick finger at the Over-Captain. 'Your last raid cost us Captain Rhodaan and Merihem, not to mention four assault boats and over a dozen of my fighters. And to what effect? The orks are still on our doorstep, as belligerent as ever!' The Skylord snapped his fingers and a pasty-faced officer from the Air Cohort stepped out from the shadow of a support column. The human bowed deeply before his master, presenting him with a gilded folio.

'This is the latest aerial reconnaissance from Dirgas,' Morax announced. 'Gathered at extreme risk to my remaining observation ships.' He opened the folio, spreading the parchment illuminations for the other Iron Warriors to examine. His thumb pressed down against one section of illuminated text in particular. 'This is what is most important to us,' he declared. 'The xenos are building another battlefortress, bigger than anything we have yet seen. Everyone in this room has fought orks before. No warlord would trust a subordinate with a weapon bigger than his own.' Morax sneered at Vallax. 'Biglug was never here,' he said. 'The bastard was down in Dirgas the whole time building this monstrosity!'

Vallax glared back at the Skylord. He wondered how long Morax had known about this, how long he had known the raid against the battlefortress was a fool's errand. Already, he could guess the plan Morax would propose to the Warsmith. The orks would undoubtedly try to bring the new battlefortress to Vorago. Every kilometre of the journey, the machine would be vulnerable to the Castellax Air Cohort and the planes Morax had been so conservative about deploying earlier in the campaign. The glory of driving back the orks would belong to the Skylord.

The ghoulish servitor acting as Fabricator Oriax's proxy approached the table, the lenses of its eyes focusing on Morax's data-scrolls. The machine-man's speaker crackled as its distant master reacted to the illuminated transcripts. 'This explains intelligence gathered by the few operational Steel Blood yet within Dirgas,' the mechanised voice declared. 'Biglug must indeed be there and he must intend to use this new battlefortress to deliver the final blow against Vorago.'

Morax folded his arms across his chest, revelling in the approbation of his chief detractor among the Third

Grand Company's hierarchy. The servitor's next transmission, however, turned the Skylord's blood cold.

'Only the presence of Biglug could explain the stores of aviation fuel the xenos are storing in Dirgas,' the servitor stated. 'No other warboss would be powerful enough to restrain so many of the xenos squadrons. There is only one conclusion to be reached. The warlord is forcing a mass concentration of his air power to provide his land fortress with protection when it leaves Dirgas.'

Vallax wasted no time pouncing on the opportunity Oriax's statement presented. 'It is vital then that we strike while Biglug is still in Dirgas. A lightning raid against the battlefortress. Kill the warlord before he leaves the city!'

'We have already tried that...' Morax started to object, but fell silent when Andraaz lifted his hand.

The Warsmith scowled at his bickering commanders. It was useful to keep them at each other's throats, but there were times when the consequent lack of cohesion was troublesome. 'An attack against the battlefortress would be costly and with no guarantee of catching the warlord,' he said. 'The surest way of destroying the machine would be through aerial bombardment. Even if the warlord were absent, loss of the battlefortress would impose a delay in its attack plans.'

'What about the ork planes?' Ipos wondered.

Andraaz stared at Vallax. 'The orks won't be able to fly without fuel,' he said. 'It will be the role of the Raptors to strike the fuel stores Oriax has located. Eliminate the fuel and we ground the xenos planes. If the orks wait to stockpile more, then we gain the time we need. If they rush ahead, then they leave their battlefortress exposed to Morax's bombers.'

The Warsmith raised one of his claws, shaking it at Vallax. 'You have been granted a rare opportunity to redeem yourself, Over-Captain. Do not squander it.'

Vallax bowed before his overlord. 'I will honour my duty, Dread Lord.'

'You will do more than that,' Andraaz warned. 'You will return to the Iron Bastion in triumph.' The Warsmith's voice dropped into a menacing growl. 'Triumph, Vallax, or do not come back at all.'

BROTHER UHLAN WAS uneasy as he prowled the halls of the Iron Bastion. The blood of one mameluke who strayed too close to the legionary still dripped from the Raptor's gauntlet, each drop being sucked down in the proto-synthetics which covered the upper halls. Marching across the fur-like morass of plastic fibres was like gliding across the top of a pond, conveying a peculiar deception of weightlessness. A Space Marine, conditioned not merely to function but to fight in zero-gravity environments, didn't find the sensation very discomfiting, but the Flesh, without the benefit of such training, with their fragile little bodies of meat and superstition, they would find the effect debilitating. The coverings were one of the more subtle safeguards in place within the Iron Bastion to defend against a slave revolt. No Flesh, however determined and insane, would be able to withstand the effects of the proto-synthetics.

Flesh, however, was not Uhlan's concern at the moment. Not even the ork hordes were foremost in his thoughts. His worries were focused firmly upon Iron. Namely upon Over-Captain Vallax.

Intriguing against the Over-Captain had been reckless, Uhlan appreciated that now. Vallax had exploited his authority and position to dispose of Rhodaan. The hopes the half-breed had pinned upon Rhodaan had perished with the captain. They were buried with the ambitious officer out there in the wasteland, forgotten and forsaken on the battlefield.

The hours since returning to Vorago had given Uhlan time to think about his position and his future. He had dared aspire to ambitions beyond the reach of a half-breed Raptor. Indeed, he had clung so fervently to those ambitions that he had even argued with Vallax against demolishing the escape route behind them. That had been a mistake. Uhlan had seen the suspicion in Vallax's eyes.

No, ambition was forgotten now. What was uppermost in Uhlan's thoughts was survival. Rhodaan's fate had given him a very clear example of how Vallax disposed of his enemies – at least once they were no longer useful. At the moment, Uhlan was trying very hard to find a way to be useful to his Over-Captain.

The emaciated servitor surged out from a niche cut into the ferrocrete wall, its chassis deeply engraved to match the murals etched across the walls. Its cadaverous face stared blankly from its brazen setting, scenes of battle stained across its features. One of its metal armatures extended across the corridor, blocking the way. It was a feeble obstacle, Uhlan could have snapped the arm in half without breaking a sweat. Doing so, however, would send alarms racing through the entire tower. The halls leading up to the Chamber of the Speaker were lined with such sentinels. Those higher up were better armed and even more cunningly concealed, designed not merely to challenge an errant Iron Warrior, but to eliminate him.

Uhlan had no need to go further up the hall. The first servitor was the only one he needed to seek out. Staring into the lenses glowing from the servitor's eye sockets, the Raptor intoned the cumbersome equations of a Lingua-Technis code. By way of response, the servitor shuddered, almost as if in the grip of a fit. When the episode passed, it leered ahead, lenses scanning the Iron Warrior's face. Uhlan could not shake the impression that it was more than a mere machine, that a cruel intelligence now stared at him from behind the servitor's face.

'Brother Uhlan,' the servitor's vox-caster crackled. 'You have something to report?'

Uhlan nodded his head. 'Yes, Fabricator Oriax,' he said. 'Over-Captain Vallax has been given a mandate from the Warsmith. He is to lead a raid against the enemy in Dirgas.'

'This much is already known to me,' Oriax's voice stated.

'Yes, of course, Fabricator,' Uhlan said. 'But what you do not know is that Over-Captain Vallax feels there is no hope of achieving our objective. Not without assistance.' The Iron Warrior hesitated before continuing, wondering even before he spoke if he had assumed too much. 'I have been of use to you before, Fabricator. You have said that while I function I have purpose. Vallax believes his mission to be a suicide run and is making his plans accordingly. With the proper support – your support, Fabricator – he might...'

A crackle of static hissed through the servitor's speaker. 'Humility, Uhlan Half-breed? No contempt from the Space Marine who stands proud in battle against the Fabricator, buried in his sanctum with his machines? Your need must indeed be great.'

Uhlan coughed, choking on the rage boiling up inside him. Yes, he was a half-breed, inferior to those crafted from pure gene-seed, but he was at least an Iron Warrior. Oriax was nothing but a metal maggot, a toad chewing at the roots of the Iron Bastion. It offended the very core of his being to grovel before such a creature. Yet he knew he must grovel if he was to avoid a useless death on the funeral pyre Vallax was preparing.

'The Third Grand Company will be ill-served by the useless sacrifice of its Raptors,' Uhlan said.

'Did you know that Captain Rhodaan has returned?' Oriax abruptly asked. 'Climbed through an old service catacomb in the Epsilon sector. Can't imagine how he found it.'

The news sent Uhlan's mind racing. If Rhodaan was alive then the entire situation might change. Warsmith Andraaz might favour him ahead of Vallax, put him in command of the raid. The realisation only brought more bitterness in Uhlan's heart. Rhodaan was sure to use his new position to avenge himself on Vallax, and the best way to conceal that revenge was to send the rest of the Faceless to share the Over-Captain's doom. Uhlan had dared to manipulate Rhodaan against Vallax in hopes of bringing down his hated commander. Now he would share in that destruction.

The servitor retracted back into the niche. 'Tell Vallax I will support him,' Oriax said. 'I will send something to guide him to my sanctum.'

Uhlan stared in disbelief at the servitor. In all his centuries, he had never heard of anyone being invited into the Fabricator's sanctum. Perhaps Warsmith Andraaz had seen it, but certainly no other Iron Warrior. At once, Uhlan appreciated the magnitude of the aid Oriax was offering.

'I will tell him,' Uhlan vowed, clamping his fist to his chest.

The servitor's lenses shifted in their sockets, fixing him in a mechanical stare. 'Impress upon Vallax the urgency of his situation. The return of Rhodaan changes everything. If he accepts failure, then he abandons the glories of victory to others. You would do well to remind him of this.'

The lenses seemed to sparkle, the voice from the vox-caster dropped to a whisper. 'Your fate is joined with that of Squad Vidarna, Brother Uhlan. All of you are creatures of Vallax in Captain Rhodaan's mind. Do not forget that.'

It was on Uhlan's tongue to argue with the Fabricator, to accuse him of manipulating the Iron Warrior into this position. Playing the two officers against one another had been a strategy Oriax had encouraged. Now that Uhlan was caught between the two, it seemed he was being left to bear the consequences of failed intrigues.

Uhlan left his outburst unspoken, however. He could sense the change that had settled upon the servitor. That feeling of malignant intelligence was absent. Oriax was no longer in communion with his machine. Arguing with it now would be like arguing with his bolter.

Angrily, the Iron Warrior turned and withdrew along the proto-synthetic floor. He would tell Vallax of the Fabricator's offer, if for no other reason than the simple fact that Oriax was right. Uhlan was bound to Vallax now. Whatever doom awaited the Over-Captain, it was waiting for his Raptors too.

CHAPTER XV

I–Day Plus One Hundred and Four

Over-Captain Vallax marched along the deserted corridor, the sensors in his helmet stifling the drone of sirens and the thunder of shells. It was a testament to the enormous calibre of the enemy guns that any sound at all could penetrate far enough to reach the bunker. Vallax wasn't certain if such an achievement was impressive or absurd. Anything of such size would be almost immobile. When the time came for the guns to be dealt with, the enemy wouldn't be able to move them somewhere safe.

The thought brought a curl to Vallax's scarred lip. As though anywhere was safe for an enemy of the Iron Warriors.

Vallax's hair bristled as raw hate crackled through his brain, a peculiar psycho-reactive mutation inflicted upon him by the baleful emanations of the warp and its denizens. Vallax rarely suffered such an irritant for long, but Rhodaan had proven himself not without a certain aptitude. He had not maintained his rank of Over-Captain for two thousand years by disposing of irritants while they were still useful to him. Still, Captain Rhodaan's usefulness was no longer equal to the menace he represented. Rhodaan had acquired quite a reputation of his own in the recent campaign against the hrud. Vallax didn't like subordinates who possessed too much renown.

The Iron Warrior glared at the ferrocrete walls, then fixed his gaze on the pseudo-mechanical flesh-drone acting as his guide. The thing was enough to nauseate even an Iron Warrior, a loathsome hodgepodge of skin and steel, cable and bone. Fabricator Oriax never assembled two of his flesh-drones quite the same way. But there was one thing the Techmarine never failed to implement. Each flesh-drone still had a recognizable face stitched onto it somewhere, a face that continually writhed in silent screams. It was said that Oriax never completely lobotomised the subjects of the conversion process, that he left just enough self-awareness in the flesh-drones for them to experience the full horror of their new existence while their mechanical programming made it impossible for them to escape it.

Even among the Iron Warriors, Fabricator Oriax was regarded with a measure of caution, a wariness that stopped just short of being outright fear. The Techmarine was an enigma to the rest of the Third Grand Company and had been so for millennia. Maimed in the crystal-swamps of Tarsis IX, Oriax was more machine than flesh, his mind driven by the strange impulses of steel, not the demands of honour and pride. Since the conquest of Castellax, the Fabricator had rarely stirred from the bunker complex beneath the Iron Bastion, and then only at the command of Warsmith Andraaz. Visitors to the bunker were even more rare.

Vallax, however, was a special case. If not for him, Oriax would never have left the crystal-swamps. The Techmarine owed his life to the Over-Captain, a fact which Vallax had exploited to his benefit many times in the past. Now, it was time for him to do so again.

The flesh-drone hesitated outside a massive titanium bulkhead, the vox-caster built into its chest spitting and crackling as it transmitted a steady stream of binary. Vallax knew the bunker was rife with traps to safeguard Oriax's seclusion. Without the flesh-drone's transmissions, nothing alive could penetrate the Fabricator's sanctum.

With a growled rumble, the bulkhead door retreated into the floor, allowing Vallax and his guide to enter a vast inner chamber, its most prominent feature being the forest-like confusion of pipes rising from its floor and vanishing into the ceiling far overhead. A riotous array of pict screens flickered from every corner of the room, presenting a thousand different views of Castellax, from the dark depths of the promethium mines to the jagged spires of the Iron Bastion and the decayed sprawl of Vorago, the city's outskirts now further despoiled by the marauding orks.

Vallax's hand shifted to his pistol holster as he saw his own visage fill one of the monitors. His hypno-trained senses immediately estimated from what location such a view of himself would be afforded. Spinning around, he found himself staring into the skeletal face of one of Oriax's grisly spies, the floating skulls he called his 'Steel Blood'. The followers of the False Emperor employed similar constructs, but Vallax doubted they had the dedication to craft them the way Oriax did. There was the stink of the warp about the Steel Blood, a daemonic taint that no mortal could experience without a twinge of uneasiness. It was a sensation too elusive for understanding, like something that could be seen only out of the corner of the eye but which hid itself when viewed straight-on.

While he glared at the Steel Blood, the metal jaw of the floating skull snapped open, exposing the metal meshwork of a vox-caster. 'Salutation and honour to Over-Captain Vallax. Deathsmith of the Faceless. Scourge of the Pox-pits. Brother Iron Warrior.'

The Iron Warrior brushed past the floating skull,

ignoring the Steel Blood's synthesised praises. 'Show yourself, Oriax!' Vallax's voice boomed through the forest of cables and pipes. 'I did not descend twenty levels and forsake the call of battle to waste words with your mindless tinker-toys.' The Space Marine marched deeper into the tangle of machinery and monitors. 'I am not the Warsmith, Oriax. I do not suffer proxies.'

In a single fluid motion, Vallax swung about, drew his pistol and sent a single shot slamming into the centre of the Steel Blood's cranium. The floating skull exploded in a burst of sparks, shards of metal and shreds of organics flying in every direction.

'Your marksmanship is as good as when you patrolled the citadels of Olympia,' a shrill, mechanical voice reverberated from the darkness.

'It is better,' Vallax said, his armoured thumb rubbing across the smoking barrel of his weapon. The optics of his helmet adjusted to filter away the chemical haze that filled Oriax's sanctum, but the compounds were so complex as to baffle even the engineering of the Legion's artificers. His anger rising, Vallax marched in the direction of the voice. 'Reveal yourself, Oriax. I want to look at what I'm speaking to.'

The chamber shuddered as fans suddenly churned into life, drawing away the obscuring gases and chemicals that enabled the sanctum to retain its preternatural darkness. Vallax's optics immediately adjusted to the natural gloom, but there was no sign of anyone where the voice had spoken.

'Is this better?' Oriax's voice came from the same place, rising from a vox-caster fitted to one of the pict screens. A moment later, the same words echoed from a spot some fifteen metres to Vallax's left. The Iron Warrior spun around, glaring through the darkness. This time there was something to reward his gaze. Nestled amidst a jumble of machinery and cogitator cabinets, their blinking lights and flashing diodes casting a diabolic glow about his body, was Fabricator Oriax.

The Techmarine presented a ghastly shape, devoid of the symmetry of rational design. His body was a mass of cables and gears fused about the remnants of a man. A confusion of spidery steel arms jutted from his figure at every angle, scrabbling at the consoles arrayed about him with dazzling speed. A massive metal claw arced upwards from his back and hung menacingly above his head, fiddling with an array of rune-boards suspended from the ceiling. A set of pincers, electricity crackling between their steel talons, projected from his right shoulder, hovering about a table resting at the Techmarine's side. Vallax felt a moment of shock when he saw that the pincers appeared to be assembling another Steel Blood – possibly to replace the one he had so noisily destroyed. Efficiency, or anticipation? Vallax wasn't sure which answer was more disturbing.

'You should count yourself favoured, Over-Captain,' Oriax's distorted metal voice declared. 'There are few I allow to see me as I am.' The Techmarine's limbs paused in their assorted duties, each curling back to point for a moment at the body to which they were attached. At the core of that trash-heap of cables and gears was a cuirass of ancient armour from the time of the Great Crusade, the skull-helm symbol of the Iron Warriors engraved across the breast. Staring from above the symbol was an iron visage every bit as inhuman and forbidding, a clutch of pale, scarred flesh surrounding a lipless gash of mouth and a torn stump of nose. A brace of mechanical eyes burned with crimson light from the pits of Oriax's mangled face.

Vallax felt no horror at Oriax's condition, only a sneering contempt. There was a good reason why the Techmarine hid himself away and tried to guard himself with a cloak of mystery. The brutal fact was there hadn't been much left of him after the crystal-swamps, less than even a normal man; much less than a Space Marine.

'I did not come here to waste time gawking at freaks,'

Vallax growled. 'Your surrogate convinced the Warsmith to allow me to lead the assault.'

'You find that prospect daunting?' The synthesised voice made it impossible to tell if there was a mocking tone behind the words.

'I worry only that Captain Rhodaan will betray his own duty,' Vallax snarled at the Fabricator. Rhodaan's return to the Iron Bastion had been something of a shock to him, but even more so had been the way Andraaz had responded to him. Rhodaan had been placed on an equal footing with Vallax in planning out the raid, given co-command in all but name. It was a final humiliation for the Over-Captain and one in which he read the seeds of his own ruin. Merely by surviving, Rhodaan had turned the Warsmith against Vallax. Andraaz might have overlooked treachery, but he would never forgive failure. 'The success of my mission depends upon Rhodaan's diversion against the ork headquarters. The vermin must believe that their command centre is our target, not the fuel dump.'

The Techmarine's claw lowered so that it could point at Vallax, shaking at him like the reproving finger of an Olympian combat instructor. 'Rhodaan won't know his is a diversion unless *you* tell him. Lead the upstart to believe his is the real attack. Provide him with enough janissaries to cover his assault. Enough serf-meat to keep the orks occupied.'

Under his helmet, Vallax's lips pulled back in a cunning smile. 'Leave him ignorant of the true purpose of the mission,' he mused. 'But Rhodaan is no fool, he will question the deployment of my own squad as a diversionary force. He may guess the deception and undermine me.' Vallax's hand tightened into a fist as unpleasant memories recurred to him. 'He has done it before,' the Over-Captain admitted, thinking of Rhodaan's ambush of the hrud.

Oriax's laugh was like a burst of electronic interference. 'You will not deploy anywhere near the blockhouse, or anywhere that might give Rhodaan warning. When the time for action comes, your squad will come to my sanctum.' The entire console around the Techmarine shifted with him as he turned to face a particular portion of wall. At an unspoken command from the Fabricator the entire wall sank into the floor, exposing a second chamber.

Even through his armour, Vallax felt a chill and knew it to be a cold born not of flesh but of spirit, a psychic frost that betokened some great effort of witchery. Warily, he came forwards to peer into the inner room. He gasped at what he saw.

'Each wall possesses thirteen facets, adorned with special psycho-reactive alloys found only within the Eye of Terror,' Oriax boasted as Vallax stared at the sharply angled walls. At the base of each facet, arrayed like the spokes of a wheel, were thirteen naked things chained to stout pillars. 'The pillars are of wraithbone plundered from the vanquished craftworld of X'amot,' the Fabricator said, but Vallax was more interested in the beings bound to those pillars rather than the columns themselves. At first glance, the things might have been mistaken for humans of the most degenerate and malformed stock, but a second look made it apparent that whatever lurked inside those twisted bodies was anything but human.

At the centre of the chamber, its surface etched in cabalistic symbols and framed with a ring of psi-circuitry, was a great disc of bloodwood. The black hue of the disc gave evidence that the timber had recently been fed, soaking up the spirit-energy of its victims. For such a mass of bloodwood, Oriax must have had at least a hundred 'donors'. Murder on such a scale didn't impress Vallax. What did impress him was the fact that he recognised this apparatus and could guess its purpose.

'You've recreated the Daemonculum,' Vallax said, glancing away from the inner chamber to stare at Oriax's corpse-like face.

'I've improved upon it,' Oriax corrected him. 'The

sorcerers of the pesedjet are too mired in superstition to truly understand such power.' The Fabricator's claw stretched out, gesturing at the bloodwood platform. 'Bring your squad to me, Vallax. Stand at the heart of the Daemonculum. I shall propitiate the thirteen daemons and harness their energies to transmit you where you need to be.' Again, the static-laughter crackled through the sanctum. 'Unless Rhodaan has developed a warp-eye, he will never guess your purpose or your objective.'

Vallax nodded slowly. 'This will bring great glory to both of us,' he said. 'The Warsmith will be impressed and will reward me greatly. You will not find me ungenerous, Oriax.'

The Fabricator's many arms spread outwards in a great spiral, his mechanical eyes glowing in the darkness. 'It is enough that I help the brother who saved my life. That is all the reward I ask.'

WARILY, THE SPACE Marines of Squad Vidarna, Vallax's infamous Faceless, stepped out onto the bloodwood platform. Their Over-Captain gestured with his chainsword, motioning Oriax to begin. The other Raptors dropped into a wary crouch, their weapons at the ready. Orders or no, they were uneasy about the Daemonculum and alert for the danger they sensed exuding from the bound daemons and the wraithbone pillars.

A burst of binary crackled from Oriax's mouth. In response, a dozen Steel Blood whirled across the massive chamber, joining the Raptors upon the platform. Another burst of binary and several of the Fabricator's flesh-drones lumbered out into the room. The servitors had been specially built for this task, equipped with ghastly mechadendrites that curled upwards from their backs to arc downwards over their shoulders. Each mechadendrite ended not in a hand, but in a great shackle of bronze. In their semi-organic natural arms, each flesh-drone bore an iron knife and a brass bowl.

Struggling in the grip of each set of shackles were the pathetic remains of human slaves. Like the servitors, they too had been especially prepared for their function. Legs and fingers had been surgically amputated to limit resistance, tongues had been removed to silence outcries that might disrupt the cadence of incantations. In stark contrast, drugs had been administered to heighten awareness in their terrified minds of the slaves, stimulants injected into their veins to strengthen vitality and frustrate the physical toll of terror on their bodies. It was important to the working of the Daemonculum that the sacrifices experience the magnitude of fear but be incapable of perishing from fright. Their deaths had another, more purposeful design.

A cabal of servitors surrounded the bloodwood discs, their armatures wrapped in heavy cloaks adorned with a profusion of archaic symbols – the arcane trappings of the pesedjet. Each servitor grasped a black candle in its claws, a candle rendered from human fat and with a wick that was only partially corporeal, having been exposed to the energies of the warp.

Oriax flicked a claw and the robed cabal began to intone a sibilant chant, a tonality that no human voice could arrange and no human mind could conceive. The sound of the immaterium was in that chorus, the whisper of empty spaces and endless darkness, the call of the hungry void. With another flick of the Fabricator's claw the flesh-drones continued their march, each drawing itself before one of the thirteen facets. They turned so that they each faced a wraithbone pillar and the daemon bound upon it. As the slaves bound in their shackles struggled futilely in their grip, the flesh-drones stood still, obedient and waiting.

The chorus rose, now invoking the names of the god-daemons of the warp, the primordial forces beyond reality, the eldritch powers of Chaos.

In perfect, mechanised synchronization, the flesh-drones

raised knives and bowls. While the naked slaves tried to scream with the stumps of their tongues, the knives flashed out across their throats. The blood of thirteen murdered mortals sloshed into the bowls, some arcane energy magnifying the sound into the roar of a cataract. The stink of blood spilled across the Daemonculum and the ethereal cold vanished, switching in an instant to a hellish, sweltering blaze.

The daemons stirred in their bindings, striving to reach the bowls. Again, the flesh-drones froze, waiting upon the cadence of the cabal, oblivious to the maddened thrashings of the daemons only a few metres away. Curses and maledictions spilled from the fanged maws of the daemons, threats and entreaties, promises and pleadings for the placation of their abominable hunger.

Only when the choir reached a certain point in the incantation did the flesh-drones act. Sconces set into the roof began to spray a pungent incense into the chamber, a smoky vapour that streamed everywhere in only a few moments but, with unnatural trepidation, refused to stray across the bloodwood disc. Obscured within the smoke, the flesh-drones raised their offerings to the daemons. Unable to resist, the daemons lapped up the gory liquid with long, wolfish tongues, slurping noisily at their hideous repast.

It was some minutes before the daemons had glutted themselves, but the delay was inconsequential now. By accepting the offering when they had, the daemons bound themselves to the ritual, subjected their power to that of the Daemonculum.

A sickly yellow light slowly began to rise about the bloodwood platform. Through the glow, Vallax could be seen snarling orders at his Raptors, demanding their courage and restraint. It was the last view Oriax had of the Iron Warriors. In the next instant the glow engulfed them all, rising to blinding intensity.

All at once, the sickly light winked out, restoring the

chamber to its normal, dingy illumination. Where the light had shone, there was nothing but the bloodwood disc. Five Iron Warriors and a dozen Steel Blood had vanished, evaporated from reality in the blink of an eye.

Oriax pivoted in his dais, stabbing a servo-arm at one of the switches on his command console. A section of wall within his sanctum slid aside, exposing a tiny observation room. From the dark space, the horned figure of Captain Rhodaan emerged, the demi-organic wings on his back fluttering nervously in such proximity to the Daemonculum.

'You have seen?' Oriax demanded. 'You have observed?'

Rhodaan nodded, turning his head towards the bloodwood dais. 'How do I know this device does what you claim? It stinks of witchery.'

Oriax recoiled into his seat, his face fairly dripping with scorn. 'Any science which is incomprehensible to a small mind is decried as witchery,' the Techmarine stated. 'The deluded slaves of the False Emperor have bound their Imperium in chains of superstition and ignorance through such conceits. Our misguided brothers in the Eye have displayed kindred ignorance, hobbling themselves with fables about gods and magic.' The Techmarine's pincers folded inwards, pointing at the decayed cuirass. 'Only I, Fabricator Oriax of the Third Grand Company, have displayed the intellect to understand. To truly understand. Witchery?' he scoffed. 'This is technology.'

'Save your speeches, Fabricator,' Rhodaan retorted. 'You haven't answered my question. How do I know this... technology... does what you claim it does? How do I know what has happened to Vallax and his Faceless?'

Oriax fixed his mechanical eyes upon the Raptor. 'You don't,' he said in a steely hiss. 'Perhaps it is all just smoke and mirrors.' The Techmarine's claw waved towards the walls of the Daemonculum. 'Perhaps they are hidden in some little spy hole, observing you as you observed them.'

Rhodaan kept his gaze fastened on Oriax. 'I was

thinking more in the nature of disintegration.'

Static crackled from the Fabricator's throat, a mechanised approximation of laughter. 'I had thought you less ignorant,' Oriax stated. 'If I wanted Vallax dead, there are far simpler ways it could be arranged. Besides, what do you think the Warsmith's reaction would be if he were to discover I vaporised an entire squad of Raptors without his permission?'

Rhodaan considered that objection to be a good one. Oriax presented an even better one a moment later.

'You have already committed yourself, captain,' the Fabricator reminded. 'The transports have already left Vorago. You and your Raptors were not on them, any more than Vallax and his. The Warsmith would take this as an act of rebellion against his authority. You don't need to be reminded what that would mean.'

'Then they have actually been teleported into Dirgas?' Rhodaan asked, still unwilling to believe what he had seen.

'They are in Dirgas even as we speak,' Oriax answered. To prove his point, the Fabricator pivoted and depressed several runes on his console. Immediately, several pict screens winked into life, displaying images of Squad Vidarna engaged in furious battle with mobs of orks in what looked to be a standard-pattern blockhouse.

'They are in Dirgas,' Oriax repeated. 'But they are not exactly where they wanted to be. As my Steel Blood transmit the images, you will note, captain, an absence of fuel drums or anything else that might store the liquid pollutants the orks require to keep their planes in the sky. No, I fear all Vallax will find in this blockhouse are orks and more orks.'

Rhodaan watched the pict screens, studying the savage close-quarters fighting between Iron Warrior and ork. 'They could fight their way clear and still reach the objective.'

'Improbable,' Oriax declared. 'First, they would have to

realise their mistake. That will take time because of the standardised layout of the blockhouses we've built across Castellax. Second, they will need to locate the correct blockhouse. Third, they will still need to win their way clear of the orks.' The Techmarine gestured at Rhodaan with his claw. 'Fourth, they will be too late, because even if they overcome the first three factors, Squad Kyrith will already have reached the target and destroyed it.'

'You are assuming I will submit my men to your Daemonculum,' Rhodaan observed.

'As I have pointed out, you have no choice,' Oriax said. He pressed another rune on his console. The flesh-drones lumbered away from the pillars and the bound daemons, shuffling back into the inner recesses of Oriax's sanctum. In their stead, another detachment of thirteen flesh-drones marched towards the Daemonculum, fresh slaves shackled to their mechadendrites.

'The moment the transports left Vorago without you, you were committed,' Oriax continued. 'Do not chastise yourself for your decision. If you had gone on the transports, you would have encountered catastrophe. Brother Uhlan, whom I believe you know, arranged to ensure you didn't catch the orks by surprise. He planted an explosive charge on one of the transports, setting it to detonate when the squadron reached Dirgas. He was too cunning to leave the charge on your transport, where it might be found, but instead chose one of the janissary ships. The explosion, will, of course, alert the orks and the air defences of Dirgas have proven quite considerable. Formidable enough to deflate even Morax's pomposity.'

The Raptor was trapped, and he knew it, but that didn't make him like the situation any better. 'How do I know you won't deceive me as you did Vallax?'

'Logic,' Oriax stated. 'If I deceive you, there is just a chance Vallax will reach the real objective. Neither of us wants that. The Over-Captain represents an older facet of the Legion, an atavism that keeps the Third Grand

Company mired in the past. We must anticipate new leadership with new ideas if we are to evolve and progress and achieve our destiny. Iron Warriors such as yourself, Rhodaan, fresh and vital without the encrustations of ancient history clouding your vision. My Daemonculum is the key to that future, if you only have the boldness to use it.'

Rhodaan stared out across the macabre device. For all of Oriax's protestations, it still stank of witchery and the preternatural, a thing of the Beyond. The daemons stirred in their chains, casting longing eyes at the flesh-drones and their captives.

'The Daemonculum hungers,' Oriax said. 'The appetite of a daemon is never sated. They are manifestations of the warp, the void made manifest, shaped by the thoughts and beliefs of physical beings. It is wrong to think of them as actual beings in their own right, they are simply shadows cobbled together from ideas and fears. Without a material mind to give them form, they cannot take shape. They exist simply as energy, flowing through the immaterium. Yet, in our ignorance we cast our minds back to the blackness of superstition and call these entities daemons and invest into them all that is conjured by such a name. Are they daemons because of what they are, or are they daemons because that is what our prejudice and fear have made them?'

'Save your philosophy,' Rhodaan growled. 'Whether arcane technology or the blackest sorcery, it matters not. You are right, Fabricator, I have no choice.'

Oriax swivelled behind his console, depressing runes on the board. 'If the discussion is over, then you may summon your men,' the Techmarine declared. 'It is time you were away.' The red lights in Oriax's face dimmed as the Techmarine stared at Rhodaan.

'I anticipate great things from you, captain,' he said. 'Do not disappoint me.'

Rhodaan stiffened under the mechanical gaze. 'I will

honour my oaths and my duty. Squad Kyrith will succeed in the mission Warsmith Andraaz has entrusted to us.'

The Fabricator shifted in his seat, his pincers flashing across switches and runes. 'The mission,' he hissed in a scratchy whisper. 'Ah, yes, I had almost forgotten.'

Processing Omega was situated in the very bowels of Vorago, a gargantuan facility nestled beneath the central terminus for the intra-city mag-rails which conducted supplies throughout the city's sprawl. The terminus was a shambles now, all but obliterated by the ork bombers and artillery. It was a blighted waste of rubble, desolate and abandoned, fires smouldering among the ruins unchecked, the dead lying abandoned and forlorn.

Five hundred metres below the surface, however, it was a very different story. Vast tunnels, a spider web of corridors and catacombs, were thronged with tractors and trolleys, push-carts and sledges, virtually every kind of vehicle that could be scrounged and scavenged. Masked men, their bodies draped in the ominous plastic dusters, marched through the gloom, indifferent to the heaped corpses they bore with them deep into the earth. Unlike the abandoned terminus, here, in the belly of Vorago, the dead were not forgotten.

Taofang stared from behind the goggles of his mask, watching in amazement as Yuxiang's tractor emerged from the dark tunnel into the hellish light of a vast cavern. He barely noticed the sentries who passed them through, the guard posts and automated defence turrets flanking the mouth of each passageway. Instead, his gaze was captivated by the ghoulish scene awaiting the tractor at the end of its run. Ahead, like a nest of serpents, a profusion of conveyor belts stretched, each belt abutting a small loading dock. Taofang watched as gangs of disposers scurried about the vehicles being offloaded in the docks, using big meat hooks to fish corpses from the cargo beds. The bodies were dumped unceremoniously onto the belts, then whisked away across the cavernous hall.

Yuxiang parked the tractor in one of the docks. He looked back at Taofang and Mingzhou, riding on the machine's running boards. Both of the janissaries had donned the uniform of disposers, Mingzhou taking that of Deacon when the overseer decided to stay behind in the tunnels. After all, he already knew what they would find at Processing Omega.

'Are you sure you want to go on?' Yuxiang asked, his voice muffled by his rebreather. The two janissaries glanced at one another, dreadful anticipation making its presence felt. They were soldiers however, their valour hardened under the cruel pogroms of the Iron Warriors. For them, there could be no fear, only death or survival.

Yuxiang nodded and emerged from the cab. Already a gang of disposers had assembled around the tractor and were quickly scooping out bodies and dropping them onto the conveyor. It was frantic, hurried activity inspired by the unreachable work quotas set by the Iron Warriors themselves. The very haste of the work made the disposers inattentive; none noticed when, after helping lower a few bodies onto the belt, Yuxiang and his companions drifted away one by one.

Taofang was the last to break clear. When he was out of sight of the work crew, he hurried to the maintenance shed where Yuxiang and Mingzhou were waiting. The former factory slave gave his companions one last chance to retreat, but their resolve held fast.

With a grim light in his eyes, Yuxiang reached down and slid back a manhole cover, exposing a slender iron ladder that descended into what seemed to be a pit of green fire. He hesitated a moment, steeling his nerve, bracing himself to revisit the horrors he had already exposed himself to. After a moment, Yuxiang climbed down the ladder, the two janissaries following after him.

They did not descend far, only deep enough that Taofang

could slide the manhole cover closed above them. Arms wrapped about the rungs of the ladder, the three rebels hung suspended a hundred metres above an enormous room. For Yuxiang, the resemblance to a factory was unmistakable: the conveyor belts and winches, cranes and pulleys, gantries and scaffolds. Masked labourers shuffled about the vast installation while pallid servitors maintained their endless vigils at control points and cogitator-terminals.

'This is where Castellax buries its dead,' Yuxiang whispered in a haunted tone.

Far below, a nest of conveyors descended from the ceiling to spill the corpses from the unloading stations onto a series of lower belts. From there the mangled remains descended another twenty metres before they were unceremoniously dumped into a gigantic cistern, a vat of bilious green liquid that bubbled incessantly, spewing a scummy froth about each corpse as it dropped into the toxic lake. Bodies bobbed like bits of cork amidst the green filth, but as the liquid seeped into the flesh, the cadavers lost their buoyancy. Quickly they sank towards the bottom of the vat.

'The chemicals in that lake will reduce a human body down to its constituent proteins within ten minutes,' Yuxiang explained to the janissaries above him, repeating the hideous commentary he'd had from Deacon. 'Only the enamel from the teeth won't be reduced.' He pointed with his hand to a great pipe jutting from the base of the vat. Through a narrow grate, a stream of green mush exuded onto another conveyor belt. Gangs of labourers stood to either side of the grate, removing at regular intervals a series of metal filter screens. The three rebels could see the white paste clogging the screens as they were removed, the only part of the human body that refused to be 'processed'.

'That sludge you see,' Yuxiang said, nodding to the mush leaving the pipe, 'will be further filtered, immersed in bio-secretions, amphetamines and adrenal-extracts. Everything a fighting man needs to maintain his alertness and aggression. Then it will be injected into tubes, ready to be distributed to the defenders of Vorago as protein-paste. Organic supplement for the synthetic diet.'

Taofang shook his head in shock, trying desperately to refuse the evidence of his eyes. He wanted to be sick. 'They are feeding us our own dead,' he groaned.

Beneath him, Mingzhou made a gagging noise, her body going limp for a moment, one of her boots slipping from the rung. Quickly she remembered herself, grasping the ladder before she could fall. She turned her gaze down upon Yuxiang.

'You were right,' she said. 'The Iron Warriors have to be destroyed.' She stared back at the bubbling vat.

'Death is too good for the monsters who would do this,' she declared. 'But it is the only justice we can hope to bring them.'

CHAPTER XVI

I-Day Plus One Hundred and Five

THE FERROCRETE HALLS of the blockhouse were alive with alien roars and the chatter of automatic weapons. Mobs of orks swarmed through the streets of Dirgas, converging upon the scene. After months away from the main fighting, their thirst for battle had reached the point of mania. News of a scrap in the very middle of the city spread like wildfire.

One after another, the Raptors of Squad Vidarna, Over-Captain Vallax's infamous Faceless, died. Fighting their way ever deeper into the blockhouse, the Iron Warriors had become the centre of a storm of death. Hundreds of enemy corpses lay strewn through the chambers and corridors of the fortress, but they were losses the orks could easily afford. There were thousands to take their place. From the start, there had been only five Space Marines. It had cost them two comrades to penetrate as far as the manufactory.

Vallax spun around as Gressil was ripped apart by the lethal chatter of a grotesque combi-weapon. The

Over-Captain regarded his underling's sacrifice with a sneer and leapt upon his killer, an enormous ork encased in crude, blocky armour. The whirling edge of his chainsword screeched as it churned into the ork's shoulder. Instead of gnawing through flesh and bone, however, it gouged a mesh of wires and cables. Lubricants and fuel spurted from ruptured hoses and pipes.

The ork grunted and lashed out with a monstrous power claw, the talons closing tight about Vallax's sword arm. With a grinding groan, the pneumatic claw began to compress the vambrace, cracking the thick ceramite plate.

Vallax's boots hammered into the ork's chest in a futile effort to kick the brute away. The hulking monstrosity didn't even flinch, deigning only to smile viciously at the Iron Warrior as it tightened its grip.

The Raptor squirmed within the ork's clutch, clenching his teeth against the pain surging from his trapped arm as he twisted his body around. The arm was crushed to a pulp when the ork tightened its grasp. Vallax's brain, conditioned to block out every magnitude of pain, ignored the mutilation, forcing himself to raise his good arm and bring the muzzle of his bolt pistol towards his captor's face.

The organic side of the cyborg's face was obliterated by the high-impact explosive shells, slivers of shrapnel and bone fragments flying from its destroyed skull. Instead of collapsing, however, the ork's metallic body simply froze in place, its mechanics powering down, another dead machine in the maze of stamping presses and conveyors which littered the floor of the manufactory. A grotesque statue, the cyborg stood, the arm of its killer held fast in its frozen claw.

Emboldened by Vallax's immobility, a swarm of gretchin came scurrying from their holes, eyes gleaming with murderous glee. They surrounded the trapped Iron Warrior, shots from their primitive slug-throwers and autoguns glancing off his power armour, clubs and axes clattering against his legs in a futile effort to pierce the Raptor's shell. Snarling in rage, Vallax gunned down a dozen of the filthy slaveling xenos, but always there were more to replace those he killed.

Uhlan's pistol suddenly roared, the report echoing across the manufactory. Gretchin burst beneath his shots, their weedy bodies blasted into gory pulp by the bolt-shells. Screeching in terror, the cowardly survivors broke and fled, darting behind presses and diving into gaps amidst the machinery.

'That is the last of them, my lord captain,' Uhlan reported.

Vallax glared at the half-breed, wondering how long Uhlan had waited before intervening. With the rest of Squad Vidarna dead, the mongrel could concoct any story to account for the Over-Captain's death. Had Uhlan bided his time until he was convinced Vallax would survive with or without his help?

Vallax strained to free his trapped arm, growling under his breath. 'Oriax's Steel Blood was late as usual.' He scowled as he thought of the spy-skulls and their notable failure to assist the Raptors. 'The Fabricator's usefulness to this operation begins to wear thin.'

Uhlan nodded. 'Indeed, Over-Captain. The failings of his servitors are inexcusable. They should have found the fuel dump for us by now.'

Vallax wrenched the cyborg's claw downwards, stretching his free arm so he could retrieve his chainsword from the floor. Thumbing the activation rune, he brought the weapon grinding against the metal wrist behind the claw.

The Over-Captain barely concentrated on what he was doing, his mind instead mulling over what Uhlan had said. It was true, the Steel Blood should have located the fuel dump by now. The blockhouses weren't terribly complex, simply mirrored layers stacked eight and ten deep. A standard pattern repeated all across Castellax.

Vallax cursed as he made the connection. The

blockhouses all followed the same blueprint, each floor plan identical to the next. There was the reason the Steel Blood had failed! The Daemonculum had transported them to the wrong blockhouse!

As that horrible certainty impressed itself upon his mind, Vallax heard the wail of one of Oriax's Steel Blood. He looked towards the sound, watching as the metal skull came flying into the manufactory – a horde of orks rushing after it. The Steel Blood was sounding an alarm all right – but it was an alarm meant for the orks. The damned things had been alerting the aliens and leading them to the Iron Warriors the whole time!

'Shoot the Steel Blood!' Vallax snarled at Uhlan. The half-breed stared at him in confusion, then cried out as blood exploded from his ruptured chest. A harpoon of steel protruded from the stricken Iron Warrior's breast. Even as Uhlan turned to fire on his attacker, the cable fitted to the harpoon snapped taut. He was thrown off his feet as the cable began to retract, dragging him across the manufactory towards the gun carriage that had fired on him and a grinning ork with a blowtorch gripped in its oily paw. Other aliens swarmed past the mekanik, loosing a fusillade of shells, solid shot and glowing plasma at the disabled Uhlan.

Vallax redoubled his efforts to cut away the cyborg's wrist. Survival was doubtful now, but at least he could die fighting on his feet, like a true Iron Warrior, not slaughtered like Uhlan.

Even as he cut away the last string of cables, Vallax flattened beneath an impact against the back of his head. As he struck the ground he could see the crumpled wreckage of a metal skull lying on the floor beside him, its cranium caved-in by a high-velocity impact. Vallax imagined his helmet must have a similar dent.

The jaw of the damaged Steel Blood dropped open, the vox-caster spewing forth the synthesised voice of Fabricator Oriax.

'This is the end, Over-Captain. Before you die, know that Captain Rhodaan even now secures the objective for the Warsmith. It is in another blockhouse, of course. The only thing in this one is death. Your death.'

Vallax struggled to rise, but found that his legs refused to respond. Learned in biology as well as mechanics, Oriax had guided his Steel Blood to the precise location to deliver maximum damage upon the Iron Warrior. The impacted helmet had delivered a paralysing blow to Vallax's spine.

Panic filled Vallax's hearts as he realised the extent of Oriax's treachery. He could hear the orks rushing into the room, rushing to seize their helpless prey.

'You found me like this in the crystal-swamps,' Oriax's voice droned. 'I should have died, but for you. Now, I avenge that crime.'

'Die, Vallax, and may the Chaos Gods show your spirit the same mercy you showed me.'

ALARMS WAILED OVERHEAD as the orks began another strafing run against the defences of Vorago. Fighters came screaming down, the chatter of their guns chewing holes in the firmament, sending slivers of ferrocrete dancing into the night. Janissaries and overseers scrambled into the shelter of bunkers and pillboxes while slaves cowered in their firing pits. The anti-aircraft crews, chained to their batteries, had no option except to stay at their posts and try to bring down the alien attackers.

Taofang watched the carnage unfold from the black mouth of a service tunnel, his lasgun held close to his body beneath the folds of his duster. He waited for the height of panic and confusion, watching to ensure that none of the Iron Warriors were going to put in an appearance and bolster the valour of their minions by giving them something more terrifying than orks to fear.

'We should move now,' Taofang said, turning to stare back into the gloom of the tunnel. Clustered around the tractor were a score of men, haggard-looking slaves for the most part but with a few janissaries and renegade disposers among the mix. It was easy to spot the ones who were armed and the ones who weren't. The armed men had a vicious gleam in their eyes, the unarmed ones simply had weary resignation. They wouldn't be very useful in a fight – not until they felt that they had a real chance to strike back. Guns would give them that confidence. Guns were the objective of tonight's excursion onto the firebreak. Yuxiang had built a small army by removing 'dead' men from the walls, but if they were to fight, they needed weapons and ammunition. Far more than could be scavenged from the firing pits.

'Are you certain this is smart?' Deacon asked in his anxious voice.

'The height of the ork attack,' Taofang stated, his tone brooking no argument. 'The soldiers will be keeping their heads down while the planes are overhead. They won't stir from their shelters. That means we'll only have the ones in the command post to worry about.'

Yuxiang fixed the janissary with a sombre look. 'You know there will be no option but to fight?' he said. 'We can't try to reason with them. Sway them to our cause. There isn't time.'

Taofang nodded, his expression grim. He glanced over at Mingzhou, locking eyes with the sniper. 'Don't worry,' he said. 'Anybody in that command post is no comrade.' He patted the barrel of his lasgun. 'Colonel Nehring has had this coming a long time.'

'Ever since Gamma-Five,' Mingzhou agreed, a cold smile on her face.

'We saw a lot of good men die at Gamma-Five,' Taofang said. 'I've a mind to watch a few bad men die for once.'

Yuxiang lifted his arm, gazing back at the men around the tractor, looking to see that each of them was watching him rather than distracted by the ork attack. In his turn, the factory slave fixed his attention on Taofang.

Even when an ork bomb exploded somewhere above the tunnel, shaking it and sending trickles of dust raining down, he didn't allow his attention to waver. When the moment came, every second that followed would be invaluable. Yuxiang was determined to squander none of them.

By his turn, Taofang maintained a tireless vigil at the mouth of the tunnel, watching as the few janissaries still in the open at last abandoned their posts and went scrambling for cover. Except for the dead and dying, the top of the wall was almost deserted now. He started to turn, started to give the nod to Yuxiang so he could signal the other rebels. It was the hint of motion from the corner of his eye that spun Taofang back around. Frustration boiled up inside him as he watched a trio of janissaries come sprinting into the tunnel.

Until now, even in the height of the attack, fear of the tunnel had kept the soldiers away. No man courted the places of the dead and the service tunnel stank of the disposers and their morbid work. That some of them should overcome their dread now, just when the rebels were set to act sent black despair flooding into his heart. It was as if all their plans and hopes were nothing more than the cruel jest of...

Taofang shivered, unwilling to finish the thought. The Iron Warriors visited the most horrible punishment upon those slaves they found practising the Imperial creed, paying homage to the so-called God-Emperor of Mankind. It was whispered among the Scorpion Brigade that there were other gods beside the Emperor, monstrous things which even the Iron Warriors grudgingly paid homage to.

In his mind, Taofang could hear the mocking laughter of invisible horrors. Having come so far, many of the rebels would never find the courage to reach this point again. Gambling their lives on this adventure, they would cherish the reprieve, hold each hour given back to them as precious and sacrosanct. No, when they retreated back into the tunnels, there would be no coming back.

The janissaries came rushing into the dark opening, their faces pale, their bodies shivering from the ordeal of battle. One of the soldiers recoiled as he saw Taofang standing inside the opening, shocked and disgusted by the sudden appearance of a disposer. His fright passed quickly, a nervous chuckle starting to rise as he turned to address his comrades.

The soldier never spoke the words on his tongue. As he turned, a bright beam of crimson light slashed through his head, searing through helmet and skull alike. The slaughtered janissaries collapsed in a heap, a new shock stamped forever in his dead eyes.

Mingzhou's shot threw the two survivors into action. One of the soldiers snapped his lasgun to his shoulder, years of remorseless training allowing him to almost instinctively pick out the direction of the shot. Before he could fire, however, the janissary was lying on the floor of the tunnel, an ugly hole burned through his stomach.

Taofang stared down at the wounded man, smoke rising from the hole where he had fired his hidden weapon through the plastic shroud of his duster. He felt no pity for the stricken man, for all that they might have fought shoulder to shoulder only a few weeks earlier. Because of this man and his comrades, Taofang had been ready to retreat before the battle was even joined. Until that moment when Mingzhou shot and restored his perspective. Now he felt ashamed of his reluctance to do what had to be done, his hesitance to be as ruthless as his enemy. Morality was the refuge of those without the strength to triumph.

Burning light cracked from Taofang's lasgun, burning another hole through his duster as it stabbed down into the face of the wounded janissary. It was a moment he knew he would carry with him always, the moment when something died deep inside him, to be replaced by something else. Something strong and cold and terrible.

'What about the third one?' Yuxiang cried, rushing up to the mouth of the tunnel.

Taofang glanced about. Unlike his comrade, the third janissary had chosen flight over fight. He could be seen dashing across the wall, his boots barely touching the ferrocrete in his haste. If the soldier had kept his wits about him, the rebels would have been undone, but in his panic the janissary simply rushed blindly past bunkers and pill-boxes filled with comrades. At any one the survivor could have stopped and sounded the alarm, brought enough armed men swarming into the tunnel to obliterate the tiny gang of rebels.

Only moments ago, Taofang had felt the claws of some unseen force wresting opportunity from them. Now, as if by the same capricious intent, an equally incredulous circumstance was handing that opportunity back to them.

'Head for Nehring's bunker,' Taofang shouted to Yuxiang. He ducked back into the tunnel as an ugly ork plane flashed across the firebreak, dropping a bomb against the superstructure. The explosive impact nearly knocked him from his feet.

'What are you going to do?' Mingzhou demanded, her hand tight about his arm, her eyes sharp with concern.

Removing the lasgun from beneath his duster, Taofang checked the power level. 'I'm going to get him,' he declared. 'Catch him before he spreads the alarm.'

Mingzhou clung to him as he tried to leave the tunnel. 'Stay here,' she told him. Before he could react, the sniper was darting out onto the wall, throwing herself into the shelter of a bomb crater. An ork fighter went screaming overhead, a little line of tracers skipping across the ferrocrete only a few metres from the woman.

She didn't even react to death dancing at her side. Tossing back her crimson hair with a roll of her neck, Mingzhou aimed down the sight of her lasrifle.

'She'll never make it,' Yuxiang groaned.

Inwardly, Taofang shared Yuxiang's doubt. The janissary

was over two thousand metres away, darting from side to side to avoid the attacking ork planes. It was absurd to believe anyone, even one of the Iron Warriors themselves, could hit a moving target at such range.

A moment later, the situation was made even more dire. Seeming to stir from his panic, the soldier glanced about wildly, looking for a bunker to dart into. He found one, only a dozen metres away. Spinning around, the janissary raced towards the fortification.

In that brief moment as he turned, the janissary doomed himself. Mingzhou could read his intention as clearly as Taofang, she could see the refugee's objective. Aiming along the route he must take, the sniper pulled the trigger of her lasrifle. A beam of red light stabbed out, whisking into the janissary. The soldier didn't even cry out, he simply crumpled to the ground.

Mingzhou leapt up and sprinted back into the tunnel, the lasrifle cradled in her arms. 'Let's go visit the colonel now,' she suggested.

Leaving Deacon and a half-dozen rebels to bring up the tractor behind them, Yuxiang led the rest at a run across the firebreak. Ork aircraft still filled the skies, fumes from their crude engines spilling down over the wall. As one of the fighters came streaking down, its guns spitting, the rebels scrambled for cover. Three of the men, former slaves who had been rescued from the pits, were caught in the fire, their bodies shredded by the heavy-calibre slugs spewing from the xenos guns.

The rest didn't have the luxury of considering their dead. Rushing past a bombed-out pillbox, the rebels converged upon the grey bulk of Nehring's command post. In the lead, Taofang hesitated before the armoured door, one last hideous thought occurring to him. So far there had been no sign of Iron Warriors on this section of wall. The reason might be that they were inside the command bunker.

'Something wrong?' Yuxiang asked.

Taofang looked at the slave, saw the eagerness and exhilaration on the man's face. No, he decided, they had come too far to be cheated now. There was no good to come from voicing his fear now. Whatever was on the other side of that door, they would face it together.

Taofang leapt down the short string of steps between the doorway and the bunker proper, surprising the sentries huddled there for protection against the orks. The stock of his lasgun opened the cheek of one sentry, a shot from the barrel settled the second. Maintaining his momentum, Taofang hurdled the bodies and dashed into the anteroom beyond.

Here, too, he found surprised and disordered men, a rabble of soldiers who had taken to the anteroom for shelter. They gapped at him as he stood in the doorway, his duster spattered in the blood of his recent foes, the barrel of his lasgun shifting between them. One of the soldiers reached for his own weapon and was cut down instantly by Taofang's laser. For a moment, shock held the other soldiers immobile. Before they could recover, Yuxiang and the other rebels came swarming into the anteroom, firing as they came.

Sounds of the massacre must have drifted into the control centre beyond the anteroom, for the heavy steel door slid back and a scowling lieutenant came storming through the portal. The officer had woefully misjudged the situation, however. Thinking he only faced some squabble amongst his men, the lieutenant was unprepared for the scene of carnage, or the victorious perpetrators of that havoc.

Before the officer's scowl could collapse into shock, before his hand could even reach for the pistol holstered at his side, a crimson beam from Mingzhou's lasrifle punched a smouldering hole through the lieutenant's forehead.

'Death to the Iron Warriors!' Yuxiang shouted, pushing past the dying lieutenant, making for the closing portal behind him. The battle cry was taken up by the dozen rebels who had made it this far, all save Taofang, who wondered if one of the superhuman fiends did indeed await them on the other side of the door.

The sizzle of lasguns hissed through the air as the rebels burst from the anteroom. The cries of dying men echoed through the confines of the command centre, mixing with the dull rumble of ork bombers being transmitted across exterior vox-casters. Tech-adepts crumpled at their stations, their archaic robes scorched by las-bolts; engineers wilted to the floor, their overalls stained with their life's blood; officers collapsed across their consoles, their black uniforms folding around them like shrouds.

There was little resistance. Beyond a few sidearms, the occupants of the command centre were unarmed, outgunned even by the sparse arsenal the rebels had possessed at the start of their attack. Now, equipped with weapons looted off the anteroom dead, the rebels overwhelmed Colonel Nehring's staff. After a few furious minutes of carnage, barely a half-dozen officers were still alive, their hands raised in defeat, pleas for mercy rolling off their lips. It would have been a different story if one of the Iron Warriors had been present, but thankfully the oversized command throne reserved for a visiting legionary was vacant.

Yuxiang prowled through the wreckage, wincing as sparks from a damaged Steel Blood flared across him, burning his scalp. Intent upon the dead men sprawled on the floor, he hadn't noticed the hovering servitor. A las-bolt tore into the floating skull, sending it careening across the room to smash itself against the thick ferrocrete wall. Taofang uttered a caustic laugh.

'It's a waste of time looking there,' the janissary barked. 'There's only one man we need, and you won't find him with the dead!'

Mingzhou marched to where the little knot of prisoners was being held. Her face bore a vindictive smile as she grabbed the breast of one man's tunic and pulled him away from his fellows. The officer's dusky skin was beaded with sweat, his eyes wide with fright. They grew still wider when he heard the sniper shout to her comrades. 'Here is the colonel! Always trust him to leave the dying to other people.'

Yuxiang and Taofang stared coldly at the terrified officer. 'This is the man who can get us weapons?' Yuxiang asked.

Colonel Nehring licked his lips, his eyes shifting from one man to the other, trying to gauge which of them was in command, to which of them he needed to appeal to save his life. Something about Taofang's posture made it seem like the janissary was in charge, but one look into the soldier's eyes was enough to make Nehring cringe. There was hate in those eyes, hate that wouldn't be placated.

'I am in command of this entire section,' Nehring said, turning towards Yuxiang. 'If you desist now... I will... will not report this to the Iron Warriors.'

Mention of the dreaded Space Marines brought gasps from some of the slaves, but if Nehring mistook fear for timidity, he was sorely mistaken.

Yuxiang buried the butt of his lasgun in the officer's belly, driving the breath from his body, smashing the arrogance and authority from his attitude. 'You will get me guns,' Yuxiang told him. 'That is the only thing I want. Not threats. Not promises.'

Coughing, trying to suck air back into his lungs, Nehring nodded in submission. 'What... whatever... want...'

As the officer started to rise, the sizzle-crack of a lasgun rasped through the room. Nehring cried out in agony, sprawling to the floor as the smoking wreckage of his knee failed under his weight. He landed hard, teeth chipping as his jaw smacked against the floor. Howling in pain, he clutched at his leg.

'We don't need his lies or his mouth,' Taofang growled, aiming his lasgun downwards, sending another bolt sizzling through the back of Nehring's hand. 'The supply caches are actuated by retinal scan.'

Nehring's dark skin grew pale, a panicked yelp escaped his bleeding mouth. Desperately he groped along the floor, trying to drag himself to shelter. His effort was thwarted when Mingzhou's rifle slammed down against his other hand, breaking every finger.

'Gamma-Five,' the sniper hissed down at him. 'You made quite an impression on everyone who was there.' She drove the rifle into his ribs. 'Unfortunately, most of them aren't here to thank you for your selfless leadership.'

Yuxiang rounded on Taofang. 'Kill him and get it over with,' he demanded. The janissary shook off his restraining hand.

'We'll need his eye,' Taofang declared. He reached down to his boot, drawing a wide-bladed combat knife. 'We need his eye to actuate the retinal scans.' He paused, glaring down at the terrified, whimpering officer.

'We need his eye,' Taofang repeated. 'But I think I'll take the whole damn head.'

THE ORK'S SNARLING face burst into blobs of meat and splinters of bone as the churning blade of Rhodaan's chainsword bit through the alien's horned helm. Like a poleaxed grox, the huge ork slammed to the floor, its stumpy fingers still tugging at the triggers of the stubbers clenched in its paws. The Iron Warrior kicked the twitching corpse from underfoot, giving him space to confront the rest of the xenos horde.

The eerie power of the Daemonculum had pierced the walls of reality, translating Squad Kyrith from Oriax's sanctum deep beneath the Iron Bastion to the ork-infested city of Dirgas. In the blink of an eye, the Space Marines had been teleported across an entire continent, shifted across the face of Castellax. Whatever the Fabricator's protestations, the thing still stank of witchery to Rhodaan.

Rhodaan spun around, opening the belly of a howling ork rushing at him with a crude axe, a shot from the Raptor's plasma pistol melting the skull off a second alien marauder. As the two creatures collapsed before him, Rhodaan lunged across their bodies, taking the attack into the midst of the alien mob. To an untrained eye, the tactic might seem reckless but it was actually a calculated exploitation of the savage xenos mindset. The ork was a creature which gloried in battle, eager to fight. At the same time, its society was one of strict hierarchy, the strong dominating everything weaker than themselves. An ork quickly understood its place in the hierarchy, deferring to the more powerful of its breed until such time as it felt itself strong enough to challenge its betters and raise its own position.

Given even the briefest pause, an ork mob would automatically adjust itself, instinctually deferring to the leaders and allowing their biggest and strongest the right to sate their blood thirst. By denying them that instant for adjustment, Rhodaan wrong-footed the aliens, put them off balance, made them hesitate ever so slightly. Before bringing its shock maul down, a scar-faced ork glanced to make certain its boss wasn't nearby. That fraction of a heartbeat was all the delay Rhodaan needed to open the brute from belly to groin.

Beside him, Pazuriel and Baelfegor wrought havoc among the aliens. The orks were pure primal savagery, raw undisciplined force. They attacked with a simple, fearless brutality – an undiluted appetite for battle that wasn't confused by consideration of tactics and strategy. Against a lesser foe, the very recklessness of the attack would have been overwhelming. Against Iron Warriors, however, it was a recipe for slaughter. Primitive might against the cold precision of tactical warfare. Beasts born for battle against men who had been trained, conditioned and engineered for war. Nature versus the deadly progeny of a thousand arcane sciences.

Even if the orks had possessed minds capable of under-standing, the Iron Warriors didn't allow them the time to understand just how woefully outclassed they were.

'All charges in place,' Brother Gomorie's voice crackled across the inter-squad vox.

Rhodaan smiled inside his helmet, blasting the growl from a huge ork warrior with a blazing beam of plasma. The report was welcome news. Any chance Vallax and his Faceless had of stealing triumph from Squad Kyrith was quickly evaporating.

Oriax had been as good as his word. The Raptors had materialised within the ferrocrete halls of the blockhouse Biglug was using to stockpile the horde's aviation fuel. Secure in their control of Dirgas, the orks had positioned their sentries on the perimeter of the blockhouse, to keep their own kind from sneaking in and stealing fuel. There had been no provision for guards inside, no thought that the Iron Warriors might pose a threat to them so deep inside their own stronghold.

If not for a pack of xenos scavengers that had managed to sneak into the blockhouse, the Raptors might have achieved their objective without alerting the enemy at all. Rhodaan was tempted to attribute their encounter with the thieves to bad luck, but it was too much of a coincidence to be so easily dismissed. He could still feel the chill of the Daemonculum clinging to his armour, the mephitic vapour of the warp. How might that linger-ing taint affect them? How might perverse warp entities amuse themselves by violating laws of causality and prob-ability? Was it coincidence that had caused the scavengers to stumble onto Squad Kyrith? Was it simply bad luck that had allowed a few of them to escape and spread the alarm?

Ill fortune or daemon-engineered doom, Rhodaan didn't care. Whatever fates conspired against him, he would defy them with his every breath. Let the gods of Chaos plot and scheme, they would not cheat him of his glory.

'Set the charges for five minutes,' Rhodaan growled across the vox. The chatter of a heavy stubber forced him to duck behind the bulk of a support pillar, chips of ferrocrete flying in every direction as the ork gunner tracked the Raptor across the storage chamber, oblivious to the cocktail of fuel spilling from ruptured drums and barrels.

'Add thirty seconds,' Rhodaan amended, the aiming reticule in his optic display picking out the ork gunner from the mob of lesser aliens. It was a big brute, its leathery chest bared to expose a network of wire piercings that formed the leering visage of an alien glyph. The weapon it carried was a massive automatic stubber, so massive that even a Space Marine would have thought twice before trying to fire it from the hip the way this monster was. That the ork could do so and maintain some rude semblance of accuracy was more a testament to its brawn than the mental agility required to compensate for the weapon's recoil.

Rhodaan seized one of the fuel drums stacked near his refuge, hefting the burden in an underhand shift, sending it wobbling across the floor. The ork shifted its aim, barking with laughter as its bullets shredded the drum. Sparks and burning drops of fuel blossomed from the disintegrating drum, lighting upon the floor. Pools of fuel blazed into hellish fury, racing through the chamber, throwing walls of flame in every direction.

Many of the orks howled in alarm, scattering before the flames. The brute with the stubber maintained its murderous barrage with stubborn ferocity, blindly sending bullets slamming through the obscuring flames.

From the midst of the fire, a vengeful figure of ceramite and plasteel came hurtling at the ork. Fire dripped from Rhodaan's power armour, smouldered against the blood-slick pinions of his demi-organic wings. Thrust ahead by his jump pack, the Raptor smashed into the surprised alien, the heavy stubber shattering beneath the Iron Warrior's impact as he crashed into the ork.

The brute was sent reeling, stumbling across the chamber, slipping in the burning fuel. Arms flailing, the ork collapsed into a pool of liquid fire. Anguished howls rose from the creature as it thrashed among the flames.

Rhodaan didn't relax. He had seen the stubborn vitality of orks too often.

The brute sloshed painfully in the pool, then rolled onto its back. Through the pain and blinding fire, the ork was able to focus upon its attacker. Its body wrapped in flames, it lunged up from the floor, meaty paws clenched into burning fists.

The Iron Warrior met the monster's attack with a sweep of his chainsword that sent the roaring head bouncing across the floor. He sidestepped as the burning body came hurtling after him. It staggered on a few paces, as though unaware that its guiding intelligence was lying on the floor. The fists abruptly fell to the ork's sides, its shoulders slumped. Almost in slow motion, the headless corpse dropped to the ground.

'My error,' Rhodaan said across the vox. He stared at the burning corpse. 'Twenty seconds.'

'We shall require all the time we can get for extraction,' Uzraal said, the sizzle of his meltagun audible across the vox.

Rhodaan was already in motion, turning to address the threat presented by a new mob of orks rushing at the Iron Warriors from the far side of the chamber. Ignoring the flames and the threat of explosion, he grabbed a burning fuel drum and threw it into the midst of the aliens. A blast from his plasma pistol detonated the drum like a bomb, splashing the mob in burning promethium. A half-dozen orks collapsed in fiery agony; the rest, many of them with burning clothes and singed skin, scattered.

'Through this pack,' Rhodaan ordered, dropping one of the fleeing aliens. In the corner of his helmet's visual display he could see the layout of the blockhouse. The lift would be nearby. In his mind, he could picture the aerial reconnaissance images provided by Morax's Air Cohort.

There was no guarantee of outside help; even if Vallax and Uhlan hadn't initiated any treachery, the valour of Flesh was uncertain. The Raptors couldn't count on them to brave the defences of Dirgas to reach the blockhouse. Certainly not in the time allowed to them. No, Squad Kyrith would have to attend to their own withdrawal, an eventuality Rhodaan had prepared for.

'We fight our way to the roof,' Rhodaan told his Raptors.

'And then?' Pazuriel demanded. Rhodaan could just see the other Iron Warrior from the corner of his vision, shooting down orks with bursts from a hand flamer. Against the backdrop of a burning fuel dump, there was something almost ridiculous about the scene.

Rhodaan scowled inside his helmet. He was depending on the orks to act true to form, aggression overruling caution. Otherwise, they were all going to die.

'Reconnaissance shows several vertical lift aircraft parked on the roof,' Rhodaan said. 'We fight our way up there and steal one of their planes.' A touch of black humour crept into his voice, humour that had nothing to do with the alien warriors he continued to gun down as they rushed at him through the flames.

'Be attentive for anything that looks like a pilot,' Rhodaan said. 'Whoever finds one better have a strong omophagea.'

There was a chorus of disgusted groans across the vox-channel.

Rhodaan smashed his way through an axe-wielding ork, then brought his chainsword down, slashing the arm off another charging alien. 'Content yourselves, brothers,' he said. 'An ork's brain isn't a big meal.'

CHAPTER XVII

I-Day Plus One Hundred and Six

RHODAAN STARED IN revulsion at what passed for controls in the ork aircraft, feeling the pit of his stomach drop out. He'd hoped the alien aircraft would be simple enough for them to fly out of Dirgas. It was simple, he had to admit that much, but it was so simple he didn't see how the xenos could make it fly. How they were going to was a question he hoped Gomorie's gruesome snack would answer. He'd been the lucky Raptor to catch the ork pilot on the launch pad, though Baelfegor's reluctance to close with the xenos might have contributed to Gomorie's opportunity. No Iron warrior shirked his duty, but there were some objectives it was more appealing to leave to another battle-brother.

The cockpit was a glass-faced box squashed onto the nose of the bomber, having every appearance of being welded onto the fuselage as an after-thought. As though the orks had built the rest of the plane and then realised they'd missed out any way to control it. The control panel was a crude box, its face pitted with a few dials and levers, an enormous and clunky-looking steering column, several vulgar-looking patches of graffiti and a bank of buttons that was missing at least three of its number with a fourth dangling from the panel by a few wires. A pair of huge foot pedals rose from the floor, one of them bolted flat by a strip of sheet metal, the other flapping limp in its fastenings. A huge copper pipe stretched along the side of the compartment, its surface pitted and scored in dozens of places, greasy rags wrapped about the worst of the ruptures. Rhodaan winced at the heavy promethium smell rising from the pipe, realising with alarm that it was some element of the plane's fuel system and that once the craft was in motion, it would start leaking all over the cockpit.

Still, Rhodaan couldn't even consider that to be the most alarming element of the ork cockpit. There was the little drawing of an arrow, for instance, scrawled across a strip of hide and nailed to a section of the fuselage above one of the levers. Whatever the meaning of the arrow, the direction it was pointing didn't correspond with the direction the lever could be moved. Then there was the little box rising from the floor beside the pilot's couch. It looked like a primitive clutch, a single control rod that could be slid into different positions to control the craft's speed. Little las-marks seemed to denote the velocity the craft would make in each position the clutch was thrown. At some point, an ork had welded a piece of pig-iron over the groove, locking the clutch into its highest speed. The Space Marine lost no time tearing the bit of pig-iron from the groove.

Gomorie wiped his mouth and placed his helmet over his head. The mangled skull of the ork pilot fell to the floor. The Iron Warrior stalked towards the controls, trying to manoeuvre around the bulky couch. From outside, the chatter of bolters rose.

'More orks on the roof,' Pazuriel reported over the vox. Along with Uzraal and Baelfegor, he was maintaining the perimeter the Iron Warriors had established around the aircraft. 'If we're going to leave, we need to do it soon.'

Gomorie's hands closed about the top of the couch. Viciously, he ripped it clear from its moorings and ejected it from the cockpit. His path clear, he pushed past Rhod-aan and stared at the controls.

'Can you make any sense of this hodgepodge?' Rhod-aan demanded.

Gomorie nodded. 'Have our battle-brothers embark, lord captain,' he said. His finger pressed one of the buttons on the panel. When nothing happened, he pressed it again, this time hard enough to make it sink into the panel. When the plane still failed to respond, he smacked the side of the panel with his fist. Abruptly, the aircraft shuddered into life, the rumble of its awakened engine, the tremor of its activated pistons pulsing through the fuselage.

'Squad Kyrith is aboard,' Pazuriel's voice announced over the vox.

The crack of bullets and shells against the plane's fuse-lage lent an immediacy to Pazuriel's words. There was no one outside to maintain the perimeter. In a matter of moments, the orks would be swarming over the plane.

'Now or never,' Rhodaan told Gomorie.

Gomorie stood confidently before the controls, the mag-clamps in his boots lending him more stability than the crude pilot's couch ever could. 'It is not a complex system,' he declared. He lifted one of his feet and brought it towards the pedal that had been bolted almost flat to the floor. 'All you need do is feed the engine...'

As soon as Gomorie touched his foot to the pedal, the ork plane roared forwards, leaping from the rooftop like a hound loosed from its chain. Rhodaan was sent reeling, his helmet crashing against the low ceiling of the cockpit. Gomorie wrapped his arms about the steering column, more to keep himself upright than to direct the craft.

'Slow this obscenity down!' Rhodaan roared.

Gomorie brought his foot smashing down on the other

pedal, but it simply flopped limply against the floor. He turned and looked at Rhodaan. 'That should have been the brake,' he reported. 'It seems the pilot took it upon itself to disable it. The ork didn't want to appear timid to its fellows,' he elaborated as some of the alien's memories stirred in his mind.

Rhodaan felt his hearts hammer in his breast. 'How do we land without brakes?' he demanded.

Again, Gomorie focused upon the mental images from the ork's brain. 'We crash,' was his far from encouraging response.

ENGINSEER HERODITUS FOCUSED his gaze upon the wondrous vision. Despite the emotional weakness, he regretted the atrophy of his organic eyes. Cybernetic implants were too stable, unable to cloud with tears of awe and devotion. Unable to exhibit the proper respect such a sight demanded.

Above him, on the causeway, being lifted upon stout titanium chains, was the graceful casing of Vindex Lartius, every inch of its shell lovingly inscribed with liturgies of power and catechisms of revenge. Dozens of purity scrolls fluttered in the sluggish breeze of the underworld's archaic filtration cycle, the lead seals binding them to the warhead embossed with the cog symbol of the Adeptus Mechanicus.

Vindication was coming, was nearly at hand. Justification for their years of subservience to the traitors, atonement for their debased survival. The works of the arch-enemy would be swept away. Castellax would be cleansed of its contagion.

'The walls shall be broken. The gate shall be opened,' Logis Acestes declaimed, his face upturned, watching Vindex Lartius slowly rising towards the distant ceiling.

'The xenos shall be the Omnissiah's instrument,' Heroditus agreed.

Logis Acestes turned towards the enginseer and bowed.

'The orks will destroy this place. They will break apart the works of the enemy, smash them to bits, pull them asunder. Nothing shall be left. The profanations of Castellax will be purged by the brute.'

Heroditus felt an upswelling of regret, a flicker of doubt that nagged on the edge of his consciousness. 'Must this be the way?' he wondered aloud.

'The grace of the Machine-God is wisdom,' Acestes answered him. 'Do you despair because Castellax is to be scoured by the alien? Would you pray even now for the armies of the Imperium, the Adeptus Astartes themselves, to descend upon this world as saviours? That is compassion, emotion, illogic. The failings of flesh.' The tech-priest drew back the sleeve of his synthfibre robe, exposing lean rods of steel and cable, the mechanical semblance of bone, muscle and vein. 'We purge ourselves of flesh to become closer to the Machine-God. To remove from us the distractions and temptations of organic existence. To gaze with unclouded eyes upon Knowledge.'

The vox-casters built into Acestes's chassis crackled to life. He turned away from Heroditus, addressing the dozens of other tech-priests ministering to the ascension of Vindex Lartius.

'Castellax must be purged, razed in the fires of the foul xenos,' Acestes pronounced. 'Perhaps you would prefer liberation from the enemy by our fellow man. That is weakness. That is selfishness. That is, itself, faithlessness and betrayal. The fear of flesh is to die and that fear cries out against what we know we must do. Castellax cannot be saved. Castellax must not be saved! The works of the arch-enemy must be annihilated, all those who laboured upon them, all those who gazed upon such profanations of technology must be exterminated. Nothing must be left!

'Liberation,' the word came as a hissing sigh from the speakers. 'What could such a thing have accomplished? Destroy the Chaos Marines, but leave their works intact!

Bear these violations against the Machine-God back into the Imperium, allow their taint to spread, their unclean concepts to corrupt! No!' The word boomed like cannon-fire from the speakers. 'Better the xenos with its axes and hammers. All must be consumed! All must be destroyed!'

Acestes raised his arms in appeal to Vindex Lartius. 'Only through total extermination can we honour our oaths to the Omnissiah!'

Heroditus bowed his head as the crackle of a Lingua-Technis prayer streamed from Logis Acestes. What the tech-priest said was true. Castellax had to be destroyed. Nothing could be allowed to survive. Fabricator Oriax and his perversions could be allowed no legacy. It all had to end here, beneath the alien paws of the orks.

The enginseer focused for a moment on the binary chant he was transmitting to the sentinel-implants buried within his own body. Oriax's little cybernetic spies. A flicker of irrational fear swept through him. If the spies weren't dormant, if they weren't disrupted by the chant... But, no, it was absurd to think their conspiracy could have come so far if the Fabricator was aware of it. Oriax would have alerted the other Traitor Marines long ago.

Still, as he watched Vindex Lartius ascend, Heroditus couldn't escape the persistent sense of alarm, the illogical feeling of unease that refused to be subdued by reason or probability.

This close to achieving their aims, Heroditus worried that something would interfere. That at the last moment the Iron Warriors would reach out and snatch their victory from them.

THE BULKY PLANE shuddered, waggling its wings, threatening to unbalance and spill itself into a sideways roll. Rhodaan clenched his teeth, reaching out and sinking the fingers of his gauntlet into the scrap-work fuselage, bracing himself against such an accident. The ork bomber was barely aerodynamic as it was, the slightest attempt at any sort of aerial manoeuvring was liable to bring it down. After their bold escape from Dirgas, to end up scattered across the desert in the wreckage of a xenos plane was too ignoble a doom to countenance.

'Brother Gomorie,' Rhodaan growled at the cockpit. 'Keep this flying junkyard stable!'

'The controls are erratic, lord captain,' Gomorie apologised. 'There is no regulation to their degree of responsiveness.' The Raptor made a disgusted hiss. 'The xenos must be mad to fly...'

'I do not care about xenos or their madness,' Rhodaan stated. 'Just get us back to Vorago in one piece.' He turned away from the cockpit, watching Pazuriel manipulating a box-like contrivance across the belly of the bomber.

'It is almost ready, lord captain,' Pazuriel said, rummaging about in the guts of a primitive relay. Wires ran from the cabinet-like device to either wing of the bomber. It had been a hazardous operation, rigging lights to the wings while the aircraft was in flight. There was no standardization to the materials the orks had employed building the plane, allowing the wings several patches built from diamagnetic alloys. Uzraal had nearly been lost when his boot slipped on one of the treacherous spots, only the speedy employment of his jump pack preventing the Raptor from being dumped into the Mare Ossius.

Yet the lights were essential. Their escape from Dirgas had been remarkably smooth once they seized the bomber and Gomorie consumed the knowledge of its pilot. Most of the ork gunners manning the city's defences were restrained enough to avoid shooting at their own aircraft and those few who were more bloodthirsty confined themselves to the odd, hasty pot-shot.

The poor communications among the orks had allowed the Space Marines to fly away in the xenos's own plane, but Rhodaan knew there would be a much different situation when they reached Vorago. There it would not be the besieging orks who would be a danger, but the guns of their own defences. Deadly, precise and coordinated, a lone bomber would be easy prey.

Somehow, if they were to survive, Rhodaan had to inform the Iron Bastion of their identity. Towards that end, he had implemented a two-fold plan. The lights on the wings were set up to flash a constant signal, a stream of visual binary that any of Oriax's servitors would be able to understand and relay. The machine-men would inform the Iron Warriors of their observation and the plane would be allowed to land.

However, that plan relied too much on chance and proximity to make Rhodaan comfortable, so he was counting upon it as a back-up contingency. His main hopes were vested in Pazuriel's current labour. The bomber had been outfitted with a vox, a primitive crystal set intended to receive the babble of ork transmissions littering the atmosphere of Castellax. A confusion of military commands and visual braggadocio it had taken time to refine the transmission stream into something that would stand out from the general discord. If the signal could be rendered powerful enough, it would be noticed by the mamelukes in the Iron Bastion monitoring ork communications. The hazard, of course, was that they wouldn't be able to drown out the other transmissions from any great distance. Like the flashing lights, they would need to be in close proximity to Vorago to be heard.

How close? That was the big question that bothered Rhodaan. It would do them little good to be identified as Iron Warriors just as their plane went diving down in flames.

The distant boom of guns rose to reach the bomber, an instant later the fuselage was rattling from the sound of flak clattering against it.

'Some overenthusiastic xenos,' Uzraal grumbled from one of the plane's gun turrets. He leaned away from the glass viewport, waiting until the clatter against the fuselage subsided. 'Don't those stupid animals understand we're on the same side?' he added in a surly hiss.

Baelfegor looked aside from his own station. The side of the Iron Warrior's armour was stained red, his shoulder spitted by a sliver of flak that had punched its way into the bomber during their flight from Dirgas. 'We could drop a few bombs on them. Then they might believe us.'

Uzraal shook his fist at the other Raptor and swung back into his station. It had been his suggestion that the bomb load be dumped shortly after they were away from Dirgas. It was a sound decision, the ork ordinance was volatile and unstable, just the sort of thing they could do without if forced into a crash landing. Even so, the other members of Squad Kyrith delighted in taunting their battle-brother over the decision.

'Nearing Vorago now,' Gomorie announced from the cockpit, at once silencing the banter between Uzraal and Baelfegor.

Rhodaan marched to the fore of the plane, staring at the black sprawl of Vorago, watching as the besieged city emerged from the clouds of dust and smoke that obscured it. Seen from this vantage, he found a new appreciation for the havoc the orks were inflicting. Except for the Iron Bastion itself, hidden behind its void shields, there wasn't a section of the city that hadn't been pounded by the enemy. Hundreds of fires burned unchecked, whole districts were blackened rubble. About the perimeter walls and firebreaks, swarms of alien warriors clamoured and fought, striving to pierce the defences and rampage through the unconquered city. There seemed to be many more of the orks than Rhodaan remembered. He wondered how many reinforcements the horde had received in the hours since he'd been transported through the immaterium by Oriax's sinister Daemonculum.

The flak that had peppered the bomber was, as Uzraal said, haphazard fire from the orks. As yet they were still too distant to take fire from Vorago's defences. Yet that would change very quickly. Rhodaan could see the black, vulture-like shapes of ork planes flying above the city, could see some of the same suddenly blazing into brilliance as they were burned from the sky.

'Brother Pazuriel!' Rhodaan shouted. 'Start transmission! If our brothers believe us to be orks, we will be shown no mercy.'

'All is in readiness, lord captain!' Pazuriel yelled back. 'Light flashes have commenced and I am making vocal transmission now.' The Raptor removed his helmet and placed the crude ork vox-transmitter up to his lips. The alien device would only recognise the loudest tones and could somehow differentiate between organic and synthetic emanations. In a thick, deep tone, Pazuriel snarled into the fat vox handset the code Rhodaan had decided upon. Something simple and direct that not even the lowest mameluke could fail to recognise and interpret.

'Iron within!' Pazuriel shouted. 'Iron without!'

The war cry of the Iron Warriors, a chant none but the Space Marines were allowed to utter. The monitors within the Iron Bastion couldn't misinterpret the message. The broadcast would be instantly relayed to their battle-brothers. The plane would be given safe passage into Vorago.

The distance continued to decrease, the walls and ruins of Vorago becoming larger and more distinct. Still all Rhodaan could hear from behind him was Pazuriel's voice repeating the battle cry. He looked through the glass, watching the flashing lights bolted to the wings. If the vox failed, then their only chance to be identified was by the sequence of lights. Rhodaan kept his eyes fixed upon the starboard wing, watching the sequence run and then repeat.

As the stolen bomber neared the reach of the batteries on the perimeter wall, the crackle of a voice from Pazuriel's receiving set brought Rhodaan away from the cockpit and back into the hold. He stared down at the vox, listening as the subservient voice of Flesh addressed Pazuriel.

'Unknown aircraft,' the slave said. 'You are requested to terminate transmission and switch to a secure channel.'

Pazuriel's face contorted into a scowl of frustration. 'If we had the apparatus for secure transmission, would we be fiddling with dark-age broadcast,' he snapped.

There was silence for a moment, then the slave was back. 'Unknown aircraft. Please transmit your Castellax Air Cohort identity code.'

'I'll shoot that flesh-maggot when we land,' Uzraal promised.

'Not if I get my hands around its neck,' Pazuriel growled back, then returned his attention to the vox. 'We are Iron Warriors returning from a raid against Dirgas. We weren't issued a daily identity code. This is an ork plane without means to process any code even if we did receive one.'

The slave transmitting from the Iron Bastion was either stubborn or afraid of straying from his training. 'Unknown aircraft. Do not approach the city without proper identity confirmation.'

Rhodaan could hear Pazuriel's knuckles crack as he clenched his fingers around the stem of the handset. 'Listen, Flesh. Do I sound like an ork?'

A moment of silence, then a reluctant answer. 'No.'

'Is there any human on Castellax who would dare say "Iron within, Iron without" except an Iron Warrior?'

The answer this time was soft, almost timid. 'No.'

'Then that means this plane is full of Iron Warriors, doesn't it?'

'Yes... my lord.'

Pazuriel grinned in triumph. 'So what should you be doing?' he demanded.

'Clearing you to land and telling the defence batteries to hold their fire.'

'Get to it,' Pazuriel snarled, smashing his fist into the receiver and shattering it into wreckage.

'Was that wise, brother?' Baelfegor asked.

Pazuriel lifted his helmet and set it back on his head, locking it into place with a twist of his arms. 'Perhaps not, brother,' he replied. 'But it was immensely satisfying.'

Rhodaan glowered at the other Iron Warrior. 'That was foolish and impulsive,' he reprimanded Pazuriel. 'Neither are qualities worthy of the Legion. I will determine suitable penance.'

Chastened, Pazuriel bowed before Rhodaan. 'Of course, lord captain,' he said.

Rhodaan turned away, marching back to the cockpit. Once more he stood at Gomorie's shoulder, watching as the bomber flew towards the perimeter wall. They were within range of Vorago's guns now. At any moment, they might expect the chatter of anti-aircraft batteries. Rhodaan glanced at the wings, assured himself the lights were still flashing their signal.

The moment passed. The bomber flew over the outer wall, into Vorago proper. Carefully, Gomorie manipulated the bulky steering column, even his enhanced physique taxed by the strength required to control the instrument. No mere human could have possessed the brawn the orks demanded, only a Space Marine could match their alien strength.

The bomber's wing tipped, the plane shuddered into a slow turn, banking towards the Iron Bastion. Still the guns below presented no menace. The bold gambit had succeeded. Squad Kyrith was returning in triumph to Vorago!

Suddenly, the ramshackle plane shook furiously, flames erupting along its side. Baelfegor cried out, his armour pierced by shrapnel. He lurched away from the gun turret, using his combat knife to saw away at the projecting slivers of steel.

Again the bomber was shaken, wobbling in the sky. Rhodaan glared through the cockpit glass, trying to find whatever ork pilot through suspicion or simple perversity was firing on them. As near as he could see, the sky around them was clear.

From the corner of his vision, upon one of the fire-breaks, a puff of grey smoke. An instant later, the bomber lurched drunkenly, its starboard wing holed by flak. One of their own batteries! One of their own anti-aircraft emplacements was firing on them!

Rage boiled inside Rhodaan's breast. Treachery. That was his first thought. If Pazuriel's transmission had been discounted or failed to be relayed, then every gun in the city would have tried to bring them down. For only a single battery to turn against them...

The hand of Vallax, or perhaps Uhlan! The Faceless might have left provision in case Squad Kyrith returned before them. A convenient accident that could eliminate Rhodaan without anyone the wiser.

'How bad are we hit?' Rhodaan snarled at Gomorie.

Gomorie looked up at him, his infected hand lengthening into argent claws. 'This rubbish shouldn't have been airborne before we started getting shot at,' he said.

Rhodaan braced himself as another salvo of flak slammed into the bomber, pitting its belly. 'Can you get us out of range?'

'That depends how well they can track a falling target,' Gomorie replied.

Rhodaan took a second to digest that report. 'Open the bomb-bay doors,' he ordered. Gomorie stabbed his silver claw against one of the many buttons littering the control terminal. He stared at it a moment, waiting for an indicator to light up. He stabbed it again, then pounded on the terminal in frustration.

'Never mind,' Rhodaan said. He drew his chainsword from his belt, thumbing the activation stud. Marching down the cabin, he snapped orders to the other Raptors. 'Make obeisance to your jump packs. We free-dive in ten seconds.' He could hear the other Iron Warriors invoking the machine-spirits of their wargear as they trooped after him, a strange admixture of respectful appeals and callous threats. Whatever was necessary to make the machines function in the crisis.

The chainsword bit into the locked bomb-bay doors, sparks flying as its churning edge sawed through the hinges. Wind roared through the plane as one of the doors ripped free.

'Bomb-bay doors are open!' Gomorie shouted over the vox.

Rhodaan growled back at him. 'No, the doors are gone. Lock those controls and get back here. Unless you'd prefer to go down with the plane.' Rhodaan gestured with his thumb and Uzraal dropped through the opening, the thrusters of his jump pack activating as he fell, turning his plummet into a controlled dive. Baelfegor followed, blood streaming from his impacted armour. Rhodaan watched the Raptor descend, waiting expectantly for the glow of his jump pack's thrusters.

The glow never appeared.

'I'll kill that filthy flesh-maggot,' Pazuriel cursed. 'I can't understand how they failed to identify us.'

Rhodaan motioned him through the door. 'I think they knew exactly who they were shooting at,' he announced over the squad vox-channel. 'Keep that thought with you on your way down and when we avenge our battle-brother's wasteful death.'

VALLAX AWOKE TO pain. It felt as though a dull knife was slowly sinking into his brain. The pungent stink of promethium, melted plastic, burned hair, corroded metal and fresh blood all assaulted his senses, striving to overcome the one stench that overpowered them all. The midden-heap scent of ork.

The Space Marine could tell his helmet had been removed by the cloying caress of foul air against his skin. The recyclers in his helmet would never have allowed such a concentration of filth to impact his senses. He could feel the dull, lethargic stirring of the air around him, the faintest hint of motion against his skin. Allied to the closeness of the smell, Vallax knew he was inside a room somewhere, a room with only the most rudimentary circulation.

Vallax opened his eyes, the action sending a sliver of pulsating agony through his skull. He was in a room, but such a room as would make Algol's private abattoir seem a quiet place of contemplation. A riotous array of hooks, pincers, blades, saws, chisels and mauls hung from the corroded walls. Shelves displayed a weird collection of jars, bottles, boxes and bags each stuffed with a deranged assortment of bones, limbs and organs. Flies buzzed about the more exposed parts of the collection, glutting themselves on the rotting flesh.

Beside the macabre collection, a long workbench equipped with a pneumatic grip and a small furnace, an assortment of gears strewn about its surface. Oversized claws, piston-driven legs, even a box with steel jaw bones, lay piled around the bench. A crate of scrap metal loomed against the wall, several pieces jutting from the mess appearing to be recycled implants from ork cyborgs. Vallax recognised the power claw that had crushed his arm lying towards the top of the heap. Hulking against the side of the crate, wheezy snoring noises hissing through its speakers, was the mechanical mass of a killa kan, its murderous arms hanging limp against its hull while its entombed pilot slept.

Gritting his teeth, Vallax managed to turn his head. The motion sent a shudder of perfect agony cascading through his skull, the dull knife seeming to press deeper into his brain. The Iron Warrior resisted the clamour of his nerves, forced his head to turn still farther.

What he saw was a ghastly ork, its apelike body draped in a filthy coat of blood-stained white. The alien's head had a squashed, flattened appearance rendering its broad face somehow toad-like. Above its enormous, toothy grin, the ork's beady eyes lurked behind a set of tiny glasses with frosted lenses. The monster was ignoring Vallax, puttering about with a tall, box-like device that seemed to be a graveyard of dials and diodes. Electricity arced between horns set about the machine's superstructure, dancing between them in random leaps.

The ork fumbled with the machine, then delivered a vicious swat to its side as the alien's patience exploded. Angrily, it started to rip out a wire running between the side of its head to the machine. The wire resisted the ork, however, and before it could complete the operation, its beady eyes noticed Vallax's awareness.

Clapping its paws together, its toad-like grin opening still wider, the ork returned to its machine, turning dials and smacking its sides.

Suddenly, it seemed as if the inside of Vallax's head had been set on fire. He clenched his eyes closed, feeling a stabbing agony rippling through his optic nerves. Strange images flashed through his mind, a deranged panoply of confused impressions of savagery and violence. Prominent among the nightmarish discord were images of orks strapped to tables, screaming as their bodies were carved to ribbons by a grinning greenskin surgeon.

The ork paused, peering at him intently. Then the creature's body began to shake, a braying bellow howled through the room. Vallax struggled to move, but was unsurprised to find that his limbs were securely chained, lashed to some crude metal armature. Even so, his pride refused to accept that he was helpless, that all he could do was sit there and let an ork laugh at him.

Then the Space Marine saw his reflection in the ork's glasses. He had expected to see himself bound, laid out upon some sort of standing frame. What he hadn't expected was to see his head bare, battered and shaved. He hadn't expected to see a section of his skull missing, the living brain standing naked and exposed. The dull knife sensation was explained now. There was a dull knife stuck in his brain, wires fastened to its hilt streaming back to the ork's weird machine.

The ork gestured with its thumb. Vallax followed the gesture, noting for the first time a rabble of orks clustered about the hatchway leading into the hideous surgery. They were big, brawny types, utterly unlike the squashed surgeon, yet each of them seemed reluctant to trespass on his domain.

Somehow, Vallax found he knew what the monsters were. Kommandos, orks that possessed a strange capacity for strategy and tactics, especially infiltration and ambush. The surgeon was called a painboy, his name was Gorflik and he was held in a weird alchemy of respect and outright terror by the orks of Waaagh! Biglug.

The Iron Warrior's mind reeled. How did he know this? What obscenity were these filthy xenos perpetrating on his brain?

One of the orks in the doorway, a massive monster wearing camouflaged leggings and a long leather storm coat, the remains of a peaked cap squashed about its cranium, leaned across the threshold and growled something at Gorflik. Vallax could tell from the painboy's reaction that the growl had been some sort of command. The ork in the coat was called Kaptain Grimruk, boss of the kommandos gathered in the hall.

Gorflik chuckled, adjusting the dials on his machine. Immediately, Vallax felt burning torment flare through his skull. Images were again rising unbidden, not the surface thoughts of the ork, but memories of his own. He could see the Iron Bastion in his mind, could see himself mentally prowling through its halls.

Immediately, Vallax knew the purpose behind this torture, the fiendish function of Gorflik's machine. Before his thoughts could solidify, Vallax crushed them down with his ferocious will. Over and again in his mind he repeated the war cry of the Legion. Iron within! Iron without!

A snarl of disgust from Gorflik told Vallax his ruse had worked. He had built the mental equivalent of chaff inside his head, blocking the ork from the information it wanted: the layout of the Iron Bastion. The secret routes into and out of the fortress. The ork's enraged thoughts came storming back across the wire. In his mind, Vallax could see the beast interrogating other captives. When they resisted Gorflik the way Vallax had done, the painboy took steps to break their defiance.

Gorflik reached to his head once more, pulling out the metal prong which connected the wire from the machine to the ork's brain. Without bothering to clean the probe, the painboy let it fall and started towards the assemblage of cutters and saws Vallax had noted earlier.

The treacherous Oriax had certainly arranged a merciless and ignominious death for him, but as Vallax watched the ork pick out its tools, vindictive determination steeled him for the ordeal. Whatever happened, he would endure. The orks would never break an Iron Warrior. They would kill him first.

But before that happened, Vallax intended to be free. There were things he had to do before he died and it would take more than millions of orks and thousands of kilometres of polluted wasteland to stop him.

Oriax would rue his treachery.

CHAINS SWAYED IN the fitful breeze created by the atmospheric modulators, clashing against one another in an eerie clangour. The dull, raw impacts as the objects dangled from the stout hooks formed a weird percussion to accompany the sound. The robed mamelukes scurrying about in the dingy, scarlet light which filtered down into the hall shivered with each note of the macabre orchestra, a shiver that owed nothing to the clammy temperature of Algol's domain.

Each man knew the Iron Warriors regarded him as nothing more than Flesh, something weak and disposable.

Skintaker Algol was worse. He found Flesh amusing and spared few opportunities to indulge his perverse humour. His demesne within the Iron Bastion was littered with the wreckage of men and women who had the misfortune to attract his attention. Through deed, misdeed or simply a tragic uniqueness of appearance, once the Skintaker's eye was upon them, there was no escape.

Algol sat upon an adamantine chair, listening to the sound of the swaying chains and the dull thumps of the things hanging from them. The Iron Warrior's eyes were half closed, his face contemplative. Around him, eyes averted from their ruinous master, a gang of slaves mended the gruesome cloak of human skin.

The heavy lids slowly pulled back, exposing the sadistic eyes. Algol smiled coldly as he studied the broken bodies suspended upon the hooks, masses of meat and muscle stripped of skin. There was discord among his grisly chimes. He suspected one of the older components was beginning to give out. It would need to be replaced. Judging by the lack of harmony, he'd require something of about seventy-three kilograms. Less the weight of five litres of blood and two square metres of skin, naturally.

Slowly, Algol lowered his gaze, contemplating the creature standing beneath the chains rather than the creatures suspended above it. Unlike the mamelukes, the flesh-drone didn't shiver in the chill of the chamber, despite the ice-crystals forming on its pallid skin. True, the face writhed and contorted in various expressions of agony, but that was some extravagance of Fabricator Oriax rather than anything induced by Algol.

The Skintaker found that fact a source of vexation.

'You may speak now,' Algol decided, settling back in his chair. He studied a chronometer fashioned from a human skull. 'The orks should make another push against the perimeter at dawn. I intend to be there to meet them.'

The flesh-drone gave no notice of Algol's depreciatory tone. All it did was open its mouth and allow the voice of its creator to issue from the speaker implanted in its throat. 'I am unaccustomed to waiting upon the hedonist indulgences of an inveterate sadist,' the voice of Oriax hissed from the speaker.

Algol rose from the chair, striding towards the servitor. 'And I do not grant audiences to a decaying meat-puppet,' he snarled. 'If you want to speak with me, stir from your sanctum. I'll leave what's left of your mouthpiece where you can salvage it.'

The flesh-drone retreated before the angered Space Marine. 'Wait, Algol!' the voice entreated. 'What I have to disclose will be of interest to you.'

The Iron Warrior hesitated, doubt flickering through his eyes. 'I will listen until you bore me, Fabricator.'

The flesh-drone eased its way back across the room, chains glancing from its lobotomised cranium. 'Would you be interested in a cell of rebel Flesh?' Oriax asked.

Algol didn't bother concealing his smile, his fingers straying across the folds of his cloak. 'I have heard claims that some of your minions have strayed from their oaths of loyalty,' he said.

'I bring you more than slave gossip and rumour,' Oriax declared. The mechadendrites fastened to the flesh-drone's torso unfolded, exposing the gleaming metal skull of a Steel Blood. The gruesome cyborg rose from the servitor's claws, hovering in the chill air of Algol's abattoir. The lens in its left eye socket began to glow, throwing a three-dimensional image onto the floor. In exacting detail, the Steel Blood transmitted a view of Colonel Nehring's command post as it was being overrun by Yuxiang's rebels.

'I always keep several sets of eyes around places of interest,' Oriax explained. 'The Flesh destroyed one of my Steel Blood that was inside the command post, but they didn't discover this one.'

'You believe these maggots are connected with the renegade tech-adepts?' Algol asked.

The flesh-drone shuffled forwards. 'These ones are well-organised and well-prepared,' Oriax explained. 'There might be someone more capable behind them.'

Algol rose to his feet, chains brushing against his shoulders. 'I will inform the Warsmith. Detach a combat squad from the walls. We will track down these overbold worms and bring them to account.' His eyes seemed to glow in the crimson murk. 'They will tell all before I have finished with them,' he promised.

The rasp of a mechanised sigh rattled from the flesh-drone's speaker. 'You disappoint me, Algol,' Oriax said. 'I thought you were more confident in your abilities. An entire combat squad to deal with a few dozen Flesh? The Warsmith will laugh at you for such excess... if he doesn't shoot you for cowardice.'

'Do not tempt me, half-warrior,' Algol snarled at the servitor. 'No organism alive mocks my valour! I have strode across the battlefields of a thousand worlds, brought death to a million souls. None can question my prowess!'

'Prove it,' Oriax's voice rasped from the servitor. In one swift motion, Algol pounced upon the flesh-drone, ripping its head from its shoulders with his bare hands. Angrily, he dashed the mangled mess of flesh and metal against the wall.

Despite the outburst, Algol found he hadn't silenced the voice of Oriax. The Fabricator's words streamed now from the mouth of the Steel Blood.

'I came here to offer you the glory of smashing these rebels on your own, with none to share in it. Think how well the Warsmith will look upon the Skintaker then.'

Algol dropped the headless husk of the flesh-drone and stared at the hovering Steel Blood, doubt in his gaze. 'Why would you bestow such a boon upon me?' he wondered aloud.

'I never forget my debts,' Oriax said. The optics of the

Steel Blood glowed a little brighter as the transmission continued.

'There are services you rendered me in the crystal swamps...'

CHAPTER XVIII
I-Day Plus One Hundred and Twenty

REMNANTS OF THE Castellax Air Cohort streaked through the brown smudge of sky, guns roaring as they strafed the orks massed before the walls of Vorago. Bombs rained down upon the scrap-work alien machines, obliterating them in showers of smoke and fire. Each sortie brought death to thousands of the invaders.

It wasn't enough.

Watching the sorry spectacle from the battlements, Captain Rhodaan could only shake his head at the futility of the air attack. The time for such tactics was long past. Like some grasping miser, Skylord Morax had held the strength of his air force in reserve. Rhodaan could easily imagine the other captain's intention. It was obvious to anyone with the least degree of observation. Morax had been waiting for this moment, when the enemy came on in full strength, to make the final push against Vorago. Then he would unleash the carefully husbanded might of his Air Cohort against them, breaking their attack and the siege in one fell swoop.

Morax's plan was typical of those who allowed their contempt for a species as primitive and uncouth as the orks to cloud any appreciation for their capabilities. Because the orks weren't subtle, because they were crude and simple and direct in their approach to warfare, many commanders made the same mistake. It was the sin of pride and arrogance. Something didn't need to be clever or complex to kill. It only needed to be strong.

The orks were strong. It offended Rhodaan to admit that, but there was no other way to say it. Where any other army would have broken under Morax's aerial assault, the orks had held fast, using great dozers to clear away the wreckage and maintain their attack. No thought was spared for their dead, no fear displayed that they might be the next to die. With stupid stubbornness, the orks threw themselves towards one purpose and one purpose only: attack.

With each sortie, the Air Cohort's strength bled away. Flakwagons and missile launchers took their toll, bringing down several fighters with each pass. Ork planes claimed their share as well, punishing each intrusion by the humans and pursuing them far out into the wastes. Morax had issued orders against any pilot leading orks back to the Air Cohort's underground aerodromes, and for many of the escaping planes the sight of an ork on its tail was a death sentence whether the xenos caught it or not.

By this stage in the siege, the sorties had become nothing more than the empty posturing of a commander in disgrace. Each time the Air Cohort sallied forth they encountered ever heavier concentrations of flak, ever more numerous swarms of ork planes eager to score a kill. The last few squadrons had barely even started their runs against the alien ground forces before they were compelled to withdraw.

Through his restraint, Morax had allowed the skies of Castellax to belong to the orks. Now, when he wanted to take them back, the Skylord was discovering that it was too late.

Rhodaan turned his gaze from the skies, focusing instead upon the perimeter wall. His section boasted some two thousand Flesh, a mix of factory slaves and janissaries, as well as the Space Marines of Squad Kyrith, minus the dead Brother Baelfegor. In his stead, Brother Merihem had been placed under his command. According to Sergeant Ipos, Rhodaan was the only officer capable of even a marginal degree of control when it came to the Obliterator.

The Raptor knew that fragile control had nothing to do with him, but rather owed itself to Merihem's unsettling fascination with Gomorie and his struggle against the corruption infecting him. Whenever there was a pause in the fighting, sometimes even in the heat of battle, Merihem would stop and stare at Gomorie, his tiny face spreading in a mocking smile. Rhodaan wasn't certain he wanted to understand the Obliterator's humour.

'The xenos are mustering for another push.' Uzraal reported over the inter-squad vox. He had been stationed within the command post for this section of the perimeter, providing him with access to the intelligence being transmitted down from the Iron Bastion. 'The big battle-fortress is taking up position on the flank of the main ork encampment. Several thousand orks are disembarking and rushing to reinforce the assault troops around the walls.' There was a pause and Uzraal's tone was tense when he continued his report. 'The xenos are unloading three walkers. Intelligence categorises them as "stompas".'

Rhodaan felt his blood chill as he heard Uzraal's statement. Stompas were gigantic ork war machines, somewhere between the hulking dreadnoughts and the Titan-like gargants in size. It was fortunate that the aliens hadn't been able to construct any of the city-crushing gargants, but the presence of the smaller stompas was still a crisis in the making. Turning his gaze in the direction of the ork camp, Rhodaan focused the optics in his helmet to maximum magnification.

True to Uzraal's report, he could see the huge, clumsy machines lumbering away from the cyclopean battle-fortress, staggering from side-to-side like drunken mutants. The stompas stood taller than the perimeter walls, scrap-metal effigies of the ork physique. Where their arms should be, immense gun carriages and power claws swung on crude armatures. Even from this distance, Rhodaan could see the scaling ladders bolted to the hulls of the primitive machines. Like all ork strategies, the deployment of the stompas was simple and direct. The aliens would march their machines right up to the walls, then use the ladders to swarm up their hulls and drop down onto the battlements. With Morax's Air Cohort routed from the sky, there was little the defenders could do to interfere.

'Lord captain,' Pazuriel's voice crackled over the vox. 'Should we prepare to assault the walkers?'

'Negative,' Rhodaan answered almost automatically. 'We might stop one of them, but while we were doing it, the others would be free to reach the wall.' His tone was grim as he made that assessment. 'Uzraal, relay our situation to the Bastion. Ask Ipos for further orders.'

'I already have,' Uzraal answered. 'He says our position has been determined to be critical to the overall defence. We have to hold, regardless of opposition.'

Rhodaan didn't deign to respond. Furious, he strode to the battlements, sending a burst of bolter-fire into the orks massed below, venting his frustration upon alien flesh. Critical to the overall defence? That assessment aroused his suspicion. He couldn't forget the reception Squad Kyrith had received on their return. Upon investigation, the battery that had fired on them was found to be littered with dead janissaries, victims, it seemed, of a malfunctioning servitor. That, Rhodaan felt, was far too convenient. Everything smelt of some hidden adversary trying to cover his tracks. The senseless order to hold the perimeter against impossible odds carried the same stink.

Over-Captain Vallax hadn't returned from Dirgas. It was assumed that he and his Faceless were casualties. It was as well, because if he had made it back to Vorago, Rhodaan felt he would need to look no further for the enemy trying to stab him in the back.

Pain had become its own reality. Dull and throbbing or sharp and burning, pain had risen to consume Over-Captain Vallax's senses. It pulsed through the corridors of his mind, pounded through the marrow in his bones, crackled down every nerve. Never had the Iron Warrior been subjected to such suffering, even during the extensive battery of surgeries that had transformed him so long ago from a mere human into a legionary.

The ork painboy had done everything its sadistic brain could conceive to break Vallax. Anything merely human would have been killed ten times over by Gorflik's tortures. Vallax, however, remained steadfast, defying the ork. 'Iron without. Iron within.' The mantra of the Legion drummed through Vallax's psycho-conditioned mind, demanding fealty to his oaths, loyalty even the Chaos gods could not break.

The room was filthy with Vallax's blood. His tormentor's green hide was mottled with splotches of gore. Shreds of the Iron Warrior's flesh were caked about the vivisectionist instruments stuffed in the ork's work belt, strips of his skin clung to the assemblage of saws and knives arrayed about the little table resting beside the cross-frame. Only the little glasses gleaming from Gorflik's face remained clean, their sheen reflecting each atrocity visited upon the Raptor's body when Vallax stared at the ork.

He accepted the burden of his wounds with pride. The more he suffered, the stronger his determination to defy his tormentor. The ork could ruin Vallax's body, but it could not ruin his honour.

Far more agonising to Vallax than the violation of his flesh by the orks was the profanation of his armour. From where he was bolted to the cross-frame, he could see the segments of his power armour strewn across a workbench, lying in the dirt and filth of Gorflik's surgery. Sometimes, when the painboy tired of Vallax's defiance, it would retreat to the workbench and tinker with his armour, opening its ceramite shell to fiddle with the mechanisms within. It had made the Space Marine's hearts crack to see the brutish alien pulling fibre bundles from the hollowed out vambraces, dumping the synthetic muscles onto the floor like so much trash. It had made his blood boil to watch the brutish alien tinkering with the breastplate, defiling it with crude tools. Often the ork would withdraw from the room in the midst of its sacrilege to consult with Kaptain Grimruk when the beast was lurking about the doorway. Always, after such conferences, Gorflik would return to the workbench with a notable attitude of excitement.

Vallax knew better than to throw himself into a rage. Fastened to the frame, all his fury could accomplish was the amusement of his captor. Instead, the Iron Warrior buried his anger deep inside himself, letting it fester in his hearts, letting its strength burn in his veins. Like pain, anger was power, fuel for the Space Marine's indomitable will.

Slowly, with a cold deliberation that bespoke his iron discipline, Vallax worried at his bonds, sliding his body back and forth, weakening the grip of the bolts binding him to the frame by enlarging the wounds around them. He was careful in his efforts, always waiting until Gorflik's vigilance was at its lowest ebb – when the creature was lost in the thrill of administering its tortures or busy with Vallax's power armour.

After weeks hanging upon the frame, Vallax was held to the bars only by the grip of his fingers and toes. Grimly, he bided his time. He knew that his prison had been moving, could feel the vibration shivering through the frame, see the sway of the chains and tools hanging upon the walls. There could be only one destination, the only objective the orks had yet to conquer on Castellax: Vorago.

Black hate surged through Vallax whenever he thought of the city. It was there, buried deep beneath the Iron Bastion, that he would find the one who had betrayed him to the orks, the one who had so carefully engineered this fate for him. Every torture, every humiliation and indignity inflicted upon him – all of it was another score to settle with Oriax. Revenge sustained Vallax when duty and honour threatened to fail him. He would see the Fabricator pay for what he had done, would cherish the sound of his screams as he cherished the memory of the Warmaster's voice.

Gorflik's surgery was buried inside some vast machine, perhaps one of the ork battlefortresses. Every second he could feel the motion coursing through the deck, Vallax knew he was drawing closer to his own objective. In the name of revenge, he clung to the frame and endured the tortures.

It was only when the room grew still, when the rumble of motion vanished, that Vallax knew the time to act was near. Now he kept his attention on Grimruk and the camouflaged orks, who were often in the hallway outside the surgery. The Iron Warrior's body had suffered hideously under the attentions of the painboy. He was under no delusion what his chances would be against one ork, much less a dozen. To have any chance at escape, he had to wait until Gorflik was alone and unobserved.

His wait wasn't a long one. Never very disciplined, the orks in the hallway showed a marked disinterest in their vigil once the battlefortress stopped and they reached their destination. Faintly, from beyond the walls, Vallax could hear the crump of artillery and the crack of gunfire. Somewhere outside there was a furious battle being fought, one the ork guards desperately wanted to be a part of. One after another, they began to desert their post until at last there were no more leering faces peering at him from the hallway.

Vallax's body grew tense, his savaged muscles burning as he flexed and tested them. Gorflik's back was to him, the alien once more probing the components of his armour, vandalising it with primitive tools and perverse mischief.

Clamping his teeth tight, Vallax kicked out with his leg. The limb flashed from the cross frame, ripping clear of the bolt that had once pinned him in place. The wet, slippery noise of the metal bolt sliding through his flesh brought Gorflik spinning around. There was an almost comical expression of wonder on the ork's face as its brain tried to come to grips with what it was seeing.

The need for caution gone, Vallax opened his mouth in an inarticulate howl and tore himself down from the frame, using his already freed leg to push away and turn his fall into a dive. Gorflik bleated in confusion as the Space Marine's mass slammed into him, smashing the alien back against the workbench.

Blood streaming from his newly opened wounds, the Larraman cells in Vallax's veins struggling to seal his injuries, the Iron Warrior wrapped a mangled hand around the ork's throat, choking off the frightened bark the alien started to utter. With his other hand, he reached for one of the ceramite sabaton lying on the bench just behind the reeling ork's ear.

Gorflik flailed in Vallax's grip, one meaty paw clutching at the hand around his throat, the other digging into his filthy coat for an instrument that looked more bayonet than scalpel. Viciously the ork stabbed the blade into his enemy's chest, penetrating the black carapace and digging into the fused ribcage beneath. Before the painboy could finish driving home his attack and put his full weight against the blade, Vallax cracked the armoured sabaton against the creature's skull. There was a gratifying crunch of bone, a pungent reek of alien blood.

The ork continued to struggle, but its strength waned each time Vallax brought the ceramite armour smashing into the side of its head. Again and again he struck the alien, relenting only when the thick skull collapsed and Gorflik's body fell limp.

Vallax staggered back, glaring down at the monster. Almost absently he noticed the surgical blade still embedded in his chest. With a savage wrench, he pulled it free. Vindictively, he brought the razored edge down to the ork's forehead. In a single downward sweep, he slashed the keen blade across the leathery green flesh, slicing away the painboy's face in a dripping sheet of skin.

The Iron Warrior rose from his victim, casting a wary glance at the doorway then at the killa kan standing in the corner of the room. The sounds of the brutal struggle had gone unnoticed. No guards appeared in the hallway. The gretchin pilot implanted inside the miniature dreadnought continued to snore. For the moment, at least, his escape was unnoticed.

Hastily, Vallax gathered the segments of his armour from the workbench. It sickened him to see the abuse they had suffered. Many of the intricate mechanisms built inside the suit – neural connectors, protein injectors, servo-motors, air purifiers, synth-muscles – had been ripped out with indiscriminate zeal. The interfaces that would bind the armour to the black carapace implanted beneath Vallax's skin were gone. Their loss, above all else, troubled the Iron Warrior. Without the interfaces, he would be unable to properly manipulate the power armour. Instead of wearing it like a second skin, it would be a dead weight dragging him down and straining his endurance.

The Iron Warrior glared at the piles of vandalised components strewn about the surgery. Strain or not, he wouldn't abandon his armour to these brutes. His decision made, he began fitting the ceramite segments about his body. It felt strange, without the synth-muscles and servo-motors assisting him when he moved, to have the armour reducing rather than enhancing his strength and agility.

Except for his helmet, every piece of Vallax's armour was represented on the workbench. Soon, he resembled an Iron Warrior once more, encased from neck to foot in sleek ceramite plates. He scowled as he felt his head, the exposed section of his brain feeling raw and somehow withered. Resolutely he wrapped his fingers around the metal probe, pulling it free with an agonising tug. The Space Marine glared at Gorflik's machine. Choosing an ugly hammer from the tools at hand, he lost himself for several minutes in smashing the dead ork's invention into so much scrap.

When he finished, Vallax scolded himself for such excess. Dropping the hammer, he stepped away from the ruined machine and turned to the crate of weaponry and recycled cybernetics. It took him a few minutes, but at last he dragged free a boltgun that appeared in working condition. A few minutes more and he had the weapon separated from the cyborg arm it was bolted to.

As a last gesture, Vallax bent over the dead painboy, stripping the coat from the ork and wrapping it around his head like a turban to protect the grey tissue of his exposed brain. He stole towards the hallway, peering outside to assure himself there had been no alarm. The corridor was deserted, the door on the other side of the hall shut. No orks moved upon the stairway at the head of the passage.

Checking the chamber of his scavenged weapon, Vallax swept into the hall and sprinted up the stairs. He knew he would have to fight his way clear of the battlefortress, that an army of enemies lay between himself and the Iron Bastion. Between himself and his revenge. For the moment, at least, the Chaos gods smiled upon him and he was unobserved.

Vallax's head pulsed with the each step as he raced for the stairs, strange sensations rippling through his body. Despite the dank, sweltering humidity he had felt a moment before, his flesh prickled with a sudden chill. A tart taste filled his mouth, blues and blacks leapt out in painful vibrancy in his vision. His ears shuddered under the impression of brutish laughter.

The Iron Warrior fought down his treacherous senses. Nothing would stop him from reaching the Bastion and his revenge. Not even his own infirmities.

The tractor came rumbling down the murky tunnel, its lights dimmed and hooded to prevent their gleam from carrying too far into the darkness. Corpses were piled high in the bed, carrion recovered from the battlements. Dozens of tractors were making the circuit between Processing Omega and wall, trying to keep the battlements clear of the mangled waste of war.

Yuxiang smiled beneath the ghastly snout of his mask. In the confusion and carnage, no one was paying attention to the disposers. They weren't watching them with the same degree of vigilance as usual. The lack of supervision allowed the rebels to scavenge weapons and ammunition from the dead, stuffing their plunder deep beneath the bodies where no one would look.

Combined with what they had stolen from Colonel Nehring's supply cache, Yuxiang estimated they had enough weapons and ammunition to equip three hundred men. As yet, of course, their numbers weren't even close to that size. Including the two slave-recruits hiding in the cargo bed with the bodies, the rebel force was only fifty-four strong. But they were strong. They were determined, committed men and women who would fight to their last breath against the tyrannies of the Iron Warriors.

'We're starting to look like an army,' Taofang commented. The janissary was marching beside the slow-moving tractor with Mingzhou walking at his side.

Yuxiang digested that observation, feeling a strange pride at the compliment. As a slave, he had despised the soldiers who exacted the dictates of the Iron Warriors, had loathed everything that smacked of war and violence. As a rebel, however, he appreciated the need for violence and understood the value of martial discipline and training.

'It doesn't matter what we look like,' Yuxiang observed philosophically. 'What matters is how we fight.'

'Leave that to us,' Taofang said, wrapping an arm around Mingzhou's shoulder. 'Every man you bring down from the wall will be trained by two of the...' The janissary's words broke off, his body growing tense. Reaching a hand to his face, he pulled down the gas mask and stared in alarm at the tunnel ahead.

Beneath the glow of an overhead lamp, a body lay sprawled, dressed in the tatters of a scavenged uniform. It was the sort of uniform the rebels had been issuing to their new recruits. How the man had come to be here, so far from their hidden refuge was a question that was of less importance to Taofang than what had brought the man to his current condition. For there was no question that he was dead, his arm nearly ripped from its socket, a pool of blood staining the ground around his prostrate form.

'I think that's one of ours,' Deacon exclaimed from the other side of the tractor, his voice pitched with excitement.

Yuxiang brought the tractor to a halt. As he started to emerge from the cab, a chilling sight strode into the little circle of light cast by the lamp. It was the figure of an enormous man, his already gigantic frame further bulked by the ornate ceramite power armour that encased his body. The helmet that enclosed his head was cast into the snarling semblance of a skull and from his shoulders hung a ghoulish cloak of flayed human skin.

Algol the Skintaker. Not a soul on Castellax could fail to recognise the most sadistic and terrifying of the Iron Warriors, by reputation if from no more direct an encounter.

Watching the slavemaster stalk into view from the darkness was like seeing Death manifesting itself. Yuxiang trembled at the wheel of the tractor. From the corner of his eye, he could see Taofang shivering in his boots.

Only Mingzhou kept some measure of reason in her head. 'He's over twenty-five hundred metres away,' she assured them. 'Someone with the best lasrifle on Castellax couldn't pick off a target from that range. We have to get out of here before he can close the distance.'

As she spoke, Algol raised his arm, the graceless bulk of a bolter clenched in his fist. Without pause or hesitation, the Space Marine fired. From the other side of the tractor, Deacon screamed and fell, his chest ripped to splinters by the bolter's explosive shell.

'Get on and keep down!' Yuxiang shouted to Taofang and Mingzhou, throwing the tractor into reverse. It had barely started to move before Algol fired again, the legionary's shots smashing into the engine block. Smoke and steam erupted from the shattered engine.

The slaves hiding in the cargo bed rose and tried to run. As each tried to leap clear, he was picked off in mid-air by a shot from Algol's bolter, their mangled bodies flying across the tunnel.

Mingzhou dropped down to the ground, rolling under the carriage of the tractor, aiming her lasrifle at the distant Space Marine. As she squinted down the sight, she cursed. 'No one can shoot like that,' she swore, pulling back the trigger and sending a crimson beam of light flashing down the tunnel. Hundreds of metres from its target, the beam faded into nothingness.

The flash of light caused Algol to pause. The skull-faced helm tilted to one side, peering more intently at the tractor. Almost casually, the Iron warrior adjusted his grip on the bolter, tilting the barrel downwards ever so slightly.

'Mingzhou!' Taofang screamed at the sniper. 'We have to get out of here!' Yuxiang leapt down from the cab and added his voice to the janissary's.

'Get to cover!' Mingzhou shouted back. 'He can't hit me under here unless he gets close! And when he does, I'll put a hotshot through his skull!'

The bolter cracked again. Taofang cried out as he watched Mingzhou's body jerk up and strike the underside of the tractor. Her body slumped back against the ferrocrete paving, blood streaming from her shattered flesh. Instead of closing upon her and coming within range of the sniper's rifle, the Iron Warrior had fired his shot into the floor several metres in front of the tractor, deflecting his shot so that it arced beneath the vehicle and struck the woman hidden there.

'She's dead!' Yuxiang shouted, trying to drag Taofang away. The janissary pulled away, his hands tightening about the stock of his lasgun. Yuxiang watched incredulously as the janissary began marching down the tunnel towards Algol, the crack of his lasgun echoing through the tunnel as he advanced, oblivious to the distance between himself and his enemy.

Yuxiang knew there was nothing he could do to help Taofang. The janissary was marching to his death, a fate he seemed now to welcome. Algol, with sadistic amusement, held his fire, allowing the doomed man to advance down the tunnel knowing he could strike the soldier down any time he wanted.

Yuxiang turned and ran into the darkness. Survival, the will to live, thundered through his veins, urging him onwards. Behind him, he could hear the steady crack of Taofang's lasgun, the reports receding into the distance. Finally, as the reports became faint, he heard the boom of the bolter one last time.

He was alone in the maze of tunnels now and somewhere behind him, coming after him as surely as Death, was the Skintaker.

A SUSURRUS OF binary echoed through the catacombs, a staccato of pious devotion and supplication filled the

346

darkness. Cowled heads were raised, mechanical eyes were bright with the fervour of zealous anticipation, cybernetic claws were twined in prayer.

Above the conspirators, who had risked all to assemble it, who had offended their own strictures to cobble it together, the warhead of Vindex Lartius hung upon its chains. Like the eidolon of some techno-barbarian cult, the great bomb beamed down upon them, seeming to revel in their adoration. Its machine-spirit would soon claim its function, the purpose to which it was formed. The perfect fusion of purpose and destiny that only the divine machine could achieve.

If it was still possible, Enginseer Heroditus might have felt envy for the purity of Vindex Lartius. Its essence hadn't been violated and abused by the obscenities of the Iron Warriors. It hadn't been coerced into labouring for the foul achievements of Fabricator Oriax, the arch-heretic of Castellax. It was clean of the blasphemy with which every man in the catacomb had desecrated himself.

Every man save one. Logis Acestes had never submitted to enslavement, had never allowed himself to be subjected to profane servitude under Oriax. He had hidden himself, bided his time until the opportunity to strike back at the heretics was presented to them by the grace of the Machine-God.

Of them all, only Acestes was clean enough in spirit and purpose to sing the psalm that would arm the warhead, to press the rune that would detonate Vindex Lartius and bring the purifying fires of annihilation to the lords of Castellax. It was an honour of which only Acestes was worthy. Only he could lead them into redemption.

The tech-priests maintained their Lingua-Technis chant while Acestes mounted the causeway and approached the gilded cabinet in which was housed the sacred rune of detonation. He folded his hands together, bowed his head in an attitude of reverence. A soft hiss of binary crackled from his vox-caster, a sonic pulse that swept through the cavernous chamber.

Instantly, the chorus of the conspirators was silenced. Heroditus struggled to speak, but every relay and servo within his body refused to respond, locked into fail-safe redundancies from which they wouldn't stir. His eyes, the only parts of him that were organic and therefore mobile, rolled in their sockets. His optic sensors observed that the entire congregation had been gripped by the same affliction. Frozen in place, solemn and silent as steel statues, none of them could even give voice to his distress.

Heroditus felt his mind shudder, aware that it was not simply motion that was denied to him. All functionality had been restricted. The orisons of distraction, the subroutine of deception he had been feeding into the spy-implants were no longer running. The implants, if they continued to function, if they weren't afflicted by the plague-protocol, might even now be alerting Oriax to what the conspirators had achieved. The Iron Warriors might even now be descending upon this place to dismantle Vindex Lartius.

Fear, that most ancient and primal of emotions, coursed through the enginseer's brain. Coming so close to fulfilling their purpose and achieving redemption only to have it all snatched away from them at the very edge of countdown! If he still possessed tear ducts, Heroditus knew he would have wept for the malicious cruelty of fate.

Then hope stirred within him, rushing through his brain without the impetus of a valve-pump to speed it along. Upon the causeway, Heroditus saw motion! Logis Acestes was raising his head, was staring across the other tech-priests, studying their predicament. Victory and redemption were still within their grasp. It needed only one voice to sing the psalm of activation, one hand to depress the rune of detonation!

Acestes gazed out across the conspirators, the lenses of his optics pivoting within the sockets of his skull. From his speakers, a voice boomed down, but it was not the voice of the logis. It was a voice that had become even more familiar to the tech-priests during the long centuries of occupation. It was the voice of the arch-heretic. The voice of Fabricator Oriax.

'We come to the end of all things,' Oriax's words crackled from Acestes's speakers. 'Your craft and efficiency in achieving your purpose have been exemplary. I knew when I first conceived this plan that your productivity would be more zealous were you to labour under an appealing delusion.' Acestes lifted his arms, extending them outwards to better display his robed chassis. 'Towards that end, I revived your Logis Acestes from the dust of dissolution, crafting a replica of his semblance and infusing it with a simulacra of his mentality. You should feel honoured. Seldom have I worked so diligently upon one of my flesh-drones.'

Heroditus felt the magnitude of the Fabricator's betrayal come crushing down upon him. Not for an instant could he question the evidence of his senses. Through the deception of Logis Acestes, Oriax had preyed upon their faith and defiance, had exploited the embers of rebellion burning inside them. Like some daemonic maestro, he had conducted the conspiracy from the very beginning, directing its every move.

'The time is at hand,' Oriax pronounced. 'The full weight of the ork attack descends upon Vorago. Now the Iron Warriors will be annihilated. Vindex Lartius shall break the walls and the horde shall pour in, overwhelming the traitors. The Third Grand Company will be blotted from existence, Warsmith Andraaz will die in disgrace knowing all his achievements perish with him.' The static crackle of Oriax's laughter hissed from Acestes's speakers.

'I tell you all of this, so that as your spirits are hurled into the void, you will understand,' Oriax said. 'Like the orks, you have been a useful tool. I would feel uneasy allowing you to die under the delusion that your sacrifice has been for your Omnissiah and your False Emperor.

Understand, as I activate Vindex Lartius, that you perish not as martyrs, but simply as pawns of Oriax!'

The Fabricator's words rang in Heroditus's audio relays as he watched the replica of Acestes reach into the gilded cabinet to depress the rune which would annihilate them all.

CHAPTER XIX

I-Day Plus One Hundred and Twenty-One

RHODAAN BROUGHT THE churning edge of his chainsword slashing across the snarling face of his adversary, sending a spray of green flesh and yellow tusks spurting across the wall. The ork crumpled, its fingers still tugging at the trigger of its pistol. Rhodaan kicked the twitching corpse out of his way and lunged at the next alien he had marked for slaughter. There was no shortage of choices. With each breath, dozens of orks were leaping down from the rusty shoulders of the stompa, howling with bloodlust as they dropped to the wall. The huge scrap metal hull of the war machine loomed high above the wall, its massive guns lobbing shells into the city, its spotlights blazing like the eyes of a mad god.

The death cry of an ork shrieked through the audio relays in Rhodaan's helmet as he opened its guts with his sword and vaporised its chest with a blast of plasma. The Iron Warrior dismissed his mutilated foe, spinning around to catch another ork in mid-drop. The alien's bullets glanced from his power armour, but the teeth of

Rhodaan's grinding sword caught it squarely as it fell, cutting it open from groin to throat. The severed halves of the ork flopped about its killer's feet, greasy alien ichor spraying from its organs.

There was no pleasure in killing the orks, however many Rhodaan slew. The deaths were meaningless, devoid of any tactical significance. The fact that the stompas had reached the wall rendered the situation untenable. If the Iron Warriors' artillery had been able to stop their advance or if Morax could have assembled enough of his strike-bombers to make a direct assault on them, then perhaps the walls could have held. But none of these things had happened. Caught in a fixed position, compelled to rely upon the fire support of mere Flesh, the Space Marines were engaged in a war of attrition now. No tactics, no strategy, not even martial discipline and superior weaponry. Everything was boiling down to a question of simple numbers. With perhaps forty Iron Warriors spread out amongst the entirety of the defences, the numbers favoured the orks by several orders of magnitude.

Rhodaan clenched his teeth as he incinerated the face of a charging ork. Reason railed against the absurdity of the commands coming from the Iron Bastion, yet there was no denying the voice was that of Sergeant Ipos, the Warsmith's seneschal. What they amounted to was 'hold and die', the sort of command dispatched to replaceable Flesh, not to hardened Space Marines. Certainly not to Raptors, the elite of the elite.

Spinning to cut the legs out from under a monster ork with a steam-powered industrial claw welded to its forearm, Rhodaan wracked his mind for some way, some excuse, to discard the orders he had been given. Some way to save himself and his Iron Warriors.

'Lord captain,' Brother Uzraal's voice crackled over the vox. 'The seismic index of the stompa's bludgeons has increased ten-fold.' Stationed within the janissary command post for this section of the perimeter, Uzraal was able to access directly the various intelligence filtering into the headquarters. Among that intelligence was the data being transmitted by the stability cogitators buried deep inside the perimeter wall. From the very start of their attack, the stompas had employed their gigantic claws to pound the wall. Now, it seemed, their barbaric efforts were finally beginning to wear down the ferrocrete.

'Estimated time before collapse?' Rhodaan inquired as his chainsword severed the roof of an ork's skull. The alien froze in its tracks, staring stupidly at the stew of blood and brains dripping down its hands. The Iron Warrior finished it with a thrust that crunched through its ribs and pulped its heart.

'Collapse within the next rotation,' Uzraal reported, 'but we can expect fractures before then. The entire front façade will probably shear off.'

Through his boots, Rhodaan could feel the steady tremor of the stompa's claw pounding away, a tattoo of destruction that was relentless and implacable. The aliens didn't care how many of their own perished when the wall came down, that was of no consequence to them at all. What mattered was breaking through this obstacle that had defied them, seeing it smashed down and brought low. Even the orks, Rhodaan thought bitterly, understand that fighting for control of the wall is pointless.

Turning to parry the assault of a screaming ork wielding an electrified mattock, Rhodaan suddenly found himself catapulted into the air, his armoured body spinning end over end as he was hurled far into the smog-choked sky. The air around him was thick with huge chunks of ferrocrete, twisted slabs of metal, gory strips of meat that could only dimly be recognised as belonging to either humans or orks. The audio relays in his helmet emitted only a soft buzz, their dampeners overwhelmed by some terrific sound.

The demi-organic wings fixed to Rhodaan's jump pack snapped open, turning his aerial tumble into a controlled descent. He was forced to shift and weave through the cascade of debris, nearly being swatted from the sky by a jagged lump of metal he slowly realised was the claw from one of the stompas. It had been sheared off at the joint, tons of steel hurled hundreds of metres into the sky. The force required to do such a thing was incredible, almost unbelievable.

Rhodaan had a full appreciation of how unbelievable a moment later. The filters in his helmet's optics pierced the thick clouds of smoke and dust, revealing the shattered landscape below. Where the firebreak abutting the perimeter wall had stood there was now just a jagged crater. Hundreds of metres of wall had been obliterated by some tremendous subterranean explosion, the force of the blast crippling the stompa attacking the nearby section, flinging it like a tinker toy to lie floundering on its side, its massive feet churning futilely at the empty air. How many thousands of orks and Flesh had been annihilated outright in the blast, Rhodaan couldn't say, but he could see their bodies strewn about everywhere. Scattered survivors, dazed and confused, crawled about the ruins.

The Raptor's mind whirled. Was it possible the orks had sent sappers underneath the wall, that the brutish xenos had managed to infiltrate the complex underground defences of Vorago to plant some planet-cracking bomb under the city? It was a theory that repulsed Rhodaan, yet what other explanation was there?

Increasing the magnification of his optics, Rhodaan forgot his questions about why and how. Beyond the blast, a vast horde of orks were gathering, drawn like moths to the violence of the explosion. At the moment, the aliens were confused and indecisive, but as soon as the smoke cleared they would know what to do. They would see that the blast had obliterated the wall, leaving the interior of Vorago wide open.

'Squad Kyrith,' Rhodaan snarled into his vox. His helmet's external audio receptors were still buzzing from the detonation, but the internal relays were still functional. 'Report!'

'Brother Gomorie. Thrown clear. I am two kilometres from your position, lord captain.'

'Brother Uzraal. Coordinating the Flesh in opening the collapsed passage into the command post.'

Rhodaan waited, but no reply came from Pazuriel. Another of his formidable Raptors squandered in a wasteful death. A sudden thought came to him as he considered the reduced strength of his command. 'Brother Merihem?'

The Obliterator's voice hissed across the vox. 'I function,' the monster growled. 'My position is five hundred metres from your location. Allow me a space for my diagnostics to recalibrate.' Over the vox, Rhodaan could hear a grisly sucking sound, like boiled flesh being stripped from raw bone. Whatever adjustments Merihem's corrupt body was making, he didn't want to know.

'Orders, lord captain?' Brother Gomorie asked.

Rhodaan stared grimly at the wall. The orders he had been given by Sergeant Ipos were to hold their position, but their position didn't exist any more. It had been annihilated in the blast. A cold smile formed on his face.

'Fall back to the Iron Bastion,' Rhodaan decided. 'Use your jump packs. We will rendezvous at central command.' A murderous edge crept into his voice. 'I think I'm going to discuss strategy with Sergeant Ipos.'

Uzraal's voice crackled across the vox. 'Lord captain, the Flesh here want to know what assistance they can render us. Shall I execute them for their impertinence?'

There was a touch of eagerness in Uzraal's tone that Rhodaan didn't feel like indulging. 'Negative. Save your ammunition. We may need it.' As he gave the command, his mind turned again to Merihem. The Obliterator's ability to generate his own ammunition would be beneficial if the monster's talents could be properly harnessed. He had a feeling that something was terribly wrong back at the Bastion, something he would need every resource to confront.

'Brother Merihem, what is your situation? Can you make your way back to the Bastion?'

The Obliterator's hiss crackled across the channel. 'I am partially extracted from a three-metre deep impact crater. There is a damaged manufactorum ten metres to my west, a smashed Air Cohort fighter fifty metres to my north and a squad of janissaries with a disabled truck one hundred metres to my south,' Merihem reported.

'Can you commandeer the transport from the Flesh?' Rhodaan asked.

The Obliterator's amusement rippled through Rhodaan's helmet. 'Do you think they can stop me, lord captain?'

Rhodaan ignored the question, staring instead at the ork horde. The smoke was clearing now and the aliens were able to see some of the damage that had been done. Already, excited orks were jabbering at their fellows, sometimes punctuating their words by firing a burst into the smoke. It wouldn't be long now.

'Squad Kyrith, withdraw to the Bastion,' Rhodaan ordered. 'Vorago is lost.'

As he ignited his thrusters and soared across the devastation, his helmet's external audio crackled back into life. Behind him, Rhodaan could hear the orks give voice to a mighty roar, a bestial cry that had heralded carnage and atrocity across an entire galaxy. He didn't need to look back to know the horde was rushing into the breach. That semi-articulate roar told him the orks were on the attack.

'Waaagh!'

DARKNESS. IT HAD become the entirety of existence, a blackness so all-encompassing that it assumed its own voice. The voice of darkness, roaring through the ears, bellowing its malignance with a thunderous dirge.

No, Yuxiang corrected himself, it was not the darkness

that roared and raged, it was the thing which lurked in that darkness. The armoured devil who stalked him through the catacombs, calling out to him with the amplified boom of vox-casters. The fiend whose sadistic taunts pursued him through the empty tunnels, mocking him for his audacity.

What was a man except weak, frail Flesh? How could mere Flesh hope to defy Iron? What hope had worms who rose against gods?

HE HAD KILLED them all. Algol boasted of the ease with which he had tracked the rebels back to their refuge. He sneered as he described the death of each rebel Yuxiang had recruited. None of them had any chance. Fifty armed men against one legionary? The fight was over before it began.

The Skintaker had hoped for an amusing diversion when he descended into the tunnels to hunt his prey. He had hoped the rebels would put up some manner of defence, at least display enough cunning and ingenuity to give Algol pause. The Space Marine hadn't even broken a sweat, hadn't even bothered to tune out the transmissions from the Iron Bastion so he could focus entirely upon the hunt. Yuxiang's rabble had been pathetic, laughable. Children playing at soldiers.

YUXIANG CLUNG TO the wall, sucking in the stagnant air, feeling the industrial pollutants singe his lungs. He'd discarded his gas mask and duster long ago, as well as anything else that would weigh him down and tax his endurance. The lasgun had been the last thing he'd cast aside, but he knew his reluctance to part with it had been absurd, giving in to his fear. There was no chance he could fight the Space Marine, Algol could pick him off any time he wanted. If Yuxiang ever allowed the Iron Warrior to get so close as to offer him a chance to shoot, he knew the giant would finish him before he could get off a shot. As though a measly las-bolt could pierce the ceramite armour encasing the monster.

No, all he could do was run. All he could do was delay the inevitable, to draw out the chase. Eventually exhaustion would overwhelm him or Algol would grow bored. Then it would all be over. Until then, all Yuxiang could do was run, to selfishly cling to each terror-soaked moment left to him. Even when death was so near, a man clung to life with a miser's greed.

'Your friends are all dead, little one,' Algol's voice thundered from the darkness. 'They have all left you. Left you alone. Left you to me.'

Yuxiang drew another lungful of polluted air and pushed himself away from the wall, mustering his strength for another effort. One hand trailing along the wall, allowing him to keep his bearings, he raced ahead into the darkness. He could hear the monster laugh, the sound echoing through the corridors.

'Tired? Is the Flesh growing weak?' Algol mocked. 'And you thought you could stand against Iron? That is such an insult that I think I will take my time. I'll start the knife at your throat and you'll beg me to dig it a little deeper and end your misery. I'll stop and listen and make you think maybe you have earned mercy. Then I'll set to work again and you'll know it will be a long time before I allow you to die.'

Yuxiang tried to block out the Iron Warrior's thunderous voice as Algol described outrage after outrage, a litany of torture that only a devil incarnate could conceive. Desperately, he drew upon unknown reserves of strength to push ahead, unreasoning fear goading him towards an escape he knew was irrational to hope for. The legionary had superior strength and endurance, enabling him to far outlast Yuxiang. The optics in his helmet allowed him to see in the dark while Yuxiang could only grope blindly down the passages. Even if he didn't have the benefit of night vision, the Iron Warrior could track the slave by scent alone, his olfactory senses heightened to the sensitivity of a canid.

No, there was no escape from the horrors Algol described in chilling detail. There was only one thing Yuxiang could do. That was to cheat his tormentor of his victory.

To do that meant to silence that urge to survive, to cling to each moment left to him. Yuxiang gripped the knife in his boot, the combat knife Taofang had given him when the janissary had seen Processing Omega and joined the rebellion. He fingered the knife now, running his thumb along its edge. The keen blade cut the skin, drawing a bead of blood from his finger.

Yuxiang knew Algol would be able to smell his blood. The Iron Warrior's cruel imagination would guess what his prey was about. Through the corridor, the sound of the armoured giant's rushing steps rumbled like the roar of a train. Yuxiang pressed the blade against his throat, determined to do what he had to before the legionary could stop him.

Then the world came crashing down.

There was a sound like the cracking of a mountain, a wave of hot air that smashed down from the roof, mashing Yuxiang against the floor. He could feel the ground jumping beneath him, the walls shivering beside him. The stink of ferrocrete dust filled the air, blotting out even the industrial stink of pollutants.

Consciousness threatened to abandon Yuxiang, but he stubbornly forced it to maintain its hold on his mind. The knife had been knocked from his hand by the tumult. Yuxiang desperately groped about in the darkness for the lost blade, still intent on denying Algol his victory.

The blade remained elusive. Each heartbeat, Yuxiang expected to feel the Skintaker's hands close about his throat, lift him from the ground and shake him like a ragdoll. Then the real torture would begin.

By degrees, even through the panic rushing along

his spine, Yuxiang became aware that it was becoming brighter in the tunnel. A sickly stream of daylight was filtering down into the passage through a jagged fissure in the roof. Some colossal explosion had caused the ceiling to fracture and come apart. Great chunks of ferrocrete lay strewn about the tunnel, several of them having missed Yuxiang by only a few metres. He wasn't sure if that was anything to be grateful for. Crushed under tons of rock would be preferable to what Algol intended.

Then, through the veil of dust, Yuxiang saw something that made his heart stop. He could see the skull-like helmet and the ceramite armour of his tormentor, the hideous cloak drawn across the fiend's shoulders. It was a moment of pure horror as he stared into the blazing optics of the Skintaker.

The moment passed and was replaced by incredulous jubilation. Yes, Yuxiang could see the Skintaker's head and shoulders, but he couldn't see anything else. The rest of the Space Marine was buried under a pile of rubble, great masses of ferrocrete and steel girders. One plasteel rod, projecting from the debris, was coated in blood too bright to belong to an ork or unaugmented human. The sight of Algol's blood drowned Yuxiang's fear. The monster was mortal after all!

Slowly, Yuxiang approached the pile of rubble, a twisted plasteel rod clenched in his hands. He stared down at the trapped Space Marine, feeling the arrogance and contempt burning behind the optics. He could see Algol struggling to move, straining to push the masses of ferrocrete and steel off his body. A disjointed, fragmented growl rasped from the damaged vox-casters, allowing Yuxiang to hear only every other word in a steady stream of threats and invective.

Yuxiang was no artificer, no craftsman trained in armourcraft. What he knew were machines, the presses of the factory. There was one simple rule to any machine: it was weakest where its moving parts were. Studying the trapped Space Marine, Yuxiang noted the slight gap between gorget and helmet designed to allow the legionary to turn his head. A cold smile formed on Yuxiang's face. He lifted the jagged twist of plasteel with its sharp point.

'This is how it ends,' Yuxiang told the imprisoned devil. 'Sometimes even the worm gets its chance. Sometimes even a god dies at a man's hand!'

Vengefully, Yuxiang drove the plasteel stake into Algol's throat, worrying it around in the wound until all the Larraman cells in his body couldn't stop the bleeding. As Algol's blood tried to seal the wound with scar tissue, Yuxiang's vicious attentions tore them open again.

Bit by bit, the Skintaker was bleeding out. It was a slow, humiliating death. The sort of death Algol had revelled in bestowing.

The irony of his own destruction only made Algol's humiliation more complete.

EVEN LOCKED INSIDE his immense suit of Terminator armour, the sound of the wailing daemons clawed at Warsmith Andraaz's ears, scratching at his mind with icy talons. He could feel their unnatural essence pawing at the core of his being, hungrily caressing that eternal spark ecclesiarchs and philosophers called the soul. He felt the urge to submit to the profane violation, to surrender himself to the call of Chaos.

The Warsmith's scarred face hardened. His tyrannical will exerted itself, driving back the temptations threatening to lure him to distraction. Chaos was a force, a power, a cosmic energy to be tapped and harnessed, exploited and dominated. Let the Word Bearers and Thousand Sons wallow in their bog of superstition and slavery. Let the World Eaters and the Emperor's Children surrender their very identity to ruinous gods, allow their minds to be devoured by daemonic desires. The Third Grand Company would remain pure. The Third Grand Company would remain steadfast. They would not lose focus upon the Long War. They would not forget the reason for their hate. It was theirs, it belonged to them. They would share their revenge with no one, mortal or god.

Andraaz cast his gaze across the Daemonculum, watching as the flesh-drones brought their offerings before the chained daemons. He could feel the throb of infernal power racing through the bloodwood platform, smell the ethereal taint of warp energy as it gathered in the chamber. Weird coruscations of light crackled between the pillars, plays of brilliance that were at once all colours and none at all.

The Warsmith flexed his fingers, the scythe-like talons of the power claw fitted to his armour unfolding in response, energy rippling down each blade. He could feel the ancient weapon's eagerness, its thirst for battle. Soon, he promised it, soon it would be sated. It would rend and tear, rip and slash until the very end, until the last breath had been crushed from his body.

He turned his gaze from the daemons and their bloody repast, looking instead upon the five armoured giants standing beside him on the bloodwood dais. The Rending Guard, veterans of Isstvan and Olympia, victors of a million battles. Each of the Iron Warriors was entombed within a hulking mass of ceramite and titanium, their archaic Terminator armour festooned with gilded skulls and runic script. Oaths of blood and honour bound them to the Warsmith, joined their very souls to serving Andraaz faithfully and without question. They would lay down their lives for the Warsmith.

Today, they would.

Andraaz stared hard at his Rending Guard, burning every spike and rivet adorning their armour into his memory. They had served him well down through the millennia, been his strong right hand in every conflict. Never had they failed him. A flicker of guilt tried to find its way into the Warsmith's hearts as the thought came to him that he had failed them in the end. Andraaz dismissed the idea. He was Warsmith. In a very real way, he was the Third Grand Company. The Iron Warriors under his command were there to serve and obey. He owed no obligations to them. They would fight and they would die to bring glory to Andraaz.

Today, they would die. Andraaz had decided that when he led the Rending Guard into the depths of the Iron Bastion and into Fabricator Oriax's sanctum. With the breaking of the perimeter wall and the firebreak, there was no longer any question of holding back the xenos scum. Castellax was lost. The Iron Warriors might hold out for a few more months in the Bastion, but the end would be the same. There was no hope of victory now.

All that was left to them was to seize a final chance at glory. To make the orks pay dearly for their triumph. A butcher's bill that would make even the aliens tremble.

In defeat, Andraaz would seize the only honour left to him. He would meet the ork warlord on the battlefield. He would slay the beast that had brought doom to his world.

Across the chamber, Andraaz could see Fabricator Oriax, the Techmarine's mechanised manipulators flying about the oval control console arrayed about him, depressing glowing runes and turning bronze dials. The original Daemonculum had required a coven of thirteen psi-witches to control it. Through his machinery, the new Daemonculum needed only Oriax.

The Warsmith's gaze hardened as he considered the Techmarine and his creation. How long had the Daemonculum been operational? How long had Oriax deceived him about its capabilities? Andraaz had been aware for many decades that the Fabricator was obsessed with the Daemonculum, but he had never suspected how deep that obsession ran. Oriax seemed unduly possessive, as though he had forgotten that the device, and Fabricator himself, belonged to Andraaz.

If he hadn't needed Oriax to control the Daemonculum now, Andraaz would have shown the Techmarine what it meant to deceive a Warsmith. Circumstances, however, had made him essential to Andraaz's final chance for glory. The Fabricator's Steel Blood had located the ork warlord, Biglug. The warlord couldn't afford to miss the final battle for control of Castellax, if he did then he would lose his hold over the other orks and some other alien would rise to challenge him. Biglug had to participate in the final attack and Oriax's Steel Blood had spotted the xenos monster leading a mob of his fellows into the breach. Even now, the servitor-spies were monitoring the ork warlord, transmitting updates directly to Oriax's sanctum.

Biglug had been cagey throughout the campaign, keeping himself away from the battlefield. Perhaps now he felt the Iron Warriors were broken, that they could pose no further threat to him. The ork was due for a grim surprise.

The Daemonculum would transport Andraaz and the Rending Guard directly to the warlord's position, teleporting them past the thousands of orks closing upon the Iron Bastion. When Oriax completed the arcane sequences and activated the eldritch machinery, Andraaz would step through the warp and meet his destiny.

Warsmith and warlord would meet and to the victor would belong the final glory.

SLAVES SCATTERED AS the three Raptors stormed into the communications centre. Uzraal tossed the mangled body of the janissary officer who had tried to stop them at the door. The Flesh had been posted there on orders from Sergeant Ipos. The man's sense of duty had brought him a hideous death. The other janissaries wisely chose to stand down.

Rhodaan's wings fluttered irritably as he cast his gaze across the hall. The pict screens bolted to the walls displayed scenes from all across Vorago, scenes of the orks rampaging through the ruins. Here and there, pockets of Iron Warriors could be seen, desperately trying to hold sections of the wall. Rhodaan's blood boiled as he appreciated the dilemma his battle-brothers faced. Annihilation or disobedience. For an Iron Warrior, it was a difficult choice to make.

With every passing moment, however, Rhodaan was convinced he had made the right choice. Upon reaching the Iron Bastion, the Raptors had sought out Warsmith Andraaz, only to learn from his major-domo that he was absent. Along with his bodyguard, the Warsmith had disappeared. He had left no word of either his destination or his intentions. In his absence, the Warsmith had left Sergeant Ipos to coordinate the city's defence.

That germ of information had brought the Raptors into the communications centre, smashing their way past doors and guards to reach the heart of the Bastion. The Warsmith had left before the explosion that ripped through the walls. That meant the suicidal, irrational orders to hold and die had come from Ipos alone. Rhodaan intended to have a few words with the seneschal. Then it was his intention to peel Ipos out of his power armour and start removing each of the traitor's implants with his bare hands.

'Where is Ipos?' Rhodaan growled over his vox, his voice booming from the speakers in his horned helmet. The terrified Flesh didn't answer, but a few of them turned anxious eyes towards the armoured nexus at the centre of the room. That told Rhodaan everything he needed to know.

Resembling a multi-faceted cyst of titanium, the nexus was designed as a final control point in the event the Bastion was invaded. Within the armoured tomb, communications could be maintained even after the rest of the tower was lost to the enemy. Designed to resist an army, it was intended as a refuge that could operate for weeks on its own.

Rhodaan glared at the armoured nexus, studying its structure. If he had been intent on capturing it intact he would have found the proposition daunting. However, despite his desire for answers, he was too practical to insist on taking Ipos alive.

'Melta bombs,' Rhodaan ordered. The Flesh in the communications centre watched in horror as Gomorie and Uzraal approached the nexus, planting the deadly explosives in the few relays projecting from the armoured shell. One of the humans screamed, the sound initiating a panicked exodus. The Space Marines ignored the Flesh fleeing past them, focused only upon their objective.

'Ipos,' Rhodaan snarled over his vox, using a general frequency that any Iron Warrior would be able to receive. 'You have betrayed the Third Grand Company. I will give you a count of five to come out and answer for your treason.' Expectant silence brooded in the communications centre as the Raptors waited. The door of the nexus remained sealed.

'Die like a traitor dog then!' Rhodaan roared. He brought his gauntlet down in a slashing gesture. Gomorie depressed the activation stud on the detonator he held.

Star-fire blazed from the nexus as the melta bombs exploded, the shock of the blast ripping through the communications centre with the fury of a hurricane. Cracks snaked across the floor, rubble rained down from the ceiling, pict screens warped and shattered. Smoke billowed from toppled control terminals and communication relays.

The Raptors strode through the devastation like armoured gods marching through Armageddon. Before them, the nexus was broken, a deep crack crawling down its face. Gomorie walked to the titanium shell, slid his fingers into the crack. With a tremendous heave, he sent the broken section of the shell crashing to the floor.

The interior of the nexus was a shambles. Machinery lay in tangles of wire and conduit, shattered bits of pict screen lay strewn across everything. Amidst the wreckage, his armour breached and torn, was the hulk of Sergeant Ipos.

Vindictively, Rhodaan moved to drag the corpse from the debris. As he approached, however, he noted the ugly burn at the centre of the dead Iron Warrior's chest, a mark that looked to have been inflicted by a close-range plasma discharge. What was more, it was an old wound, at least several hours.

Rhodaan recoiled in alarm as he heard Sergeant Ipos's voice rising from the wreckage, enjoining the Iron Warriors on the walls to maintain their positions. He stared at the dead Space Marine for an instant, then noticed the servitor lying a few metres away. The flesh-drone was broken, its steel legs snapped from its pelvis, its chest crushed by a section of titanium plate. But it still possessed a semblance of functionality, enough at least to continue issuing orders to the Iron Warriors.

Orders in a perfect imitation of Sergeant Ipos's voice.

How long had the seneschal been dead? Who had set the servitor in his place?

Rhodaan's hearts turned cold. He had a feeling he knew the answer to both questions. It answered many things, such as the renegade gun battery that had fired on them when they returned to Vorago.

The squad vox-channel crackled, the steely voice of Brother Merihem rumbling through Rhodaan's helmet. 'I have secured the transport hangar,' the Obliterator reported. 'The Flesh could not stop me. When you have finished your business with Ipos, the survivors will enthusiastically put themselves at your command.'

Rhodaan smiled at the sound of Merihem's voice. He had worried that the Obliterator would forget his purpose and try to seek out Andraaz on his own. There was bad blood between the two and with everything collapsing around them, duty to the Legion might not be enough to restrain the monster. Rhodaan needed him, coherent and obedient, if he was to have any chance at all of bringing the Third Grand Company's betrayer to task.

'Hold position,' Rhodaan ordered the Obliterator. He turned to Gomorie and Uzraal. 'Establish communication with our battle-brothers. Tell them to disregard their last orders. They are to extract themselves from Vorago in whatever way they can. Tell them... tell them to rendezvous at the Oubliette.'

The two Iron Warriors scrambled among the debris to find a working relay. Rhodaan watched them for an instant, then turned his attention back to Merihem. 'The situation is more complicated,' he told the Obliterator. 'Make your way to the grand hall. We will rendezvous with you there.'

'I obey,' Merihem answered. 'And I am bringing along a complication of my own. I think it will amuse you. Give me a few minutes to discipline the surviving Flesh.'

Rhodaan could hear the first screams across his vox before the Obliterator shut off his vox-bead. Yes, it was a good thing the monster was on his side.

And a very bad thing for the battle-brother who had betrayed them all.

Rhodaan hoped Fabricator Oriax liked his sanctum because very soon it would become his grave.

VALLAX BROUGHT HIS shoulder smashing against the metal grille, feeling its rusty surface crumble under the ceramite plate. He hesitated, turning his head to stare back down the industrial sewer. Even without the augmentation afforded by his missing helmet, his superhuman senses pierced the darkness like the sharp edge of a knife. He could hear the slosh of the slow-moving sludge running through the passage, smell the caustic vapours rising from the mineral waste, see the streamers of corrosion dangling from the roof of the tunnel, feel the sluggish draught created by the sewer's recycling systems. Concentrating on his senses, he waited. His hearts slowed, his body tensed as he anticipated the howl of orks, the rush of blood-crazed aliens down the tunnel.

After a few breaths, the Iron Warrior was satisfied. Nothing had heard the impact against the grille. Turning, he brought his shoulder smashing against the obstruction once more.

The oversized drains connected to every factory in Vorago, a network of sewers that stretched deep beneath the city. Nothing human could survive in the stagnant, toxic air. Only the small multi-lung implanted in every Space Marine allowed Vallax to breathe the poisonous filth. Even so, the Iron Warriors had been thorough in their construction, implementing numerous baffles and obstructions throughout the sewer. Experts at siege warfare, they had applied that same knowledge when it came to constructing their own defences. Vallax knew there were other, more lethal diversions hidden in the tunnels, traps the recognition code being transmitted by his armour disabled as he neared them.

The grille gave way beneath his shoulder and Vallax thrust the crumpled mess of rusty bars into the sludge. He studied the intersection that opened beyond the tunnel, taking a moment to orient himself. Unerringly, he set himself upon the northward passage, the tunnel that would guide him back to the Iron Bastion.

It had been a dangerous route that led him into the sewers. His escape from the battlefortress had been at the edge of catastrophe every step of the way. He had lost count of the orks he'd slaughtered in the confusion of corridors and passageways, the other aliens he'd killed while stealing through the ork encampment. Many times, he had wondered if he would be able to overcome the perils of his ordeal. Always the thought of Oriax sustained him. Vallax couldn't die beneath the paws of the orks. Not while the Fabricator was still alive.

Vengeance. It was a purity of purpose that had sustained the entire Legion for ten thousand years. Now, Vallax drew strength from sacred vengeance, cherished it as he cherished his personal honour and martial pride. Oriax would suffer for what he had done. When Vallax finished with him, the maimed Iron Warrior would truly wish he had perished in the crystal-swamps.

Bloody thoughts driving him onwards, Vallax stole through the polluted tunnels. He didn't see the camouflaged shapes moving through the darkness, following his trail in the sludge, didn't hear the low grumble of ork lungs choking down the toxic air, didn't smell the sour-stink of alien flesh in the synthetic draught.

CHAPTER XX

I-Day Plus One Hundred and Twenty-One

A WEIRD FLASH of green light strobed through the Iron Bastion as the Raptors ran down the tower's stairs. It was an after effect of munitions striking the void shields. The orks had brought some of their heavy artillery into the city and turned it upon this last point of defiance. Rhodaan could tell by the rich jade hue that the force field could withstand much more than the aliens were firing at it. Perhaps if the orks concentrated their fire they could bring the shields down, but such restraint was going to be hard for their warlord to impose now that the brutes could smell victory.

The Iron Warriors had several hours to do what they needed to do before the shields were reduced to even three quarters of their present strength. That suited Rhodaan fine. When he got his hands on Oriax, he didn't want to feel rushed.

Brother Merihem's techno-organic bulk awaited them in the grand hall, looking immense even beside the towering pillars that supported the vaulted ceiling fifty metres above. Patches of the Obliterator's armour undulated like the surface of a troubled stream.

'I have done my duty and waited, lord captain,' the Obliterator said, his pallid face spreading in a steel smile. His body pivoted at the waist, spinning with an unsettlingly machine-like motion. He pointed a clawed finger at one of the pillars. 'Others have waited too. Though their sense of duty had to be encouraged somewhat.'

Rhodaan saw a lone Iron Warrior standing beside the pillar. He recognised the elaborate armour at once and though his face was concealed behind his helmet, Rhodaan was certain that Skylord Morax's expression was anything but happy.

'You sent this... abomination... to...'

Rhodaan glared at the outraged Morax. 'I sent him to secure transport for our extraction,' he corrected the Skylord. 'Finding you was just an unexpected bonus.'

'Captain Morax was preparing to quit the Bastion,' Merihem explained. 'He seemed intent on commandeering all available transport.' The Obliterator's little face arched forwards in a weirdly boneless fashion to stare at Morax. 'He had a considerable amount of bric-a-brac he wanted to take away with him.'

'Supplies to sustain my forces while I conduct a guerrilla war against the orks,' Morax protested. As he moved, Rhodaan could see the stiffness in the Skylord's body, the way he favoured one leg over the other. Whatever Merihem had done to subdue him hadn't been gentle.

'The Speaker is versed in guerrilla tactics?' Merihem marvelled.

Rhodaan didn't need to hear anything else. Abducting the Speaker revealed Morax's intentions plainly enough. The Skylord was going to bury himself in one of his underground aerodromes and use the psyker to send a message to Medrengard. Once that was done, he would be able to sit back and wait for a relief force to come and drive the orks from Castellax.

It wasn't a bad plan. Rhodaan decided he would adopt it just as soon as his business with Oriax was completed.

'He says the Warsmith left to confer with the Fabricator hours ago,' Merihem reported. Morax was quick to elaborate the point.

'Andraaz took the Rending Guard with him, all wearing their Terminator armour. I could hear them reciting the Olympian Death March as they descended into the sub-cellars.'

'Do you think the Warsmith knows about Oriax's treachery?' Gomorie asked. 'Maybe they've gone down there to stop him.'

Rhodaan shook his head. 'No, if the Warsmith knew Oriax was a traitor he would have stopped the false orders being transmitted to our battle-brothers. There was some other purpose in their going to the sanctum.'

'The Daemonculum!' Uzraal exclaimed. 'Oriax must have offered to use the Daemonculum to get the Warsmith to safety.'

Again, Rhodaan shook his head. 'The Warsmith wouldn't run,' he stated resolutely. 'The Rending Guard were singing the Death March. No, it wasn't escape Oriax offered them. It was a chance to die with full honours.'

'But Oriax is a traitor,' Gomorie objected.

Skylord Morax limped away from the pillar, drawn by the Raptor's statement. 'If that is true, then the Warsmith is in danger.' He looked from one Space Marine to another, sensing the suspicion staring back at him from behind each helmet. 'Whatever you may think of me, I am an Iron Warrior. I know where my loyalties lie. I would have left the Warsmith to seek a hero's death, but I won't abide murder at a traitor's hand.'

'What can Oriax do?' Uzraal asked. 'The Warsmith has the Rending Guard with him. They are more than a match for a crippled Techmarine.'

Rhodaan didn't answer at once, instead dashing towards the lifts that would conduct them to the sub-cellars and the Fabricator's sanctum. The other Iron Warriors rushed after him, the limping Morax trailing behind the Raptors, the hulking Merihem following behind Morax.

'If the Fabricator gets them into the Daemonculum he can teleport them anywhere on Castellax,' Rhodaan explained. 'Maybe even off-world. Power claws and Terminator armour won't help much if the Daemonculum drops them into the planet's core or deposits them in orbit around the sun!' The thought of the Warsmith suffering such an ignoble death was obscene to Rhodaan. Loved or hated, as Warsmith, Andraaz's death had to be a thing of glory and consequence, not a farce engineered by a cold-blooded manipulator. Such a blemish on its honour would never cease to haunt the Third Grand Company.

Rhodaan fairly leapt into the cage, his fingers depressing the activation runes as Merihem lumbered across the threshold. The Obliterator lurched forwards, almost slamming into the opposite wall, as the mag-lift hurtled downwards.

The green flashes from the void shields faded as the elevator descended past the surface, dropping down into the foundations of the Bastion itself. The hum of the field generators surrounded the Iron Warriors as the cage passed into the sub-cellars and the labyrinth of tunnels that formed Oriax's domain.

The first thing Rhodaan noticed when the cage doors opened was the hellish crimson glow cast by the hazard lights set into the ceiling of the crypt-like receiving bay. The second thing he noticed were the broken servitors strewn across the floor and draped across cargo containers. His third observation nearly took his head off as a bolt-shell whistled through the exposed cage and detonated against the wall behind him.

'Cover!' Rhodaan roared, lunging from the cage and throwing himself behind one of the steel cargo boxes. Uzraal and Gomorie kept close to the sides of the cage as they provided covering fire for their captain.

'So the usurping lapdog comes rushing to defend his master!' The hatefully familiar voice echoed through the bay. 'Why am I not surprised?' A bolt-shell slammed against Rhodaan's refuge, blasting a chunk of steel from the crate and sending shrapnel spraying in every direction.

Vallax! Rhodaan had given up the Over-Captain as dead, an earlier victim of Oriax's treachery. Understanding the full measure of the Fabricator's lies, Rhodaan felt a pang of guilt for his own complicity in the Techmarine's schemes. Even his hatred of the Over-Captain wasn't enough to accept the magnitude of Oriax's betrayal.

'We have all been betrayed, Vallax!' Rhodaan called out. 'The Fabricator has lied to us all. Through his deceit, many of our battle-brothers lie dead.'

Another bolt-shell slammed into the crate, driving Rhodaan from his shelter and sending him leaping behind the hull of a cargo lifter. Shells tore into the floor around him as he was momentarily exposed. Thankful as he was, he was surprised at Vallax's poor aim.

From the mag-lift cage, the metallic bellow of Merihem thundered across the bay. The hulking Obliterator stormed from the cage, both of his arms formed into the blocky feeds of dual storm bolters. Vallax shifted his aim, firing at the charging monster. Merihem's exposed bulk was too great a target to miss and slivers of his techno-organic armour sprayed from the explosive impacts.

Rhodaan seized the opportunity offered by Merihem's distraction. Powering over the top of the cargo loader, he used his wings to dive down upon Vallax's position. The Over-Captain's marksmanship might be compromised, but there was nothing wrong with his reflexes. He was aware of Rhodaan's move the instant the Raptor cleared the loader, darting back behind the cover of a cargo container as his enemy fired.

Rhodaan adjusted his dive, throwing himself forwards, crashing down into the lip of the container and sending it crashing down into Vallax. The Over-Captain was startled, but hardly surprised, catching the container as its fell and shifting his body so that the heavy steel box rolled away from him rather than directly down onto him.

In his manoeuvre, however, Vallax was compelled to drop his weapon. Rhodaan was surprised to see that it was a battered, almost unrecognizable boltgun of Imperial manufacture, defaced with ork glyphs and with an absurdly large blade welded beneath the gun barrel. Where and why the Over-Captain had acquired such a weapon was a mystery to him, though hardly as perplexing as Vallax's own condition. A quick glance showed the sorry violation of Vallax's power armour and the mutilation committed against the Iron Warrior's head.

Vallax rounded upon Rhodaan, grappling with the other Raptor before he could bring his plasma pistol to bear again.

'The Fabricator didn't expect me to survive,' Vallax snarled at Rhodaan. 'But I endured. I escaped the orks. I returned. I bring doom to Oriax.'

'We share common cause,' Rhodaan growled back. 'Oriax has betrayed us all. He plots against the Warsmith. Even now it may be too late to stop him.'

Vallax strained against Rhodaan's grip. Without the assistance of his armour's servo-motors, the Over-Captain could feel himself being overcome, but the stubbornness of hate refused to let him relent. 'We share nothing,' Vallax spat. 'Oriax's death belongs to me!'

The sudden roar of Merihem's guns startled the two combatants. For an instant, Rhodaan feared the Obliterator had lost any sense of purpose or duty and opened fire on the other Iron Warriors. The pained howls of orks sounding from the far side of the bay told a different story. For an instant, he glanced away from Vallax's scarred face, watching instead as a mob of orks dressed in camouflage came charging from one of the maintenance tunnels.

'So, you escaped from the orks,' Rhodaan sneered at Vallax. 'They used you, fool! You've led them past the Bastion's defences.' He could see the horror on Vallax's face, horror that drowned even his hate. Loyalties and oaths that had been burned into the Space Marine's psyche echoed Rhodaan's words, crushing individual thought and emotion beneath the shame of dishonoured obligation.

Rhodaan thrust Vallax away from him with a disgusted shove. Even when he had plotted against the Over-Captain, he had felt a certain respect for him. Now there was only loathing. Any Iron Warrior who could so blind himself with hate as to be used by orks was beneath contempt. 'Gomorie, Uzraal,' Rhodaan growled into his vox. 'Establish a perimeter. Try to keep the xenos at bay while Brother Merihem and myself attend to Oriax.'

The two Raptors came rushing from the cage, firing as they went. Anguished howls rose from the ork kommandos unlucky enough to be on the receiving end of their shots. Captain Morax limped after them, furiously cursing his lack of a weapon.

Rhodaan stared grimly at the little cluster of Space Marines. That they could hold back the orks wasn't in doubt. What troubled him was his force's resultant reduction in strength. He had been counting on the other Raptors' support when they confronted Oriax. There was no telling what sorts of defences the Fabricator had installed in his sanctum.

'Take them with you,' Vallax said, his voice low, his tone chastened. The Over-Captain pointed to the scavenger bolter lying on the ground. 'I will hold back the xenos scum.' His eyes glistened as he stared into Rhodaan's snarling mask. 'Please, brother, allow me this chance to atone for the hurt I have done the Legion.'

Rhodaan lifted the bolter from the floor, handing it to the Over-Captain. He didn't have the luxury of doubting Vallax. There wasn't time for that. 'Hold them as long as you can, brother,' he said. Vallax nodded, then turned and began firing at the kommandos.

'Brother Gomorie! Brother Uzraal!' Rhodaan called out over the vox as he darted among the crates. 'A change in plan. Over-Captain Vallax will engage the xenos. You will fall back and support Brother Merihem and myself in breaching the Fabricator's sanctum.' The restoration of his Raptors to the raiding force instilled a new confidence in him. Even if it was for the last time, he felt good to be leading Squad Kyrith into battle.

'What about me?' Captain Morax's voice hissed across the vox.

Rhodaan smiled. 'Try to keep up,' he told the Skylord.

Corrosive gas spewed from vents set into ceiling and floor, while titanium panels slid out from the walls to seal either end of the corridor. The glowing, yellowish vapour sizzled as it settled against the Iron Warriors' power armour, stripping away the smooth veneer and bubbling against the raw ceramite beneath. Rhodaan could well imagine that the gas was specially created to penetrate power armour. He didn't like to think what it would do to mere flesh and bone.

'Brother Merihem,' Rhodaan snapped, pointing his gauntlet at the titanium panel blocking the way ahead.

The Obliterator surged forwards, his armour steaming as the gas billowed around him. Merihem's left arm rippled, its mass contorting into a nest of slender metal shafts tipped with blocky focusing arrays. A mechanical whine sounded from his shoulder as he swung the multi-melta towards the titanium panel and unleashed its hideous energies against it.

For an instant, the panel glowed white hot, then it cracked and crumbled, smashing to the floor in a heap of smouldering cinders. The Space Marines rushed through the opening, heedless of the heat continuing to rise from the edges of the hole. Streamers of gas clawed at them as they escaped the trap, as though trying to draw them back with phantom fingers.

Beyond the corridor was a small anteroom, devoid of all adornment. Rhodaan's suspicions rose to the fore. Every hall and passage leading to Oriax's sanctum had been trapped, testing the Iron Warriors' mettle every step of the way. Even for Space Marines, Rhodaan considered it almost miraculous they had suffered no casualties in their approach. Now there was this room, with its deceptive tranquillity. What hidden menace lurked here?

Rhodaan glared at the walls. No, he was tired of playing by the Fabricator's rules. 'Brother Uzraal,' he growled into the vox. 'Melta bombs. North wall.'

Uzraal checked the dispenser on his belt. 'Two left,' he reported.

'That should be enough,' Rhodaan said, motioning Uzraal to proceed.

Morax grabbed Rhodaan's shoulder, spinning him around. 'There's no cover,' he objected. 'We'll be caught in the blast.'

Rhodaan removed the Skylord's hand. 'Better than whatever Oriax has prepared for us,' he stated. 'If you haven't noticed, his traps are worse the further we go. It's time we stopped doing what he expects us to do.'

Uzraal came dashing back to the other Raptors, the bombs placed against the wall. They dropped down into a crouch, covering their heads. Morax looked at them for a second, then hastily followed their example. Merihem turned his back to the wall, the metallic morass of his body coalescing into thick armour plates.

The detonation of the bombs was deafening. Again, the external audio relays in his helmet crackled and went silent, shielding him from the worst of the din. Chunks of ferrocrete and bits of plasteel glanced from his power armour. The optics in his helmet dropped filters across his vision to penetrate the dust boiling from the ruptured wall. When he saw what was beyond the breach, Rhodaan clenched his fist in vicious jubilation.

Behind the anteroom was a chamber Rhodaan recognised, a place he had been once before. By blasting their way through the wall, they had bypassed the labyrinth of halls and passages and penetrated directly to the heart of Oriax's domain.

They were in the sanctum.

As soon as he stepped through the breach, Rhodaan knew they were too late. He could feel the clammy, unnatural clutch of warp energies that saturated the sanctum. Turning his gaze towards the chamber that housed the Daemonculum, he could see the weird afterglow emanating from the bloodwood dais. He could see the flesh-drones marching away from the bound daemons, the dead husks of their offerings swaying limply from their mechadendrites.

The Daemonculum had already been used, and recently. Warsmith Andraaz and the Rending Guard were gone, transported to whatever fate Oriax had chosen for them.

'You are fortunate, Captain Rhodaan,' Fabricator Oriax's voice crackled through his sanctum, echoing from a hundred vox-casters. 'I was aware of your intrusion into my domain, but I wasn't at liberty to give your trespass my full attention. Other, more pressing matters required my undivided devotion. One does not draw upon the forces of the warp simply by flicking a switch. Neither are those energies so easily dismissed.'

Rhodaan spotted one of the macabre Steel Blood gliding towards him, its optics glowing crimson in the darkness. A blast from his plasma pistol sent the skull-like machine crashing to the floor. 'You have betrayed the Legion and the Warsmith,' Rhodaan accused. Another Steel Blood came diving down towards him and quickly shared the fate of its predecessor. 'You have forgotten your duty, forgotten your honour!'

'Forgotten?' There was a static crackle as the Fabricator laughed. 'I have not forgotten them. I have simply evolved past such archaic conceits. Duty, honour, loyalty. As a Legion, we should have cast them aside long ago. There is only one thing that is of consequence in the galaxy. Knowledge. That is the only true power. The genesis of creation and destruction.'

From behind him, a third Steel Blood hurtled towards Rhodaan, diving at the base of his helmet. Before it could strike him, however, the metal skull flew apart in a burst of sparks and flame. He could see Gomorie standing just beyond the breach, staring at his corrupted hand, a hand that had now fused itself around his bolt pistol and was slowly absorbing the weapon into itself. The other Iron Warriors pressed past Gomorie. There was a look of vicious amusement on Merihem's little face as he passed by.

'This way,' Rhodaan told the others, guiding them through the nest of machinery and around the periphery of the Daemonculum. If the uncanny device truly demanded Oriax's attention, then the Fabricator should be seated behind the same command console he had used when transporting Squad Vidarna and Squad Kyrith to Dirgas.

'You think you have come here as my executioners?' Oriax's voice bellowed from the vox-casters. 'Your ignorance pains and upsets me.'

Morax cried out in alarm as the wall beside him suddenly dropped away. Through the opening lumbered the hulking flesh-drones Oriax employed to feed the Daemonculum. Dead slaves still shackled to their mechadendrites, the cyborgs struck with the steel talons that replaced their natural limbs. The Skylord reeled away, mashing the head of one servitor with the fist of his gauntlet.

'You are here to die,' Oriax declared. 'All who share the secrets of *my* Daemonculum will die. I shall share that power with no one!'

Merihem swung around, his left arm rippling as it transformed into a heavy flamer. Sheets of fire engulfed the flesh-drones, immolating their organics, shorting out their electronics and melting the fibre-plastic nerve-bundles that provided them with motion. The flesh-drones stumbled on a few paces, then crashed in burning heaps.

'The superstitious pesedjet never understood what they had,' Oriax crowed. 'It was left to me alone to unlock the secrets of the Daemonculum, to understand its power and its potential!'

A second phalanx of servitors emerged from behind the walls. Rhodaan left the other Iron Warriors to attend to them. There was only one enemy they had to kill, and he intended to kill him. Across the periphery of the Daemonculum, he could see the Fabricator behind his console, the Techmarine's confusion of artificial limbs flying across the rune-panels.

Fighting down the revulsion that filled every atom of his being, Rhodaan drew his chainsword and charged across the Daemonculum. He could feel the bound daemons grab at him with ethereal tentacles, struggling to draw his blood to them, to consume the vibrancy of his soul. Their siren wails thundered through his body; begging, threatening, entreating, promising. Only his obligation to the Third Grand Company gave him the will to resist, the strength to plough through their invisible snare. Purity was anathema to the creatures of the warp and nothing was more pure than vengeance.

'Warsmith Andraaz would not allow me to continue my work,' Oriax's voice droned from the vox-casters. 'He was impatient to exploit the Daemonculum's power. He didn't appreciate the need to understand its secrets, to know how it worked.'

Rhodaan leaped across the boundary of the Daemonculum, using Eurydice to propel him straight across the sanctum to Oriax's command console. There was a look of almost comical incredulity on the Fabricator's face as he looked up and saw Rhodaan's chainsword slashing down at him.

'I don't care how it works,' Rhodaan snarled at the traitor. 'I only care how *this* works!'

Suddenly, a fist of steel slammed into Rhodaan, hurling him away from the console. He crashed into a ring of pict screens, smashing them into shatters beneath his armoured weight. It was the Raptor's turn to stare incredulously at his foe. Oriax was stepping from behind his console, his withered legs thickening with each step. By contrast, the Fabricator's left hand began to shrivel, assuming a more natural size than that of the fist which had sent Rhodaan flying.

The optics sunk into Oriax's face fixed themselves on Rhodaan's sprawled figure. 'That,' the Fabricator hissed, pressing a mechadendrite to the wound in his forehead where the edge of Rhodaan's sword had grazed him, 'was inconvenient.'

WHEN WARSMITH ANDRAAZ emerged from the Daemonculum, he found himself in a wasteland of rubble and torn bodies, wrecked machines and ruined buildings. In the distance, rising from the ruins, he could see the spire of the Iron Bastion, its structure illuminated by eerie green light as ork artillery shells impacted against the tower's void shields. Everywhere the howls of orks filled the air, the triumphant roars of beasts gone mad with the thrill of victory.

The Warsmith's power claw crackled with energy as he brought its talons shearing through the greenskinned alien standing almost at his very feet, gawking at him in amazement. Ribbons of orkoid flesh exploded into the air as the claw's field shredded the alien. Andraaz raised the storm bolter in his right hand and sent a salvo of explosive shells slamming into a mob of orks trying to pry their way into a disabled tank. Alien blood sprayed across the hull as the Iron Warrior's shells tore the vandals apart.

'Biglug!' Andraaz shouted, his voice thundering through

the rubble, hurled down the streets by his armour's vox-casters. 'Show yourself, you craven vermin!'

The Warsmith's armour was rattled by a fusillade of bullets and shells, orks springing from the rubble to assault the hulking Space Marine. Andraaz's Terminator armour withstood the motley barrage, the Warsmith's storm bolter sending a far more lethal response slamming into the greenskinned aliens. 'Concentrate fire on the larger groupings,' Andraaz growled into his vox. 'We'll try to draw out their warlord.'

Only silence answered the Warsmith. He sent a last salvo ripping through a mob of yellow-garbed orks, then turned to snarl a reprimand at the Terminators behind him. What he saw sent a rush of blood pounding through his hearts. The Rending Guard were there, but they couldn't answer him. The reason they couldn't answer was that they hadn't quite made the transition through the Daemonculum as cleanly as the Warsmith. In fact, from the appearance of the gory puddles of flesh and ceramite, it looked as though they'd emerged from the transition inside out.

A fierce bellow sounded somewhere down the street. The rattle of small arms crashing against the Warsmith's armour lessened. At the sound of a second bellow, they stopped altogether.

Andraaz turned away from the bloody mush that had been his retinue, turned his enraged gaze upon the creature at the end of the street. It didn't matter that the ork had nothing to do with their deaths, the alien would pay for the Rending Guard just the same.

The alien was gigantic, easily the biggest ork Andraaz had ever seen. It was like a living Dreadnought, its arms as thick around as tyres, its legs built like ferrocrete gambions. The brute's thick neck was as wide across as a man's chest, the lantern jaw hanging down from its face was stuffed with yellow fangs the size of bayonets. Slabs of pig iron, steel, titanium and armaplas had been cobbled together into a rude sort of armour to match the ork's mammoth frame. The ork's arms were bare to the shoulder, exposing a riot of primitive tattoos and scars. The monster's face, what little of it was visible under its horned helm crunched down around its ears, was similarly marked. Beady red eyes gleamed from behind the vented visor that hung from the rim of the helmet.

A bandolier of chains crossed the ork's torso, festooned with hooks from which a collection of trophies rattled against each other. Andraaz recognised the yellowed skull of a genestealer patriarch, a cracked cranium segment ripped from an eldar wraithguard. Ork skulls clattered against kroot jawbones. The Warsmith scowled as he noted the helmets of Space Marines mixed among the trophies, those of rebels and loyalists alike. His anger swelled as he found that he recognised one of the helmets as belonging to Over-Captain Vallax. Beside the Iron Warrior's helmet was the grinning death's head of a Steel Blood.

The ork lumbered forwards, growling orders at the aliens around it. A mob of scarred brutes trailing behind it fell back but kept their weapons at the ready.

Biglug, for Andraaz knew this beast could only be the ork warlord himself, stared at the Warsmith for a time, like a fighting dog taking in the scent of its opponent. The ork's massive paws tightened about the heft of the power axe he carried, the promethium generator fastened to the weapon's shaft belching black smoke as it strove to maintain its energy field.

Suddenly, Biglug threw back his head, barking with laughter. He grunted something in his crude language and pointed at the slop-heap that had once been the Rending Guard. The aliens in his retinue took up their warlord's laughter, the mockery spreading to the lesser aliens scattered about the ruins.

Andraaz felt a rage such as he had never known flare up inside him. He had come here prepared to die, to fall in battle to this xenos rabble, but he was damned if he would be laughed at by them.

'Iron within! Iron without!' the Warsmith roared, charging down the street at the laughing warlord. Shells from his storm bolter smashed into the brute's armour, their impact only slightly lessened by whatever field generator protected the monster. Biglug staggered back under the impacts, blood gushing from an arm pitted by one of the shells. The mob behind the warlord surged forwards, but the monster turned on them, howling in anger and chopping one of them down with his axe.

Far from being frightened by Andraaz's bold attack, Biglug exulted in it. The warlord raised his arms to the polluted sky and bellowed his own war cry. Then he was charging down the street, ignoring the bolt-shells slamming into his armour, intent only upon closing with his foe, matching his axe against the Warsmith's claw.

The Warsmith rushed at the alien monster, one final victim before the dark claimed him. One last sacrifice to the pride of Andraaz, Lord of Castellax.

CHAPTER XXI
I-Day Plus One Hundred and Twenty-One

OBLITERATOR! THE REALISATION struck Rhodaan like a physical blow. Oriax was an Obliterator!

The Fabricator must have sensed Rhodaan's shock. He grinned at the prostrate Raptor, holding his right hand up so that Rhodaan could have a clear view of it as Oriax willed it to change. Metal bubbled up from the pores in his skin, expanding to engulf the entire hand. More and more silvery metal oozed up, thickening the hand until it was a massive cudgel. Still the transformation wasn't complete,. The cudgel lengthened and flattened, expanding until it took on a hammer-like shape.

'One does not stare into the abyss unchanged,' Oriax said. 'A little bit of it comes back with you, changes you.' The static crackle of his laughter echoed through the sanctum. 'Perhaps as I studied the Daemonculum, it was studying me in turn.'

'You are infected,' Rhodaan spat at the Fabricator.

The grin crumbled into a scowl. 'I am enhanced, more than what I was. More than what Vallax pulled from the crystal-swamps of Tarsis.' Oriax glanced at the mammoth hammer on the end of his arm. 'Andraaz was most obliging. He brought me souvenirs from every campaign fought by the Third Grand Company.' He stalked towards Rhodaan, raising the hammer. Energy crackled about the weapon, sending arcs of electricity snaking across the sanctum. 'This, you should remember. Before the virus claimed it for its own, this was a thunder hammer. It belonged to the Silver Skulls you helped annihilate on the planet Karkus.'

Rhodaan waited until the Fabricator was only a few steps away, until Oriax lifted the hammer and was about to strike. At that moment, he sprang into action, blasting Oriax with his plasma pistol and using the thrusters of his jump pack to burst from the tangle of collapsed machinery.

The burning ball of plasma seared through Oriax's hand, sending fingers clattering across the floor. As the thunder hammer came slamming down, it pulverised the machinery but failed to strike the Raptor as he propelled himself away. Everything worked almost as Rhodaan had hoped. It was the mechadendrites that brought him to calamity. The artificial arms, like the rest of Oriax's wargear, had become infected by the Obliterator virus. Like his armour, like the thunder hammer, they had become a part of the Techmarine's corruption.

Striking like some jungle serpent, the mechadendrites shot at Rhodaan as he burst from the wreckage. Coils of plasteel and titanium wrapped themselves about the Space Marine, driving him first against the ceiling, then smashing him to the floor. The short blast of propellant wasn't enough to defy the wiry strength in the tentacles. Dazed by the impact against the ceiling, arms pinned to his sides by the coils, Rhodaan could only watch helplessly as the mechadendrites dragged him back to their master.

Oriax's hammer was twisting and changing once more, becoming thin and narrow. His other hand bubbled and steamed, the techno-organic substance of his body reeling from the bite of superheated plasma.

'You only delay the inevitable,' Oriax scolded his captive. 'Castellax is doomed. The orks will destroy everything.' He turned his head and stared at the Daemonculum, beads of oil dripping from his optics like black tears of rapture. 'No one will learn the secrets of the Daemonculum. They shall perish here, with us!'

Rhodaan struggled for breath as the coils began to tighten. 'The orks are inside the Bastion, Oriax. Do you want the xenos to take your little toy?'

The coils tightened as Oriax hissed his contempt. 'It would be disappointing if the orks didn't come. I took great pains to bring them here. First with the deep range scouting probes to establish contact with them, to give them the bait to draw them here. You have to be careful with orks, give them information too openly and they distrust it. Make them work too hard to gain it and they become bored and kill their prisoners. It took great patience to train Flesh to withstand just the right amount of torture.'

Rhodaan stared in disbelief at the Fabricator. 'You lured the orks here? The entire invasion was your doing?' His fists clenched at his sides, his body thrashed in a futile effort to break the bonds that held him. 'Why?' he demanded.

'I already told you,' Oriax said. 'The Warsmith was going to take my Daemonculum away from me, let others defile it. I couldn't let that happen. Better that Castellax should burn, that the Third Grand Company should be no more, than the unworthy be allowed to share my knowledge.' Oriax tilted his head to one side, his optics glittering as he watched Rhodaan being crushed in his grip. The arm that had been a hammer now churned into life, a whisper of light flashing from its tube-like extremity.

'A monofilament wire,' Oriax explained. 'A little something to remember the dying eldar race. In a moment, I will project this wire through your helmet's right optic. Then I will use it to puree you inside your own armour.' The icy grin was back on Oriax's face. 'I just thought you might like to know.'

'No!' The word roared through the sanctum, rumbling across the broken machinery. Oriax swung around, the Fabricator's brow knotting in concern as his optics focused upon the hulking monstrosity marching slowly across the floor of the Daemonculum.

Rhodaan felt a surge of relief rush through him. Brother Merihem. Once again, the Obliterator had arrived at just the right moment to snatch victory from the jaws of defeat. As he marched across the bloodwood platform, Rhodaan could see Merihem's body sway, his legs struggling with each step, as though he strode through an unseen mire. How hungry Oriax's daemons must be to turn their attentions upon an Obliterator! For a moment, the Raptor wondered if Merihem would be able to resist the temptations roaring through his mind, the siren call of the imprisoned daemons.

Merihem's will was stronger than the daemons, a will forged in iron and hate. The pale little face glared at Oriax, the steel teeth shining in a cold smile that gave even the Fabricator pause.

'Why do you stand against me, brother?' Oriax asked. He extended his hand, displaying its oozing mush of flesh and metal for Merihem to see. 'We are truly brothers. We share the blessings of the machine made flesh and the flesh made machine. These others,' the Fabricator shook Rhodaan in his grip, nearly breaking the Raptor's neck, 'are nothing to us. They are no different than the Flesh from which we were chosen. They are the clay from which the true Iron Warrior may rise. Those like us, who are truly iron within and iron without.'

Merihem lumbered forwards, dragging his feet clear of the bloodwood and the spectral clutch of the daemons. 'I care nothing for the Legion,' he growled. 'I care nothing for the kinship of false brothers who betray their oaths.' His steel smile became even more vicious, the little black eyes twinkling in the pits of his face. 'What I care about is that trash in your hand. I want him.'

As he heard the Obliterator's growl, Rhodaan knew he listened to the voice of Death. The monster had warned him when they left the Oubliette that there would be a reckoning. He had been a fool to ever think Merihem could be trusted, that a beast like him could ever be bound by such noble concepts as duty and honour. The abomination had simply been biding his time, waiting for the moment when Rhodaan stood at the edge of victory before he struck in order that his revenge might be even more complete.

'You are not here to avenge the Warsmith?' Oriax demanded, his voice crackling with doubt.

Merihem took another lumbering step forwards, the claws of his left hand splayed in a gesture of murderous readiness. 'I am here to avenge myself,' he declared. 'To avenge my exile and imprisonment. To avenge the denial of my purpose, the squandering of my potential. To avenge centuries abandoned in the darkness, locked away like some keepsake. To avenge the shame of my condition. If the Warsmith was here, I would peel the flesh from his bones and drink the blood from his torn hearts.' Merihem's black eyes glared into the lenses of Rhodaan's helmet. 'Since Andraaz is not here, I shall content myself with his lapdog, the mongrel who brought my disgrace so long ago and left me to rot in the dark.'

The monster shifted his gaze to Oriax. 'Stand aside, "brother," and I will show you what it means to hate.'

* * *

THE WARSMITH'S CLAW came slashing across the ork's chest, energy flaring in a nimbus of cobalt as the blades struck the power field generated by the alien's armour. Andraaz grunted in pain as electrical feedback crackled down his arm, searing every nerve. He bit down on his pain and forced his talons through the power field. For an instant, the field resisted, then as the attack persisted, the scythe-like blades went tearing into the ork's body.

Biglug reeled back, howling in surprise as much as pain. Tatters of armour flopped from the gashes left behind by Andraaz's power claw, blood bubbled from the ork's torn flesh. Trying to defend himself, Biglug brought the power axe chopping into the Iron Warrior. The ceramite surface of the Terminator armour shuddered at the impact, but the Legion's artificers had maintained the artefact well. Biglug's energised blade barely penetrated a few milli-metres despite the monstrous brawn behind the attack.

Andraaz fired his storm bolter into the ork's roaring face, the rounds smashing against the force field that pro-tected the brute. The assault did, however, distract Biglug, keeping his tiny brain occupied while the Warsmith brought his claw shearing through the ork's leg.

Or at least such had been Andraaz's intention. As he brought his power claw slashing down, the Warsmith was aware of a strange, all pervasive crackle of static. Dimly he recognised it as a pulse of binary. The servo-motor in his arm seized and shut down, refusing to complete the murderous strike. From a supercharged engine of destruction, the left arm of the Warsmith's armour had become an inert lump of metal. If his reactions were any slower, his reflexes less honed by the battlefield, Andraaz's equilibrium would have collapsed under the transformation, the dead weight of his raised arm and its suddenly thwarted momentum dragging him down to the ground. As it was, he pivoted, swinging his entire body around to prevent such a disaster.

In preventing his fall, Andraaz exposed himself to his foe. Biglug howled with delight as he lunged at the Iron Warrior's unprotected back, the power axe slashing through the sensorium relays and diagnostic bundles running along the left side of the armour. There was a stabbing pain along Andraaz's spine as the axe sheared through a mass of fibre-bundles, sending electricity crackling from the compromised machinery.

Andraaz swung back around, firing his storm bolter into the alien's body. Against the point-blank barrage, even the force field was overwhelmed. Biglug snarled in pain as explosive shells smashed into his armour, sending splinters of plasteel and armaplas flying. The brute was staggered by the onslaught, but even this wasn't enough to subdue his savagery. As he reeled back, Biglug twisted his power axe around, hooking the edge of the head in the adamantium ribs that supported the Terminator's thick layers of ceramite and plasteel. The Warsmith stumbled forwards as the ork dragged him after it.

Andraaz resisted Biglug's pull, digging his feet in the shattered earth, using the full weight of his Terminator armour to defy the ork's brawn. Pivoting in place, he turned the ork's exertions into a lumbering swing, flinging Biglug into the broken wall of a processing plant. The xenos's impact was like that of a cannon, chunks of ferrocrete crashing down about the ork's head. The Warsmith added to Biglug's ordeal, raking his body with shots from his storm bolter. With a loud wail and a strobing burst of light, Biglug's force field fizzled, smoke rising from the overwhelmed mechanism.

The Warsmith smiled coldly and took a lumbering step towards the staggered Biglug. Andraaz lifted the storm bolter, picking a spot between the brute's beady eyes to deliver the killing shot.

Before he could fire, Andraaz heard the binary shriek crackle through his armour's sensors. The massive

Terminator suit froze in mid-step, the limbs locking in place as their motivators powered down. The Iron Warrior struggled to move by sheer force of his muscles alone, but even his superhuman strength was unequal to the effort.

The ork warlord extracted himself from the rubble, shaking his head as he tried to clear away the cobwebs. He glared at Andraaz and smacked a meaty paw against his alien chest in a token of violent challenge. Snarling, the ork rushed towards the Warsmith.

Biglug hesitated when the Iron Warrior failed to move or respond in any way. The ork actually took a few paces backwards, his eyes darting from side to side in search of a trap. Finally, his gaze turned to Andraaz once more. He cocked his head to one side, scratched at his jaw with a stumpy finger. Then, angrily, the ork slapped his hand against his chest once more, as though daring the Warsmith to shoot him again.

Still, Andraaz couldn't move, the binary pulse was paralysing the machine-spirit of his armour, imprisoning him inside. He howled in frustration, wracking his brain for some way to force the armour to act.

The ork warlord's fragile patience wore out, his desire for a good fight overwhelming his suspicions of a trap. Roaring with fury, Biglug charged the dozen metres between himself and Andraaz. He brought the power axe smashing down in a brutal sweep that shattered the Terminator's shoulder and nearly sheared the Warsmith's arm from his body.

Biglug jumped back, bracing himself for the Iron Warrior's counter-attack. When his enemy still failed to move, the warlord stood straight and barked at Andraaz, cursing and jeering the Iron Warrior who refused to fight. Contemptuously, Biglug brought the butt of his axe cracking into his foe's head, unbalancing the Terminator and pitching him over into the dirt.

Falling, Andraaz had a good view of the trophies lashed to Biglug's chest. He could see the Steel Blood chained there beside Vallax's helmet. The skull's optics were aglow, its jaw open to expose the speaker buried in its mouth. Andraaz knew the source of the binary pulse that had paralyzed his armour, had made the machine-spirit betray its master. He knew that the shameful death of the Rending Guard had been no accident or malfunction.

Biglug hooted with contemptuous mockery as he brought his axe smashing down into the prone Terminator, each blow sending tremors through the thick ceramite plates. Blow after blow, the alien was battering his way through the armour and to the defenceless Space Marine trapped inside.

Warsmith Andraaz had thought to make a heroic end for himself, but Oriax had arranged things differently. The orks would remember him, all right, but not as some mighty foe who had stood proud upon the battlefield. Andraaz would be the arrogant coward, who in the end had cowered before their warlord and not even put up a fight when Biglug started to pull him piece by piece from his ruptured armour.

Andraaz hadn't liked the orks laughing at him, but they would be doing it for a very long time.

MERIHEM'S STEEL GRIN widened, stretching from ear to ear, his little black eyes glaring malevolently from the ghostly pallor of his face. The Obliterator clenched his claws, each finger bubbling into a little chainblade. Rhodaan struggled in Fabricator Oriax's grip, trying to reach his belt. He might not be able to stave off death, but he wouldn't go down like this, butchered like a grox by a subhuman abomination.

The monster began to descend from the Daemonculum when there was a sudden blast of bright light. Merihem's chest exploded in a pool of bubbling metal and molten meat. The Obliterator staggered, swinging around and firing his autocannon across the chamber. Uzraal, his meltagun still smoking from its violent discharge, dived behind one of the wraithbone columns.

'Now, while it is weak!' Uzraal shouted.

In response, Captain Morax and Brother Gomorie came charging across the bloodwood platform. Clenched in their arms was the frame of a flesh-drone, its mechadendrites extended, frozen into position at the moment of the servitor's destruction. The effect was like a three-metre long lance and the two Iron Warriors drove it straight into the wound Uzraal's meltagun had blasted in Merihem's body.

The Obliterator's corrupt essence had already started to flow back into the injury, fibres of steel and flesh knitting back together. The lance stabbed into Merihem's regenerating chest, piercing clean through the monster. He swung around, his tiny face pulled back in a sneer.

'Laugh this off, obscenity!' Morax cursed. The Skylord's hand smashed the power plant still fixed to the flesh-drone's frame. The two Space Marines hastily released their improvised spear as thousands of kilowatts of electricity crackled down the servitor's frame.

Merihem shrieked in agony as the discharge seared his body, burning through every synapse and wire. The Obliterator lunged forwards, his chainclaw catching Morax, the whirring blades chewing into the Skylord's armour. Merihem lifted his prey from the floor, glaring into the lenses of his helmet. 'Clever worm,' Merihem spat. His other hand began to shift, reforming into the crazed confusion of the ork combi-weapon he had absorbed in the wasteland.

Bolt-shells smashed into Merihem's back, driving splatters of liquid meat from his regenerating wound. Merihem pivoted, aiming his new weapon at Gomorie. There was a frown on the Obliterator's face as he blasted

Gomorie with the full malignity of the combi-weapon. Crude, unpredictable in its original state, the ghastly virus in his body had refined and stabilised the weapon, allowing it to reach its full potential. Gomorie's armour shredded under the impact, his body tossed through the air to crash at the foot of a wraithbone pillar.

'Such wasted potential,' Merihem commented. 'I had expected better things for you, little brother.' The Obliterator clenched his fist, bringing the sawing chainblades tighter about Morax's body. The Skylord flailed in his grip, blood streaming down his legs as the blades ripped into his flesh.

Another blast from Uzraal's meltagun slammed into Merihem, reducing his shoulder into a steaming morass of metal and muscle. The Obliterator's arm went limp, dropping Morax to the floor. Vengefully, Merihem sent a salvo from his combi-weapon chasing after Uzraal, but again the Raptor was behind cover before the monster's aim could come true. Maintaining an incredible rate of fire, Merihem chased Uzraal across the Daemonculum, ravaging the arcane machinery with each burst.

'IT SEEMS I will not have to depend on the orks to destroy my Daemonculum,' Oriax observed with bitterness. He turned his attention back to Rhodaan, savouring the Raptor's struggles. His eyes narrowed as he focused them on the wings of Eurydice, a covetous gleam creeping into them.

'I have long admired your archaeotech,' Oriax said. He extended his hand, caressing the closest wing. His palm was already collapsing into a liquid mash, spreading to coat the demi-organic pinions. 'You don't mind if I take it. You won't have any further use for it, I assure you.' A touch of amusement flickered on the Fabricator's face. 'When they are mine, do you think I'll fly?' he asked.

Rhodaan glared back at him. 'I think you'll burn,' he

snarled, slamming his hand against the Techmarine's chest. The magnetic clamp on the haywire grenade he'd removed from his belt locked on to Oriax's armour. The Fabricator was just able to look down at the device before it sent its pulse flaring through his body.

The same discharge roared through Rhodaan, conducted into him by the Fabricator's grip. As he was hurled away by the electrical shock, he slammed into one of the pict screens, feeling it shatter behind him in a shower of crystalline shards. Every nerve in his body felt like it was on fire. Half the systems in his armour had shorted out, the optics in his helmet flickering through different colour spectrums. Agony rippled through his muscles as he lifted his hands and removed his helmet. Groggily, Rhodaan regained his feet.

As terrific as the effect of the haywire pulse had been upon him, Rhodaan had been spared the grenade's full fury. The Fabricator had borne the brunt of the discharge. Oriax stood shuddering and writhing amid the wreck of his console, his mechadendrites spasming in an insane display of claws, pincers and drills. The metallic substance of his corrupt body undulated, throbbing like a pool of lava. His face was frozen in a silent shriek of agony.

Defying the pain in his own body, Rhodaan lunged across the chamber, snatching his chainsword from where it had fallen. Fury flung him at the Fabricator: the fury of the betrayed, the fury of the loyal for the disloyal, the fury of a warrior against a comrade who has forsaken his duty.

'This is how you die, traitor!' Rhodaan shouted as he brought his chainsword hacking into the paralyzed Oriax. He never understood the strange look in the Fabricator's eyes or the terrible irony that he should be struck down in such fashion, defenceless and without honour.

Rhodaan's chainsword bit into Oriax's head, slashing

through his mouth and cleaving the skull along the jaw-bone. The roof of Oriax's head went spinning off into the darkness, while the rest of his mangled body simply slumped to the floor like a broken toy. Electricity continued to sizzle through the corpse as the haywire grenade expelled the energies of its power plant.

The victorious Raptor stared down at his handiwork for a moment. Again, he reached to the floor, retrieving his plasma pistol. One traitor had been settled. Another was still to be reckoned with.

Sheets of flame billowed across the Daemonculum, pursuing Uzraal as he strove to elude the monster. Merihem had given up trying to shoot the Raptor, instead adopting the muzzle of a flamer to burn the Iron Warrior from his hiding places. There was a murderous grin on the Obliterator's face as he stormed across the charred planks of the bloodwood platform.

'You will die,' Merihem promised. 'All flesh will die. In the end there will only be iron!'

Uzraal threw himself from the cover of a pillar as a stream of fire came rippling towards him. The wraithbone blackened and charred under the blast, emitting an eerie wail of inarticulate agony. The stream of fire shifted, searing along the wall as it chased after the Space Marine.

'Run, rabbit!' Merihem roared. 'Cower like all flesh. Hide from true strength. Hide your face from true power!'

A ball of superheated plasma slammed into Merihem's arm, burning it clear to the bone. The stream of fire erupting from the flamer was choked off as ruptured hoses sent the same fire spilling across Merihem's body.

'For a homicidal sociopath,' Rhodaan spat at the burning monster, 'you talk too much.' The demi-organic wings on his back flexed as he marched out into the Daemonculum and watched the Obliterator burn. Before he had taken more than a few steps, he was using Eurydice to leap into the air, hovering above the line of bolt-shells ripping into the floor.

Wreathed in flame, Merihem came storming across the chamber. The Obliterator had abandoned the flamer, reforming his arm into a combi-bolter. If anything, he presented an even more grisly sight, the pallid flesh of his face burned and charred, bits of steely bone protruding from the cracked skin. One eye had been fused closed beneath a shapeless lump of burned meat. The other glared balefully at the hovering Rhodaan.

There was no need for words as Merihem raised his weapon and aimed at the captain. Mere words could not have expressed the hate boiling inside the Obliterator's breast. Mere words could not have voiced the cold defiance of the doomed Raptor.

As Merihem's weapon started to spit its rain of death upwards, the Obliterator was struck from the side and dashed to the floor. His techno-organic body shifted as he fell, pivoting so that he might glare at his attacker. All emotion had been burned from the monster's face, but there was shock shining in the black depths of his eye.

What had struck the Obliterator down was a creature even bigger and more massive than himself. Steam sizzled from its scaly hide, strange coruscations of light flashed from its pores. Thick ropes of wiry grey hair hung from its limbs, weird runes crawled across its flesh. Great horns stabbed from a narrow forehead like some gruesome crown. A face inhuman and fiendish, pulled into a long muzzle of fangs and tusks, leered with diabolic malignity. For all the horror of the entity's shape, to the Iron Warriors the most horrible thing of all were the fragments of broken, shattered ceramite clinging to it, scraps of armour that bore the heraldry of their own Legion.

Struck down by Merihem, dying beneath the wraithbone pillars, Rhodaan could only wonder what obscene promises the daemons had made to Gomorie. That his battle-brother had accepted was all too evident. A quick glance at the pillars showed the withered husks of the daemon-hosts lying limp and abandoned in their chains.

If the daemons had promised Gomorie the strength to overcome Merihem, then they had exceeded their vow. As the possessed Space Marine loomed over the fallen Obliterator, it brought its talons slashing down, ripping great goblets of molten metal from Merihem's body, flinging the corruption in every direction. Very quickly, the charred platform was becoming littered with lumps of molten ooze.

Despite the havoc inflicted upon his body, Merihem did not submit to the daemon's abuse. With a fierce bellow, the Obliterator surged up from the floor, his chainclaw ripping into the daemon's steaming flesh. Gobbets of ichor and flesh flew from the churning blades. The Obliterator brought his other arm around, blasting the creature point-blank with a full burst from each barrel.

The daemon was sent reeling backwards, strewn across the platform. The terrible energies of the daemons alone were ripping apart Gomorie's body, dissolving it with each breath. A mortal shell could barely contain the energies of a single daemon, even that of a Space Marine was unable to play host for long to the abomination that had poured into Gomorie's flesh. As the fiendish creature drove through Merihem's barrage, it seemed to be corroding from within, its substance dripping away with each step.

Rhodaan didn't wait to see what the result of this ghoulish contest would be. Tightening his grip on his chainsword, he dived down upon Merihem from behind, adding his velocity to the downward sweep of his blade.

The chainsword crunched down into Merihem's charred skull, burying itself in his neck. Rhodaan left the churning blade embedded in the Obliterator and pressed the muzzle of his plasma pistol against the wound. Grimly, he pulled the trigger and sent a blast scorching through Merihem's head, incinerating the abomination's brain.

The withering fire from the Obliterator's guns fell silent. The hulking mass of metal and meat staggered forwards a few paces, Rhodaan's sword buried in the wreck of his head. Then, with a great crash, the monster fell, slamming through the charred bloodwood panels and hurtling into a sub-cellar far beneath the Daemonculum.

'Rot in agony,' Rhodaan spat at the fallen beast. He thumbed a grenade from his belt and tossed it into the cellar. With something like an Obliterator, there was no such thing as being too careful.

Turning away from the pit, Rhodaan braced himself to confront the daemon. There was no knowing what the creature would do now that their common enemy was vanquished. There was no knowing if it would feel a sense of kinship simply because Gomorie had been an Iron Warrior.

His caution was unnecessary. Before Rhodaan's eyes, the battered, broken body of the daemon began to collapse. Perhaps, with their promise fulfilled, the daemons were withdrawing back to the warp. Certainly after all the centuries bound to the Daemonculum, it was understandable that the entities might have experienced enough of mortal reality for a long time.

In the space of only a few heartbeats, the daemon was nothing more than a pool of greasy putrescence from which the odd bit of ceramite plate protruded. It was a miserable legacy for a battle-brother who had died so well. The daemon's dissolution hadn't even left anything to bury.

Uzraal marched across the chamber and joined Rhodaan beside the greasy morass. He stared down at the muck, then looked up at his captain.

'What is your command, Grim Lord?' Uzraal asked.

Rhodaan stared at the other Raptor, wondering if

the fight had driven him mad. Only the Warsmith was addressed that way. As he stared at Uzraal, however, understanding came to Rhodaan. If Oriax's plot had worked, then Andraaz was dead. There was no question that Morax was dead. So were Gamgin and Nostraz. Algol was missing and far too unbalanced to lead anyone. That made Rhodaan the last of the Third Grand Company's captains. As Over-Captain, Vallax was outside the line of succession, expected to function as the Warsmith's second-in-command, not his heir. Even if he survived, Vallax couldn't become Warsmith.

Uzraal was right, Rhodaan realised. Except for the orks, he was now Lord of Castellax, commander of the Third Grand Company. Or whatever was left of it.

'Fall back to the hangar,' Rhodaan ordered. 'We will rendezvous with the other survivors at the Oubliette.'

Rhodaan cast a last, contemptuous look at the shattered ruin of the Daemonculum. They had suffered much because of this fiendish creation and its crazed master, but the Third Grand Company would endure. They would rise from the ashes stronger than before. Under his leadership, they would recover and return to fight the Long War.

Turning from the Daemonculum, Rhodaan marched towards the inner recesses of the sanctum, Uzraal close behind him. 'We'll use the maintenance tunnels to make our way back to the upper levels. I want to be away from here before the entire Bastion is crawling with orks.'

IT WAS SOME hours before Kaptain Grimruk and his kommandos made their way into the wreckage of Oriax's sanctum. The lone Iron Warrior in the receiving bay had put up an impressive fight, impressive enough that Grimruk had taken the dead Space Marine's head as a present for Warlord Biglug.

The orks began to fan out through the sanctum, ripping

down anything that looked portable, smashing anything that looked like it wasn't. Grimruk paid them scant attention, prowling among the wreckage, kicking over the disabled husks of servitors and flesh-drones. It was only when the kaptain drew near the Daemonculum itself that he became more attentive.

There was a strange energy, a sense of power and danger emanating from the chamber. Grimruk removed the peaked cap from his head and scratched his leathery brow. Privy to Biglug's inner councils, Grimruk knew that the warlord was searching for something on Castellax, some weapon that would make Waaagh! Biglug mightier than Waaagh! Kogtoof. The problem was, none of the orks knew exactly what it was they were looking for. They'd captured immense stores of weapons and ammunition, even put some of the captured humans to work making more. The fleet had been expanded with captured ships. Despite the millions of ork dead, Waaagh! Biglug was already more powerful than before the attack on Castellax.

Still, Biglug insisted there was something special, something secret hidden somewhere on the planet. As his body recoiled from the Daemonculum's emanations, Grimruk wondered if this was the weapon the warlord was looking for. He would have the mekboyz come down here to have a look at it.

Grimruk glanced across the sanctum, watching the kommandos pulling the place apart. He looked again at the Daemonculum, feeling the evil of the thing oozing across his leathery skin. The ork growled angrily. He didn't like this sensation that the device stirred in his mind, this feeling of fear. What Grimruk didn't like, he destroyed. Biglug would get over his disappointment.

Howling orders, firing his weapon into the machinery to set the kommandos an example, Grimruk began the demolition of Oriax's Daemonculum.

EPILOGUE

I-Day Plus Three Hundred and Fifty-Seven

WARSMITH RHODAAN STUDIED the holographic display being projected above the obsidian table. Several of the Iron Warriors' deep-space observation satellites had escaped the orks, being too small to attract their attention when they still had entire ships to chase around the system. Most of Admiral Nostraz's fleet had been captured by the xenos, rearmed and repaired in the Iron Warriors' own shipyards. It was a final indignity for the lords of Castellax to endure, but Rhodaan was determined that others would soon share his pain.

A large part of the ork fleet was already gone, though he suspected the aliens hadn't planned it that way. A few months after the fall of Vorago, the orks had hastily assembled their fleet midway between Castellax and its sun. It was a typically orkish manoeuvre – impulsive and utterly lacking in preparation. The most junior naval captain would have cringed at the wild, haphazard action and at the dozens of collisions resulting from it.

The vanguard of the ork fleet, however, was too

impatient to wait on those ships too slow or too damaged to join them. Under the impatient urging of Biglug himself, no doubt, the ork ships had pushed ahead with their strange operation.

What happened next would have astonished anyone who had not seen the Daemonculum in operation. One instant the ork fleet was there, the next a hundred of their biggest ships were gone, as though they had simply winked out of existence. Sensors detected warp energies, but without the telltale signature of a warp gate, allowing that one could have been opened so deep within a planetary system. Moreover, there were a few dozen wrecks floating about that hadn't quite made the transition with Biglug's ships. From the satellite representations, the wrecks looked strangely twisted and mangled, as though caught in a tug-of-war between Titans.

Biglug was gone. For several weeks, the remaining orks fought amongst themselves as they tried to find a new leader. Rhodaan never did learn the name of the new warlord, but it showed an unusual streak of humour for a xenos, calling its warhost the 'Rustbustas'. Rhodaan would have liked to feed the creature its own organs for that joke.

Instead, Rhodaan decided to feed the orks something else. Scavenging resources wherever they could find them, the surviving Iron Warriors of Castellax began assembling vox-transmitters all across the planet, staffing them with whatever Flesh they could find. The slaves were charged with transmitting distress signals, not to Medrengard, but to Obestrus, the nearest inhabited world controlled by the Imperium. There was no chance that the low-powered signals would actually reach Obestrus, but that wasn't important. What was important was for the orks to discover the direction those signals were being sent.

It didn't take long. The orks were growing bored since the fighting on Castellax had ended. With the vox-signals promising another world nearby to sack, the aliens threw themselves into a frenzy of activity. Ships were repaired, stores transported off the planet, ork warriors loaded onto transports and ferried up to the waiting fleet. Before they were done, every ork on Castellax would be up there, ready and eager to take the fight to Obestrus.

Through the orks, the weapons of the Iron Warriors would strike the Imperium. They would decimate their armies, cripple their fleets and devastate their worlds. It was revenge by proxy. And while the Imperium sent its resources to deal with the orks, they would leave other sectors exposed and vulnerable.

The Iron Warriors would find those weak points. The Iron Warriors always found an enemy's weak point. Maybe it wouldn't be the Third Grand Company, but the Iron Warriors would be there to prosecute the Long War and remind petty humanity that the sins of their past were still with them.

For in all the galaxy, nothing endures like hate.

ABOUT THE AUTHOR

C. L. Werner's Black Library credits include
Mathias Thulmann: Witch Hunter, Runefang,
the Brunner the Bounty Hunter trilogy and
the Thanquol and Boneripper series. Currently
living in the American south-west, he continues
to write stories of mayhem and madness set
in the worlds of Warhammer and Warhammer
40,000. He claims that he was a diseased
servant of the Horned Rat long before his first
story was ever published.

A SPACE MARINE BATTLES NOVEL

THE DEATH OF
ANTAGONIS

DAVID ANNANDALE

An extract from The Death of Antagonis
by David Annandale

On sale February 2013

THE DRAGON CLAWS slammed into the ground with the force of judgement, punching craters in the enemy army. They came in at staggered distances, with Volos closest to the caravan. The goal: blast away the dead and form a chain along which the caravan could move once more. A jump pack assault normally called for close combat weaponry, but for this deployment Volos had ordered a maximum ammo load and flamers for all. He straightened from his landing, unshouldered the flamer and let spray in a single movement. His back to the mountainside, he played the fire out over 180 degrees, incinerating the dead and pushing their masses back.

The leading Hellhound started up. Its cannon was silent, the promethium tank long since depleted. Volos stepped forward, the flamer on full, and the dead retreated still further. The Hellhound drew level with him. Volos glanced up and saw Colonel Kervold salute his thanks. Volos gave a slight nod and returned his attention to the enemy. The Hellhound passed at his back, between Volos and the cliff wall. Toharan's voice crackled over the vox-link. 'We're advancing. Fine work.'

'So is yours.' He tried to picture the journey his fellow sergeant had made. It was song-worthy.

The Hellhound stopped. Its engine stalled out. Not letting up with the flamer, Volos turned his head. Kervold was looking down inside the vehicle, his expression a jagged mix of fury and puzzlement. He opened his mouth.

The order never came. His eyes widened. Volos saw something new wash over the colonel's face, emotions that should have been foreign to that scarred stone. The first was fear. The second was doubt, and somehow, this seemed more intense and terrible than the fear. Kervold convulsed with spine-snapping force, his body shaken by the fist that was seizing his soul. His eyes glazed as his face twisted into the shape of blank fury. He thrashed himself free of the hatch and turned with a snarl towards the refugees who were just now passing the Hellhound.

His right hand holding down the flamer's trigger, Volos pulled out his bolter with his left and shot Kervold, turning his skull into mist. As he acted, he processed what he had seen. The contagion had struck from the inside of the Hellhound, where no injury had been sustained. The implications staggered him, but they would receive his attention later. The consequences demanded a response now.

The plague spread through what remained of the Mortisians with the speed of a shock wave. The last of the Imperial forces succumbed in seconds. The disease leaped from man to man without needing injury or even contact. It was as if the fall of the colonel signalled the death of the companies' collective spirit. Commissar and conscript alike frothed and lunged for the civilians.

Volos's flamer ran dry. The enemy surged with renewed strength and reinforcements. Clawing for their prey, the dead slammed in a wave against Volos, knocking the bolter from his grasp, lifting him off the ground and throwing his weight against the Hellhound. Volos slid off the vehicle's hull. The flood tried to crush him. 'Toharan!' he voxed. 'The Guard is lost! Grab anyone and *go*!' Buffeted by the infinite enemy, he vowed to the Emperor that he would give his life in the service of any victory that might yet be claimed from this day. Then he crossed his arms against his chest and flexed his wrists, fists down.

There was a familiar moment of agony so pure it bordered on ecstasy, and his bone-blades shot out from his wrists, passing over his knuckles. They were a metre long and sheathed in adamantium. He swung his arms down and out. Limbs and heads went flying. Arterial fountains burst around him, drenching his armour, covering his visor. He ducked his head and lunged forward, a maddened bull. His helmet had a large slit near the top, and from it protruded his forehead's bony growth. He had sanded it into the shape of a crescent horn, the tips and edge as lethal as the blades that grew from his arms, and here too he had added the extra kill strength of adamantium. The dead fell before his charge. His vision became a specialised tunnel vision as the euphoria of war descended on him. He saw nothing that wasn't the next thing he was about to butcher. His fangs extended, hungry for the mangled flesh and blood whose sight and smell had become the sum total of his world. He was the destroyer, and however numerous his foes, they were pitiable in their fragility.

A moment came when he had nothing to kill and his mind cleared with a neuronal snap. His system quivered with the residual ecstasy, but he was already thinking tactically again. Corpses in the dozens surrounded him. The army in his vicinity had staggered, and would need a few seconds before the torrent could flow again. Volos retracted his blades, recovered his bolter and vaulted to the top of the Hellhound.

The Mortisians were all part of the dead army now. There was still occasional weapons fire, but it was all sloppy, and all aimed at the refugees. There were precious few of them left. The brothers of Squad Pythios carried a civilian on each shoulder and were moving at a good pace toward the pass. They had just reached the next of the Dragon Claws. Brother Nithigg's clearing was about to collapse as the onslaught closed in, but the dead were still seconds behind, and the Space Marines were gaining momentum. Handfuls of civilians ran in howling clusters, desperation giving their sprints a speed that was almost that of the Black Dragons' jog.

Moment by moment, their numbers dwindled.

Volos joined the race. He came up behind a pair of scrambling humans, a man and a woman. They had been high administrators, to judge by their shredded finery. They held hands as they ran, as if that fragment of comfort was worth what they lost in speed. The gesture was so futile in the face of inevitable massacre, and so touchingly human. It was, Volos thought, the epitome of what he had been created to protect. A group of frenzied dead closed in on the couple. Volos swatted the enemy away, pulping the bodies. He scooped up the two humans. They screamed when they first felt his grasp. They seemed hardly more reassured when they realised what was happening. They stared at him with eyes that were near mindless with fear. But they didn't struggle.

Volos ran faster, barrelling through the dead, exploding bodies with his juggernaut run. He reached Nithigg, who grabbed two civilians and joined the race. Behind, more clusters of humans fell off the pace and were swallowed by the horde.

By the time Squads Pythios and Ormarr reached the pass, the only refugees left were the ones they carried. Two each, except for Toharan, who had three: there was a small child perched on his head. Thirty-seven survivors. A poor showing.

The Black Dragons pounded along the broken, twisting path of the defile. Behind them, the dead raged and followed, but lost ground. The walls of the pass closed in, barely a few metres apart at moments. They leaned in from the vertical, black stone slicked with moisture. Misting waterfalls thickened the air. The Temple chain was taking the intruders into its hard embrace, hugging them tighter and closer. Even with his enhanced vision, Volos found it difficult to see more than a few dozen metres ahead. But that was enough.

They ran for hours, outdistancing the enemy by kilometres, but not slowing even then. They still didn't slow when the pass opened out into the bottom of a vast canyon. The path turned here and snaked thousands of metres up the near canyon wall. It led, at the top, to the narrow, graceful span of the Ecclesiarch Alexis XXII bridge. From this distance below, the bridge was as insubstantial as human hair. Stretching kilometres across the canyon, it was the unique access to Lexica Keep. Its lights glowering in the night, the fortress crouched against the far cliff face like a bird of prey. From between the dark wings of its walls, it peered with cold, contemptuous majesty at the warriors and their charges.

It offered no comfort.

STEEL BLOOD

C L WERNER